**THE PIRATE AND THE
MERMAID'S TAILOR**

1

THE MERMAID'S APPRENTICE

L. PALMER

Copyright

Cover developed by Miblart. See: https://miblart.com

Printed in the United States of America

KDP: 978-1-961446-05-2
IngramSpark: 978-1-961446-06-9
IngramSpark Hardcover: 978-1-961446-07-6

http://lpalmerchronicles.com/published-works

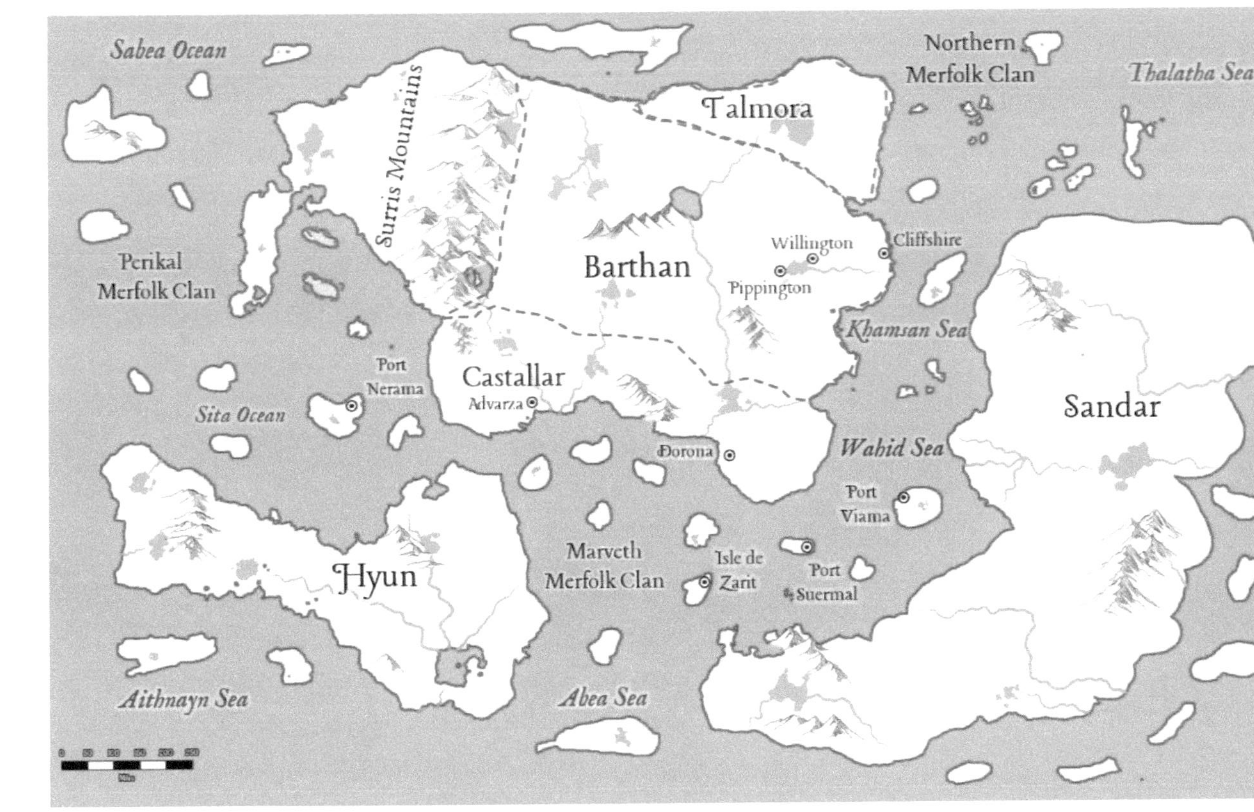

Sabea Ocean
Northern Merfolk Clan
Thalatha Sea
Surris Mountains
Talmora
Perikal Merfolk Clan
Barthan
Willington
Cliffshire
Pippington
Sita Ocean
Port Nerama
Castallar
Advarza
Khamsan Sea
Sandar
Đorona
Wahid Sea
Port Viama
Hyun
Marveth Merfolk Clan
Isle de Zarit
Port Suermal
Aithnayn Sea
Abea Sea

TABLE OF CONTENTS

Part 1

CHAPTER 1

In Which Mabel Sinclair Goes to Sea

Cliffshire, along the coast of Barthan

April of the Year 306 of the Barthanian Republic (B.R.)

Every woman in the room, except Mabel, was in love with Malcom Sinclair.

She knew her arrogant oaf-of-a-brother better than anyone. Sitting on a silk-padded chair at the edge of the small ballroom, she contemplated how to ruin his chances with the women in matching, lacy ball gowns. It was a rescue mission, really, to save them from the sweet-spoken lies Malcom sold with his charming smile, tall frame, and sweeping, dark red hair.

Mabel sighed and switched which hand she rested her chin on. She was always amazed her elder brother could tell the young women apart. Their hair had the same set of ironed curls pulled into a bun, and their gowns only varying by color. The cut and drape of the skirts or curve of the bodice should be sculpted to the woman, instead of how these women were crammed into their dresses. No one was apparently bold enough to tell half the women they resembled overstuffed sausages.

"Maybe I should," Mabel whispered.

However, being so rude would just infuriate her mother further. Mabel never meant to let honest words slip out at inopportune times, but there were moments when it was necessary. Like during tea today, when no one would tell Mrs. Flemham how the pearls on her hat, hanging from behind a stuffed red cardinal, looked like bird droppings.

Once Mabel had spoken, Mrs. Sinclair covered her horror with false laughter and patted her arm. "My daughter has such a unique way of seeing things."

Given how several respected women at the tea table eyed Mrs. Flemham's hat and tried not to giggle, Mabel didn't think her observation was unique.

But Mabel found it best to horrify her mother only once per day. So, she kept her silence as other young women strutted past in variations of the same gown.

At least she wore a unique dress, made in close collaboration with her father's tailor. The narrow blue pinstripes complemented her light-blue eyes and didn't accentuate her dark red hair. Her hair called enough attention on its own. The dress's lines ran along her slim, seventeen-year-old frame, designed to give her a hint of curves where she had little. Though, her mother had scoffed at the lack of layers of skirts, saying, "How can you catch the eye of a young man when you look like a child?"

Surveying the room, Mabel was the only sophisticated woman there. Her friend Hazel was not as vapid as some women, but still giggled every time a handsome young man spoke to her. The rest of the women mimicked porcelain dolls in their infantile lace, powder, and paint.

Not that Mabel's sophistication mattered much with this crowd. She'd grown up with most of the young men in their polished tuxedos, watching them laugh and joke with her brother. Knowing the exploits Malcom and his friends boasted about after parties like these, she preferred remaining forgotten in her chair.

A hush fell over the ballroom and all men seemed to turn their heads at once. Stunning was an understatement as a woman in her early twenties strode in. Her golden hair gleamed, her blue eyes sapphire-like as the candles reflected on the dark blue satin of her gown. It had a full, sweeping skirt, the fabric gathered as if the sea were forming around her. Mabel stretched up, trying to see past others along the edge of the room, seeking a better view of the finely made clothing.

This woman knew how to dress, and Mabel wanted to learn from such a master.

Malcom's grin was bright as he broke from the crowd of women around him and strode to this newcomer's side.

"Madame Cassandra." He held his arm out to her. "I was afraid you wouldn't come."

"I made a promise." She took his arm with one hand and unfurled a gold fan with the other. "And how could I miss this opportunity to see you again?"

Malcom's smile broadened as he raised her hand to kiss it. As his gaze turned away, a shadow of disdain rose in Cassandra's eyes. It was just a moment, but it sent a chill down Mabel's spine.

At least, though, she seemed the only other person in the room who saw through Malcom.

Cassandra's warm but thin smile returned as Malcolm led her deeper into the crowd. All men in the room forgot the females beside them as their gazes followed this statue of a goddess come to life.

As the evening wore on, men crowded around Cassandra, preening and posing, their voices growing louder as if that would charm her. The women migrated into clumps, each group taking turns glaring jealously. Mabel strolled along the room's perimeter, observing how deftly Cassandra faked a laugh or stroked Malcom's arm, keeping full control of him.

Mabel froze as Cassandra's blue eyes focused on her. Staring straight back, Mabel hoped her gaze said, *What game are you playing at?*

Cassandra gave Mabel an appraising look before turning to laugh delightfully at Malcom's latest attempt at being clever. Mabel narrowed her eyes. Something about this woman didn't sit right. Though, Mabel was impressed by whatever game she was playing. All she needed to do was figure out the game.

"Isn't it horrible?" Hazel came to Mabel's side and took her arm. "I was just getting Stewart Bafford to notice me, and she walks in. It's as if I don't exist."

"None of us exist," Mabel said. It was eerie how the men followed Cassandra with such blind devotion. The woman was skilled at drawing attention, but the men were nearly hypnotized. "Not with her in the room."

"Who is she, anyway? I haven't seen her in Cliffshire before." Hazel looked hopefully to Mabel. "Your brother seems to know her."

"I don't think he does." Mabel sighed as Malcom laughed loudly at something Cassandra said. "They might have met before, but nothing more. He would have bragged for days if he knew her."

Hazel leaned toward Mabel. "Do you think you can get her to disappear? Make one of your clever remarks, maybe? It'd be a great service to us all."

Mabel glanced at her friend. "I'm only rude for honesty's sake."

Hazel gestured toward the crowd of men. "Then honestly tell her she's ruining the evening."

Biting back a laugh, Mabel said, "Hazel, be patient. Given Malcom's lack of quality, I doubt she'll return to ruin another night."

She squeezed her friend's arm before continuing her circuit of the room.

The men's attention on Cassandra only worsened as the hired quartet began to play. A few other couples joined Malcom and Cassandra in waltzing across the small dance floor, but the men kept knocking into each other as their gazes tracked Cassandra.

Dancing fizzled out as women turned down their chance to make a fool of themselves. Hazel looked to Mabel with a silent plea, as if there was something she could do.

The reprieve Hazel asked for came as Malcom and Cassandra slipped out a side door. Something about the glance Cassandra took to ensure no one was watching made the hair on the back of Mabel's neck rise. Glad to be an invisible slip of a girl, she stepped out another side door to the garden.

Her efforts would likely only bring her own embarrassment if she found Malcom and Cassandra kissing somewhere. However, something felt off as she followed the sound of giggling, along with Malcom saying, "Why do you tease me? Don't you know all I want is to kiss you?"

"Not yet, my dear." Cassandra's voice was smooth as silk, and she let out a flirting laugh. "Soon, you'll give me all I desire."

Mabel came around a set of hedges as Malcom and Cassandra left the grounds. They crossed to the harbor and strolled along the private docks. Mabel followed, keeping to shadows.

"That is my family's small yacht." Cassandra pointed with her fan. "Do you want a tour?"

"Does this include a look inside the cabin?" Malcom tried to land a kiss on her cheek, but Cassandra was a step away before his lips could reach her.

Mabel tracked the pair as they walked to where the yacht was moored, the hull gleaming in the moonlight. It looked light on the water, with a single sail and small cabin.

"What a beautiful night for sailing." Cassandra looked up at the stars. She tugged at Malcom's arm playfully. "You've told me what a fine sailor you are."

Mabel rolled her eyes as Malcom puffed up his chest. "The best in town. I even won a sailing competition last month."

Cassandra laughed with delight and clapped her hands. "Oh, such greatness you so often speak of."

"Would you like to see me sail?" Malcom gestured toward the harbor. "One turn around the cove?"

"Just you and me?" She playfully tapped his nose. Malcom stared at her with eyes longing for a kiss.

"As it always should be." He kissed her hand before helping her onto the yacht. Humming to himself, he set the rigging and unlooped the rope holding the vessel to the dock. Taking his post at the helm, Malcom looked ahead and began steering the small yacht away from shore.

Mabel crouched as she hurried down the dock. Whether Cassandra or Malcom was planning something, it would be better if someone else was on board to help the victim. Or, if both were innocent, she'd jump out and scare them when Malcom finally got his kiss. He'd be furious, but it would be fun.

Pulling up her skirts, she leapt and grabbed onto the back of the yacht. She hung with her knees curled up and the hem of her dress dragging in the water. Once she climbed onto the yacht, she tucked herself under the tarp covering the dinghy.

"Do you know what beauty is?" Malcom had one arm around Cassandra as he guided the boat along the familiar curve of the harbor.

"I've never had anyone dare explain it to me." Cassandra had a dryness in her voice. Mabel bit back a giggle at the quiet sarcasm. "What is beauty, my dear?"

"It is the moonlight as it caresses the curve of your neck." Malcom leaned his lips closer.

"I'm told the moonlight often does that."

"It is the starlight reflected in your eyes, even after dawn, when the stars have disappeared."

"If I've so many little dots in my eyes, I may need to see a doctor," Cassandra said with a laugh.

Malcom's voice purred as he said, "It is the perfect curve of your waist."

He began to pull her into a kiss, but Cassandra pushed him away and tapped her finger on his lips.

"Concentrate on sailing. We'll get to such things when the time is right."

Pulling down her hand, Malcom said, "The time is now."

He grabbed her by the shoulders and tried to pull her against him. She brought her elbow between them and shoved him back with far greater strength than Mabel expected. Malcom laughed as he fell against the side of the ship. Mabel gripped the dinghy's oar, ready to assist Cassandra.

"One kiss is all I ask for." Malcom grinned as he pushed off the wall and shoved her against the cabin.

"Mr. Sinclair," Cassandra said as she pulled a handkerchief from her pocket, "before we engage in exercising our lips, can I give something to you?"

"If I accept it, will you give me the greater gift I seek?"

"You will have more than you'd ever expect."

Malcom held out his palm and Cassandra placed a golden bauble on it. He glanced at it with a laugh before tossing it in his hand. As the bauble flew up, Cassandra caught it in her handkerchief. Mabel's eyes widened as her brother shrunk, transforming into a fat toad. He hovered in the air a half-second, his now bulbous eyes panicked. Cassandra caught him in her hand and walked to an unlit lantern hanging from the cabin. She patted his head with a finger.

"This form matches your character far better, Mr. Sinclair." She set him inside the lantern and shut the door.

Mabel's heart pounded as she stared at her brother.

Part of her wanted to laugh, considering how well he deserved it.

However, he was also now a toad. Which was far past impossible.

As a panicked ribbitting echoed from the lantern, Cassandra took the helm. "Don't worry, Mr. Sinclair. Your kiss will come in time."

She switched a gold lever on the helm. A gleaming light ran along the rigging as the sail drew tighter, taking full wind and pulling the yacht faster toward the open sea.

Mabel gripped the oar. It wouldn't be long before the yacht was too far for her to swim back to shore, and who knew where Cassandra was taking them. She rolled out from behind the dinghy, oar in hand, and dropped into a crouch. Her pulse thudded as she carefully approached the golden-haired young woman and raised the oar.

Cringing, she swung as hard as she dared, which was not as hard as it needed to be.

Cassandra caught the oar, her blue eyes glaring coldly at Mabel.

"I thought I heard someone jump on the yacht." She yanked the oar from Mabel's grip. "You're his younger sister. Mabel Sinclair, wasn't it?" Gesturing with the oar, she said, "I've no business with you. Go on and swim to shore, if you wish."

"Where are you taking my brother?" Mabel said, trying to have more courage than she felt.

"Your chances of swimming are becoming less, and I'd rather not lose the dinghy. I recommend you go." Cassandra tilted her head. "Though, who designed your dress?"

She prodded Mabel's side with the oar, motioning for her to turn around.

"I did, with my father's tailor," Mabel said as she complied. The shore was disappearing quickly. She was a strong swimmer, but the distance was growing swiftly. And she'd have to leave behind her dress. Another could be made, but she rather liked this one.

Also, there was the matter of her brother sitting as a toad in the lantern.

"Whose idea was the drape of the pinstripe?" Cassandra said.

"It was a collaboration." Mabel's brow furrowed. "My brother may be an oaf, but he doesn't deserve to be a toad. If you give him to me, I'll tell no one what happened tonight."

Cassandra raised an eyebrow. "And who would believe your brother was turned into a toad?"

Mable grunted. "I'd still say you kidnapped him."

"Me?" Cassandra blinked innocently. "The heiress all the men fawned over tonight? Kidnap anyone? Who would believe it?" She gave Mabel a clever grin. "Especially coming from a teenage girl?"

Mabel glanced at her before leaping toward the lantern on the cabin. Cassandra grabbed Mabel's collar and yanked her back easily. Mabel's feet kicked in the air as Cassandra pushed her onto the bench next to the helm.

"We're too far from shore to send you back safely," Cassandra said. "You may as well sit. If you cooperate, I'll make sure you return home."

"With my brother?"

"I've far more important uses for your brother." Cassandra waved a dismissive hand. "Your parents are likely better off without such an odious young man."

"He's still my brother."

"Did you use padding to accentuate your hips in the dress?"

Mabel glared. The questions about her dress were only a distraction. "Where are you taking him and how did you turn him into a toad?"

"Your dress is an unusual style and is far better than what other women were wearing tonight."

"Where are you taking Malcom?"

"Where I need to." Cassandra reached inside the cabin and pulled out a large wooden box. Opening it, she said, "Have you designed other dresses?"

Mabel folded her arms. "I am considering myself being kidnapped and will not answer any other questions."

"Then I don't see a need to explain where we are going." Cassandra pulled out a set of golden wires. They unfolded to look like a weathervane as she attached it to the base of the helm. She then pulled out a pearl half the size of her head and set it in an indent.

Cassandra hummed as she ran two fingers over the pearl and yellow lines of electricity ran along the golden wires. Mabel's eyes widened further. This could not be real.

"Where are you taking us?" she said.

"I'll trade an answer for an answer." Cassandra reached up and adjusted the wires. Mabel fell back against the cabin as the boat lurched forward and sped across the sea at an impossible speed.

"I have designed other dresses," Mabel shouted, her palms flat against the wall.

"We are headed toward Marveth."

Mabel stared at Cassandra, the name meaning nothing. "Where?"

As she sat on the bench next to Mabel's, Cassandra pointed in the direction they were headed. "Marveth. It's off the sea bordering Castallar."

"Castallar is at least a week's sailing from here," Mabel said.

"It is, when not using magic." Cassandra rested her hands in her lap as if they were having a nice chat. "Are you interested in designing dresses as a profession?"

She looked to Cassandra. "Will you just give me my brother and let us go home?"

"I think it's clear we're past the point of going back." Cassandra pulled at Mabel's skirt, admiring its drape. "You've an excellent eye for shape and a clear talent. I'd like to see other designs."

Yanking her skirt away, Mabel said, "You kidnapped my brother and me! Why does my dress matter?"

"I did not kidnap you, Miss Sinclair. You stowed away on my vessel." Though Cassandra's appearance remained the same, her eyes had the weight of someone far older than twenty. "We are headed to a place where fashion is in high demand. If your talents are what I think they are, I could help you build a profitable business."

"I just want to go home." Mabel wasn't sure if Cassandra's magic or her focus on clothing design was stranger.

"As I said, that will be arranged." Cassandra leaned toward her. "But I learned long ago to not let an opportunity pass me by."

"I'm not going into business with someone who kidnapped my brother."

"Do you want to bring your brother home?"

Mabel nodded. This was all too strange. Maybe she should have stayed on the dock.

"I have a business arrangement that I need to use him as payment for," Cassandra said.

Mabel's mouth hung open. "You're selling my brother?"

"Which means you could buy him back. But you need the right currency to do so." Cassandra gestured at Mabel's dress. "I have connections and can arrange for several acquaintances to commission outfits. One or two commissions should be enough to trade for your brother's return. A few more, and you should have passage back home." Cassandra smiled. "Never let it be said I am without kindness."

Mabel stared at the woman. She was definitely mad. "What are you trading my brother for?"

Cassandra looked off into the distance. "After many years of searching, I think I've found the secret to correcting the spell keeping me from my true love." She pulled a locket from underneath her dress and opened it. A young man of Castallan origin stood beside Cassandra in a wedding portrait. "There is my Arturo. Isn't he handsome?"

"You're married?" Mabel shouted.

"Of course." Cassandra looked at her as if this were obvious. "Why do you think I wouldn't let your brother kiss me?"

"Because he's an oaf!"

Cassandra laughed lightly. "I normally don't share quite so much of my plans, but I have a feeling about you, Miss Sinclair. If you will learn to trust me, I think you could be quite helpful."

"I'm not helping you sell my brother."

"There are only two ways to save your brother," Cassandra said. "You can buy him back, or you can help me steal."

Mabel shook her head. "You truly are mad."

"I'm sure I appear to be." Cassandra leaned her elbow on her knee and rested her chin on her hand. "Miss Sinclair, do you think you are clever enough to steal from mermaids?"

"What?" Mabel watched the electric lines and glowing pearl orb before looking at the toad her brother had become. "Mermaids are real too?"

"Of course they are," Cassandra said. "Because I am one myself."

Mabel found herself staring at her captor's legs. "You don't look like one."

"My legs cost me much, Miss Sinclair," Cassandra said. "And now there are some who hope to steal them from me. If you want to save your brother, I suggest you help me."

A numbness filled Mabel's head as she prayed this was a dream. However, she doubted it was. Instead, the most likely answer was magic and mermaids were quite real, just like how her brother was now a toad. Grabbing him and jumping off the yacht wasn't an option, nor was trying to overpower Cassandra.

Deciding to take the only remaining choice, Mabel muttered, "How do we steal from mermaids?"

CHAPTER 2

In Which Antonio Cortez
Leaves for the Navy

Antonio Cortez grinned as he carried the pair of long paper boxes down the cobblestone lane of Dorona, his home city stretching across the valley and hills beside the sea. Sofia Gutierrez rose from her porch steps, her white dress with red embroidery flowing around her, her smile mirroring Antonio's. He had spent hours making the dress for her and it matched her beauty perfectly. Reaching the porch, he held the boxes with one arm as he used the other to twirl her before he gave her a kiss.

"Mama and Papa are just finishing breakfast," she said with an excited giggle.

Antonio took in her dark brunette hair and brown skin a shade darker than his own. She was truly the most beautiful girl in all of Castallar.

"How do I look?" he whispered.

"Handsome and impeccably dressed as always." She brushed his shoulder.

"But do I look respectable?" He swallowed. "I want your papa to see me as a man."

"You are nineteen and shipping out with the Navy tomorrow."

She kissed his cheek. "How could he not see you as a man?"

Still, Antonio sweated as Sofia opened the door, bringing him into the house smelling of cinnamon and fresh tortillas. She squeezed his arm before stepping into the small dining area.

"Mama, Papa, Antonio Cortez is here. He wanted to speak with you."

"Tell him to come back when he's done with the Navy in two years," Mr. Gutierrez grumbled in his gravelly voice.

"He has going away gifts." Sofia gestured toward the common room. "Please, Papa."

"He's a nice young man," Mrs. Gutierrez said. "We can give him a few minutes to say goodbye."

"I don't think that's what he's come for."

Antonio's stomach clenched. He had come for far more than to say goodbye. He and Sofia had discussed it yesterday as they sat on the breaker wall overlooking the harbor, his arms around her as they watched ships roll in and out, including some of the newer steam ships with their spouts of white smoke. He had felt more confident of it when he helped her sneak from her room in the evening and they had gone dancing. As their hips moved in sync to the rhumba and salsa beats, he focused on her brown eyes and bright smile. Dancing with her eased his fears of entering the Navy as he dreamed of their future.

The only obstacle between Antonio and his hopes was Mr. Gutierrez and his broad, short frame.

Mr. and Mrs. Gutierrez entered the living room. Antonio stretched himself up, his height taller than most men. It was not enough to balance Mr. Gutierrez's girth.

"I'm needed at the firm in half an hour." Sofia's father glared at Antonio. "What do you want?"

Forcing his smile to remain, Antonio laid out the boxes on the sitting table.

"First, I wanted to thank you and Mrs. Gutierrez for opening your home to me these past six months."

The words were polite, but it was a lie. The first five times Antonio had called on Sofia, Mr. Gutierrez had shouted him away. However, after a month of Antonio sneaking Sofia out her window to go dancing, Mrs. Gutierrez had convinced her husband it was worth allowing Antonio in so he could be watched.

"Sir, you have asked me dozens of times what a seamstress's son can do to provide for your daughter." Excitement ran through Antonio as he opened the first box. "I thought it best to show you my craft."

He raised a bright yellow dress, Mrs. Gutierrez's favorite color, and held it out to her. One of his mother's wealthier clients had cancelled a gown but already paid for the fabric. After he pleaded, his mother, Leticia, let him use it and the final result was worth the effort. Especially with the embroidery he had added on the ruffled sleeves and skirt.

The dress had taken many hours, even with him sneaking away where he could hide and use his magic. Antonio kept his powers hidden just as his late father, Manuel, had always told him. No one else believed in magic, and Antonio couldn't frighten them. Even for him, it was strange to watch the needle glow as it sewed in and out of the fabric on its own. But it helped him quickly create these mosaics of colorful thread.

Mrs. Gutierrez gasped and took the gown. "It is beautiful."

"It is ridiculous," Mr. Gutierrez said. "A child's dress. My wife is more sensible."

"And for you, sir." Antonio opened the second box and pulled out the bolero jacket sized for Mr. Gutierrez, designed for his boxy frame. He laid out the jacket on his arm, making sure to show the red, white, and yellow embroidery on the sleeves designed to complement the yellow dress. Then, he pulled out the matching pants, also showing the embroidery.

"And where am I supposed to wear this circus outfit?"

Antonio kept his smile. "During Carnivale night, or out to a fine restaurant. Wherever you and Mrs. Gutierrez wish to look your finest."

"Did you cover it with all this thread?"

"I did all the embroidery." Antonio motioned at the sleeve. "If one of the wealthiest customers ordered this, it would cost—"

"And what could you have been doing?" Mr. Gutierrez grunted. "Looking for real work, like a man?" He pointed. "The Navy will teach you to sweat and think for a living instead of patching threads."

"This is real work," Antonio said. "I'm going to save my money while in the Navy and come back and open my own shop. As I see the world, I'll collect fabrics and see styles this small city has never seen, and everyone will want the clothing I make. I will be poor at first, but, if I work hard and get my clothing in the right hands, I will be able to provide a good home for your daughter, sir."

"You will provide nothing for my daughter."

Sofia came to Antonio's side and took his hand. "I love him, Papa and—"

"Who said you could love this boy?" Mr. Gutierrez's face swiftly turned red. "I should have pounded him in the ground when he first came by. He is a dreamer and will leave you penniless in the street, and you will come to me to beg for food for your children." He pounded a fist against his chest. "My daughter will marry a man with a good income who can give her a proper home. Not you, boy. Now go on your ship."

"Sofia and I've spoken," Antonio said. He would stand as a man, even if the answer was already obvious. "We've promised ourselves to each other, and, with me leaving tomorrow, we hoped we might have your blessing to marry today."

Mrs. Gutierrez pressed her hand to her chest as her face paled. "My niña is only sixteen."

Taking the opportunity of Mr. Gutierrez's furious silence, Antonio said, "I have nothing now, and she will need to live with you while I'm away. But we have already decided to be husband and wife. Why not begin now, and I can travel with the comfort of knowing I will come back to the woman I love? Our home will be small when I return, but I will do all I can to provide for her and make her happy."

Antonio put his arm around Sofia. "I love your daughter. Please. Give me the chance to build a life with her."

Mr. Gutierrez grabbed the two paper boxes on the sitting table and whacked Antonio with them. Antonio pulled Sofia into his arms and turned his back to her father to protect her. While Antonio was stronger than most men, punching his future father-in-law, even in self-defense, seemed unwise.

Weeping, Sofia held him tight. If only he could have waited to leave till after her eighteenth birthday. Then she would be an adult and could marry without her parents' permission.

"Mama has offered you a home." Antonio kissed Sofia's cheek. "Remember that."

"Let go of my daughter!" Mr. Gutierrez grabbed Sofia by the shoulders and yanked her from Antonio's arms. Antonio was strong enough he could have held her, but that might also hurt her, so he released the girl he loved.

"Mama! Please!" Sofia yelled as her mother grabbed her and held her in place.

"Your father has spoken," Mrs. Gutierrez said, cradling her daughter. Antonio's heart broke as Sofia sobbed.

"I love her, sir." Antonio moved to step toward Sofia, but Mr. Gutierrez landed his thick fist against Antonio's jaw. Next Antonio knew, he was half-lifted off his feet and carried out the front steps. He shouted as Mr. Gutierrez tossed him into a mud puddle.

"You are banned from my house!" Mr. Gutierrez spat at Antonio. "Never come near my daughter again."

Sofia's weeping tore at Antonio as it echoed from the window. He had doubted Mr. Gutierrez would say yes, but this was harsher than he had imagined.

"I will be back in two years," he yelled through the open window. "Once I get off that ship, I will walk to this door, and I will claim

Sofia."

Mr. Gutierrez slammed the window shut, breaking one of the panes of glass. He glared at Antonio. With a grunt, Antonio relented and marched away.

After winding from the newer, larger homes of middle-class bulls like Mr. Gutierrez, Antonio jogged his way to the tighter packed apartments and shanties where he had been raised. The smell of the sea and fresh fish filled the air as he walked through the ramshackle neighborhood, some of the shacks having been built on the rubble of others. There was a brightness and liveliness as he passed through the market and waved to shopkeepers and friends he had known his whole life.

He came to his mother's shop and home, samples of her skill hanging outside alongside a faded sign with prices. He smiled at the panels of wood he had replaced and painted in the past few weeks, brightening the small building. It had been sweaty work, but the result was bright and would help his mother while he was gone.

At least he had accomplished one thing before leaving for the Navy.

A deep disappointment washed through him, and he stuffed his hands in his pockets. Dreaming of marrying Sofia had helped him escape thoughts of the dreary life he was about to enter as a sailor. Now, his heart was doubly heavy. He kicked a rock before winding to the back alleyway and the small yard just behind the shop.

"Didn't say yes?"

Antonio glanced at his eldest half-sister, Luisa. She held a basket of clothing next to her round belly carrying her second child.

"I showed him my best work." Antonio shook drying mud from his embroidered coat. The fabric was worn but he had tailored it to accentuate his lean build. "He has no vision."

"You have too much of it." She ruffled his hair. "Just like Papa."

Antonio pushed her hand away. He wished his father, Manuel, hadn't died five years ago, when he was fourteen. Today would have been easier if he could have spoken with his father, gotten his steady advice. He could just see Manuel storming into the Gutierrez home and defending their way of life.

A knot formed in his throat, picturing his father standing and holding a beam on a broken ship under construction right before the ship collapsed. Thirty men had been saved, but not Antonio's own papa.

Since then, Antonio had to stand in his father's place for his mother and two older half-sisters. They managed well on their own, but he still had duties. Those would be harder to meet while trapped on naval ship.

At least he only had two years to serve instead of the seven his father had signed up for.

"What happened, Antonito?" Luisa shook out a skirt and hung it from the laundry line.

Antonio grunted before dropping onto a stool near the back stairs. "What is wrong with our way of life? It is honorable work, and everyone needs clothing."

"Not everyone's clothing needs the embroidery and ruffles you like to add."

"Every person deserves to dress grandly at least once." He held out his hands, gesturing at his outfit. "All of my clothes are cast-offs, but I have found ways to polish them."

"And everyone walking by cries out, 'What is El Emperador Antonio wearing today?'" She gave him a mock-stern look. "I don't think they let you embellish your uniforms in the Navy." She raised her eyebrows. "Or are you going to embroider the sails?"

"Steam ships don't have sails," he muttered as he folded his arms.

His other half-sister, Juanita, leaned out the back door. She gave a mock-pout. "Did Emperador Antonio not carry off his princess?"

She broke into snickers and Antonio groaned.

"You are three years older than me. Where is your prince?" he said.

She gestured toward the harbor. "Somewhere on a ship. He's going to arrive and come to this shop to repair his clothes. He'll take one look at me and carry me off to some beautiful island he secretly owns."

"The only man who can afford that is likely a pirate," Luisa said with a laugh. "What about Paulo? He's been bringing you some very nice fresh fish these past few weeks."

"The fish he smells like as he carries them across the city in his cart?" Juanita snorted. "I'll take a man who at least smells decent."

"My Fernando reeks of sweat when he comes home from repairing ships, but he's not bad after a quick wash."

Waving her hand at Luisa's belly, Juanita said, "We all can see you enjoy your husband."

"You'll find your own man too. And stop fancying after all the handsome ones. Fernando's not the best looking of men, but he works hard and treats me well." She nodded to her two younger siblings. "And his family is generous to us. It's very kind of his mother to be planning Antonio's farewell dinner tonight."

"I just wish Sofia would be there," Antonio muttered as he slouched. "Two years without her will be a lifetime."

"Then go like a grand hero and steal her from her window," Juanita said, biting back a giggle. "That will surely please her parents."

"Don't encourage him." Luisa looked to her brother. "Antonito, she will either write to you or not. If she does not, you are lucky you're not married to her."

He met his eldest sister's gaze. "I love her and will my whole life. That will never change."

Juanita reached over and squeezed his cheek. "Until you get on shore and see a woman for the first time after months at sea."

He pushed her hand away and stomped up the back stairs. Reaching the top, he said, "I love Sofia Gutierrez. We will write to each other each week, and the minute I return, she will be my wife." He pointed. "You will see."

He grabbed the door to try to slam it open, but the door was locked. His two sisters giggled at him as he fumbled for his key and unlocked it before storming inside.

He crossed the small living area stuffed with a couch and table. To the left were his mother and Juanita's own narrow rooms. On the right, was the linen closet, with the bottom shelves removed to make room for his cot. He opened the door and pulled out one of his other three suits.

Entering the small bathroom, he washed his face before glaring in the speckled mirror. His mother deserved better than this small home. Her work was excellent and deserved higher prices. He would make sure she had something better when he returned.

Tears came as he leaned against the door. "I don't want to go. I don't belong in Navy."

But he had the conscription letter and two years of required service ahead of him. If he did not go, he would be put in prison. If he ran off after starting training, he would be shot for deserting.

The sailor's life was not for him, but he had no choice. His only hope had lain with marrying Sofia and having the comfort of knowing she would still be his when he returned.

He changed out of his mud-spattered clothes and combed his hair. The care he took to smooth the wave of his dark locks would be mocked once he was a sailor, but he would maintain his sharp looks. He might not have much, but he could manage that.

"Antonio?" came his mother's voice.

"I'm cleaning up. I'll be out in a moment."

He wiped his wet cheeks and blew out some air to try to gather himself. His mother had already wept too many times the past few weeks as they talked of him leaving. His sisters might tease him, but they would miss him. And he would miss them too. Even when they ruffled his hair and pinched his cheeks like he was still nine.

Stepping out, he forced a brave smile. His mother's worn face gave him a sympathetic look. "Her father said no, didn't he?"

For all his attempts to hold composure, he broke into tears again as his mother opened her arms to him. He embraced her and kissed the top of her head.

"I will make a better life for us," he whispered.

"Of course you will." She kissed his cheek. "You are my Antonio and are meant for great things."

Antonio laughed with his friends and family as they crowded together in the small back yard of Luisa's in-law's home. It was a joyful time, his tears from earlier broken by old stories and jokes being swatted back and forth.

With another cry of, "To Emperador Antonio, the next ruler of the sea!" his friends left to drink in his honor, and he walked his mother and Juanita home.

He took in the starlight along with the lights of the ships on the water. Despite the smallness of their home, he loved this city. He loved the shanties around him with the busy market shops and the people with little of their own willing to give everything to help another. He loved the beaches, where he often had gone swimming with his father and sat talking for hours afterward. He loved the row of outdoor clubs where music played, and he could dance half the night if he wanted. And he loved Sofia, who was likely lying in her room weeping for him.

That thought brought a sharp pain, but he kept his smile and pushed away his own sorrow as he arrived in the apartment above his mother's shop. There, he talked with his mother and sister late into the night.

The conversation lulled, all three of them knowing they should go to bed. Antonio pulled from his pocket a bent photograph of Sofia.

"Two years is a long time," he said.

His mother carried over the wedding photograph of her and his father. She looked far less worn by the years in her lace, white dress, a sweet joy in her eyes even while standing stock still for the old-style camera. His father stood in his naval sailor uniform, looking as handsome as Antonio remembered, his cheekbones even more pronounced than Antonio's.

"I was a new widow, Juanita barely born when I met your papa," his mother said while sitting beside him. "I didn't mourn my first husband much, considering he was a drunk and was murdered by his partner in a smuggling run gone wrong. Still, I wasn't ready for a man as stunningly handsome as Manuel to look at me with a warm spark in his eyes."

Juanita smiled sadly. "Papa always said, 'Meeting my Leticia was like seeing a star had fallen from the skies.'"

"You're still just as beautiful," Antonio said with a wink. He grinned, loving when his mother spoke of his father.

"I'm over twenty years older and forty pounds heavier." His mother turned to Juanita and pointed. "And Paulo might smell of fish, but he's a good man with the same spark in his eye."

"Juanita's waiting for a handsome pirate." Antonio laughed and Juanita bit back a smile, trying to look angry as she hit his arm.

Their mother gave them a tired look before continuing, "I was charmed by him, though how could anyone not be charmed by Manuel Cortez?" She sighed with a soft smile. "I was afraid to give my heart again after how cruel my first husband had been. Still, for two years while he was on a boat patrolling the nearby harbors, my Manuel would come by the shop every few weeks. He'd find excuses to stay a few hours, by fixing things my first husband had neglected for years, or just standing at the door chatting with me. After I began to soften, he'd play with Luisa, running with her and getting her to giggle, or he'd mind you, Juanita, as you'd get bigger and be a menace as you learned to crawl and walk.

"So, my heart broke when he came to me after two years of me trying to pretend all that was between us was a dear friendship and told me he was being transferred to a different ship far away. He'd be gone his last two years of service." She wiped tears from her cheeks and Antonio gripped her hand as his own cheeks were wet. "We'd never kissed till that day, when he proposed to me, but I knew I loved him and was glad to marry him a few days later, with his captain doing the honors."

She looked to Antonio. "Two years, even with writing letters every week, was a long time, but I was the anchor keeping him steady on hard days at sea."

Antonio looked at the wedding photograph. "Sofia is my anchor. I only wish I could leave with her as my wife, as Papa did with you."

"Maybe it's better you're not." His mother rested her hand on his. "Because Manuel also left me with you, though we didn't know it yet. And you were a small terror on two limbs by the time he came home. I don't know if I was more relieved to have him home because I loved him or because he could help me mind my three children."

Juanita smiled even while wiping tears from her face. "I loved playing with Papa, and how he'd swing me around so I could pretend to fly."

"When I marry Sofia," Antonio said, "I'll be as good a husband and father."

"You will be that way with whoever you marry," his mother said, her brown eyes meeting his. "I think Sofia's a pretty girl, but the pair of you are young. You're entering a much bigger world and might change, or you might meet someone."

Antonio shook his head. This wasn't the first time his mother had said this. "I love Sofia. She is my true heart and I'll come home to her."

"I've no doubt of what you feel," his mother said. "But be honest with your heart. If your love starts to fade, listen. If your love stays true, then you'll be sure of your choice."

"I'll always be true to her, as Papa was to you."

His mother put her arm around him and kissed his cheek. "My life has been blessed by a good husband and three good children. I hope your life can be just as happy."

Antonio embraced his mother. "I will make a better life for you, Mama. I promise."

She rubbed his shoulder before releasing him. "It is an early day tomorrow. Go sleep and we'll say goodbye in the morning."

He hugged Juanita. "I hope your handsome pirate comes for you."

She giggled and kissed his cheek. "You're a fool but a good man, Antonito."

He held on to her a little longer before entering the closet he used as a room and lying on his cot

However, worries kept sleep far from him.

After a restless hour, he sat up. Perhaps there was one worry he could have better peace with before he left.

With his mind determined, he dressed quickly and crept out the back door before sprinting across the city, the night still warm despite the early morning hour. He grabbed a handful of small rocks and tucked them in his pocket before climbing up to the roof across from Sofia's window. Crouching there, he tossed the pebbles toward the window frame, creating a tap. His pocket was nearly empty and his heart sinking as he tossed the second-to-last rock. As he reached for the final one, Sofia pushed out the windows.

Grinning, Antonio stood and waved. Her face was worn by tears, but she broke into a warm smile and waved back. He motioned for her to wait, and then, as he had many times since meeting her, he jumped the gap, catching his fingers on the roof's gutter. Sofia moved out of the way as he slid his feet through the open window and dropped into the room.

"Shh," she whispered. "Papa is listening."

Antonio kissed her, the tenseness in his shoulders easing as he held her close. She truly would be his anchor.

"I made this for you." He handed her a small package wrapped in paper. "I was going to give it to you if we got married today."

He kept his arm around her as she opened it with an eager smile. She held out the fine silk handkerchief, embroidered with a map of the sea around Castallar.

"I will kiss it every night." She held it to her breast before pressing her head against his shoulder. He rubbed her back as he held her.

"I wish Papa had let us marry today," she said.

"Be patient and look for me in two years," he said. "Even if I have to take you from this window, we will be married."

Her gaze lowered. "I long to be married, but, listening to Father, I do worry."

Antonio kissed the corner of her forehead. "I will return from sea." He pulled his sketchbook from his pocket and flipped it open. "And, when I am home, I will make for you the perfect dress for the wedding. It will—"

She placed her hand over the drawing before closing the sketchbook. "We need to talk of more serious things than your little drawings."

A pang hit Antonio's chest. Her attention often wandered when he tried to show her his sketches of clothing he planned to make. Once they were married and he began his tailor shop, she would understand.

"These sketches are the path to our future." He tapped the sketchbook. "Once people see the clothing I make, they will ask who designed it, and we'll have the whole city coming to us. It will take time, but we will succeed."

"There are other professions." Her eyes were worried. "You can write and do numbers. Perhaps, when you return, you can get a clerkship, or—"

"Be patient, Sofia, and hold to our dream." He tucked his sketchbook in his pocket before taking her hands in his. "Do not let your father's doubt cloud your vision."

"Two years is so long." She released his hands and went to her nightstand. There, she pulled out a square, palm-sized box. "I bought this for you a few days ago, to help you remember me."

"I need nothing to help me but am glad to have it." He grinned as he opened it to find a locket containing a lock of her hair and her portrait. "There could be nothing more beautiful."

"I shouldn't have, but—" Her cheeks reddened a bit as she opened another drawer and pulled out a silk nightgown. It was made of soft fabric, and he began picturing how it would rest on her curves. He shoved aside this thought, tucking it away for their wedding. Yet, her pleading eyes turned to him. "I bought it for tonight."

He took it from her and folded it carefully before placing it between her hands. "I will long to hold you as you wear this, but it must wait."

"What if—" Her large tears fell, and his heart ached. "What if you don't come back and we miss—"

"Then remember this kiss." He pulled her close and pressed his lips to hers, letting himself caress her back as his other arm held her around the waist. "And dream of it each night until I return."

He kissed her softly again before going to the window. Looking back, the sorrow in her eyes pulled at him. Forcing a grin, he said, "I love you, and I will return."

He jumped from the window, catching the roof on the neighbor's house and pulling himself up. He blew one last kiss before hurrying back toward his own home. In his hand, he clutched the locket, holding the symbol of the promise between them.

He would keep it, and, when he returned home, he would marry the woman he loved.

CHAPTER 3

In Which Mabel
Attends a Merfolk Festival

"Stay at my side," Cassandra said as she led Mabel through a dim tunnel. "This place is extremely dangerous for humans. Do not eat or drink anything. And keep an eye on your brother."

Walking down a set of stairs carved into stone, Mabel wondered if she should have stayed on the yacht, keeping watch on the barren island. Although, the echo of violins and laughter coming from deeper in the caves marked this a lie.

Maybe Cassandra was mad and was going to murder Mabel. That seemed a more real possibility than mermaids, despite the enchanted yacht and her brother sitting as a toad inside the lantern.

Her eyes widened as they came to a glistening door covered in seashells and Cassandra knocked three times. It rolled aside, no hand touching it. The stone room beyond appeared empty until ripples ran across the pool at the center. A tanned, dark-haired woman rose from the water, her pronounced cheekbones similar to Cassandra's.

"Good evening, Isabella," Cassandra said as she entered. "Is everything prepared?"

"It is, Mother, but you are late again." The woman gave her a tired look while moving to the edge of the pool. She pulled herself up to the side, revealing a long fishtail where her legs should be. Mabel tried not to stare while her pulse quickened.

Apparently, merfolk were real.

And this one was Cassandra's daughter, though she appeared nearly the same age.

Mabel wasn't sure which fact was more bewildering.

"Being late makes for a grander entrance." Cassandra picked up a tri-corner hat sitting on a shelf and handed it to Isabella. "And is far more fun."

Glaring, Isabella pulled on the hat. Mabel jumped as Isabella's gleaming fishtail shifted into legs while a ballgown formed around her.

"Who is the girl?" Isabella rose to her newly-formed feet and assessed Mabel with a wary glance. She tilted her head. "That is an unusual dress."

"Isn't it interesting?" Cassandra gestured. "Look at the angle of the pinstripes on the bodice. She designed it herself, with the help of her father's tailor."

"Why did you bring her?" Isabella focused on Cassandra. "You know how dangerous it is for humans here."

Cassandra raised her lantern. "This is her brother, who is a toad whether in human or amphibian form. He is tonight's bait."

Isabella's eyes narrowed. "Did you change the plan again?"

"We should never be predictable when High Witch Randala is involved."

"Of course not." Isabella stepped inside and picked up two small cages filled with about a dozen frogs each. She handed Cassandra one of the cages. "Shipwrecked smugglers are getting harder to come by, with these steam ships puttering about. Next time, it will help if you can supply your own entry fee."

Cassandra lifted the cage, analyzing the frogs inside. Mabel felt the amphibians staring at her, pleading to be set free.

"I'll do what I can," Cassandra said, "but having to move to hide my lack of aging is wearing and takes so much effort."

"You have many estates on land. I thought you had a regular rotation."

"I have a plan, but there's the trouble of getting rid of perfectly good servants and finding new ones who know to not ask questions." She glanced at Isabella. "And there's the new business manager Arturo hired, Mr. Hedley. He's competent but does not trust me."

"He may have some wisdom in that." Isabella tapped the lantern holding Malcom. "If he does give you real trouble, a few hours as a frog may inspire him to be more cooperative."

"I tried," Cassandra said with a sigh. "But he's too clever and was warned by Arturo."

Isabella let out a small laugh. "A reminder that while Father loves you, he knows you well."

Cassandra shot her a glare. "Are you here to help me tonight or not?"

"I will help distract Eduardo and the High Witch as promised." Isabella's face grew more serious. "Let's pray it is enough."

"It is only one step out of a thousand but will help both of us." Cassandra motioned toward the tunnel. "Are you ready?"

Mabel stood by the door as the pair of women, or mermaids currently wearing legs, strolled down the tunnel, their walk elegant. As she followed, Mabel glanced back the way she and Cassandra had come. Perhaps she was forgotten and could sneak back to the yacht.

"Miss Sinclair, do stay with us," Cassandra said, her voice friendly. "You never know what's wandering these tunnels. One wrong turn, and you're a squid's dinner."

That was as unpleasant a prospect as following Cassandra and Isabella. However, if Mabel wanted to rescue her brother and escape the island, following them was her best path.

The stone stairs shifted to a transparent crystal before leading to a pair of engraved, silver doors gleaming in the ambient light. Laughter and chatter echoed from beyond.

Isabella tapped the doors. A porthole slid open, and a man glanced out, only his eyes visible in the slit.

"Do I see a beautiful pair of sisters?" He laughed. Mabel tried not to roll her eyes. Apparently, people were just as false among merfolk as those at home.

"Oh, Reginald, you know I'd prefer to age a little," Cassandra said. "But my daughter does look lovely, doesn't she?"

Isabella unfurled a fan and fluttered it before raising her cage of frogs. "May we enter, or shall we stand here and be flattered more?"

"The pair of you do provide the finest of views, however, I imagine you would rather enjoy tonight's pleasures." He looked to Mabel. "I see you've brought a human girl."

"You know me," Cassandra said. "Always bringing unique entertainment."

Isabella gestured at Mabel, a dryness to her voice as she said, "She designed her own dress."

"A fashion artist?" Reginald squinted.

"She's a young woman of great promise," Cassandra said. "May she join us?"

"Of course."

The porthole closed and the doors opened as if they had no weight. Cassandra motioned for Mabel to come to her side and touched her arm while whispering, "Stay wide-eyed and do not join any games."

Mabel glanced at her before putting on a gawking expression. "Will this do?"

The corner of Cassandra's mouth rose. "It will do very well."

They walked through the gilded doorway and Mabel had no trouble staring wide-eyed at the ornate, open hall. Gold was everywhere, crafted into statues and elaborate decorations on balconies and chandeliers. Beneath the glass floor passed several broad fishtails attached to human torsos.

Apparently, merfolk spent quite a lot of time on their hair and clothing. The mermen and mermaids wore shirts or bodices made of gleaming skins, their necks drenched in pearls and jewels. Most mermaids wore elaborate hats atop pillars of hair adorned with starfish, shells, and glittering jewels.

"One fun game," Cassandra whispered, "is to guess how many are wearing wigs."

Nothing in this massive room appeared fun to Mabel. There were many wondrous things, but she felt sick, a prickling along her back warning of danger.

They walked down the lush, red carpeted stairs to the main floor. Merfolk glided through the water beneath the glass to raised pools ringed by short, marble walls. Each wall was used as a gaming table, merfolk on one side, human men and women on the other. On the gaming tables sat individual cages holding frogs, lizards, birds, and other small creatures. It sent a chill through Mabel as she watched them being exchanged for bets.

Mabel wanted to run over to each of the tables, hit the humans, and wake them up. How they could flirt and laugh with the merfolk was beyond her understanding. Danger filled the air, yet no one else appeared to notice.

As they crossed the floor, several women in gowns and wearing tri-cornered hats smiled at her and offered sweet-smelling drinks. Based on Isabella's hat, these were mermaids too. Other humans, whether in fine suits or patched sailor uniforms, drank freely, laughing more with each sip. The transformed mermen and mermaids watched her with predatory eyes and Mabel moved closer to Cassandra. At least she was a threat Mabel was familiar with.

"Mother! Isabella! I'm so glad you came!" A merman pushed out from one of the pools and pulled on a tri-cornered hat. As he shifted out of the pool, his outfit transformed into a dark suit molded to his broad shoulders and his fishtail transformed into legs.

"I'm surprised Eduardo is acknowledging you," Isabella whispered as she smiled at her brother.

"What do you think he is plotting?" Cassandra said.

"Something to stop whatever you're plotting."

His grin was broad but false as he came and kissed both women's cheeks. His gaze turned to Mabel, and he smiled while baring his teeth like a shark.

"Who is this delicacy?" He approached and reached for her hand.

Mabel wanted to step back, but something about the intensity of his eyes held her in place. She jumped as Cassandra swatted Eduardo's hand.

"She is a protégé," Cassandra said. "And barely past being a child." She gestured around the room. "There are finer vintages of human females here tonight."

"She is a beauty in the making, then." He bowed to her. "I am eager to meet you again, Miss—?"

Mabel's tongue pressed to the tip of her teeth, starting to say her name, but stopped. There was something unsettling keeping her mouth shut.

"What of the males wandering?" Isabella took her brother's arm. "Any admirable specimens?"

"Of course, but Vivian's already hunting them. We may have our bond, but you know how she is."

"Take me to them. You know how she loves competition."

Eduardo gave Cassandra a wary, knowing glance, but guided Isabella away.

"I often don't understand how he is Arturo's son," Cassandra breathed as she took Mabel's arm. "Child, in the future, be more careful what yachts you jump on."

"Can I just have my brother?" Mabel whispered, holding closer to Cassandra. "And go home?"

"If my fate were not tied to this exchange, I would." Cassandra placed a guiding hand on Mabel's shoulder. "Stay with the plan and I will have you home by morning. All of this will become a strange dream."

Cassandra led her to a side room with another marble-lined pool.

She tapped the lantern holding Malcom against a bell hanging near the door and a low tone filled the room.

"Tap that sconce," Cassandra whispered while pointing, "and the servant's tunnel will open. Go right and follow it straight no matter what. Hide on the shore until I come with my yacht."

Mabel nodded, recounting in her mind the plan Cassandra had walked her through on the yacht. Hopefully, it would work, and Cassandra would take Mabel and her brother home.

Several towers of hair rose from the water followed by three mermaids who appeared less than pleased to see Cassandra.

"The halfling came," one said, looking to the others. "Do you think she kept her word?"

"One man, fresh from shore," Cassandra said holding up the lantern. "When do I not keep my word?"

The three mermaids all glared at her, as if asking if she really wanted an answer.

"What of this child?" The mermaid with deep brown skin tilted her head. "That dress fits your form well, girl. Who designed it?"

"I did." Mabel's voice squeaked out. She had never expected merfolk to be so intrigued with fashion. Either they were, or they were saying it to gain her trust.

"She is an artist worth noting," Cassandra said. "I think we shall see much of her designs."

The mermaid with a purple tower of hair moved toward the lantern holding Malcom. She sniffed the air and grinned. "He smells fresh."

"And very much enjoys kissing." Cassandra smiled. "You'll be quite pleased."

The three mermaids glanced at each other.

The brunette leader said, "It seems a fair exchange." She reached into a pocket hidden within the pool and raised a scroll encased in gold. Cassandra's eyes were hungry as she stepped toward them.

Mabel readied herself. They were nearing the moment she had to act.

Cassandra raised the other cage, having unlatched the door, a finger holding it closed. "I also have this batch of healthy young men; in case you are interested."

The purple-haired one sniffed the cage and wrinkled her nose. "Those all stink of years of salt."

Cassandra began to pull back the cage, but the door flipped open, and frogs leapt out.

"Give me my brother!" Mabel yelled as they had planned and rammed with full force against Cassandra. The mermaid tumbled forward into the pool of water and Mabel grabbed the lantern holding Malcom as Cassandra passed it to her.

The three mermaids in merfolk form screeched at an ear-piercing pitch as Mabel ran to the sconce and shoved on it. The tunnel door open and she sprinted to the right. Shouts broke out behind her, but she ran as swift as she could while gripping Malcom's lantern.

Mabel glanced back. Shadows in the dim tunnel approached swiftly. She focused straight ahead, trying to get more speed, but the footsteps were gaining on her.

Slipping on the rock as she ran, she sought some alcove or opening to hide in. The tunnel ran on, and the footsteps grew closer.

There was a zapping noise and Mabel looked over her shoulder. A pair of tall men carrying gleaming tridents sped toward her. One of them carried an eel covered in lines of electricity and raised it to throw at her. Looking ahead, she tried to speed her step. Her foot snagged on a crack in the stony ground, and she tumbled, scraping her knees and palms.

"Cooperate and we may be kind," one of the guards said.

Mabel scrambled to her knees while grabbing a rock. The guards approached her with a steady sureness. She was trapped but would fight before being captured.

With a yell, she threw the rock toward the nearest guard. He twisted his hand and the rock skewed to the side. As she edged away, the second guard pulled back his arm to throw the eel at her. Mabel turned to run, hoping she might dodge.

A broad-shouldered man leapt out from a hidden alcove and threw a net at the two guards. They raised their tridents, but the net caught them, and the pair jolted as if shocked before falling.

"Won't hold them long and more will come." The hard-faced man with a gold earring held out his dark-toned hand, his skin a far richer color than most in Cliffshire. His clothes were worn and smelled of the sea.

She took his hand and he helped her to her feet. As they ran down the tunnel, more shouts came from behind them, matched by the clang of swords.

"This way!" He led her around a corner while a few guns went off followed by a cannon.

"What's taking so long, Paulson?" a bleating voice called from ahead.

"There was a girl in trouble, Gregson." Paulson pivoted as he ran and fired a pistol toward the ceiling. Mabel held her arms over her heads as she kept her swift pace while rocks fell from above.

"Pretty one?" There was a hopeful tone in the other man's voice.

"She's nearly a child." Paulson grunted as they continued running. He led her around another corner and through an opening camouflaged by vines. She breathed in as they came outside, the air cool and fresh. A ship was visible in the moonlight, the cannons blasting toward the water, a black flag with crossbones rising above the full sails.

"She is very young. Too young for this sort of trouble." A grey-haired man bearing the bleating voice came out from behind the trees, hooves where his hands should be. "Where'd you find her?"

"In the hallway. Seemed in as much trouble as we are." Paulson pulled out his pistol and reloaded it. "Gregson, what'd you do?"

"Thought a nip of the drinks merfolk were serving would be worth the risk."

"And now you've no hands for rowing back to the ship."

"You always row faster without me." Gregson gave an apologetic shrug.

A booming sound came from the tunnel behind them, and Mabel jumped. The shouts and clashing of swords grew louder.

"Come on, girl." Paulson waved for her to follow as he sprinted toward a longboat waiting onshore. Gregson hobbled beside him, his legs bent like the back-legs of a goat. Mabel frowned, shock running through her. The man had a small, fluffy tail behind him.

"You coming, young lady?" Gregson turned and grimaced. "I'd not stay here when the Marvethan Hunters join the guards. There are worse things than being half-transformed into a goat."

Mabel gripped the lantern holding Malcom, wondering what merfolk might do beyond transforming a human. It would be best not to find out.

She ran after the pair of men and helped Paulson push the longboat into the water before climbing aboard herself. Paulson's powerful arms pulled the longboat away from shore.

Perhaps Cassandra would take her home if Mabel waited on the shore as ordered and was lucky enough not to be found. However, given how Malcom sat as a toad in the lantern, it was unclear how far Cassandra could be trusted.

Mabel was sure of her choice as merfolk guards ran along the shore, hunting fugitives.

"They're sending the orcas!" Gregson held onto the side of the boat with his arm. "Get down, girl."

Mabel hunkered down while Paulson pulled harder.

A black fin rose in the water nearby and a tail splashed, splattering the boat and rocking it. Mabel gripped the side of the boat as something beneath nudged it. Paulson gritted his teeth as he rowed, the oars flying through the water. A thump hit the bottom of the boat tilting it up. Mabel leaned toward the upward side along with Gregson. Water sprayed up as the boat landed.

She looked ahead, the sail ship now close. A rope ladder hung from the side and crew members fired guns and spears toward the water. At least three orcas gleamed in the moonlight, circling the ship. Mabel glanced around the longboat, seeking any weapon. A rifle lay nearby, and she grabbed it with both hands, trying to remember everything from the few shooting lessons she'd had while Malcom was out hunting.

Her heart quickened as she rested on one knee, holding the rifle ready. The sleek, black form of an orca approached, speeding through the water. Panic rose within her, but she shoved it down while aiming the weapon. Once the orca was close enough, she fired toward its head. The gun recoiled, slamming into her shoulder. She cried out while trying not to wince.

Her bullet must have hit because the whale turned off course, twisting in the water and sending a surging wave toward them. She barely kept hold of the rifle as she fell back into the boat.

"Grab the rope!" Gregson yelled.

Mabel squinted, trying to see the rope in the moonlight. A wave splashed over her, blinding her for a few seconds.

"The rope, girl!"

With her vision cleared, she grabbed the rope swinging from the side of the ship. It slipped from her hands and thunked against the wooden hull before the crew above swung it again. This time, she caught it.

Another orca hit their longboat from beneath and there was a loud crack followed by Paulson letting out a curse.

"Grab hold of me." Paulson held his arm out to Gregson. The hoove-handed man wrapped his arms around Paulson's shoulders and held on. Paulson then grabbed the rope from Mabel and said, "Grab hold of me too. Keep tight."

Mabel nodded and kept a firm grip on the lantern with Malcom before holding her other arm around Paulson. He wrapped the rope around his leg and gripped it with both arms. She felt his strength as the rope yanked upward, pulling them from the boat.

As they dangled beside the ship, an orca crashed through the longboat and the small vessel splintered apart. Mabel clung tighter to Paulson and shut her eyes. Within seconds, members of the crew pulled her and the others onto the deck.

"Grab a rifle!" the captain bellowed as he stood near the mast wearing a large, wide hat with embroidery, his coat flapping in the wind.

A crew member tossed a rifle to Paulson who swiftly took it and joined other crew members along the edge of the ship. Then, the crew member handed a pair of rifles to Mabel along with a box of bullets. "Reload for Paulson."

With the weapons slipping in her grip, she knelt beside Paulson and stared at the rifle, trying to remember how to load it.

"Like this." Paulson pulled back on the hammer, pulled a lever, and opened the breech chamber. He dropped the bullet in, closed it and raised the rifle to fire. Mable stared over the edge of the ship. Merfolk were visible beneath the waves, swimming alongside the orcas as if guiding them.

"Either fire or load, girl!" another crew member shouted.

Paulson fired while Mabel's wet fingers fought with the hammer and lever on the second rifle. Once the breech chamber was open, she dropped the bullet in, closed it, and handed it to Paulson.

"You'll get it. Just keep steady." Paulson gave her a nod before leaning over the side of the ship and firing.

"Tighten that sail!" the captain yelled. "Get this blasted ship moving!"

The wind grew harder as if he had summoned it, the ship gaining speed as they drove further from shore. She fell into a steady rhythm of reloading and trading the rifles with Paulson. He had to often load for himself, but she was getting faster.

"They're heading off!" a crew member yelled.

She panted while falling against the side of the ship as the orcas and merfolk relented. A cheer grew among the crew, a few of them hugging each other. A few patted some donkeys standing on the deck, wearing striped shirts across their upper half.

"Those're our crewmates we came to rescue." Paulson nodded toward them before slapping Mabel's shoulder. "You did a fine job helping, girl."

As he turned to another crewmate, Mabel picked up the lantern holding Malcom and moved to the nearest mast, trying to be as invisible as she could. Exhaustion dragged on her and she tried not to shiver in her damp dress under the cold wind.

She had gone from a common ballroom to a merfolk gala to a pirate battle in a matter of hours. Looking down at her brother, half of her hoped closing her eyes would lead her to wake up and discover this was only some exhausting dream. However, a freezing gust of wind battering her face reminded her how real everything was.

"This here's the lass." Gregson hobbled toward her. "Heartier than she looks, Captain Stenton."

The captain's heavy footsteps approached, and Mabel pushed herself to stand and appear more confident than she felt. He rested his hands on his hips as he looked her over, a scowl on his grizzled face, a few scars nicking his skin.

"What's your name, miss?" Captain Stenton eyed her.

"Mabel Sinclair, sir." There was no point in lying. She raised the lantern holding Malcom. "I'm just trying to get my brother and myself home to Barthan."

He tapped the lantern. "Got you mixed up with merfolk, eh?"

"It's not the first trouble my brother's gotten into, but it is the most dangerous."

A small smile cracked Stenton's hard face. "I know the sort. And you got dragged along?"

"Somewhat." It had been her choice to jump onto Cassandra's yacht. "Can you help us find passage home?"

"Perhaps. When we're in less dangerous waters." He scratched his nose. "Any special skills, besides being the slowest rifle loader I've seen?"

Mabel stared blankly. It would be fair to contribute what she could on the ship, while traveling to some port where she might find a passenger vessel headed to Barthan. Thinking through what she had to offer, she said, "I can read and write, sir. And do a bit of accounting, if needed and I—" She tried to think of something else as he squinted at her. Glancing at her drenched skirt, she said, "And I have two hands and can sew."

"Tonight, two hands that aren't hooves are in short supply." He held out his hand. "Welcome aboard the Gray Moon, Miss Sinclair."

CHAPTER 4

In Which Mabel and Antonio Learn Their Trades

The Sita Ocean, between Castallar and Hyun

July of the Year 306 B.R.

Sitting on his bunk, Antonio signed his weekly letter to Sofia before folding it into an envelope and kissing it. In three months at sea, he had only received a pair of letters from her. His mother wrote every week and his sisters sent letters often, plus a few notes from friends.

Most likely, Sofia just hadn't been able to sneak the rest of her letters past her parents. More would come later. He was sure of it.

The letters she had sent were rare treasures, despite being less than a page each. They were marked with a kiss from her lipstick and held ink smeared from a teardrop. He had already memorized her brief words, but it was a comfort to read them again.

The boatswain's whistle marked the early morning shift. While other sailors groaned, Antonio hopped from the bed, checked his lengthening hair in his pocket mirror, and hurried up the stairs. He had already shaved hours ago, instead of joining other sailors in singing bawdy songs. It was one of the few ways he could manage his appearance.

He joined the other seamen in heading to the deck of the wooden frigate. The vessel was large and impressive despite the worn rigging and creaking at every smack of the waves. He'd been surprised the ship was still in service when he had first come aboard. Yet, there was a beauty to the frigate which the new steamships lacked.

"Pretty fingers." The deckhand pointed toward Antonio and then at the foremast. "Staysail's got a small rip. Go manage it."

Antonio ran below deck and grabbed the satchel carrying his sewing kit. While other men swabbed the deck, pulled ropes, and repaired the ship, he climbed up the rigging for his most common task.

Reaching near the top of the mast, tied in by a rope harness, he took a moment to look out over the water. Islands stood in the distance, but the mainland was far behind them. He smiled, trying to compose how he would describe the view to Sofia in his next letter.

The wind was strong at this height as he pulled on the ropes holding the sail, making it loose while the rest of the sails on the ship carried it forward. Carefully placing his feet against the wood rod holding the bottom of the sail, he held onto the top with one hand while he pulled out his needle and thread. Squinting, he analyzed the small tears in the thick canvas. With the right stitch, it would be as if the tears had never existed.

He glanced behind him while pressing the needle into the sail and hummed. A glimmer of light ran along the needle as it guided itself through the thick fabric.

He pictured himself sitting with his father, Manuel, explaining how to focus his magic and guide the needle with music. As a child, Antonio had thought everyone else did the same until his sister Luisa had screamed at seeing the needle move on its own. Since then, he had learned to hide when he used his power, covering it with his hand, hiding in a corner, or working late at night.

Keeping his hand close to the curved needle winding in and out of the fabric, making it look as if he were sewing, Antonio sung to himself.

I'll return to my love one day again,
Some place where the sea meets the sun,
Just stay true to me and watch the stars,
And I'll be home to be in your arms.

"Oh, my sweet darling," Pieras said from about ten feet below as he fixed some rigging. "Your eyes shine like a polished buckle and your hair waves like the weed of the sea."

The sailor at least twenty years older than Antonio laughed, his skin rough from years on the ocean.

"You just envy that I've found my true heart," Antonio called back.

"I've found my true heart," Pieras shouted over the wind. "It sits at every port in a bottle of rum and a plump barmaid in my lap."

"Even barmaids deserve true respect," Antonio said. "Why not try talking to one?"

"I communicate plenty with my lips." Pieras grinned. "You should try it at the next port. With your pretty face, you'll find a girl to enjoy right off. And, if she's friendly enough, maybe the night too."

Pieras gave a hearty laugh as Antonio focused on his work, hiding his embarrassment.

"I'm returning home with two things you lost long ago," Antonio said. "My honor and my money."

Piers laughed even harder. "You should try tossing both away. The reward is worth it."

Antonio shook his head while Pieras began singing one of the rougher sailor shanties, and several other deep-voiced, longtime seamen joined in from various parts of the ship. They were good men in their own way, doing honest work for the Navy. However, few of them looked beyond the next day, with their plans only to live and die on the open sea.

"Keep your head straight," Antonio whispered. "Save your money. Get home. Marry Sofia. Open the tailor shop. Build your future."

It was a mantra he said at least a dozen times a day, and it kept him focused while other men teased him, trying to tempt him with the pleasures at post. His father had spoken of having a similar focus that had helped him get through long days at sea. Antonio knew his future was with Sofia, and nothing would push him from his path.

The Khamsan Sea, between Barthan and Eastern Sandar

Mabel placed some small bits of cooked fish into the lantern holding Malcom and refilled the cup of fresh water.

"I'm sorry it's taking so long to get home," she said as her brother's chin expanded while breathing. "Captain Stenton says if I kiss you, you'll become human again. If I could trust you not to make an idiot of yourself, I'd try it. But I'm afraid of what stupid scheme you'd come up with to get us off the ship." She shut the lantern. "You'll be more comfortable here, anyway."

"How's your brother today?" said Gregson, whose hands were fully formed again, though he still had black hoof-like shells over his fingers.

"Still a toad."

Mabel rose from her bunk tucked in with everyone else's. There were only three other women in the thirty-person crew. Six of the crew members were still transformed into donkeys three months after leaving Marveth. Mabel joined the others in not having much hope they'd return to being humans.

"Thanks again for the alteration in my trousers." He turned around, showing the hole she'd helped him sew into his pants for his small tail to stick out of. "Doesn't seem to be going away any time soon, and I sit on it much less often."

Mabel tried not to laugh. "I'm glad to help."

"Have you changed your mind about the song for tonight?" A grin crossed his weathered face as they walked through the narrow passage, shifting around the barrels and crates strapped along one side of the crew quarters. "I've heard you sing while working on deck. Your voice is lovely, and with Paulson on the accordion, it'd warm us all."

"I'm not a singer." She went up to the deck, pushing open the door and taking in the fresh ocean air. It was a beautiful day.

"Neither am I, but I still do my best." He attempted a few notes, his goat's bleat nearly on tune.

At this, Mabel couldn't help but laugh. Gregson joined her laughing, more bleats coming.

"Stripes!" Captain Stenton barked from the helm. "Come here."

Mabel jogged across the deck before saluting. "Aye, sir?"

Stenton handed a velvet vest to Mabel. "This is my favorite vest." He pointed at a break along one of the seams. "I repaired it last week with the stitches you showed me, but it keeps breaking."

"Did you talk to Henrietta about giving you less pie?" Mabel said as she analyzed the rip. "Good stitches can only do so much when your clothes get too tight."

Stenton's frown deepened as he held a hand to his stomach. "A man's life at sea is hard. Don't make him give up his sweet pies."

Mabel bit back a giggle. "I'll see about adding a panel to the sides. Give you some room to grow, if you need it."

He patted her shoulder. "It was a good moon when we brought you on board, Stripes. What'd an old sailor like me do without a sharp girl like you watching out for him?"

"Not wear his favorite vest," she said.

Stenton barked a rough laugh, showing his yellow teeth. He waved for her to follow him. "Want to guess where we are today?"

She joined him beside the helmsman. He held up the sextant and pocket watch before making marks on the navigator's log. She leaned over the log, analyzing the markings before following him inside to where the map lay on the table. Rubbing her chin, she made a few calculations before drawing a line with her finger from one of the markers sitting on the map.

"Looks like we've traveled twenty miles east of Isla Azul."

Stenton grinned proudly. "Twenty-four miles east, but close to spot on. We'll make you a pilot just yet."

"I don't mind learning to be a pilot, but I would like to get home."

"All in good time." He waved his hand. "Just a few more ports to stop through, and you'll be there."

Mabel raised an eyebrow as she drew a line following the ship's path. "It looks like it'll be another six months."

"See? I told you I'd get you there."

"My parents probably think Malcom and I are dead."

"We forged that ransom letter to prove you're alive. If any money comes through, we'll have enough to book your passage at the next port. But at least they've had word you're alive."

"And supposedly being held ransom by pirates."

Stenton shrugged. "You can tell them what a fine time you had while we held you."

Mabel bit back a laugh. She was having far more fun than she should while traveling on a pirate ship in the middle of the ocean. Many of the days were hard and long, the work sometimes backbreaking, but there was a freedom here she didn't have back home as a banker's daughter. Instead of classes in etiquette and history, she had lessons in navigation and firing cannons. It was far more interesting and challenging.

A whistle came from the deck followed by a shout of, "Bounty off the port bow!"

Stenton clapped his hands together. "Finally. If it's the right ship, we'll have our full complement of crew by tonight."

"Back under deck, then?" Mabel said.

Stenton squinted at her before opening a drawer and tossing her a red leather mask and black scarf. "If you want to keep your hands clean, yes. But aren't you curious how the work is done?"

Mabel bit her lip. She should keep her hands clean of their work, but her curiosity was great. She always heard the scuffle of battle above deck while holed up in her bunk. To see a real sea battle herself would be an experience. Especially when traveling with pirates as friendly as these.

"What if I—" She swallowed. "I don't want to kill anyone."

"Neither do I. I've told you how we work. We get them to shake in their boots a bit, take some spare goods, and then leave them with a good story. What's so troubling about that? Then, they'll gouge the prices of what's left when they reach shore."

Mabel took a breath before pulling on the black scarf followed by the mask. It covered her whole face except her chin and mouth. Stenton grinned with excitement as he pulled on his own mask made of silver and a hat with large feathers, matching his decorated coat. Mabel pulled on one of the cabin boy's longcoats and the weapon belt.

"Make sure to point it at the enemy and not yourself." Stenton handed her a pistol before pointing at where various swords and cutlasses hung from the wall. "Pick your blade."

Mabel hesitated before taking the hilt of a wide-bladed cutlass. It was heavier than she expected as she tried to lift it from the wall. If she could barely pick it up here, it would be better not to carry into battle. Instead, she took the worn-looking rapier.

"A good blade for you." Stenton laughed and tapped her shoulder.

Mabel hefted the rapier, hoping the few rounds of fencing training her parents had indulged her with would do her any good. She slid it into the sword loop on her belt. Hopefully, she would leave it there the whole battle.

Her heart pounded as she joined Stenton on the deck while crew members lowered the Barthanian flag and raised the Jolly Roger. Mabel rested her hand on the rapier's hilt. She shouldn't be excited, but there was something intoxicating in how her adrenaline rose while the rest of the crew assembled for battle. Half the crew ran below to man the cannons while she was handed a rifle and sent to the edge of the ship.

"Half-size merchant ship. Count ten cannons," came the lookout above.

"Out for a bit of fun?" Gregson grinned as he knelt beside her and held his rifle ready.

"I don't want to hurt anyone."

"That's why you practice your aim." He held a hand over his hair peppered with gray. "Go for flipping the hat off. Extra points if they wet their pants."

Several of the other crew chuckled.

"Got six last time," Paulson said with a proud grin.

"One of those counted as mine." Gregson pointed. "I got him first."

Stenton shouted commands as forward cannons were raised. "Fire the grappling hooks!"

The forward cannons fired, harpoon-length grappling hooks flying out, attached to chains. The hooks stabbed into the aft of the merchant vessel, digging into the wood. Shouts and cries came from the ship while their crew fired back.

"Drop anchor and reel them in!"

Several men pulled on cranks attached to the grappling hook chains to drag the ship to them. Mabel raised her rifle alongside Gregson and Paulson as the pair fired just above the heads of the other ship's men. Mabel kept her finger on the trigger, but her hands shook, ruining her aim. Better to not fire and needlessly risk a life.

Another cannon fired from the Gray Moon, hitting the foremast of the merchant vessel. Shouts broke from the other ship and Stenton raised a brass megaphone as he stood on the ship's railing.

"This be your only warning, or Captain Ghost'll knock your arses under the sea."

Mabel joined the crew in letting out ghostly howls. The sailors on the other ship cowered, their eyes wide with fear.

"Pay a bounty and you'll be spared! No need to be brave! Cowards are the true heroes!"

"Fire!" shouted the captain of the other ship.

"Paulson, show them what you're made of!" Stenton yelled.

As several cannons fired from the other ship, Paulson knelt and fired, shooting the captain's hat from his head.

"Last chance to spare your ship and crew!" Stenton said. "If you want to make a profit of this voyage and spare your hide, I suggest you surrender!"

"Now we fire some warning shots," Gregson whispered.

Mabel winced before aiming for the broadside of the ship and firing her rifle. The recoil hit her shoulder hard, and she cried out while many sailors' hats flipped off their heads.

"What do ya say, dear captain?" Stenton yelled. "All we want is a few pieces of cargo, then we be on our way."

The captain snarled before yelling to his crew, "Stand down and stand aside!"

"Come along, Stripes. Let's give them a visit," Gregson said.

Mabel yelled as she and Gregson grabbed ropes and swung across to the other ship while other crewmates worked to lash the pair of ships together, setting a gangplank between them. She joined him and six other crewmen in holding pistols on the sailors while Captain Stenton and other crew members came across on the gangplank, a swagger in the captain's step. Once onboard, Stenton motioned for her to follow him. She walked with her back to his alongside Paulson as they entered the captain's quarters. Gregson pushed the captain inside and held a knife to his throat. Stenton whistled to himself as he gathered a few gold coins sitting out. He knocked along the side of a set of drawers before opening one and felt around for a switch.

"There it is."

There was click and a panel opened on the side of the cabinet. Stenton wiggled his fingers and pulled out a set of three vials carrying a thick, sparkling liquid the color of apple cider.

"Smuggling amber syrup?" Stenton tsked as he gave a mock glare at the captain.

The captain yelled as he shoved off the pirate and raised a small gun from his pocket. Without thinking, Mabel aimed and fired her pistol. The captain cried out as he grabbed his upper arm. Mabel's eyes widened and she shook.

She had just shot a man.

"I'm so sorry," she said. "Are you all right?"

The captain snarled as he grabbed a knife and started to rise. Gregson shoved him back down with his right hoof.

"Don't you harm Stripes," he growled.

"Get back on the ship," Stenton barked. "We'll manage here."

Mabel stared at the wound she had created till Paulson nudged her shoulder.

"Get on, Stripes. You've done enough.'

Breaking from her daze, Mabel ran from the quarters and grabbed the rope to swing back to their ship. Leaping from the railing she sped through the air, her mind recreating the pistol firing and the captain jerking back as her bullet hit his arm. Her side bashed into the hull of her ship, and she lost hold of the rope before falling into the water.

"Come on, Stripes! The rope's right there!" said one of the crewmen while trying not to laugh.

Mabel grabbed the end of the rope and began climbing up. She was grateful as a pair of crew members pulled on the other end and helped her on board.

Several of the crew wrapped a blanket around her and guided her to the captain's quarters. There she sat shaking for an hour, wishing she hadn't been so brave and hadn't fired the pistol. What if she had killed the man?

Within an hour, their ship rolled away from the merchant vessel. She found herself relaxing the further they went.

"They'll be shouting to the Navy," Stenton said as he came in and hung his hat. "But we'll be long gone and have changed the name of our ship before we reach port."

He put his hands on his knees as he bent over and looked her in the eye, her mask sitting next to her. "How do you feel about being a pirate, Stripes?"

"I'm not a very good one," she muttered.

"Your quick shot kept my hide alive." He patted her shoulder. "I think that's fine work for your first time around."

He opened up a cabinet and pulled out a pair of bottles. "Come, celebrate with the crew."

She looked up at him. "What if I had killed him?"

"Then that's the poor trade the fellow made by trying to shoot me." Stenton rested a hand on her shoulder. "You did right as part of the crew, Stripes. You were quick on the trigger and protected your captain. It is troubling the first time you strike a man but know you did right and keep on. Don't dwell on the matter." He pointed at her. "And why we work so hard to spare the lives of those we attack. We're only there for a profit. Not for blood."

Mabel nodded. His words helped, but unease still filled her. Rising, she followed Captain Stenton out of the cabin and onto the main deck. As she reached the helm, Gregson raised his own bottle of stolen wine and shouted, "To the mighty pirate Red Stripes who helped save our captain!"

The other crew members joined his cheer and applauded.

"Before dumping her own arse in the ocean!" Paulson called out.

Laughter followed and Mabel pulled the blanket over her head to hide her reddening face.

Stenton nudged her shoulder. "Come on, girl. You know in your heart you're one of us. Brave, strong, and don't mind nipping a bit of fat off wealthy merchants."

Maybe she wasn't one of them. Maybe she had made a terrible mistake. Maybe she should have followed Cassandra's instructions and stayed onshore. If she had, maybe she would be home already.

"And with this syrup," Stenton shouted, "we can save our crew members those vile mermaids cursed! Thirtieth raid with no man lost, and now we'll have six men found!"

The crew broke into cheers again. Mabel pulled back the blanket and looked at the vial Stenton raised.

These weren't heartless pirates. They were men and women making their way in the world, free of the rules of others. And they cared for each other. And her.

Though it had been frightening, the adventure had been fun.

If they went too far, she wouldn't join them. And, considering all the wrong in the world, maybe she and this group of brave men and women could do some good.

This wasn't piracy. This was freedom.

She bit her lip before raising her fist and joining the crew's cheers.

CHAPTER 5

In Which Mabel Makes a Bet

Port Nerama, Island in the Sita Ocean, colony of the Castallar Protectorate

October of the Year 306 B.R.

Antonio strolled along the market at Port Nerama, on a large island far from the coast of Castallar. A dozen languages were spoken around him as sailors bartered with the shopkeepers for goods. He paused at a cart full of rolls of fabric. His fingers brushed one, feeling the finely woven linen. This was genuine Gathrayan fabric from Sandar and quite expensive back in Castallar. His mother would love working with this soft fabric. It would be so easy to mold and drape.

"How much per yard?" he said.

The merchant shouted a far more reasonable price than Antonio expected. It would cut deep into his pocket money. He did have his savings tucked in the ankles of his calf-length boots, keeping them safe from thieves. With it, he could spend a bit extra for a gift to send his mother.

Maybe he would buy a yard or two more for one of the dresses he had sketched for Sofia. He could send the design back to his mother and pay for it to be made, and then have it taken to Sofia on her birthday.

Her third letter had finally reached him this morning. It was as brief as the other two from his past six months at sea and held no explanation of why her letters were so rare. But it gave him hope to plaster over his crack of worry, even while it kept growing.

She was still his and this gift would remind her of his adoration.

The thought brought warmth as he reached for his pocketbook tucked in his trouser pocket. His heart jumped. Nothing was there. Not even the wrapped candies he had bought earlier.

Spinning on his foot, he stared at the ground behind him.

It had to have fallen out. He just needed to find it somewhere in this crowd of hundreds packed together.

Unless a pickpocket had stolen it.

But he had kept his hand in his pocket the whole time.

Except for when that older woman had dropped her packages and he helped her.

A dread rose in Antonio as he backed away from the fabric stand. Someone had used his moment of kindness against him, and now his pocketbook, and his half-written letter to Sofia, were gone.

"What have we learned of the young sailor?" Mabel said in Castallan to Paulson and Henrietta as she sat on the brick wall overlooking the market. She smoothed her red hair woven into a crown braid, making sure everything was in place. Meanwhile, the handsome, young Castallan sailor patted his pockets and began to look around him in panic. "Hurry. He's figured his pocketbook is missing."

Henrietta chuckled as she unfolded a half-written letter. "He has a darling Sofia and is counting down the days to marry her."

Mabel harumphed while Henrietta pressed her hands to her heart and gave a mocking sigh.

"Oh, young love." Henrietta cackled, one-third of her teeth missing in her wrinkled mouth.

"What else?" Mabel said. It was unfair for a young man so good looking to already have a girl.

"Other sailors talk about his young love." Paulson leaned his elbows on his knees, a red scarf covering his bald head. "Say he loves his mama."

"Must be a nice young man, he was so helpful with my packages." Henrietta cackled again before patting Mabel's cheek. "If you're aiming for your first kiss, he's a good one."

Mabel's face grew warm. Perhaps she shouldn't have made a bet with the pair of them to gain her first kiss while here at port. It had been hard to say no while they had been teasing her onboard the ship, with other crewmembers telling tales of romances at port. Now, picturing herself kissing some strange man, her cheeks felt hot. However, losing and having Henrietta rub it in might be more embarrassing. It would be better to push through and succeed.

"Not that I want to lose the bet, but I'd pick a different target." Paulson pointed to another Castallan sailor who was leaning to the side drunkenly and winking at a woman whose cleavage was barely contained by her dress. "He'd kiss you right off."

"If I'm to get my first kiss, I want it from a gentleman." She might be traveling with pirates, but she did have standards. Snatching the pocketbook from Henrietta, she pulled out two of the one mac bills and handed one to each of her companions. "And what's the fun if it isn't a challenge?"

"You've a true pirate's heart," Henrietta said proudly. "And don't you worry. We'll be watching you and that boy. If he turns out not to be a gentleman, we'll come swinging."

"As will Captain Stenton." Mabel waved to their captain as he strolled through the market, pretending not to watch her with a worried eye. "And Gregson." She waved to him.

Still wishing they hadn't goaded her into agreeing, Mabel crouched on the wall. "Wish me luck."

"I just wish you a good kiss." Henrietta tapped Mabel's behind. Mabel shot her a glare before jumping down onto a patch of grass and then dropped into the market crowd.

"I'm going to make a fool of myself," she muttered while winding through the crowd. But this was nearly the same as the sort of thievery she helped with on the ship. And the tingle along her spine as she wondered if the gambit would work was exciting. Once she pushed through the crowd and had a better view of the tall, young sailor with chin-length dark hair framing his cleanshaven, angular face, he seemed worth seeking a kiss from.

She was eighteen and certainly wasn't going to kiss any of her grizzled and yellow-teethed crewmates. They acted more like uncles, aunts, and older siblings. After six months at sea, it was worth trying.

"Señor," she said in Castallan, hoping her two years of lessons at home along with six months of practice while at sea would help her speak clearly. "Is this yours?"

The sailor's brown eyes brightened as she held up the pocketbook. He jogged over and smiled. "Where did you find it?"

Her truthful answer would have been, *in your pocket*, but she said, "I saw it fall out on the ground when you helped that poor old lady."

She faintly heard Henrietta's cackle through the crowd.

"Thank you," he said as she handed it to him.

He glanced through the pocketbook. Relief grew in his eyes as he pulled out the letter to his Sofia and kissed it. Disappointment hit Mabel's chest. Maybe he would be a harder target than planned. But she had committed and would complete her mission.

"I swear I had a few oners," he said.

She glanced behind her. "Maybe they fell out."

"Even so, thank you, señorita." He smiled at her and her heart skipped a half-beat. "How can I repay you?"

"I wouldn't mind a stroll through the market." She grinned. "And, perhaps, dinner?"

His smile fell and his tanned face paled a shade or two. "I am grateful, but—" He pulled at a chain around his neck and showed a locket. "I am spoken for, señorita."

"Married?" She raised her eyebrows.

A sadness washed through his eyes as his fingers rested on the locket. "We had hoped to be, but—" He forced a smile. "Thank you, again."

He turned to walk away, and Mabel cursed under her breath. She couldn't give up now. Not with six macs on the line. She wasn't going to give Paulson and Henrietta the satisfaction of winning so quickly.

"I saw you looking at that fabric cart when I was trying to find you." She hurried to keep at his side. She was taller than most women, but still a half-head shorter than him. "Do you mind if I look with you?"

"I'm just purchasing a few yards to send home to my mother."

Reaching the cart, Mabel pulled at a sheer, pink fabric. "This is quite nice. Would make a good layer."

The sailor went to a pile of fabrics in various earth tones. "I was looking at these Gathrayan linens."

Mabel moved to his side and pinched a corner of the linen and frowned. She rubbed it with her fingers before looking closer. "This is Sandarian, but the weave isn't right to be Gathrayan."

The sailor's eyebrows pinched together. "I've seen Gathrayan linen only once, but this is it."

Mabel glanced at him before holding up a section of fabric. "My mother has a few dresses made in Gathrayan linen. This is good quality fabric, but do you see how the weave slants this way?" She pointed with her pinky. "Real Gathrayan linen weaves back and forth every inch or two, which gives it's unique texture while breathing well."

"My mother is a seamstress," he said. "I know my fabric. This is Gathrayan."

Mabel snapped to the shopkeeper. As he looked to her, she said, "Do you have any Gathrayan linen?"

The shopkeeper nodded before walking into the back of his tent and returning with a bolt of off-white fabric. Mabel smiled as the sailor's eyes widened and the shopkeeper set the bolt in front of them, keeping a hand on it.

Leaning closer, the sailor said, "You're right, and it is beautiful."

He moved to touch it, but the shopkeeper slapped his hand and wagged his finger. "You buy first."

"How much a yard?" Mabel said. She joined the sailor in wincing at the price. The shopkeeper glowered at them before carrying the bolt of fabric back into the tent.

"Well, you've rescued my pocketbook and stopped me from buying fabric that isn't Gathrayan," the sailor said. "Perhaps I do owe you dinner."

Mabel grinned. "I suppose I must accept."

A small smile crossed the sailor's face and he held out his hand, lightly callused from being at sea. "Antonio Cortez."

She placed her hand on his and gave a mock-curtsey, though she wore trousers she had tailored after buying them second-hand at the last port. "Mildred Stripes."

He nodded to her. "It is an honor to meet you, Señorita Stripes."

She wished to hear her real name in his smooth voice, but it was better to keep an alias.

He offered his arm, but she motioned for him to wait as she turned to the shopkeeper and pointed to the off-white linen. "How much?"

"One mac per yard."

"I'll give you sixty skoons a yard. And I want two yards."

"Ninety."

"Eighty."

The shopkeeper frowned at her but nodded. As the merchant cut the fabric, Antonio said, "But it's not Gathrayan."

"It's a good price, and it's better than most of the fabric I've found." She pulled at the sleeve of her pinstripe shirt. "I've only three shirts, and all of them are made from a dress I had."

"You made your own shirt?"

"They don't hand out shirts on merchant vessels like on naval ships."

Antonio leaned back, his eyes assessing. "Would you pull off your jacket?"

"Señor Cortez," she said with a teasing smile, "aren't you spoken for?"

"I'm a tailor by trade." He let out a laugh. "I only want to see your craft."

"Then, I've even less reason to show you. I don't want my sloppy stitches judged."

The shopkeeper returned with the fabric and Mabel handed over her coins before putting the folded fabric into her satchel.

"There's a cart up the way with some magazines from the mainland," Antonio said, offering his arm. "I think I saw an issue of *Modan*."

Mabel eyes grew wide as she took his arm and walked with him. "I read it every month back home. My favorite are Mr. Hartavo's designs."

"I don't like how he crowds a woman's neck with ruffles." Antonio waved his hand down, as if crafting a flowing skirt out of air. "Ruffles should be light and complement a woman's figure, flowing with her as she walks, not making her look like a henpecked crane."

"Yes, but how he structures the shoulders complements the stiff ruffles around the neck. It's not right for every figure, but if you want a woman to look long and lean, he does it well."

"Most women in my hometown are shorter and, well—" Antonio laughed a little. "My sister Luisa always says she's, 'complimented by curves.'"

Mabel chuckled. "I could see where Madame Pellon's designs would suit that silhouette better. In my hometown, women are always trying to seem taller and more elegant."

"Tallness is not elegance. That comes from giving the woman a grace, and letting the clothing complement her." He raised a finger. "Now, men's fashion appears simple, but there is much more structure involved. You have to consider how wide the shoulders are compared with the waist. And if a man has—" Antonio motioned around his nicely trim waist. "A lot of waist, it needs to be smoothed with a properly sized waistband, instead of having a waistband so tight the gut becomes a shelf that looks as if it will topple over."

"But isn't that how a man proves he's still young and strong?" Mabel said with a giggle. "By wearing the same pants he did as a youth no matter how much of his stomach folds over?"

Antonio stuck out his gut. "And you must make sure the buttons on your shirt stretch a bit, otherwise the look isn't fully made."

They laughed together and Mabel wished he didn't have the locket sitting under his shirt. Even if she didn't get a kiss by the end of their time together, she was glad she had chosen his pocketbook to steal.

Reaching the magazine stand, he led her to a section where sat a whole rack of *Modan*. Some of the issues were a few years old and faded, but they had fun looking at the covers, comparing notes on the clothing and its construction and on the changes in trends.

He gasped as he uncovered two copies of the annual review from three months before. "Look at this."

Mabel grinned at the thick issue. "I always love looking through the annual issue."

"It appears checkers are in style." He flipped through before waving to the shopkeeper. "How much?"

"One mac each."

Antonio held onto the magazine as if it were precious. As he reached for his pocketbook, Mabel said, "Fifty skoons each."

They settled on a price of seventy skoons. Mabel frowned as Antonio handed over one mac and forty skoons.

"You're buying one to send to your mother?" she said.

He handed one to her. "Consider it part of my thank you gift."

Her eyes widened. Rumor was naval sailors only made five macs a week, with some pay being docked for extra food, clothing, and blankets. This was too much.

"And," Antonio said, "it makes me feel better for it to be in the hands of someone who'll appreciate it."

She cradled the magazine, holding it delicately. If he didn't initiate a kiss by the end of their time together, she might.

Tucking the magazine into her satchel, she glanced at Paulson as he pretended to look at a booth covered in jewelry. She gave him a small grin and he winked back.

Holding out his copy of the magazine, Antonio ran his fingers over the headline. "Someday, this will have the words, 'Antonio Cortez' across the cover."

"Or," she said while waving her hand over the cover, "'Mabel Sinclair.'"

Antonio frowned at her. "Why would it say that?"

She playfully pushed his shoulder. "Because that's my name."

He stood straighter. "You said your name is Mildred Stripes."

Mabel sucked in her cheeks and glanced away. She needed to be more consistent in lying. "That's the name I signed onto the ship under." Her stomach churned as she thought quickly. "I—um—ran away from home."

Which was somewhat true. There had been a ship at the last port which would have brought her home in a month. With the pickpocketing skills her friends had taught her, she could have gathered enough to buy passage. Yet she had chosen to stay with Captain Stenton. He had promised to get her home eventually.

"You chose to go to sea?"

"It seemed more fun than planning my debutante ball." And it was. Her debutante would have been two months ago and each time her mother ever spoke of the night, it sounded a horrendous spectacle.

"You come from a family that could afford a debutante ball?"

"Why I am at sea is a long, complicated story," she said quietly, her head lowered. His disapproval somehow hurt. "I was trying to save my brother from being kidnapped, and—" Explaining her brother had transformed into a toad and how she had escaped merfolk might not be wise. "Well, the ship I'm on rescued me and is working to get me home."

"If you were kidnapped," Antonio said, his eyes shaded by concern, "we should take you to the authorities. I can talk to the officers of my ship. They will—"

She touched his arm. "The ship I'm on is taking me home. I'd rather not say anything more because—" She glanced behind her and whispered, "I gave you a false name, in case my brother's kidnappers are hunting him. That's why he's still on the ship."

"And you came to port alone?" He glanced back and narrowed his eyes. "I've noticed a few questionable looking men who've stayed a while. Always need to keep an eye out for thieves."

She bit her lip, deciding not to remark he wasn't very good at that. By now, she could have snatched his pocketbook at least three more times.

"That's just my friend Paulson." She waved at Paulson and gave him a friendly smile. He pretended not to notice. She gave him a bigger wave and he scowled at her as if to ask what she was doing. "He's like an uncle."

"I meant him." Antonio nodded toward a man holding a bottle and leaning against a wall while scratching his rear end. "He's been following me half the day. I don't think he's as drunk as he's pretending."

Mabel was disappointed she hadn't noticed the man. She had been watching Henrietta, Paulson, Gregson, and Stenton taking turns keeping an eye on her.

"Stay close by my side," Antonio said. "I'll get you back to your ship safely."

"I still want dinner," she whispered. "Even if I did lie to you."

"I will keep my word, but I will also keep you safe."

Mabel's heart fluttered a bit as Antonio put a protective hand on the small of her back and deftly guided her as he moved out of the market.

"What if he's following me and not you?" Mabel said.

"I'm a sailor in the Navy. Always makes me a target for those looking to punch a face in."

"You've a very pretty face," she said. "I'd prefer if they didn't punch it."

"Might make me look tougher," he said. "And make my crewmates tease me less."

Despite the small sense of danger, she giggled.

He tucked his copy of the magazine into his own satchel before they walked to the shops along the wharf, and he led her toward a wood building.

"I promised my mother to stop by a photography shop. Do you mind?" he said.

"If there are thieves inside waiting to attack, then yes. Otherwise, no."

He laughed but glanced over his shoulder before leading her inside a shop with photographs posted in the window. At the shop counter, he paid for a package of three photographs.

Mabel held his satchel and stood back as Antonio smoothed his sailor uniform and combed his hair before standing in front of an off-white sheet. He appeared quite noble and handsome as he looked at the camera and two of the photographs were taken.

"Don't you want your girl in one?" The shop girl gestured at Mabel.

Antonio glanced at her as he frowned.

"Don't you want one to remember her by?" the shop girl said.

Antonio smiled as he motioned for Mabel to come over. "I only need two to send home. Why don't you take one of your own?"

"Let's take one together. For fun." She walked toward him.

He hesitated as his eyes focused on hers. His hand rested on where the locket lay under his uniform, but he nodded. He posed beside her and stood at attention. She waited till the photographer had put a new plate in the camera before shifting her pose so she was puckering her lips near Antonio's cheek. The flash went off and Antonio glanced at her.

"What were you doing?"

"Making it a photograph worth remembering." She bit back a giggle while keeping her face innocent.

Antonio tried to glare at her, but the corner of his mouth curled into a smile.

"Photos will be ready in an hour," the photographer said.

"There's a good view of the harbor if you go up the street. Nice benches there," the shop girl said.

Taking Mabel's arm, Antonio said, "Let's enjoy a nice bench."

She wished that meant more than just sitting and watching ships. However, given the locket he wore and the note in his pocketbook, sitting with him and having a nice conversation was all she would likely enjoy.

CHAPTER 6

In Which Antonio
Dances with a Pickpocket

Antonio felt the weight of Sofia's locket against his chest as he sat on the bench and inspected the tailoring inside Mabel's jacket. If her name was Mabel. He hoped it was. The name fit better than Mildred.

"The outside counts the most," he said, "but the sewing inside is atrocious."

"Back home, I'd draw what I wanted and give it to a tailor or seamstress," she said. "Out here, all I have are my own hands. Unless I want my crewmates to use the same stitches they use on the sails."

"My time in the Navy's made me an expert at stitching sails." He flipped over his lapel and pulled out a needle with some thread. Mabel raised an eyebrow. "A tailor always has his tools on hand. You never know when something will need a quick repair."

"Even while fixing rigging?"

"Especially then."

He smiled, trying not to meet her light-blue eyes, so intelligent and bright, nor glance at the light line of freckles lining her nose and cheeks. Focusing on the seam, he demonstrated a small stitch.

"If you fold the fabric a bit and pull the needle under, like this, it will hide the stitches better. If you pin it properly, it'll be easier to keep your lines straight."

He pulled out his needle and tucked it back into his lapel. "If we had more time, I'd fix this."

"You could always jump ship," she said with a wry smile. He wished it were less charming. "Join our mercantile ways."

"And be shot for deserting." He handed back her jacket. "I'm six months in. Eighteen more months and I'll be home."

A pang hit his heart. Usually, he finished with, *I'll be home to marry Sofia.* However, the thought felt more distant than before as he enjoyed the way Mabel's red hair bound in a crown braid framed her long face, softening her defined cheekbones. She wasn't a traditional sort of beauty like Sofia, but she was striking and her wit enchanting.

Sitting with her made him realize how lonely the past six months had been, without anyone on the ship to hold a real conversation with. He had learned to play games and join songs on deck but went to his bunk whenever the conversation turned to poor taste and foul words. There were a few sailors he traded books with, but no one whose eyes lit up at seeing an issue of *Modan* or could educate him on Gathrayan linen.

All he needed was a bit of companionship before returning to the drudge of sea life. That's the only reason why he was sitting here with a girl who wasn't Sofia, wanting to put his arm around her as his eyes drifted to her lips painted a pleasant sort of red.

Shifting his gaze away, he pulled at a fold of fabric on the back of her shoulder. "Your shirt is draped well, overall, but the tailoring is off here."

He tugged at a corner near her waist and smoothed the fabric. He tried to ignore the tingle in his arm as his hand ran down her shoulder before resting on her hip, lingering longer than needed. It took more will power than he liked to pull his hand away.

"If you remove the side seam and re-lay the back to take out the extra triangle near your hip, it should lay flat." He wished his voice wasn't so hushed as her blue eyes met his. Her eyes were hard to look away from. "It will look quite sharp."

"Until it gets snagged on some rigging and I have to repair it." Her gaze broke from his as she looked down. "Señor Cortez, what will you do when you get home in eighteen months?"

His throat felt thick as he said, "I'm saving every mac and skoon I can so I can open my own tailoring shop."

He pulled a notepad from his pocket and flipped to a sketch. His stomach clenched. Each drawing in this notepad was meant for Sofia to wear someday. These dresses wouldn't sit on Mabel quite right, since they were made for Sofia's rounder hips and bosom. Mabel would need straighter lines and some padding to shift her silhouette to match modern trends. Though, her silhouette was quite admirable as it was.

Catching his thoughts, he said, "Sometimes, when I'm lying in my bunk, I'll sketch out designs."

He offered his notepad. She took it and flipped through, taking time to analyze and admire each one. Sofia always glanced at his sketches and said, "Oh, that is nice," before talking about the house she wanted someday. While he would build the house she deserved, it always hurt to have her dismiss his sketches so quickly.

Looking at the fifth drawing, Mabel said, "I like how there's movement in the way the ruffles sit. It's a very Castallan fashion, but I think there are ways to adapt it to the straighter lines women in Barthan prefer. Could open a whole market to you."

"I hope if I put out the most beautiful clothes, people will come from everywhere for a Cortez design," he said. "I'd be content, though, earning enough for a nice house, with room for my mother to have her own space and for my wife and children to be comfortable. But, if I did get into *Modan*, maybe I could have a whole hacienda, with a few servants to make my wife's life easier."

"I think your wife will be well taken care of, whether in a hovel or hacienda." Mabel turned the page. "All of these are so well-drawn."

Antonio sat up. "You think so? I've worked hard, basing my illustrations on sketches in *Modan* from Señor Valdez. It took me a long time to get the gesture lines to look right."

"They really are excellent. Though, if you saw my sketches, you might not want my opinion."

A warmth ran through Antonio. "I think I'd often want your opinion."

"You won't after you see my scribbles."

She reached in her satchel and pulled out her own notepad. With a knowing look, she handed it over. Flipping through, Antonio held his thumb to his mouth as he bit back a laugh. Most were stick figures and messes of lines, but some were recognizable as dresses.

He squinted as he turned one sideways, trying to decipher the mess of scribbles and color.

"It goes this way." Mabel moved it a quarter-turn. "And was meant to be a gown."

"Now I see it." At least he was attempting to while he traced the lines with his pinky. "I see how it widens out here, and the details along this side. If executed well, would be lovely."

Mabel rested her chin on her hand. "That is a very kind lie, señor."

"I like the ideas behind your sketches," Antonio said, "even if they take a while to decipher."

She gave him a skeptical look. "My drawings are atrocious."

"They have potential." He pressed his tongue against his cheek before pulling his colored oil pastels from his satchel. Flipping to a blank page in her notepad, he said, "Tell me what you meant the gown to look like."

As she spoke, the vision of the gown unfolded in his mind like unfurling a bolt of fabric. His hand moved with little thought, taking in her description and transferring it onto the paper. When they finished, a red and white striped gown spread across the page, a sense of movement to his sketch, details hinted at along the bodice and on one of the skirt panels.

A softness entered Mabel's eyes and she grinned. He found himself returning the smile.

"That's just how I picture it." She took the notepad and admired the sketch. "Better, actually."

"With some practice, I think you'll improve."

She let out a wry laugh. "I've been trained in drawing since I was a child and practiced figure drawings for three years. I want to be a designer, but who would take a chance on sketches like these?"

"Maybe you need a better tutor."

She chuckled. "And where am I to find that while traveling at sea?"

He touched her notepad, his fingers close to hers. "You have the ideas. The drawings just need finesse. If we take time over the next few days, I can teach you some tricks to help, how to use circles and shapes better to build your figure. It'll take some work, but you'll have a better foundation."

A weight rested in her gaze. "Señor, both of our ships are leaving tonight. All we have is a few hours."

An ache ran through him, and he rested his hand next to hers. If he were only Antonio, and not a naval sailor, he would find a way to spend more time with her. However, he had to return to his ship tonight and was unlikely to meet her again.

This thought brought a deeper pain than expected as her blue eyes met his, holding the question of what could be. He nearly reached over to take her hand but stopped himself.

Looking away, she tucked her notepad in her satchel. "Do you get many letters from her?"

He frowned, trying to puzzle through who Mabel meant. Shame filled him as Sofia's locket hit his breastbone. "Oh. I just got my third when the post came yesterday."

Antonio kept his head down and set his hands in his lap. He thought of Sofia nearly every moment, yet she had flitted from his mind like paper caught by the wind.

"Three letters in six months?" Mabel said.

"Her parents must be stopping her from writing me." He rubbed his neck, trying to clear his head. "I had to sneak her out the window to go out dancing when we first started courting."

Mabel's eyebrow rose. "She'd climb out a window to go dancing with you, but can't figure out how to sneak a letter more than once every two months?"

"Maybe they've locked her in her room." His face felt warm, feeling his own lie. "Or burned her letters. Or sent her away, though my mother says she's still in town." He shrugged. "There likely is a good reason."

"There might be," Mabel said softly. "But, if I were at home waiting for a sailor, I'd write him at least every week. If not more, considering how lonely life can be while at sea."

Sweat dotted Antonio's neck where his collar hit, Mabel's words prodding at doubts he'd been shoving down for months. The worst part was, sitting here next to her, he wanted those doubts to be true.

Rising, he straightened his uniform coat and glanced at the sunset. "The photographs should be done."

Another blast of cold wind came as Mabel pulled on her coat and stood. "I've already taken up more of your shore leave than I should have. We don't need to do dinner."

Antonio looked to her. As long as he didn't kiss her, he was still being true to Sofia, wasn't he? There were only a few more hours left, and then their ships would sail, taking them far from each other.

"I made a promise." Both to Sofia and to Mabel. He offered his arm. "Let me keep it."

"The magazine's enough." She pointed. "I can—"

"Mabel." It felt good to say her first name, especially as a softness entered her eyes. "Let me buy you dinner."

Her jaw was tight as she nodded.

He forced a smile. "And get you out of this cold wind."

She took his arm and they hurried down the wharf and back to the photography shop. He wished he could put his arms around her and warm her as she stood next to him, rubbing her arms. However, temptations were enough for the moment.

The shop girl giggled as she laid out the three photographs for Antonio's review. The first two were stately pictures of him as a sailor. His mother would likely frame hers and put it up in the shop. The third picture, however, would not go anywhere Sofia might see it.

Antonio stood in a noble pose while Mabel held laughter in her eyes and leaned toward him, her lips puckered as if about to kiss his cheek.

Rubbing his jaw, Antonio tried to hide his smile.

"I'm so sorry," Mabel said. "I'll cover the cost of that one."

"It's your photograph." He handed it to her. "To remember today, like you said."

Her cheeks were tight as she took it and placed it in her satchel. Antonio's own chest ached as he took the other two photographs and thanked the shop girl.

"Dinner, and then back to our ships," he said as they walked down the wharf toward several restaurants. "What would you like?"

Mabel shrugged as she kept her head turned away and tried to hide while she brushed her cheek with her sleeve.

Though his stomach grumbled with hunger, he pulled her into a small alleyway between buildings. He wished he had a handkerchief as he lifted her chin and brushed away a tear with his thumb.

"I'm sorry," he whispered, standing closer to her than he needed to. "I wish—" He swallowed, trying to sort out everything he wished for. "If I hadn't promised my heart already—"

"It's just the wind in my eyes," she muttered.

"I've enjoyed our time together, and if I didn't have Sofia waiting, I—"

He couldn't bring himself to finish the sentence, not even sure what he wanted to say.

Mabel focused on his shoulder. "Truth is, all I wanted was to win a bet with my crewmates."

He smiled a little. "What was the bet?"

She winced. "That I could get you to kiss me."

His stomach clenched as his eyes focused on her round lips. "How much is riding on it?"

"We bet three macs each, so I'd get six."

"That's more than I make in a week."

She nodded and brushed away another tear with the back of her hand. "It was a foolish joke, and only meant to be fun, but I—" She focused on his face before looking away. "You deserve better."

He glanced out. Paulson was pretending not to watch. As was the drunk.

Antonio tapped his hand against his leg. It was a good sum, and assisting a lady was honorable. This had nothing to do with the pressure building in his chest or how his gaze kept coming back to her red lips. All he would be doing was helping her.

"Maybe six macs changes what it means to be a gentleman," he whispered as his fingers brushed her cheek. The painful longing in her eyes matched his own. But this had to be only a brief indulgence, an acknowledgement of what could be if matters were different.

He rested his palms on her cheeks before leaning toward her and tenderly kissing her lips. Her touch in return was tentative as she trembled. He lingered longer than he meant to, even as he drew his lips from hers and kept his face close.

His heart thundered as he lowered his hand and rested it on her hip before pulling her into a second kiss. He pressed harder this time and wrapped his arms around her. She stiffened before putting one hand on his chest while leaning against him. Her warmth and presence brought a rush of fire through him. Every other worry or thought disappeared, and all he wished was that they weren't leaving on separate ships tonight.

Though his instincts called for more, he pulled his lips away. Trying to gather control, he forced himself to let go of her and take a step back. She stood with her eyes wide, shock on her face.

"We should be heading to dinner." He straightened his coat, fighting the temptation to kiss her again. "There's—"

"I stole your pocketbook," she said.

His forehead wrinkled.

"I stole your pocketbook." She cringed. "And your candy. So that I could meet you."

She reached into a hidden pocket and removed a few bills. "I've been lying to you this whole time. I even took a few oners to pay my friends who helped, but I'll pay you back. And for the magazine."

"Is your name really Mabel Sinclair?" He couldn't stop a grin from forming. It was an odd way to meet but flattering, and only made him more grateful to have kissed her.

"That's true, but I didn't run away from home. My brother was kidnapped by—" She grimaced. "As I said, it's a long story."

He took her hand. "Tell me over dinner."

She pulled her hand away. "But I lied to you, and now—"

A thump and cry came from down the alleyway. He glanced over while Paulson brawled with the supposed drunk who'd been following Antonio.

Mabel's face went hard, and she pulled a pistol from her satchel. Antonio's eyes widened and he touched her arm.

"You have a pistol?"

"A young lady alone at port should be careful to protect herself." She held it in both hands as she watched the brawl, moving into a fighter's stance.

"No need for that, Stripes," a gruff voice behind Antonio said. "He's a recruiter for a smuggling crew and was looking to kidnap your sailor. Paulson's persuading him otherwise."

Antonio turned slowly to face a middle-aged man with a grizzled jaw behind a gray beard. He had the look of a man who'd had his own share of fights at port.

"I could have handled him, if needed, captain," Mabel said.

"You could have." He squinted at Antonio. "But you were distracted by this fellow, who was getting a bit handsy for a man who already has a girl back home."

Antonio's cheeks grew warm, which was worsened as an older woman cackled while entering the alleyway from the other side. He glanced at her. She was the woman he had helped with her bags.

She must have distracted him while Mabel stole his pocketbook. He glanced at Mabel, wondering what business her crew really conducted. It would be better not to ask.

"Given that second kiss, I think we owe her extra," the older woman said with a husky laugh.

The captain pulled back one of his coat flaps and rested his hand on his pistol. "Young man, are you a gentleman or a scoundrel? Cause it's looking like the second might be true, and Stripes deserves better."

"He was just helping me win the bet." Mabel took Antonio's arm and tugged him the opposite way from the brawl. "And now, if you don't mind, we're going to dinner."

The captain eyed Antonio. "Just know, we're watching you, sir."

"Yes, sir." Antonio tried to ignore the sweat along his back. "I will treat her honorably, sir."

While the captain held a sharp eye, Antonio kept his arm with Mabel's as they walked to the open street.

Once they were past a few shops, Mabel let go of his arm. She scanned the street before pointing. "That restaurant looks quieter. The food likely isn't as good, but it will be easier to rest a moment."

He nodded while glancing back. Other members of her crew were probably tracking them. This only made the heat on his face worse.

Mabel walked a few steps ahead as they went to the restaurant. Antonio hurried to keep up, wishing she would let him take her arm again. Maybe he had gone too far with the second kiss.

He should walk away, but he wanted to finish the night and enjoy time with Mabel before he couldn't anymore.

Once they entered the restaurant, he and Mabel tucked themselves into a dim booth on the second story. The waitress brought them some water and cider while Mabel hid behind her menu. Antonio scratched his jaw, wishing she would at least look at him, giving him a clue of what her thoughts were.

The waitress came and took their order along with the menus. Facing Mabel, Antonio wanted to reach across the table and take her hand. However, he fidgeted with his napkin ring and stared at his fingers.

"I'm sorry," he said. "I shouldn't have—" He ran a hand through his hair. "I didn't mean to get so caught up in—I am sorry."

Mabel set her elbows on the table before resting her palms on her forehead and breaking into giggles. Antonio sat up, the twisting in his stomach only growing worse.

"I lied to you." She shook her head with a wry laugh. "I stole your pocketbook, and my captain threatened you. I am the one to be apologizing."

He met her blue-eyed gaze and couldn't bring himself to look away. There was an anxiety in her eyes matching his own.

"So, we're both at fault?" He let the corner of his mouth curl up. "Mabel, your thievery has led me to the brightest day I've had since leaving home."

Her cheeks grew pinker even as she returned her own smile. "It has been a good day."

Pushing down another urge to reach for her hand, he folded his arms and rested them on the table's edge. It would be better to simply make conversation and enjoy the time they had left.

"I've been wondering," he said with a soft smile, "how a refined young woman ended up on a merchant's ship?"

Her eyes searched his. "It's a long, strange story."

"We're waiting for dinner to be brought," he said. "What else is there to talk about?"

"Patricia Evanwind's picture in last spring's issue of *Modan* where her dog had a matching dress."

Antonio laughed hard and he let Mabel lead him into a discussion and debate of fashion trends and styles. It was a comfortable place he didn't mind sharing with her before they parted. Whatever her true story was didn't matter. He only had two hours left of shore leave. If he was wise, he wouldn't dare kiss her again. Though, as they talked so easily, the hope kept coming back.

The conversation paused as the server brought roasted fresh fish on a creamy pasta with common vegetables. As they ate the bland but decent food, they spoke of ports they had been to and life at sea.

Feeling the end of the meal approaching, he said, "How long will it be before you return home?"

"Months." She shrugged. "It would be faster on a passenger ship, but I'm enjoying seeing the world and traveling with my crew."

He smiled. "They clearly care about you."

She chuckled. "It is often like traveling with a set of overprotective aunts and uncles."

"Who taught you how to pickpocket?" He raised his eyebrows and grinned.

"They have taught me many valuable skills." There was a teasing glint in her eye.

"And do you plan to keep up your pickpocketing when you return home?"

She rested her chin on her hand as her face grew more serious. "When I go home, I will endure whatever plans my parents have for me."

"What of your career in fashion?" he said.

"You've seen my sewing and my drawing." She shook her head. "It is a dream I am far from achieving."

"You'll find your way." He hesitated before pulling his notepad out and writing on a piece of paper. "When you do, whether it's home or in the world of fashion, will you write a Castallan tailor and let him know how you are?"

He finished writing his name, ship, and naval identification number and passed it to her. Her eyes were contemplative as she slipped it into her own notepad before pulling out an envelope.

"I try to send letters to my parents now and then, to let them know

I'm all right. But—" She swallowed. "I'd rather they didn't know where I was exactly. In case the kidnappers are still looking." She held out the letter to him. "Will you send this at the next port you go to?"

He took the letter and rubbed his thumb on the corner while staring at the address. Here was a chance to stay connected to her beyond this evening. The thought of having a small thread keeping him tethered to her was a comfort, even if it would just be a letter to make sure she was home and safe.

"I will send it," he said.

His gaze met hers again and a spark of warmth ran through him. He glanced at the clock at the center of the room. His heart sank. Only one hour remained of his shore leave.

Good music echoed from a tavern across the street. He laid out money to pay the bill before rising and holding out his hand. "A bit of dancing before I ship out?"

The tightness in his chest eased as she took his hand and he guided her down the stairs and across the street. The dance floor inside was packed with couples dancing to a jig and bouncing across the floor. Antonio preferred a good salsa or samba, but the beat was fun and Mabel's steps matched the quickness of his. They laughed together as they jumped, doing the kicking steps. Her movements were smoother than the dances called for, marking formal training. How he wished there was salsa music to see how her hips could move with the rhythm.

The music slowed and he took her around the floor in a simple waltz. The straight line of her back and firm hold of her arms also marked her skill while other women and men flopped together. Though, some of their flopping was due to drunken couples sloppily kissing while dancing. Antonio tried to ignore them, even as his eyes kept drifting to Mabel's lips. A temptation rose to follow their example, though more politely.

But, if he did that with this quick-witted, beautiful red-head, he'd risk losing track of time and be late reporting back to his ship. His heart sank as Sofia's locket weighed heavier on his neck. Even if her letters were rare, she deserved to be honored.

Even so, all he wanted was one more kiss with Mabel.

Their steps slowed as her blue eyes held onto his. He was unlikely to ever see her again. This would just be a fleeting moment, a memory to share as they moved onto their separate lives, a whisper of what could be if their paths were different.

He leaned his head toward hers as a nervous tingling rose in his breast.

"In your next letter," Mabel said, "tell Sofia she may have your heart, but a thief stole a kiss."

She planted a quick kiss on his lips before dashing from the tavern. Antonio blinked before rushing out the door. His heart pounded as he sought a sign of her red hair or any of her crewmates. However, in the dim lamplight, there was no trace of either.

He rested a hand on his chest where the locket sat. "Let her go. Sofia is waiting for you."

However, as he strolled back toward his ship, the guilt he expected didn't come. Instead, he kept glancing around corners and alleyways, hoping Mabel had decided one last kiss wasn't enough.

CHAPTER 7

In Which Antonio Receives a Letter

The Abaea Sea, south of Sandar and north of Hyun
January of the Year 307 B.R.

Mabel gripped the rope and swung toward the deck. Her feet pounded one of the smugglers in the chest, sending him flying back into a stack of crates. Letting go of the rope, she rolled across the wet deck before rising and crossing her rapier with another smuggler's cutlass. The stub-nosed man swung toward her stomach, but Mabel parried and shoved his blade away.

"Stripes!" Gregson yelled from behind her.

Mabel pivoted on one foot and leaned back while Gregson fired a pistol, hitting the stub-nosed smuggler's shoulder. As he cried out, she turned and caught her blade against the first smuggler's as he clambered from the broken crates. Mabel dodged a punch before spinning behind the larger man and leaping onto his back. Holding her arms around his neck, she pulled tight, cutting off his air. The man fought against her, but she held on until he lay unconscious on the deck.

As she rolled off him, cheers broke out from her crew, marking victory. Mabel accepted Captain Stenton's hand as he helped her stand.

"Fine job, Stripes." He grinned. "Done like a real pirate lass. Now, let's see what bounty we've won."

Mabel sheathed her rapier and adjusted her red leather mask as she followed him down into the hold. Several other crew members were already sifting through the stolen goods, some enjoying the bottles of rum.

"If this ship has what I think it does, we've gained more than a fine haul of gold." Captain Stenton tapped the wood floor with his sword. He paused at a hollow sound and motioned to some of his men as he gave commands.

Within minutes, crates were moved, revealing a trap door. Mabel joined her crewmates in holding a pistol steady on the opening. She half-smiled to herself. Nine months ago, she'd have shook holding the pistol. While no lives had been taken in her pirating career, and she prayed none would be lost, she no longer feared protecting herself and her crew. If firing her pistol was the difference between Stenton living or dying, she would take the shot.

Stenton broke out in a triumphant laugh. "Stripes, you've got to see this!"

Mabel twirled her pistol as Gregson had taught her before setting it in its holster. A strange glow filled the small hideaway and she crouched beside Stenton in the tight space. Her eyes widened as he opened one of several wooden chests, revealing six head-sized pearls, just like the one Cassandra had used on her yacht.

"Those are merfolk pearls," she whispered, glancing at Stenton.

"Aye, they are, lass."

"Were they stolen or are they being shipped?"

Stenton shifted over to one of the other trunks and opened it. Inside were golden devices. He squinted at the engraving beneath the lid. "This is authentic Perakan Clan handywork. Must have been stolen, since these match the bounty notice."

"What bounty?" Mabel said.

"The one the Perakan Clan sent out for these goods. If it were a Marveth bounty, I'd not touch it even with a ten-foot harpoon. But other merfolk clans are far more reasonable and less likely to transform you after your business is done."

Mabel eyed the strange devices. "What do these do?"

"Other than give us a good haul of gold? Don't know." Stenton snapped the chest shut and pointed at her. "And a wise man never fiddles with merfolk devices that he don't understand. Though—"

He laughed in triumph, clapping his hands as he approached a long tube. He opened it and unrolled a map, whistling in admiration.

"What is it?" Mabel looked over his shoulder. Her eyes widened as ships with names above them drifted across the map, marking where the vessels were in real time.

"Lookee here." Captain Stenton chuckled as he pressed his finger to one of the ships. "There's your pretty sailor's ship."

Mabel's tried not to picture Antonio's brown eyes moments before she stole a final kiss. In the months since, she had tried dancing with other men at ports. A few had kissed her, but those sloppy, wet messes would have been more tolerable from dogs. She had pulled a knife on several who had tried to go too far and taken their pocketbook for her trouble.

It was clear Antonio had spoiled all other kisses, and, possibly, all other men. His tall frame and good looks were admirable alone, but he was also kind, charming, and had a sharp eye for fashion. So many good things shouldn't be contained in a single man. Especially one she would never to see again.

Looking down, she hated her own disappointment as she said, "He's not my sailor."

"What of the dozen or so notes you've sent to this Antonio?"

"I've only sent eight." Mabel was glad her mask hid the reddening in her cheeks. "They're only meant in friendship." She shrugged. "And who's to say he's gotten them, or if he'll ever answer?"

"If the fellow's wise, he'll be writing back." Stenton winked at her. "If I were still a young sailor and had kissed a girl as pretty as you, that'd be all I'd think of."

Her stomach clenched. "He doesn't know I'm a pirate."

"You're only a pirate for now." Stenton pressed a finger to where their ship stood and drew a line to her hometown off the coast of Barthan. "Soon enough, we'll return you home and, if this fellow's wise, you'll have a whole stack of letters waiting for you."

Mabel stared at where Cliffshire sat as just one dot in the world. She didn't have to go back. She could stay out here at sea, find out where her life might take her.

Then she pictured Malcom sitting as a toad in a lantern and imagined the worry in her mother's eyes. She looked down at her own gloved hands, worn lines where she'd held her sword and swung on ropes. This was far from the social clubs and formal tutoring she would be going back to.

Stenton put his arm around her shoulders. "You're an excellent pirate, Stripes, but keeping you as part of my crew is holding you back. Besides, these days of swinging on ropes and stealing from ships are getting trickier. I'll miss you when you go, but you've a bright future waiting for you at home. I can feel it."

Mabel leaned against him. "I'd feel better about going home if I could take you and the crew with me."

Stenton let out a laugh. "What would an old sea rat like me do in such a dandy world as that?"

"You'd outdress all the men if you showed up in your fine coat." She forced a smile and pushed away worries of things to come. "Now, what do we do with this merfolk contraband?"

"We get it to its rightful owner. Merfolk are enough trouble even when you don't double cross them."

Mabel turned to helping the crew move the precious cargo to Stenton's cabin. Lugging the chests to the longboat and onto their ship was hard work and kept her mind busy. She needed all the distraction she could to not ponder questions of returning home and wondering if Antonio Cortez thought of her as often as she thought of him.

The Wahid Sea, between Southern Sandar and Castallar

Rain pelted Antonio as he pulled back on the oar and water swelled beneath the longboat. Beside him, Pieras rowed in unison, helping pull them and ten other sailors toward the merchant ship. This was only a standard boarding, checking for smuggled goods, but too many sailors had whispered stories of these going foul.

The hard-faced third mate, Corporal Hernandez, beat out a rhythm on the edge of the rowboat, shouting, "Faster! Dig harder!"

One year and three months.

That was all Antonio had left of his miserable duty as a sailor, made worse by his drenched clothes. He only needed to keep following orders and he'd be home soon enough to start his tailor shop.

As the boat tilted along a wave, he felt Sofia's locket press against his cold skin. It was three months since her last letter. Reading her stagnant words was losing its comfort, leaving questions on if it really was her parents fault her letters were so rare.

Which left his mind often wandering to Mabel Sinclair. Maybe she had returned home by now, or she was at a port charming another sailor by stealing his pocketbook. Wherever she was, he often found himself scanning crowds at ports, seeking her red hair, or sifting through his letters from his mother and sisters, wanting one of the envelopes to be from her.

It was a fool's hope, but he held on tight. He needed something to help endure days like this.

Pieras yelled beside him, the tendons in his neck straining as he dragged the oar through the water. Antonio's back ached from his own effort but was grateful his strength remained greater than others. The challenge was keeping his pace even with Pieras struggling effort.

As they reached the other ship, Pieras grabbed the mooring rope and tied it to the longboat. Antonio grabbed the rope ladder and held it steady as the other sailors climbed aboard before following, leaving Pieras to watch the boat.

He stood at attention on deck with the other sailors, rifle against his shoulder, while the third mate spoke to the captain.

"There's a storm growing and you're boarding?" The blonde man glared at the third mate. "We should be tying down the rigging and holing up. Not opening our doors to navy bureaucrats."

"The manifest, please." Hernandez gestured toward the captain's cabin.

Within minutes, the manifest was provided, and the third mate led Antonio and his crew into the hold. Antonio joined the others in moving boxes and knocking against the sides and bottoms, seeking signs of hidden compartments.

He paused at the edge of a stack of crates as a child whimpered followed by a shushing sound. Frowning, he moved toward the sound and crouched beside a large crate. He ran his fingers over the side, seeking an opening. There was a small lip and he pulled on it, sliding the box open.

Two children sat inside, both about ten years old, underfed, and staring at him with fear. The girl held the tanned features of Sandar while the boy had the dark hair and crescent moon-shaped eyes of Hyun. Over the boy's palm rested an orb of yellow light, floating in the air.

Antonio stared at the orb until the boy closed his fingers and the light disappeared.

He had magic. Just like Antonio.

Which seemed a good reason someone would kidnap a child, hide them in a crate, and smuggle them who knows where for a dark purpose.

"I'm here to help." Antonio smiled gently and held out his hand.

The children stared at him. It was unlikely they spoke Castallan.

Antonio motioned for them to come out.

The boy hesitated before reaching for Antonio's hand. The girl grabbed his arm and shook her head, fear in her eyes. Antonio needed to gain their trust quickly.

He placed a finger over his lips, as if sharing a secret, before holding out his other hand. Concentrating, he gathered a line of green light, letting it weave through his fingers.

The girl's eyes widened, and she punched her palm forward with a whistle. A hard force of wind shot out, hitting Antonio in the chest and knocking him away. His back hit another stack of crates, sending them toppling over.

"Cortez?" another sailor called. "What are you doing?"

Antonio stumbled to his feet as the children scurried from the crate and ran. He hurried after them. In seconds, another Castallan sailor grabbed them by the collars.

"What are you running about here for?"

"I think they're one of the goods," Antonio said, his ribs still hurting from the girl's attack. "Found them in a crate."

The sailor grunted in disgust before kneeling. From his pocket he pulled a couple hard candies wrapped in wax paper and handed them to the children.

"You're safe now, in the care of the Castallan Navy."

Antonio rubbed his aching lower back as the children accepted the candy before taking the other sailor's hands timidly. He grunted to himself. Candy would have been far wiser than revealing his magic.

He followed the other sailor and children to Hernandez and the merchant captain. The children shook, cowering as they came closer.

"Found them in a crate, sir," Antonio said while saluting the officer.

Hernandez scowled at the captain and the pale man's face grew whiter.

"Must be stowaways." The captain moved toward the children, but Hernandez raised a pistol.

"You're not moving out of sight." Hernandez nodded to Antonio. "Good work. Leave the children here and see if there are any more."

After an hour of checking, some contraband was found, but no more children.

"Captain, you are under arrest by the Castallan Navy." Hernandez held pure disgust in his eyes. To Antonio, he said, "Take the children to the main ship. You found them. You play nanny to them. Have the captain send over more sailors to secure the ship."

Antonio nodded and guided the children to the longboat and across to his ship.

Within an hour, the Castallan Navy fully seized the merchant vessel. The sea was calmer by the time all merchant ship sailors were locked in the Navy's brig and both ships set sail for the nearest port, ten hours away.

Antonio joined the children in Hernandez's small officer's cabin, the corporal volunteering to sacrifice his bunk for the trip.

Over the first hour, the children sat quietly, their eyes wide with fear. It took nearly a half-hour for Antonio to coax their names out of them. The girl was named Rithara and the boy Chi-sol.

"Have you heard the story of the bear who became a cat?" Antonio said, forcing a smile. He tried to pantomime the silly story, and the boy giggled while the girl stared blankly.

Antonio finished and scratched his head, trying to think how to next entertain them. He hesitated before doing a one-handed handstand. As a boy, this feat of strength had impressed his friends. Chi-sol laughed, his eyes bright. Rithara glared.

Over the next half-hour, Antonio helped Chi-sol do his own handstand. The boy giggled as he wobbled.

When he finished, Antonio held his hand out to Rithara. She glared before humming and drawing a horizontal line in the air. Light glowed beneath her as she sat cross-legged and began to float. Chi-sol gasped and chattered. Lowering back down, Rithara stared at Antonio as if to challenge him.

He gave her a small bow of respect. He'd never considered using his power for levitating, or other tricks. He wasn't even sure he could.

Still, maybe he could try something else. He motioned for the girl to stand. With her unimpressed stare remaining, she rose. Antonio held his hand out as if holding a needle. He'd experimented with this during nights he couldn't sleep at home, using the dress forms in his mother's shop as a base. Perhaps it would help him now.

He hummed to himself, the sound guiding his magic as tendrils of green light formed around the girl. Within minutes, a dress woven of light fluttered around her. It was airy and wouldn't hold long, but he grinned as Rithara gaped. Apparently, she could be impressed.

Over the course of the remaining hours, Antonio and the children swapped small illusions of light. There were breaks for food and walks along the deck, where other sailors did songs and tricks to try to charm the children. Down here, though, there was a feeling of camaraderie as they all shared the same secret power.

The hour was past midnight as Hernandez knocked on the door, announcing, "We're docking at port."

Antonio found himself disappointed as he took both their hands and guided them to the deck, watching the lights of the port reflect on the water. Once the ship was moored, Hernandez led Antonio and the children down the dock to the naval office. There, a friendly-faced woman waited for the children.

Holding out her hands, she said, "Come with me. We've got beds made up for you and will work on getting you home tomorrow."

Antonio's throat clenched as the pair of children looked up at him in worry.

Kneeling, he forced a smile. "You'll be safe. Just trust her."

He embraced the boy and then the girl. Rithara clung to him, nestling her head against his shoulder as if it would protect her.

"It will be just fine." He squeezed her shoulder before releasing her. His heart ached as the children walked away. He wished he could go with them and protect them.

As Antonio stood, Hernandez came to his side.

"You're better at being a nanny than a sailor."

"I'm proud to serve however is needed, sir." Antonio saluted, keeping to himself his real thoughts on his life at sea. "What will happen to them, sir?"

"They'll be sent to the mainland and inquiries will be sent out for any relatives. Most likely, they'll be adopted by families in Castallan." Hernandez nodded to Antonio. "You did well to find them."

Antonio tapped his thumb against his leg. "Where do you think they were being smuggled to?"

"Most likely to be labor." He scratched his broad nose. "There're rumors of children being captured by criminal organizations to be taken and trained as operatives. If that's true, we've saved their minds as much as their lives."

A prickling ran along Antonio's neck. "What sort of work do those operatives do?"

Hernandez glanced at him. "The sort it's our duty to stop."

Antonio nodded and Hernandez tapped his shoulder.

"You've the makings of a good sailor, Cortez. You try to blend in, but I've noticed how you keep to your duty and don't get distracted like the others." Hernandez looked him in the eye. "I was drafted twenty years ago but made the Navy my choice. Took me fifteen years to become an officer. Could've been faster if I'd allowed my nose to get dirty."

He pointed at Antonio. "The Navy needs honest men with good courage. If you're willing to step-up, I can give you some extra duties that'll get the captain's notice. Maybe get you to boson in a year or two."

Antonio bowed his head. "I am honored, sir. But my life's not meant to be on the sea. Once my two years are up, I plan to head home."

Hernandez grunted. "Rumor is you've a sweetheart you keep mooning over."

The cold chain of Sofia's locket weighed on Antonio's neck. A deep guilt rose in him as he said, "I do my best to keep my promises."

He hadn't done so for Sofia. While she hadn't written him, it didn't give him excuse to have kissed Mabel or think of her so often. There was no promise with the young woman he had only met once, and he had little reason to hope for a future with her. If he was a true man of honor, he would resist any more thoughts straying from his oath. Even if Sofia wasn't true to him, his duty was to be true to her.

But there had only been three letters.

"Sleep on it." Hernandez nodded to Antonio. "Just remember an honest man is rare. I'd hate to lose you."

Hernandez strode away and Antonio remained on the deck, letting the cool night wind wash over him. He soon returned to his small bunk on the ship, lying on a row beside other sailors. Holding his blanket over himself, he held a finger above his face, letting a bead of green light form.

All his life, he thought he was alone. But there were others with similar powers. Someone had stolen their children for their magic. For what purpose was unclear, but it meant there was a whole world he didn't know.

He rolled onto his side, his thoughts keeping him awake. He wished he could talk to his mother and hear her wise words. But what did a seamstress in Dorona know of magic? He wished he could write to Sofia of what he had seen. It had been so long since he'd spoken to her, but he felt sure she'd either be afraid or wouldn't believe him.

Perhaps Mabel would. She hadn't flinched when pulling her pistol from her satchel. It was a large leap to think she knew magic was real, but, if he made the evidence clear, she might believe him.

Catching the train of his thoughts, Antonio groaned and crossed his arms. He shut his eyes and tried to force himself to clear his mind and fall sleep. He dozed before the bell rang, marking roll call.

In the early morning fog, he stood on the deck alongside the others and the second mate handed the stacks of mail which had arrived from port. Many men were skipped, but as usual, a small stack of letters were passed into Antonio's hands.

"Two hours extra shore leave, for your work with the children," the second mate said.

Antonio tried to smile. He'd rather stay on the ship and work than be stuck on shore leave, alone with his jumbled thoughts.

However, within a few hours he was released and wound his way to the edge of the docks, staying clear of the merchants trying to separate sailors from their money. Finding a quiet place on an empty dock, Antonio sat at the edge, his legs dangling over the water.

Enjoying the breeze and quieter setting with the echo of voices from the wharf and gulls going by, he pulled out his mail.

The first letter was from his mother, paired with one from both of his sisters. His heart leapt as he stared at the fourth letter, the handwriting rare but familiar.

He tore open the envelope and unfolded Sofia's letter.

My Darling Antonio,

How I miss you and dream of dancing with you when you return.

He read through the one-page letter full of her usual mentions of daily life, of how she wore her hair, and which dress she chose to wear to a friend's party. There was only a brief mention of his weekly letters, and no word as to why she wrote so rarely, or if he should expect more letters.

He had thought getting her next letter would be a comfort and reminder of how he loved her. However, the words felt empty, and the stories were nearly identical to ones she had shared before. Some of the sentences were exactly the same, almost as if being copied from a book.

When he returned home, it had to be different. He would be standing in front of her, and she'd throw her arms around him, explaining why her letters were so rare. His misery as a sailor had to be fogging his view of the letter. That was all. He should be grateful, especially with the lipstick marks in the corner.

He slid the letter back into the envelope and pulled out the next. The handwriting was unfamiliar and there were a number of ports written along the top, marking it as having gone through many to reach him. There was no return address.

Frowning, he opened the envelope. Inside was a swatch of reddish-orange silk along with a short letter. The bottom half of the page had a rough drawing of a figure in a reddish-orange blouse with a dark brown skirt below. If his mother had seen the sketch, she would have ordered it remade. But the concept was clear. The words inside were written in neat handwriting, though many words were misspelled or scratched out and replaced.

Dear Mr. Cortez,

I saw fabric at port. Asked myself what outfit a tailor would make. Did not steal it—I am an honest pickpocket. Merchant gave to me. I've drawn my design. What do you think?

Hope your journey is good,

M. Stripes

P.S. Sorry for scribbles. Writing Castallan harder than speaking.

Antonio's heart quickened. Mabel had written. It was little more than a note, but, even in rough-edged Castallan, her wit shone through.

Rubbing the fabric between his fingers, he could already picture the dress he might make from such a fabric.

His hands shook as he picked up the remaining letters. There were two more from his mother, but three others were in Mabel's handwriting. Each was brief, with a bit of a quip in her writing. Her illustrations improved in each letter, the concept and lines becoming more precise. He laughed at the drawing in the last one of a woman in a dress and a dog in a matching outfit.

Given the numerous port names stamped in the corner, she was still traveling and far from home. Still, he pulled out his sketchbook and flipped to where he had written down her address all the way in the nation of Barthan. Her letters had been sent weeks ago and who knew how long it took the mail to travel between nations and then to ports.

But her designs needed answers.

As he gathered Mabel's letters, Sofia's locket knocked against his breastbone. Hernandez had called Antonio honorable. Would writing to Mabel hold his honor?

The answer had been clearer last night, without knowing Mabel had written him. They were lighthearted messages, yet he could feel the personality of the young woman he'd spent an afternoon with. And kissed three times.

"You promised yourself to Sofia."

His chest ached as he looked at Sofia's letter again, the words feeling so flat compared with Mabel's. He put the letters inside his satchel before resting his forehead against his hands.

To be a man of honor, he had to make a choice: the girl he'd dreamed of marrying for so many months, or the lady pickpocket who he'd spent only a few hours with and might not see again.

"Make the choice," he whispered, but he could not bring himself to do it. Instead, he stared out at the sun gleaming on the ocean, lost between the life he had pictured for so long and an unknown future.

CHAPTER 8

In Which Mabel Returns Home

Cliffshire, Barthan

April of the Year 307 B.R.

Mabel rested her hand on her head as she looked over her belongings. She had already given most of her shirts to the other women on board, after adding panels to broaden the stomach and sleeves. Now she wore the dress and hat she had bought at the last port, the outfit simple, proper, and appropriate for returning home in. Though, she did love the bold, dark red color and broad white panel along the front.

Picking up Malcom's lantern, she said to her brother, "Captain Stenton says you'll be dressed the same as when you were transformed and won't remember much." She sighed. "I'm sorry it took so long to get home, but we'll be there later this morning."

She wished she were happier to be returning to her parents but feared how much she was going to miss Captain Stenton and his crew.

"You must go home," she whispered. "It's been a whole year."

Pulling in a breath, she placed her few remaining belongings into the worn carpet bag Gregson had bought for her. She sorted through the books and magazines. Most of these, she would leave for the crew. More had taken up reading while she was aboard, and this would help them remember her.

She picked up the annual review issue of *Modan*. A fond smile formed as she flipped through the dog-eared pages, remembering her day with Antonio. If they were aboard the same ship, she probably would have kissed him many more times. Too bad he was a naval sailor she was unlikely to ever see again.

Though, perhaps he had gotten the notes and sketches she had sent. Hopefully, they brightened the life he was trapped in. A small part of her hoped she would find letters from him waiting when she returned home. Any word from him would be far more exciting than reuniting with her family.

Reaching the magazine page announcing a competition hosted by the Fashion Society of Willington, she laughed. On a whim four months ago, Mabel had mailed her own design to be accepted and shown as part of a collection during fashion week. The prize included a paid trip to Barthan's capital for a month, culminating in having the outfit shown at fashion week itself.

The trip to Willington started sometime next month. There was no chance she had won. Her skills had improved after using Antonio's sketch in her notepad as a model and starting to use more circles and other shapes to help build her drawings. However, she was still far from professional and many entries into the contest would be better than hers.

Yet, maybe she could convince her parents to take her to fashion week. Even a single day of watching the greatest designers present their fashions would be a prize.

As she began putting the magazine in the carpet bag, a paper fell out. Picking it up, she laughed at the photograph of her pretending to kiss Antonio's cheek.

If this handsome sailor showed up on her doorstep and asked her to run away with him, she'd gladly go. Right now, that was mainly to avoid returning to her parents. Still, she wondered how Antonio was.

"Mabel, they've been waiting a year," she whispered. "Go home."

She finished packing the carpet bag and snapped it shut. Picking up the lantern carrying her brother she left the cramped crew quarters one last time and stepped out on deck.

Cheers came, the whole crew was assembled and waiting.

"Three cheers for the pirate Red Stripes!"

The crew shouted together, and Mabel was grateful she had a handkerchief to catch her tears. There were what felt like a hundred hugs as they sailed toward Cliffshire, the ship repainted to be named, *The Green Goose,* and appear an honest vessel.

The last person she reached was Captain Stenton who pulled her into an embrace and wept as he held her.

"There's no girl in the world more like a daughter to me, Stripes," he whispered.

"There's no pirate captain more like a father to me," she said with a laugh.

He chuckled and kissed her cheek. "You belong out there, but, if you need it, there's always a home for you here." Releasing her, he handed her a folded-up map. "If you have trouble at home, you find your way to us, you hear?"

She smiled sadly while tucking the map into her carpet bag. "I'll miss all of you every day."

"Your mama's going to spew tears when she sees what a lady you are." Captain Stenton hugged her again before walking to the helm and shouting, "Let's get our girl home!"

The docks and buildings of her hometown were still familiar as Mabel walked down the plank to the dock. She embraced Gregson, Paulson, and Stenton one more time before waving to the gathered crew on the ship.

Taking in a breath, she forced herself to march away from her friends and toward the town. She hailed one of the horse-drawn cabs.

A driver pulled his horse to a stop and said, "Young lady, where are you headed?"

Her stomach tingled as she gave her home address. He helped her into the cab, and she held tight to her carpet bag and Malcom's lamp as the carriage rolled toward home. Looking out the window, it was remarkable how much of the town hadn't changed. It was quiet this Sunday morning, with the same old men sitting at the café patio and the same crowd at the church pretending to be pious.

The cab turned up the lane of her home and she stared at the largest house on the street, the pillars feeling more ostentatious than she remembered. The cab stopped next to the long, gated driveway and Mabel paid her fare as she stepped out.

She walked to the front and moved to unlatch the gate, but it was locked. She glanced down the quiet street before tossing her carpetbag over and hooking Malcom's lantern on the top of the gate. Then, just as she had many times growing up, she went to the large oak tree and held onto the black, wrought iron fence as she used a bend in the tree's trunk to boost herself up. She grabbed onto a thick branch and pulled herself onto it, her arms far stronger than before. Once on top, she slid along the branch and dropped into the yard.

She unhooked Malcom's lantern from the fence and picked up her bag before moving to the small gazebo. There, hidden from view of the street and house, she pulled Malcom from his lantern.

Praying this would work, she kissed her brother's wet, toad nose.

She dropped him as he began to grow, swiftly returning to his true form, still in his dinner clothes from the night he'd been transformed. He crouched as he blinked, his eyes bleary.

"I must have been knocked in the head hard," he said. "I've had the strangest dream."

His face paled as he stood fully. "Cassandra!" He spun on his heel. "Where is Cassandra? Is she all right?"

"She's fine." Mabel swallowed, trying to remember what she'd written to her parents. "She drugged us and sold us to pirates. You—" How did she explain? There had been much debate with the crew of what story to tell. She went with, "They treated us well, but you hit your head and then got a fever. You forgot the past year and I was worried I might not be able to bring you home." She gestured toward the house. "But here we are."

He scratched his head as he glared at her. "If your story is anything close to true, how is my suit so well preserved?"

"They put it away for you so we would look our best when we came home." She nodded toward the house. "Mother and Father are waiting. Three months ago, I wrote when we had gotten on a merchant ship and would be home soon."

Malcom barked a condescending laugh. "Is that the best you could come up with?"

"That, or I could say you were blackout drunk for a year." Mabel slapped her arms against her sides. Leaving him a toad while traveling had been the best choice. Maybe it would be worth turning him back.

Malcom grunted and glanced at the gazebo walls. "I passed out in the yard again, didn't I? Explains the strange dream where I was a toad."

He smoothed his hair and straightened his suit. "I hope I didn't botch things with Cassandra. I'll have to go in and change before I call on her."

"Of course. You were drunk last night," Mabel said flatly. She could try persuading him the truth, but it would be a futile effort. "And Cassandra sent a letter asking for you to run off with her."

"Of course she did. I shall have to answer her, won't I?" Malcom pointed at Mabel and laughed. "I was so delirious, I nearly believed you about being gone a whole year."

"We'll see what you believe when we head inside," she muttered.

Malcom patted his stomach. "I am starving. I think I smell bacon and some good, fresh scones."

He left the gazebo and walked toward the side door leading to the kitchen. Mabel grabbed the carpet bag and followed a few steps behind.

He opened the door and said, "I'll need a hearty breakfast this—"

Mabel couldn't help but giggle as the cook and kitchen maid screamed. Slipping inside, Mabel sat on the wood chair by the door, as she often had as a child when chatting with the cook. Shouts rang through the house as the housekeeper and butler ran in. The housekeeper cried out and Mabel's father's heavy steps echoed.

"What's all this noise? Is there a mouse in the kitchen?" He came to the door. "Mrs. Sinclair and I are trying to have a quiet brunch."

His jaw dropped as he stared at Malcom and tears came to his eyes. "My boy! My Malcom, you're home."

"It was just a bit of youthful foolishness last night," Malcom said with his charming smile. "Nothing to get upset over."

Mr. Sinclair stared at his son as he walked toward him and then pulled him into an embrace. "A whole year a prisoner of pirates! I'm so glad you're home and safe."

"What?" Malcom said as his forehead wrinkled.

Mabel was glad no one had noticed her yet. This was a good show.

"Mrs. Sinclair!" The housekeeper ran from the room. There was a gasp and Mabel's mother ran in, her hair the same red as her daughter's. She gasped again and embraced Malcom.

"My son." She broke into sobs as she held him. "We were so worried for so long, but you're home."

"I was only gone one night." Malcom pushed from her embrace and gave an uncomfortable laugh. "I've been out just as long before. Now, I hear there's a note from Miss Cassandra, and—"

"Has she sent a note?" Mrs. Sinclair's eyes widened, and she held a hand over her mouth. "That treacherous woman. Selling you to pirates. How did you escape?"

Malcom frowned at her. "Are you well, Mother? What pirates?"

"The ones who kidnapped you!" Mr. Sinclair gripped his son's shoulder. "Sounded like a daring escape, you fighting ten pirates off at once. I'm glad all those fencing lessons I paid for saved you."

Mabel tapped her thumb against her mouth, trying not to giggle. She had forgotten the embellishments she had added in some of the letters home. Many were made while Henrietta and Gregson sat with her, the pair making suggestions as Mabel crafted the battle where she and Malcom had escaped. She was glad she hadn't gone with Gregson's suggestion to say they'd captured a pair of dolphins and ridden them to safety.

"Is this some game?" Malcom scowled. "Last I remember, I was touring the harbor with Cassandra."

"And that's where she hit you on the head with the paddle, isn't it?" Mr. Sinclair leaned, as if seeking the injury from a year ago. "Did the damage hurt your memory?"

"Will you stop teasing me?" Malcom rested his hands on his hips. Moving to the door, he said, "Now, I'll be off to clean up and get some real rest."

"Calm yourself." Mrs. Sinclair took his arm. "Let's have breakfast. I'm sure a full meal will do you good."

Malcom grunted but accepted as his mother began guiding him from the room.

Rising, Mabel frowned. She had expected to be noticed once all the fuss over Malcom was done. Yet, after a year away, she may as well be invisible.

"I'm home too," she said.

The kitchen maid and cook gasped while her mother held a hand to her breast.

"Oh, of course the pirates would bring you home too." Mrs. Sinclair held her hand out. "You must have been so glad your brave brother was with you in such an ordeal."

Mabel stared at her mother. "He did nothing." She waved her arm. "He's the one who got us in trouble in the first place but doesn't remember." She pointed at herself. "I'm the one who got us—" She had to keep the lies straight. "Out of the pirate's hands and onto the merchant vessel. He was in a stupor from his—illness and doesn't remember a thing."

Mrs. Sinclair gasped and placed her hands on Malcom's cheeks. "You were sick? We must call a doctor and make sure you're all right." She sighed. "I'm so glad we installed a telephone last month."

"I feel quite fine, Mother." Malcom held a hand to his head and glanced at Mabel. "Though, I don't understand and can't believe this."

"It is true, Malcom." Mabel glared at her brother. "You and I were stolen by pirates a year ago. It took us months to escape, and you had fallen ill by the time we found a merchant ship to bring us home. You had a high fever and were in a daze and forgot everything." The lie needed a bit more. "I think you were sick for home, because once you saw our house, the fever broke, and you returned to yourself."

She held her breath, praying this lie would stick. Given how sorrowfully Mrs. Sinclair looked at Malcom, it was quite sticky indeed.

"You missed home so much?" She kissed Malcom's cheek. "We have missed you so much, my darling son."

Malcom's eyes searched his parents. "I was truly gone a whole year? This is impossible."

"It is." Mr. Sinclair kept his hand on Malcom's arm. "We've only had the ransom letter and a few notes from your sister. Your mother has wept with grief often, and we began to fear we'd never see you again."

Taking Malcom's hand, Mrs. Sinclair said, "But you're home now and we'll send for a doctor. Make sure you are all right after so terrible a fever."

"And the police. There must be an investigation," Mr. Sinclair said. "But first, breakfast with our long-lost son." He glanced at Mabel. "And you, of course. We are so glad you are here."

Mabel's parents guided Malcom out of the kitchen while the servants stared after him. Mabel stood with her carpet bag. After a year away, she was alone and an afterthought.

She glanced at the kitchen door leading to the yard. Captain

Stenton might not have left the dock yet. If she walked out, would anyone notice she was missing?

Her throat felt thick, but she shook her head. She had decided to come home. Her parents had always favored Malcom and would care about her in an hour or two when they'd finished doting over her brother.

"Miss Sinclair, how are you?" The cook approached and pulled Mabel into her arms. "We've all prayed for you, dear girl."

Tears fell down Mabel's cheeks as she returned the cook's embrace and rested her head on the woman's shoulder.

Mabel repeated the same lies for the fifth time as the inspector sat in her parent's sitting room and her mother held her hand.

"I'm just grateful to be home safe." She forced a smile.

The inspector smiled back. "We're quite happy to have you here, Miss Sinclair."

Hours later, dinner came, along with several of Malcom's friends and a few young women eager for his return, including some of Mabel's friends. Sitting in the parlor afterward, Mabel remained in the corner, still in her red dress, sipping her raspberry water while Malcom stood before the enraptured crowd.

"We wrestled on the deck, the grizzled pirate's hands gripped my throat." Malcom mimicked the peril, his own hands to his throat. "But I shoved him off of me and stabbed him through."

Several young women gasped in awe, Malcom's supposed bravery apparently making him more handsome. A few young men grinned, flexing muscles as they whispered, "I'd have done the same."

Mabel glanced at the patio door. Opening it might balance all the hot air coming from her brother. Maybe she should have returned to Stenton's ship this morning. The crew was rough and the work hard, but they'd tell the truth. When they didn't, it was an elaborate boast made with a twinkle in their eye.

She missed them already.

As the group broke into smaller conversations, Mabel's friend Hazel sat beside her.

"You must have felt much safer with your brother at your side," Hazel said with her innocent smile.

Mabel worked not to spit out her water. Keeping her face polite, she said, "I always made sure I knew where he was."

Hazel touched Mabel's hand. "It must have been frightening."

"It was, but the pirates were kinder than you'd think."

"Was there a dashing one?" She leaned closer and grinned. "Who fell madly in love with you?"

Mabel chuckled, picturing Antonio Cortez's bewildered face in the seconds after she kissed him before running off. He would likely be comforted to know she was home. When she wrote him next, she would send along a few copies of *Modan*.

"I see that blush." Hazel giggled and leaned closer. "There was a sailor, wasn't there?"

Mabel forced a smile. Here, maybe she would tell a bit of the truth. "I did meet a sailor at a port. We only had half a day together, but he was quite charming and a gentleman."

Hazel grinned. "Did he try to rescue you?"

An emptiness ran through Mabel. "He would have, if he had known I was in danger."

"Sounds very dashing." Hazel patted Mabel's arm. "But you wouldn't believe how dashing a man I met a few weeks ago."

Mabel tried to appear interested as Hazel recounted nearly falling in a puddle, only to be rescued by a handsome young man. She then ran on about the dinner they had afterward and walks on following evenings. Mabel tried not to let her mind wander as Hazel then ran through local gossip from the past year, of who married who, and a few scandalous rumors. Hazel spoke as if all of this had grand importance, but it all felt so trivial and empty. Not when compared to marauding a ship or sailing to escape notice of the Navy.

There was a whole world beyond this town and Hazel was fixated on the ugly dress another young woman wore to a luncheon the week before. While the dress did sound like a crime against good fabric, it didn't matter. Not compared to everything Mabel had seen.

Mabel was relieved as the hour drew late enough for her to rest her hand on her friend's arm. "Thank you for coming. It was great to see a friend, but I'm quite tired."

"Oh, of course." Hazel grinned. "What if I take you to lunch and a bit of shopping tomorrow? Help welcome you home."

"I'd enjoy that." It would get Mabel out of the house and away from her parents as they fretted over Malcom.

She walked Hazel to the door and kissed her friend's cheeks goodbye before heading to her room, untouched in the past year except for a bit of dusting. She opened her closet and picked at her dresses. These clothes did not feel like hers. Not anymore.

With the help of the housekeeper, she set up a long bath and soaked a while before changing into a soft nightgown. As she lay in her ruffled blankets, she stared at the ceiling, missing the way the ship would rock on the water.

A gentle knock came at the door before her mother opened it. "Are you asleep, Mabel?"

"Not yet." Mabel sat up as her mother entered and sat primly at the edge of the bed.

Taking Mabel's hand, Mrs. Sinclair said, "We're so glad to have you home." She patted Mabel's cheek. "You're still a bit on the thin side, so we'll work to plump you up, but you're going to make a lovely debutante."

"I don't want to be a debutante." Mabel closed her fists. "I want to design clothes and—"

Mrs. Sinclair patted Mabel's hand. "You're just distraught from all the trouble you and Malcom have been through."

"He's been through far less trouble than you think," Mabel muttered.

"Rest, my love." Mrs. Sinclair bopped Mabel's nose with her finger. "We'll have your debutante debut and start getting the young men to notice you. In a year or two, we'll make sure a man with a good inheritance snatches you up as his wife."

A deeper emptiness ran through Mabel. This was far from what she wanted. Her chest ached as she pictured Antonio. "What if I married a sailor with nothing to his name?"

She didn't plan on marrying Antonio, but he would be far better as a husband than the annoying young men who hovered around her brother. That was likely the pool her mother hoped to pull from.

Mrs. Sinclair laughed. "Don't let everything you've been through fill your head with fancies. You're home now. Set your sights higher."

She kissed Mabel's forehead and said goodnight. Mabel rolled onto her side and stared at the wall as she contemplated the future her mother wanted for her. It sounded miserable. She needed to make her own future. How to do it was another question.

After an hour of tossing and turning, her mind calculating and churning, she switched on the lamp by her bed. If sleep wasn't coming, she may as well use the time wisely.

She moved to the bookcase and found her Castallan dictionary. Carrying it to her writing desk, she sat down and pulled out paper, ink, and a fountain pen.

Dear Antonio,

I have finally arrived home. My parents are glad to see my brother. I think they are pleased to see me too, but the focus, as always, is on Malcom.

I miss the sea already. My dresses in the closet feel like they belong to a stranger. Maybe I will settle in over time, but only if I can stop my mother from managing my future.

She raised her fountain pen as an idea formed. From the carpet bag, she pulled out the photograph of Antonio and her. Biting her lip, she tapped the picture against her hand.

There might be a way to free herself from the vapid ballrooms and forced courtship her mother would subject her to. Succeeding would take carefully threading together a string of lies and require borrowing Antonio's likeness. It was a very handsome likeness, and she wouldn't mind standing in front of him once more, looking into his brown eyes, and—

"Focus, Mabel," she whispered. "You'll likely never meet him again."

Which meant he never had to know how she planned to use the picture. If she did tell him, he would understand. At least, she hoped he would.

Though nerves ran through her, Mabel pulled out more sheets of paper. As she crafted the pieces needed, an excitement grew in her. With each word she wrote, she saw herself pushing back against the bars closing in around her. She would have her freedom and her future.

CHAPTER 9

In Which Mabel Is Offered a Deal

The next morning, Mabel sat at the breakfast table and ate quickly but politely as Malcom "remembered" harrowing moments from their adventures. Their parents gasped at Malcom's proclaimed courage while he briefly glared at Mabel, warning her not to contradict the heroic persona he was building. Mabel raised an eyebrow and flipped through the latest issue of *Modan*. She smiled at some of the high-collar ruffles still in style, wondering what Antonio would say about them.

She also wondered again what he would say about how she had chosen to use his photograph last night. Glancing at her mother and father, she waited for them to step on the trap.

She turned the pages and came to the preview of next month's fashion week. Sitting up, she read the interview with Mr. Hartavo. Her eyes widened at the ad in the corner for his show, a line at the bottom reading, *And introducing an alluring design by our contest's winner, Mabel Sinclair.*

Mabel jumped to her feet.

"Dear, breakfast isn't done yet," her mother said. "We're at home, not on a pirate ship. Please be civil."

She looked to her mother. "You said we have a telephone?"

Her mother nodded. "We have all the modern conveniences. You have returned to a civilized place."

Mabel grabbed the magazine and flipped to the contact page. Her heart pounded as the housekeeper guided her to the phone sitting in her father's study. Her hand shook as she picked up the handset. She had seen these at a traveling exposition and hoped she was operating it right as she moved the round dial and called the operator.

Somehow, through a series of secretaries, transfers, and operators, the line on the other end at last said, "Pierre Hartavo's studio."

"This is Mabel Sinclair. The contest winner."

"Miss Sinclair! We've been trying to reach you for weeks." The warm-voiced woman on the other end laughed. "I was starting to think you were a phantom after trying to contact you for months. We hoped you would see the advertisement."

Mabel's stomach bubbled with excitement. "I did. I've been—" She clenched her teeth before saying, "I've had some unexpected travel abroad and I never thought—I will be there. Just tell me what I need to do."

"We'll send you a new package immediately. It will come in a day or two. What's your address?"

Mabel bounced as she said her address. "I'm so excited, and grateful, and—"

"We are excited too. We can reach your telephone at this address too?"

"Yes. Absolutely." Mabel grinned. "I can't—this is the best news I've had. Ever. I—thank you."

"We will see you early next month, Miss Sinclair."

"Yes!"

There was another laugh on the other end and the woman ended the call. Mabel grinned as she stared at the advertisement with her name on it while walking back to the breakfast nook. She paused in the door and her smile fell as her parents scowled at her.

An open envelope addressed, *To my beloved Mabel,* sat beside them.

The plan had felt wise at midnight last night. It had taken nearly an hour to write the letter and use tea and a candle to age the paper and envelope, making sure to drop some water on it to make it look like it had come from a ship. She had felt confident while slipping it into the stack of letters in the housekeeper's desk.

Now, however, her cleverness could ruin the real news.

"Who is this?" Her father said as he held up the photograph of her and Antonio.

Malcom smirked while watching her squirm.

"Clearly, I am in the photograph," she said. "But forget it. I have wonderful—"

Her father slammed his hand on the table. She had expected his anger, but it still worried her. She wished she had a rapier at her side. Or at least a knife.

He unfolded the letter she had quickly written, trying to make it sound like broken Barthanian.

"My Beloved Mabel," her father read, his voice stern. "My words no express my love, and how I miss you, my corazón and wife.'" Mr. Sinclair glared at Malcom and hit his shoulder. "How could you not protect your sister? This young man surely recognized her name and knew of our fortune. This is a letter to extort us."

Malcom's mouth hung open. "I was sick! I don't remember when she met this—" He squinted at the envelope. "Anton."

The drops of water had blurred the last part of Antonio's name.

"Antonio Montero." She had at least not used Antonio's actual last name. She squared her shoulders. The lie had already been given. She may as well remain committed. "We met at Port Nerama. We knew it was right as soon as we met and eloped by noon. We spent the rest of the day—" Her stomach clenched, and she avoided her mother's gaze as she whispered, "And night together. And I love him and he's coming to claim me in a year, when his commission's over."

"Where is your marriage certificate?" Mr. Sinclair scowled.

The marriage certificate was going to be made by a forger Captain Stenton had mentioned several times who happened to live in the next town over. "Antonio's sending it once he can get a copy. It's very hard while he is at sea."

"How long ago was this?" Her mother said, her eyes wide with worry. "Are you—do you—" She gestured at Mabel's stomach.

"We haven't started a family yet, if that's what you're asking." She hadn't meant to make her mother worry about such things. However, she had planned to make her parents believe it was a fully established marriage, making it harder to break. "I had a ring but traded it for medicine for Malcom."

If Malcom could make up ridiculous things for their year apart, she could too.

"This is why young women should not be trusted alone in the world," Mr. Sinclair growled as he slammed down the letter.

"I told him of our troubles, and we did fall in love, but he also married me so I could travel without people questioning me," Mabel said. "The marriage certificate was why the merchants treated me so well." She forced tears, grateful for the lessons Henrietta had taught her in how to fake crying. "I was heartbroken when I lost it but know my dear Antonio will come."

Antonio Cortez would probably come home to his Sofia in a year, when his enlistment ended. Antonio Montero would tragically fall off his ship and die in a year or two, as confirmed by a forged death certificate. By then Mabel would be twenty-one and a widow, creating more flexibility for her future.

"I will send his name to my lawyers," Mr. Sinclair said. "And they will make sure this blemish on our name is annulled and no one hears of your foolishness."

Hazel would hear of it at lunch, ensuring her parents couldn't hide it.

"I sought to honor you the whole journey," Mabel said. "But I was so alone and afraid, and Antonio is a good man. When you meet him, you will admire him."

They would admire Antonio Cortez, if they met him. Antonio Montero, however, did not exist.

"I'll write to the Castallan Navy too." Mr. Sinclair tapped his fist against his leg. "Let them know their sailors are running off with vulnerable young women."

Mabel's fingers tensed. She hadn't thought of that. What if there wasn't an Antonio Montero? Her eyes widened. What if there was?

"Please, Father," she said, trying to look as innocent as possible. "Life at sea is hard and—" She thought quickly. "And thinking of me is his only hope on days fighting pirates and smugglers. He only has a year or so left of his commission. Even if you must annul the marriage quietly, can you wait at least a year?" She looked to her mother and forced large tears. "I love him, but, if it means not breaking his heart while his life is so hard, I'll submit to whatever you want."

This appeared to win her mother over. Especially as Mrs. Sinclair took the photograph from where Mr. Sinclair had left it and handed it to Mabel.

"I've been young and foolish with my heart too," Mrs. Sinclair said quietly. "Not as foolish, but I also wasn't stolen by pirates. Your father and I will talk." She touched Mabel's cheek. "You have been through much. You must tell me everything later."

Mabel forced out sobs as she embraced her mother. "Oh, Mother. It has been so much to hide. I will tell you everything."

Before she did, she would write 'everything' in her journal so she could make sure to keep track of the details. And so her mother could read it when she went snooping in Mabel's room.

"Oh, my dear Mabel." Hazel held her hand over her mouth, her lunch of a light salad forgotten on the table. "What you must be enduring with such a secret!"

Mabel dabbed the corner of her eyes with a handkerchief. "I love him so and I fear what father will do to break us apart." She pressed a hand to her breast. "On the darkest of days, knowing my Antonio was out there would bring me great hope. Without him, I don't know how Malcom and I would have made it home."

"Mabel Montero." Hazel rested her chin on her hand and sighed before looking at the photograph again. "He's so dashing."

"You mustn't tell a soul." Mabel pressed her hand to Hazel's arm. "For my father's sake."

That sealed the trap.

Mabel excused herself to the powder room and took her time. Once she returned, Hazel rushed back to her seat from whispering to a group of older women sitting at lunch. By the time Mabel and Hazel paid their bill, the whole restaurant was whispering of Mabel and her sailor.

As Hazel and Mabel took a turn down the street and browsed a few shops, every middle to upper-class woman they passed whispered to their companion and pretended not to glance at Mabel.

They entered a dress shop. As Hazel flirted with a well-dressed young man, who must be the hero who had so nobly rescued her from a puddle, Mabel strolled through the store. She analyzed the out-of-date dresses and pictured her own designs on the manikins. She wondered what Antonio would think of this clothing.

Her stomach clenched. What would he think of borrowing his name and image to create her fake husband?

She would write to him and explain. He would either be angry or amused. Or never get her letter.

It was disappointing to come home and have no answer from him after she had sent him at least a dozen notes. Perhaps he was trying to be true to Sofia. But Antonio seemed the sort of man who would write to make things clear.

"You only knew him for a day," Mabel muttered as she rubbed the cheap silk of a scarf between her fingers. Yet, she wished she could analyze the weave of the fabric with him.

Trying to clear these worries, Mabel looked toward the street. It was quite silly for there to be a separate shop for gloves, hats, shoes, jewelry, and dresses. Most women were looking for full outfits. If there was a way to combine everything into one store and present whole looks people could mix and match, someone could make a fortune.

Her thoughts broke off as giggles came from one of the dressing rooms, followed by a whisper of, "Oh, Malcom, how much you have endured."

"It was nothing compared to my longing for you," came her brother's voice.

Mabel sighed before walking over as kissing noises increased. She pulled aside the curtain. Malcom's hands were holding several inappropriate places of one of the young women who had appeared so demure last night when visiting the Sinclair home. Her head was tossed back as Malcom kissed her neck and whispered her name.

Mabel gave a thin smile. "Isn't my brother quite adept after practicing such skills with so many women at ports?"

The young woman cried out and covered her mouth, her eyes wide with fear. Malcom glared at Mabel as if he might punch her. Part of Mabel wanted him to try. One of them had learned quite a few ways to fight in the past year while the other remained a toad, though now in human form.

"And what of you and your sailor?" he growled, gesturing toward the street. "Seems the whole town has heard."

"I married him before he kissed me anywhere further than politeness allows." She blinked innocently at the young woman whose face was growing paler. "But I will allow you to compose yourself and be discreet."

She bit back a giggle as she closed the curtain. Ruining her brother's romances was just as fun as she remembered.

Humming to herself, she moved back to the front of the shop. Hazel was absorbed in flirting with her young man, with him just as lost in the conversation.

"I'll wait outside," Mabel said. Hazel waved her hand distractedly and Mabel exited. She sat on a nearby wood bench and waved to old friends of her mother's as they passed. The women whispered to each other with scandalized faces.

If any of them had eligible young men in their families, there was little chance they would let them marry a tainted woman like Mabel. In a few hours, Mabel had likely destroyed her chances of marrying any reputable families in town, and it felt quite freeing.

"Miss Sinclair?" A tall woman with a strange elegance appeared beside Mabel. Her dress was plain gray with a bluish hue. "May I join you?"

"It's a public bench." Mabel motioned to the open seat beside her. "Though, I fear my reputation has become questionable."

"Actually, I've come to assist your reputation, if I can, Miss Sinclair." The woman sat and gave a warm smile. It sent a prickling on the back of Mabel's neck. "I am Mrs. Snow, and I might be able to help you with your troubles."

She held out a business card. Mabel took it and her eyes narrowed at Mrs. Snow's name above the words, *Fairy Godmother Society*. If she remembered right, the organization had been on a few shipping manifests for ships smuggling amber syrup. It had taken her a while to learn amber syrup was quite a powerful liquid for carrying spells and fetched a high price on the black market.

"I'm managing my troubles quite well." Mabel waved to another familiar woman her mother's age and the woman's eyes widened before she turned away in haste and walked the other direction.

"We can help you with your troubles with your young husband," Mrs. Snow said with a hollow smile. "If you'll help us track a young lady pirate by the name of Red Stripes."

A chill ran down Mabel's spine.

"Apparently, this young woman got caught up with pirates whose ship matches one that left the dock yesterday after delivering you." Mrs. Snow tilted her head. "Our informant didn't mention your brother but did remark on a toad in a lantern. How is that toad?"

As if summoned, Malcom stumbled out of the dress shop, still fixing his collar and wiping lipstick from his cheek. He glared at Mabel before marching away.

"No one else mentioned seeing your brother," Mrs. Snow said, "but everyone remembers the red-headed young woman in a red dress."

"I'm just glad to be home," Mabel said. "It was a frightening journey."

"Which took a whole year?" Mrs. Snow's painted eyebrows rose near to her too-light blonde hair. "So long with pirates must have been terrifying for you and your brother. Though, there are rumors your brother doesn't remember a thing of it. Some say it's an illness, but those who are transformed by merfolk magic rarely have a memory of the time they were a creature."

Mabel forced a laugh. "Merfolk don't exist."

"There are also whispers of a red-headed young woman in a pinstripe dress who made quite a scene in Marveth nearly a year ago."

Mabel tried to hide her shaking as she kept her eyes on the street. Mrs. Snow was digging far too close to the truth.

"The High Witch Randala doesn't like to be tricked by humans."

Mabel found herself turning to stare at the woman.

Mrs. Snow's expression still appeared friendly. "I'm sure bringing her the girl would fetch a price. Perhaps enough to cover the cost of the amber syrup that a certain pirate ship stole from the Fairy Godmother Society."

"I don't understand these strange things you speak of." Mabel looked down, rounding her lips and trying to appear innocent.

"Oh, I think you do understand me." Mrs. Snow's smile turned cold. "And that we can come to an understanding. Especially with your father managing a bank."

"I have nothing to do with the bank. I'm just—"

"Just a girl who joined a crew of pirates, stole from the Fairy Godmother Society, and will pay for the cost of what is stolen unless she can give us the location of the captain and crew, plus a few other favors." Mrs. Snow raised her shoulders. "All we want is to give you a chance to be with your dear Antonio. Isn't that what a young bride like you wants?"

"I do love Antonio Montero." Mabel forced tears again. She would play this game with all she had. "Please don't do anything to my dear husband."

"Oh, we'll leave the young sailor on his ship. But what a heartbreak it will be when he returns and something terrible has happened. Your father's business could be ruined. You could be in prison for piracy."

Mabel dabbed at the corner of her eyes. Mrs. Snow had pieced together most of the truth but hadn't seen through Mabel's latest lie. Mabel might have a chance to outmaneuver this organization.

"How much does the Fairy Godmother Society claim is owed?"

"A thousand macs, plus interest."

A deeper chill ran through Mabel. "I can pay a few hundred, but it will take time. And give you a map of the next ports the ship will be in."

She could give a false map which looked real enough. How she would get a few hundred macs was another question.

Mrs. Snow leaned closer. "Isn't your dowry worth three thousand macs?"

Mabel wanted to glare but kept her eyes as innocent as she could. This woman had done her research. "My parents won't hand me my dowry."

"Not even for Mrs. Montero to start her life with her dear Antonio?" Mrs. Snow patted Mabel's arm.

Mabel drew away as her heart quickened. When creating her false husband, she hadn't considered her dowry. It had always felt like an amount of money stamped on her forehead by her parents, reflecting how good of a marriage investment she would be. Since she was supposedly married, why not invest it for a better purpose? Protecting Captain Stenton and his crew was a worthy cause.

First, however, she needed to convince her parents to provide the funds. With her father's anger that morning, this would not be simple. If Mrs. Snow really wanted the money, perhaps she could help.

"If I could, I would use the dowry to pay you," Mabel said. "But my parents will never give it. They don't approve of my husband."

Mrs. Snow squeezed Mabel's hand. "Then it is good I have come, for I can solve two of your troubles at once."

Mabel forced a sob, adding to her façade of being the pathetic prey Mrs. Snow believed her to be. "I can't see how."

"All it will take is an extra thirty percent and we will smooth things over with your parents. Just you trust in me. Your parents will receive testimonials of Mr. Montero's future prospects, and all will change. What is his trade?"

"Welding." It seemed a good enough lie. "He's on one of the newer steamships."

"We'll have to adapt his profession. Claim he's headed to university to be an accountant or lawyer. Which would your parents prefer?"

"Something with banking." That would please her father greatly. "Maybe a job lined up after his enlistment is over."

Mrs. Snow tapped her fingers. "Such arrangements will raise our cut to fifty percent but will help you start your new life with your handsome young sailor." She let out a soft laugh. "I know I've frightened you, but our aim is always the happiness of our clients."

Mabel forced more tears. "I only want a happy future with my Antonio. If I had known—" She sobbed into her handkerchief and Mrs. Snow's cold hand patted her shoulder. "I didn't know what the pirates were doing. They forced me to cooperate. Please, help me."

"I'll have documents written up and find you tomorrow. After you sign, we'll work to clear away all of your troubles." The woman rubbed Mabel's back. "Do not worry. Once we have an agreement with a young lady, the Fairy Godmother Society becomes very invested in her future."

Mrs. Snow left her card in Mabel's hand and strolled away. Mabel's fist shook as she grasped her handkerchief. Once the Fairy Godmother Society discovered her lie, she'd likely be in deeper trouble. She had to keep a step ahead. But Mrs. Snow clearly had informants. Mabel would have to move carefully, but she would find her way out of this.

"So sorry to keep you waiting," Hazel said as she stepped out of the shop and giggled as she waved at the young man again. "I was—"

Hazel gasped and hurried to Mabel. "What happened?" She pressed a hand to her head. "It's my fault, isn't? I'm so sorry. Mrs. Flemham was there, and she's a dear family friend, and I—I didn't mean to let it slip."

"Everyone would have found out eventually anyway." Mabel rose. Fortunately, her false-marriage and her dowry might also be her way out of her trouble with Mrs. Snow. She forced a smile. "I don't care what they think of me. I just want my Antonio to come in a year and be accepted by my parents."

Hazel grinned and took Mabel's hand. "They must, once they see how you love him." She leaned toward Mabel and giggled. "Your boldness has made me braver too." She glanced into the shop before whispering, "My beau and I are going ring shopping tomorrow, and then he's going to talk to my parents."

Mabel's eyes widened. That was not what she wanted out of this. "You're three months younger than me. Be wise, Hazel."

"If I have love, why wait?" Hazel giggled. "That's what you did, isn't it? Met the man of your dreams and married him in hours."

"I suppose I did," Mabel muttered. "But they were very different circumstances."

"You were escaping pirates; I was escaping a puddle." Hazel bounced with giddiness. "We all have our own adventures."

"We certainly do." Mabel hated the growing worry in her stomach as she and Hazel walked back to where the carriage waited to take them home. Once inside, Mabel stared out the window, praying there would be no more unexpected consequences of her lies.

CHAPTER 10

In Which Mabel Receives a Package

Mabel's palms sweated as she stood waiting in front of her father's desk at the bank. It had taken two weeks, but there sat the forged marriage certificate. Though, it said Antonio Cortez Montero. That had been a slip of her tongue when talking to the forger, yet at least it wasn't his actual name. Hopefully, the false last name would protect the real Antonio Cortez.

Who still hadn't written her. But it was unlikely the pair of letters she had sent after coming home were anywhere near him yet. She just wished he at least had answered her earlier notes.

Though, she wasn't sure how he would feel about her mother submitting the photograph of Antonio and Mabel this morning to the local paper along with the marriage announcement. It would be packed in with a number of other hasty wedding announcements which had been filling the local paper's society page ever since a version of Mabel and Malcom's year with pirates had run in the paper. Young women appeared to be following Mabel's boldness in seeking the fellows they fancied.

"This admiral's letter is remarkable." Her father held his spectacles in his hand and looked up. Given the proud smile, the letter Mrs. Snow's associate had sent was quite believable. "Your young man saved his ship from smugglers single-handedly and is on track to be an officer if he stays in the Navy. They've asked a few thousand macs to pay for his commission. Of course, I must have the lawyers check it, but to have a naval lieutenant as a son-in-law!"

"He's far more interested in banking." She pressed her hands together, feeling the weight of the gold ring with a small diamond her mother had bought for her this morning. "And, of course, I would like him to be safe with me."

"Perhaps there could be a transfer." Her father tapped his spectacles against his chin. "He could join the Barthanian military. I've some influence with the commander of the nearest fort. With such an impressive record, maybe I could pay his commission and have him become a lieutenant there."

"Nearer home is better." The words felt sickening to say, but she had to play the part. Her dowry was the shield protecting Captain Stenton and his crew from the Fairy Godmother Society. For her to win, her father had to be fed what he wanted to hear.

Mr. Sinclair laughed. "Of course. And, if I work with my lawyers now, I think I could have it all arranged within six months." He rose and grinned at Mabel. "My dear, I'm so sorry about how angry I've been. When you came home so strangely, and then turned out to have eloped with some sailor, I feared for you." He held up a set of three letters. "But, after the endorsement of his captain and two admirals, I think you've made quite a catch out at sea." He chuckled. "Do you get it? He's a sailor on the ocean? Where men go fishing?"

"It's quite clever." Mabel kept her forced smile. She was getting better at making it look genuine.

Coming around the desk, he put his hands on her shoulders. "Your mother and I talked earlier this morning. She's already planning a grand wedding when he returns. Perhaps a parade."

"Oh, a parade?" Mabel's fingers pressed against each other till her knuckles whitened. "He'll love that."

"He is a hero of the Castallan Navy. And—" He picked up another letter. "This arrived today too. He had a letter translated and sent to me. What an eloquent young man."

"He is, isn't he?" For the extra payments, Mrs. Snow was outdoing herself. If only Antonio were actually coming.

Mr. Sinclair handed it to her. "I read what he wrote of you over the telephone to your mother." He pressed a hand to his chest. "My first priority has always been to ensure you married a man with good, steady investments. I do wish he was wealthier, but after these letters of endorsement, I am sure such things will come. You are so fortunate, my dear. See how he writes of you."

Mabel took the letter and skimmed through it. The words seemed stolen from some dramatic romance. In fact, she recognized one or two lines from somewhere. She had never thought her stern father would be so infatuated by her imaginary husband.

Dabbing the handkerchief at the corner of her eyes, as she had often done in the past two weeks of playing the part of a sailor's wife, she said, "He certainly loves me."

"If he does come as a banker, we'll have to teach him Barthanian very quickly. I'll set him up as one of my clerks and train him myself. He'll learn while assisting Malcom as I help him take over some of the operations."

"That sounds wonderful." She would not subject anyone to assisting Malcom. Even her imaginary husband. "But, as he mentions here and I've told you, his family has very little. I've been in contact with his mother. I'd like to setup a transfer of the dowry."

"The dowry should wait till the proper wedding."

"But how heartbroken my dear Antonio would be if something happened to his widowed mother." She raised her eyebrows. "If not the dowry, perhaps the money you would spend on the commission?"

"Send me the information and I'll have my lawyers double-check it."

"I have the address and account here." She opened her sketch book and pulled out the slip of paper Mrs. Snow had given her in the park two days before. Her stomach clenched. It was one thing to lie to her parents to get out of being sold off for marriage. It was another to do it to steal money.

But the money was what they would be spending anyways, wasn't it? And how much had they invested in Malcom's education? This wouldn't cost much more. Picturing Captain Stenton and her other friends steadied her resolve.

"Also, as I told you a few days ago," she said, "I need to leave in three weeks for Willington."

Mr. Sinclair waved his hand. "Are you still going on about that fashion nonsense? All you did was win some contest."

"It was a nationwide contest. Also, it's a great opportunity and could build my future."

He squeezed her shoulder and smiled. "The future we need to invest in is Antonio's."

"What if—" She let her anxiety show on her face, though the cause was different. "What if he dies at sea, before he can come?"

"A man that brave?" Mr. Sinclair patted her cheek. "The duty of a man is to provide for his wife. Let me manage your husband's future. All will be right."

Mabel was amazed with how much she pitied her fictional husband. Mr. Sinclair was already controlling him while he was allegedly at sea.

"I'd like to go." She gave another forced smile. "It would distract me while you work on helping Antonio get his commission."

"Stay here. Your mother has wonderful plans for preparing for you to be the wife of a respected man. There are so many responsibilities." He grinned. "There's a small cottage down the street from our house that was just foreclosed on by my bank. Normally we would sell it to cover the loss, but I am transferring it to my name and will rent it to you and Antonio while he's getting established as a lieutenant or here at the bank. Won't it be wonderful to be so close to your parents?"

He chuckled and patted her stomach. "And won't you look fine as a young mother? It will allow us to send servants to assist you."

"This is the future I've always dreamed of." She fluttered her eyelids to cover her sarcasm. "To have a brood of children for you and mother to dote over."

"Isn't it a wonderful future?" He laughed. "They'll be a bit tanner than I ever thought my grandchildren would be, but, given the looks of your Antonio and my own good looks, those boys will be strapping young men. They might follow their father into the Navy or join the bank and learn from me and their Uncle Malcom."

"I definitely want my future sons to learn from their Uncle Malcom." She tried to keep the dryness from her voice. Her children would be kept as far from her brother as possible.

Mr. Sinclair kissed her forehead. "Put aside thoughts of the larger world. You have such good things here, Mabel."

Letting her father embrace her, Mabel felt hollow. She was going to need Antonio Montero to die sooner than planned. However, that could only happen after her dowry was handed to Mrs. Snow and the pirate crew was safe.

Three weeks later, Mabel took a stroll around the neighborhood as she looked through the documents Mr. Hartavo's design firm had sent. She needed to get to Willington by noon tomorrow. There was even the train ticket for eight in the morning tomorrow. The three-hour train ride felt impossibly far away.

In the time since her marriage certificate had arrived, more false stories were posted in the paper of Antonio Montero's greatness, leaked by her suddenly proud father. Malcom glowered more each day as Mr. Sinclair bragged about his son-in-law, her brother often muttering, "I fought pirates too."

Mabel missed the fresh sea air and a pistol in hand while helping commandeer a few spare crates from a hapless vessel. Though, if she went back, she might reconsider what they stole. There had to be a way to make it a more honest version of piracy.

She paused as hammers and saws echoed nearby. Looking up, her face paled as she stared at the cottage her father's bank had foreclosed on, workers already fixing the roof. Once repaired, it would be a pleasant cottage, but the wrought iron fence made it feel more a prison than a home.

Shaking her head, she walked back to her parent's house. This time, at least, the gate was unlocked. Entering the yard, she waved to the gardener, and he grinned as he said, "Good afternoon Mrs. Montero."

She stared at him and then the diamond ring on her finger. All the evidence he knew pointed to this being true. Yet, she missed her own last name.

The lie that should have set her free now felt like a trap.

She entered through the front door and skirted around the decorators and caterers setting-up the reception room for the night's dinner party.

"Congratulations, Mrs. Montero," one of the workers said as Mabel passed. Several other voices joined the chorus. Mabel accepted the goodwill with a smile but hurried to the second floor and the refuge of her room.

Her heart sank as her mother and the housekeeper stood together, unpacking the pair of suitcases Mabel had hidden under the bed while packing over the past few days for her trip to Willington.

"What are you doing?" she said.

Mrs. Sinclair motioned for the housekeeper to leave before picking up the sea map Captain Stenton had given Mabel. "Darling, were you planning on sneaking away to find your Antonio?"

Mabel tucked her papers from Mr. Hartavo's office into her top drawer while gathering tears. She was getting too much practice at this.

"I miss him so, Mother. I thought I might find a passenger ship to take me to where he is."

Mrs. Sinclair opened her arms and Mabel forced herself to accept her mother's embrace.

"I can't imagine how you long for him, especially after two admirals endorsed him. But be patient. Your father will have him home. He was on the phone with the admiralty in Castallar this morning."

Mabel's eyes went wide. If her father had called the admiralty, the truth would come out far too soon. She needed to order the death certificate.

"What did they say?" she said.

"Your father's waiting to hear back, but the assistants to the admirals confirmed how remarkable your future lieutenant is." Mrs. Sinclair kissed Mabel's cheek. Mabel froze, wondering how Mrs. Snow had arranged that. "So, there's no need to run off. He'll come to you, and—"

Mrs. Sinclair pulled away and moved a few things on the bed before holding up a package. It was wrapped in weather-worn brown paper and strings.

"This came an hour ago." Mrs. Sinclair grinned. "He must truly love you, though—" She pointed at the return address. "I'm surprised he left out 'Montero' on his name."

Mabel's heart jumped as she grabbed the package from her mother.

This was from the real Antonio.

She cut the string and ripped open the package. Underneath was another layer of paper and an envelope with *La Ratera*, or "lady pickpocket" in Castallan, written across it.

Her mother laughed. "He used that pet name for you in the other letters."

Mabel's back straightened as she stared at her mother. "What other letters?"

Mrs. Sinclair's face paled and her smile fell. "Oh, I—you know that I love you and everything I do is for your own good, don't you?"

Mabel's eyebrows pinched together. With how her mother avoided uncomfortable topics, she might need a rapier to threaten her and find the truth. "Antonio sent letters?"

"Several came during the two months before you returned." Mrs. Sinclair attempted a smile. "I paid for the first few to be translated and was shocked that my missing daughter received letters with such warm words from a common sailor. I had to watch over you, even when I wasn't sure you'd ever come home."

"Where are his letters?" Mabel's neck was taut as she glared.

"If I had known how admirable the young man was, and that he would soon be an officer, I would have had them sitting for you when you came home."

"Where are they?" Mabel's pulse quickened.

Mrs. Sinclair looked down. "I regret it now, but I burned them."

Mabel's fists clenched, her arms shaking as she fought to not attack her mother. "How many did he send?"

"Four." Mrs. Sinclair raised her palms as if to defend herself. "It was done as a mother who must protect her daughter. You do understand, don't you?

"No. You lied to me." Mabel's chest tightened. Perhaps she should not judge hiding the truth. "I've been home a month, and you told me nothing. I thought, perhaps he—"

"I was wrong, but all is better now." Mrs. Sinclair rested her hands on Mabel's shoulder. "You are his wife, and he will soon return to you as a lieutenant. And, based on his letters, he does care for you so dearly."

Tears came to Mabel's eyes. Antonio had written sweet words to her that her mother had read and then burned.

"Let's see what he sent." Mrs. Sinclair tapped the package and winked. "Maybe it's a nightgown for his return home."

"I will open it alone," Mabel growled.

"My darling, I was only doing my duty as a mother."

"Please. I need time by myself."

Mrs. Sinclair gave a weak smile as she left the room.

Now alone, Mabel's hands shook as she used her letter opener to tear the envelope's edge. Inside was a ripped-out page of *Modan* with the advertisement bearing her name and a note in tight handwriting. On the paper was a sketch of her in the outfit she had worn on their day together. With her Castallan dictionary in hand, she read the letter.

Señorita La Ratera,

Congratulations on winning the race to having your name in Modan. I'm hoping this means you've made it home or will be returning soon. All I have is your parents address to send my letters to. I hope it is your parent's address and not a front for your thievery. Wherever you are, I found this fabric and thought it a worthy gift to congratulate you.

With how you charmed me in one day, I am sure you will win over the leaders of fashion. I look forward to seeing your designs come to life.

They will be better than Hilda Gladston's dress at the White Banquet, won't they? A hat shouldn't also be a nest. And those ruffles! When will the great designers remember clothing should flatter a woman?

Maybe, when I leave the Navy, you will be a great designer yourself. You've the eye for it. If you do, would you think about hiring a Castallan tailor? His recent experience is mostly in sewing canvas sails, but I hope the package I sent proves he still has an eye for fabric. I think the color will highlight your blue eyes and red hair.

I am excited for you, Mabel, and wish I could be at your side as you enter Willington's fashion world. Even if I'm just there to see what a woman with your cleverness will achieve.

Hoping your days of thievery are over,

Antonio Cortez

As real tears came, Mabel whispered, "I hope Sofia is married and fat with her first child."

The tears fell heavier as she opened the package and revealing dark green Gathrayan linen.

Mabel fell on the bed as a loud sob broke from her and she clutched the fabric to her chest. He couldn't be fully in love with Sofia if he sent her this. Not with the words in his letter. Her chest ached as she wondered what he'd written in the letters now lying among the ash in her mother's fireplace.

A while later, her mother tapped at the door before opening it. Mabel's tears had eased, but she glared at her mother.

"I was wrong, sweetheart," Mrs. Sinclair said as she entered. "But maybe I can tell you what I remember he wrote about."

Mabel sat up, surprised by her mother's sincere apology.

Mrs. Sinclair rested beside her. "They weren't written as love letters, but his interest was clear with how often he mentioned your blue eyes and clever smile. The letters mostly went on about some outfit or fashion trend."

Mrs. Sinclair's cheeks went tight. "It hurt to read, because it reminded me of how you'd often go on about the clothing in the latest issue of *Modan*. It made me miss you even more. But it also proves you and your Antonio are well-matched."

Mabel let herself rest her head against her mother's shoulder. They didn't agree on much, but she enjoyed moments like this, where they felt connected. The burned letters still hurt, but at least her mother was trying.

"I only had one day with him," Mabel whispered.

"He is your husband." Mrs. Sinclair ran her hand over Mabel's hair. "A man of his honorable reputation will come home to the woman he's chosen as his wife."

A deeper pain ran through Mabel. He would likely go home to his chosen bride, but that girl wasn't her. Yet, there was the mention of him coming to her.

Mrs. Sinclair touched the fabric. "This is fine linen. Is it Gathrayan?"

"He bought it for me." *Not for Sofia.* "It's for winning the contest for fashion week."

"That's very expensive fabric."

"I know," Mabel said. "And all he has is a sailor's salary. I'm sure he sends some money to his mother, and—"

"Don't you worry about his mother." Mrs. Sinclair rubbed Mabel's back. "Your father heard from the investigators he hired and wired the dowry this morning. It'll be released to her in weekly payments, so she has a steady income, but the money's hers now."

Mabel cried out, a spike of pain in her chest, guilt rising, knowing the money would never reach Antonio's mother.

"Just rest and be patient." Mrs. Sinclair kissed Mabel's cheek. "If everything goes right, you'll wake up one morning and there he'll be, standing in his officer's uniform, so happy to see you. You'll move into the cottage down the street, and soon make me a grandmama to beautiful children."

A deep ache ran through Mabel, and she whispered, "I think I love him."

"I should hope so, you silly girl." Mrs. Sinclair squeezed her arm. "You just sit here, and we'll get you some water."

Sitting alone on her bed, Mabel pulled her knees to her chest and rested her head against her arms. Holding her hands over her eyes, she whispered, "I wish the real Antonio were the same as the fake one."

Each toast to her marriage dug a knife deeper into Mabel's chest as she endured the dinner party followed by visiting in the parlor. Malcom grumbled each time and got more sullen and drunk through the evening. At least, until he and one of the young women disappeared from the party for a while and returned with the lady nervously checking her lipstick and a smirk on Malcom's face.

The telephone rang and Mr. Sinclair disappeared from the party. Mabel forced a smile as another set of women hovered around her and rattled off marriage advice and asked empty questions. Mrs. Sinclair stood with a crowd of other women, cooing over the gift Antonio had sent and how soon she hoped grandchildren would come.

Mabel wished she were old enough for others to accept her drinking alcohol. Especially as her father returned and clapped for everyone's attention.

"Admiral Guerrero of the Castallan Navy was just on the line," he said with a broad grin. Malcom groaned loudly and looked to his friends for sympathy. Mabel's hand tensed on her glass of sparkling lemonade. "They've agreed to the commission I've arranged for my son-in-law, Antonio Cortez Montero, to extend his service by three years, but as a Lieutenant, with a good chance he'll be a captain by the end."

Mabel trembled. The admiral was likely just an actor, but it was still worrying.

Raising his glass toward Mabel. "And don't you worry, my darling. He'll be home for shore leave, coming soon directly here to you, his beloved Mabel."

Mabel dropped her glass and it crashed on the floor while everyone else joined her father in toasting Lieutenant and Mrs. Antonio Cortez Montero.

"You must be so proud," several women said, everyone squeezing around Mabel.

It took a half-hour for Mabel to escape the crowd. She made it outside in the brisk, fall air and panted as she walked her parent's yard. She groaned as she passed Malcom in the larger gazebo, sitting on a bench with a different young woman than earlier on his lap, their lips locked together and his hands again in inappropriate places. How were there so many foolish women in this small town?

Mabel turned on her heel and marched to the gazebo in the front yard where she had transformed him from amphibious form. As she dropped on the bench, she held her hands to her head and yelled.

"We did more than you asked," Mrs. Snow said.

Mabel looked up at the woman standing in the opening of the gazebo.

"And while we wouldn't prefer for the payment of your dowry to be made weekly, we find it acceptable." She held out a thick envelope full of cash. "Here is the remainder."

"How did you get the admiral to endorse him as a lieutenant?" Mabel stared at the money. Somehow, it felt dirty. "Was it an actor?"

Mrs. Snow's eyebrows rose as if she were offended. "Mrs. Montero, the Fairy Godmother Society is just one arm of a much larger network of associates. We have ties to many places, including the Castallan Naval headquarters."

A chill shot through Mabel. "That was a real admiral?"

"Yes, my dear. I told you we make the dreams come true of those young ladies who make agreements with us." She smiled. "Though, it took a bit to find Mr. Montero, until we realized the last name was wrong on the marriage certificate. But such things happen in port offices, busy with hasty marriages." She tilted her head. "I was surprised to learn Antonio Cortez's trade is sewing sails on an old clipper ship. You must be very proud of your husband."

"His name is Antonio Montero." She had to hold onto this lie in front of Mrs. Snow. For the sake of Captain Stenton. And Antonio.

"Is that what he told you?" Mrs. Snow said. "Or what you told everyone to cover for your forged marriage certificate?"

Mabel raised her hand with the ring on her finger. "My husband is Antonio Montero and we married in Port Nerama."

"Your husband is Antonio Cortez, and my suspicion is he doesn't know you are his wife."

Mabel held Mrs. Snow's gaze. "How much will that cost?"

"Oh, nothing more. Your dreams have been achieved, haven't they?" Mrs. Snow tilted her head. "Unless you need assistance with the death certificate and news of his death. We can make it quite noble. A fire on his ship where he saved his whole crew, the day after getting his lieutenant's commission."

"And who is collecting the commission payment from my father?"

"Admiral Guerrero, of course, who will make sure it is sent to the appropriate account." Mrs. Snow stepped further into the gazebo. "You almost had me fooled, by the way. If there had been an Antonio Montero who had been at Port Nerama on the day the marriage certificate was signed, I would have believed you. It took a little digging, but the hint of 'Cortez' as his middle name led us to the real young man in the picture." She laughed. "Won't he be surprised when he gets his lieutenant's commission paid for by his father-in-law."

"No, please." Mabel gestured at the large envelope. "Take the rest of the dowry, if that's what it costs. All I used was his name and his picture. Leave him out of this."

"The lieutenant's commission must go to someone. All the paperwork has been filed and your father is so proud." Mrs. Snow sat on the bench beside Mabel. "And you fancy this young man, don't you?" She gave a sparkling laugh. "I can see it when you speak of him, which is why I believed you at first. He can be yours, Miss Sinclair. We can arrange everything."

"No." Mabel rose. "I have paid my debt, and that of my friends. We have no more business with each other."

Mrs. Snow tsked. "The Fairy Godmother Society does not let go of good assets. A girl with your wits has great potential. We don't have a task for you quite yet but will be contacting you to make the arrangement. As an advance on a long, shall we say, friendship, let me give you the kindness of making your marriage a reality."

"And what will you do to him? And to me? And how much more will you extort from my parents?" Mabel crossed her arms. "The answer is no. We are finished."

"Your dreams are so close to coming true, Miss Sinclair. Everything you could ever want is about to tip into your lap. And, for now, I ask nothing of you."

"And someday you will ask everything." Mabel shook her head. "I've gotten tangled enough. I am done."

She left the gazebo and ran back into the house through the kitchen door. Using the servant's stairs, she snuck into her room. Grateful she had already repacked her suitcases, Mabel checked her room for anything else she needed.

This was her life. She would take charge of it. No one, including her parents and Mrs. Snow, would manage it for her.

She changed into traveling clothes and double-checked the train ticket in her pocket. The train station was three miles away. A good walk might be a nice break. Even with two suitcases.

The hour was past midnight as the crowd cleared and the last guests said goodnight. Her parents came to the door and knocked.

"Dear Mabel, I know tonight was overwhelming, but you must be so happy," her mother said.

Mabel sat silent in the darkness, tears falling down her cheeks.

"We're so proud of your choice in husband. We can't wait to meet the handsome, young lieutenant," her father said.

Once they left, she turned on her desk lamp and wrote two letters. One telling her parents she was grateful for all they did for her, but she had to give the fashion world a try. She would be home in time to welcome Antonio and settle down.

That lie stung deeply, but she couldn't break her parents' hearts yet.

The second letter required the Castallan dictionary, and she hoped her sentences made sense as she sent a letter of apology to Antonio, explaining it was all a grand misunderstanding and had grown out of her control. She hesitated before adding, *I pray Sofia treats you kinder than I have*, and sealing the envelope with a kiss.

Leaving the envelope for her parents and taking the one for

Antonio, she picked up her suitcases and crept down the servant stairs, through the kitchen, and into the yard. Only crickets could be heard. And giggling along with a moan.

She glanced over at the large gazebo. There her brother sat with yet another girl on his lap, the two having been kissing for a long time.

Malcom did not deserve her parents, no matter how controlling they sought to be.

Leaving her brother to his impulses, she marched from the yard and toward her own future.

CHAPTER 11

In Which Mabel Arrives in Willington

Willington, Capitol of Barthan

Mabel's arms were sore as she carried her suitcases into the lobby of the tall, granite building on a busy road in Willington, the capital of Barthan. If she'd been the girl who had jumped on the back of Cassandra's yacht nearly a year ago, she would have gawked at the street full of fine carriages, with a few strange, motorized vehicles puttering through and honking at horses. Having visited a mermaid gala and traveled with pirates, she just added this to the strange things in her experience.

Though, she did gape as she reached the third floor and the long hallway leading to Mr. Hartavo's studio where dress forms in glass cases lined the hall. Each was a dress she recognizes from the pages of *Modan*. Up close, the details and stitching were meticulous. The most magnificent was the costume made for an empress in an opera.

"Miss, may I help you?" A voice said from down the hall.

Mabel hurried over to the tall woman in a violet dress which contrasted with her dark complexion. "I'm Mabel Sinclair. The contest winner. I'm a half-hour early, but—"

The woman smiled and motioned for Mabel to follow her. "We thought you would be early. Have you not been to the hotel yet?"

"I came straight from the train. I'm sorry I didn't have time to freshen up, but I—"

"I was just as excited on my first day as a design apprentice. I'm Elona Cantor. I'm one of the lead designers. Mr. Hartavo is intrigued to meet you."

"I'm no one."

"I doubt you will be for long. Some powerful people have already taken an interest in your work."

Mabel frowned. "Who? I only submitted the one design."

"Set your suitcases here, in my office." Elona opened the door to a room with fabric swatches and designs covering the wall. Mabel grinned. She wished Antonio could be here and see this too.

That brought a twinge of guilt.

At least she had sent the letter to him once the post office had opened. It had been quite expensive to send but would reach him. What he might think of her after all of her lies was another question.

"How was the train ride?" Elona led Mabel further into the workshop. Seamstresses sat at mechanical sewing machines powered by electricity. They were faster than the peddle machines Mabel had seen. Other crew members stood at tall tables, some wearing eyepieces with magnifying glasses as they hand-beaded onto bodices pinned to dress forms. Mabel was impressed with how fast their hands moved.

"I slept for most of it." After sitting on a hard bench at the station for the last few hours before sunrise until the train came, the padded seats onboard had been a luxury. "I could barely sleep last night, and it caught up with me."

As they reached a wall of glass enclosing an office, curtains blocking the view of the interior, Elona frowned and looked closer at Mabel's hand.

"I didn't realize you were married."

Mabel forced herself not to hide her hand behind her. "To a sailor I met seven months ago."

Elona smiled warmly. "Do you have a picture?"

Mabel hesitated before pulling her sketchbook from her pocket and showing the photograph of her and Antonio. Elona's eyebrows rose in admiration.

"He is more than handsome." She laughed. "I would have quickly married him too."

"He's a designer himself." Mabel flipped her sketchbook pages to the note from Antonio and showed Elona the drawing.

"A lady in trousers? How scandalous."

"Not while on the sea." Mabel tucked the photograph and note away. "We bonded over an issue of *Modan*. He's proud I made it here."

"Of course he is. Will he be coming to see the show in four weeks?"

Mabel's smile fell. "He's in the Castallan Navy. He has another year of service."

Hopefully, he wouldn't be locked into the three years of the lieutenant's commission too.

"Do you write him often?"

"I sent him a letter this morning." Here, the truth helped the lie.

Elona smiled. "You are already quite intriguing, Miss—" She raised her eyes in thought. "Your last name isn't Sinclair anymore, is it?"

"I prefer using Sinclair as a designer."

"Mrs. Sinclair, then?" Elona tapped her fingers together in thought. "Though, that is rather plain, isn't it? I don't feel it fits you."

"Neither do I." Her marriage wasn't real and being called 'Mrs. Sinclair' felt as stuffy as one of her mother's tea parties. She could use 'Ms.', but that felt so drab. Her title and name needed to fit who she would become in this world of fashion.

A wry smile formed. "Aren't all of the great female mistresses of art called 'Madame'?"

"Madame Sinclair." Elona let out a laugh. "There is an air of mystery to it."

Mable grinned and held the point of her hat as she posed. "I'm a girl of many secrets."

"Aren't we all? An air of mystery gets many far in the world of fashion." Elona gave Mabel a conspiratorial wink before knocking on the glass door. There was a muffled voice and she leaned in. "Madame Mabel Sinclair, sir."

Mabel tried to appear composed as she entered and stood in front of Pierre Hartavo. He wore an orange checkered suit and blue shirt, his white and black striped hair slicked back as he stood beside the window.

He glanced at her. "You are a whisp of a girl, aren't you?"

"Thank you for inviting me." Mabel curtseyed. She bit back a curse at herself, falling into childhood protocol her mother had hammered into her. As an adult, she likely looked a fool.

Given Mr. Hartavo's glare, Mabel's guess was correct.

Mabel pulled her shoulders back and folded her hands in front of her. Hopefully, that would make her look professional enough.

"So much brown tweed." He strode toward her.

"I'm in my travel dress, sir."

"And the cut." He tsked. "Makes you look built as a stick."

Mabel's jaw clenched. While it was true, it didn't mean he should prod her like this. "That is what I most resemble. I normally pad my hips, but I didn't want it rubbing against the seat on the train."

His dark eyes analyzed her. "Pragmatism and fashion are far separate concerns." He gestured at the shop. "You are in the land of high fashion and the couture, Madame Sinclair. If I am to be burdened with you in my studio, I expect you not to be an embarrassment."

"I'll work to improve my clothing, sir." Perhaps she should have gone to the hotel first. But it felt more important to be here, to see this genius at work. "I'm grateful to be given this opportunity."

"Given?" He raised an eyebrow. "You weren't even in the top one hundred submissions. And yet, here you are, with little fashion and little sense."

Mabel's brow furrowed. "I'm sure it was a fair contest."

"I'm sure it was not." He gestured toward his studio. "My assistant designers all submitted and are exponentially more skilled and talented than your little scribble demonstrates. I'm not sure how you managed to catch the eye of someone with influence, nor how many on the committee walked away with a heftier pocketbook." He sighed tiredly while waving his hand. "But you are the winner, aren't you?"

"I'm not sure—" Mabel's fingers tensed. Such bribery could be the work of the Fairy Godmother Society, weaving a net around her. No. This had come before her conversation with Mrs. Snow. Either he was wrong, and she had won fairly or somebody else wanted her here.

Why someone would manipulate things for her to have her dream role, was another question entirely.

Her thoughts broke off as Mr. Hartavo gestured limply and said as if it were a bother, "We must go through the motions, though, don't we? Welcome to my studio, and I'm so glad for you to join us for a behind-the-scenes look at the world of fashion." With a glare, he added, "That is a look, by the way. Do not dare touch anything without permission."

"Of course not." Mabel tried not to glare. He was an icon of fashion, no matter how rude. She was here to learn, not consider how his arrogance would disappear if she had a pistol at her hip.

"I'll have Elona set you up a station in the corner. You will stay there most of the time, out of the way. You can watch as much as you like. Just don't bother me. Fashion week is my opus, and my muse must be right."

Unsure how else to answer, Mabel said, "Thank you, sir. I will learn everything I can."

"Learn to stay out of the way." He gestured toward the door. "Elona seems taken with you. She'll be your keeper." He sighed. "I suppose you can leave your station as long as she is with you."

He wiggled his fingers at the door, and it took Mabel a moment to realize she'd been dismissed. She nodded to him before exiting. Once the door was shut, she let out a breath.

"Did he greet you with icicles?" Elona smiled.

"He says the contest was rigged." Mabel looked to her new mentor. "It can't be. No one knows me."

"I've seen your sketch." Elona motioned for Mabel to follow her and led her to a small desk in the corner. "It shows promise, but it's not at a professional level yet. However, your answers to the questionnaire are why I recommended your submission go past the first round."

"Thank you. It seems your word sent my submission far."

"Judging is anonymous. My vote meant the same as some of the top designers here in Willington."

Mabel shrugged. "He claims someone manipulated mine to the top, but I don't know who would."

Elona patted the stool at the small drafting table. "Madame Sinclair, there are three things to know about the world of fashion. First, if someone's giving you a leg up, take every chance you get, whether you deserve it or not. Second, there is always someone better than you. Third, hard work and learning the craft will keep your career. I've been here ten years and have seen hotshots who have a quick success and then burn their bridges and career into ash."

Mabel nodded, taking in Elona's words. "I may not deserve to be here, but I want to learn."

"I saw that in your questionnaire, which is why I volunteered to guide you." Elona smiled warmly. "Keep out of Mr. Hartavo's way and absorb as much as you can. The next four weeks are going to be a master class."

Mabel found herself smiling. The next few weeks would be hard, but, if others were like Elona, she could find her way. And, if there was trouble, she'd find her way out of it. She had survived a year with pirates. She would survive this.

Three days later, Mabel bent over the worktable, her tongue pressed against the inside of her cheek as she concentrated on the stitches. Her back, fingers, and feet were sore from following Elona through the studio and doing the exercises to improve her design and sewing skills. It was endless but fascinating work. It was so easy to get lost in helping drape or design or discussing how a fabric would move down the runway. There were some in the studio who gave Mabel cool glances, but most had warmed to her, answering her thousand questions every day.

"It's nearly seven." Elona knocked against the worktable. "Even if you do plan to stay through the night working, shouldn't you at least get dinner?"

"I'll be fine." Mabel's stomach grumbled, marking that a lie. Her internship included a weekly stipend for food, but she hadn't received it yet. At least she got free breakfast at the hotel every day. She had stowed away some muffins and fruit each morning for lunch and dinner, but she longed for a hearty meal. However, there had been days of sparse food while on The Gray Ghost. She could endure. If she had to, her pickpocket skills might help her get through. Though, she didn't want to resort to thievery yet.

"Did you have lunch today?" Elona's eyebrows lowered.

"I wasn't hungry." That was only somewhat a lie. "I was so busy working on the drawing exercise you gave me, I lost track of time."

Elona tapped Mabel's arm. "Next lesson: A good designer takes care of herself. She can't get work done if she's collapsing from exhaustion."

"I just want to get this stitch right." Mabel held up the practice fabric covered in lines of stitches, most of them jagged. "It looked so simple when you did it. I'm sure I can master it in a moment."

"It took me years to gain my skills. Be patient and get some rest."

"I've only a month at this internship." Mabel's throat tightened. "I must have a job in fashion when this is done. I can't go home."

Elona gently pulled the practice fabric from Mabel's hand. "You'll gain more from this month if you take time to eat. There's a café across the street. The food is decent and the benches soft."

Mabel's heart sank. It sounded lovely, but she couldn't pay for it without stealing. "It's better if I stay here."

Elona's eyes narrowed. "To work or to hide that you've no money for food?"

Mabel focused on the worktable. "I've dinner waiting at the hotel."

Pickpocketing from the rich seemed more honorable than taking from the underpaid designers likely at the café. Maybe she should have taken the remainder of her dowry when Mrs. Snow offered it. Yet, the money felt dirty.

"You need a hot sandwich and a good dessert." Elona nodded toward the studio door. "Get your coat. Dinner is on me."

Mabel raised her head. "I couldn't."

"I'm offering." Elona leaned toward her. "I ate only eggs and bread nearly every day for my first two years working at a design studio and couldn't even buy that on some days. Let me help you."

"My stipend should come in a few days," Mable said. "I'll pay you back."

"And I won't take it. The Fashion Society Board might have put you in a fine hotel but have no idea what a meal costs. You'll probably need every skoon."

Tears came to Mabel's eyes. She was hungrier than she realized. "Thank you. And I'll pay you back, somehow."

"Win over the fashion world when your dress goes down the runway, and that'll be payment enough." Elona gestured toward the table. "Clean up your station and I'll meet you at the door."

Mabel hurried to pack up her scissors and pins. When this internship was done, she would owe Elona more than she could ever repay. Mr. Hartavo might have his name on the studio, but it was Elona who everyone turned to for advice and help. She assisted deftly, easing the tears of those who'd just been shouted at by Mr. Hartavo or assisting with a seam gone wrong. Of anyone Mable could meet in Willington's fashion world, she was glad to find Elona.

A shadow loomed over the table and Mabel glanced up. Mr. Hartavo glared at her, dressed in a dinner jacket embroidered with orange and blue peacock feathers. He looked nearly as ridiculous as some of the high-neck ruffles on his gowns.

"This is what you are wearing?" He scowled at her.

She would not be intimated by him as others were. Standing straight, she said, "Yes, sir. As I have done all day."

He waved his hand at her. "At least it is better than that tweed ensemble. And it will be hard to make a worse impression after being late to the dinner where you're the guest of honor."

Mabel frowned. "What dinner?"

Impatience flared in his eyes. "The Fashion Society dinner and reception to welcome the contest winner. Do you have any idea how embarrassing it is to arrive and have everyone ask where the little ingénue is, as if I am your governess?"

Mabel's stomach tightened. "There was a dinner tonight? No one told me."

Mr. Hartavo let out a disbelieving scoff. "It was in the welcome packet announcing you won."

"I never got the original packet." Mabel leaned on a standing stool and held a hand to her head, trying to push away a wave of dizziness. Elona's offer of a sandwich sounded far better than this dinner she'd already missed. But, if she was the guest of honor, she needed to go.

"Never got the packet?" Mr. Hartavo laughed derisively. "Then how did you know you had won?"

"She saw it in *Modan*." Elona hurried toward Mabel's worktable. "Which is why it took so long for her to confirm. I told you that after she called a few weeks ago."

Mr. Hartavo waved a dismissive hand. "No matter what happened to the invitation, you've already embarrassed me enough. Ms. Cantor, can you help this wispy girl into one of our sample gowns and get her to the gala down the street? I shall have to stall everyone and say she is arriving soon."

Without waiting for a reply, he strode out of the studio, slamming the door behind him. Mabel held her hands to her head as she glared after him. He treated it as her fault she never had information about the reception.

"Hurry." Elona led Mabel to her office. "There will likely be no food by the time you arrive." She opened a cupboard and pulled out a basket with some apples, fruit, and cheese. "I keep these for long days. Take what you want. I'll be back with something suitable for you to wear."

Mabel took an apple, the taste sweet and texture crisp as she ate quickly. It helped ease the pang in her stomach, but a hot sandwich sounded delicious too. As she ate a few slices of cheese, she sat with her brow furrowed.

Knowing Mr. Hartavo, he was painting Mabel as some wide-eyed fool with no talent. She had come to Willington to build her career and every minute meant a higher chance Mr. Hartavo would succeed in squashing her future in the eyes of the Fashion Society.

Elona returned with a dark blue evening gown with silver beading and hung it from a rack.

"This is from a couple seasons ago, but the bust should match your size better than newer ones." Elona set a make-up kit on the desk. "I'd offer my makeup, but with how much lighter your complexion is than mine, it would look odd. I hope we have the right colors in here."

"He could have reminded me," Mabel whispered, her anger deepening. "But didn't. He wants me to fail, doesn't he?"

"He wants everyone to bow to him or fail." Elona flared out the skirt of the dress. "But so do most famous designers."

Mabel's fists clenched. "I will not bow, and I will not fail."

Elona glanced at her and smiled. "Good. Mr. Hartavo bullies

enough new designers out of the business."

Mabel frowned. "If he's so cruel, why do you work for him?"

"He respects my work, so treats me better." Elona began unbuttoning the gown. "And he's no worse than most of the famous designers in Willington. They battle each other with their sharp tongues and large egos, while myself, and other anonymous designers make the clothing."

Mabel rose and began removing her own dress. She was glad her slip hid the small knife she kept strapped to her thigh, just as Paulson had taught her. "So, he puts on the show while others do the work?"

"The show is as important as the work itself." Elona pulled the dress from the hanger and carried it over to Mabel. "Some designers are excellent craftspeople. Others are better show people. Someone who has both skills can go far."

Mabel pictured Captain Stenton in his long coat and large captain's hat, putting on the show of a fierce marauder.

"So, the fashion world is little different than life as a pirate?" Mabel muttered to herself.

Elona chuckled while lowering the gown over Mabel's head. "I've never been a pirate, so I can't compare. But it is probably good wearing a sword is out of style."

"There are other weapons to fight with." Mabel tapped her fingers against her side as Elona buttoned the gown. If this crowd was anything like the parties her parents hosted, Mabel would have to carry wit as a sword and charm as a shield.

Elona adjusted the shoulders on the dress before grabbing a needle and tacking some of the fabric into small pleats to adjust the fit. "Tonight, is an opportunity to meet those who consider themselves powerful in the fashion world. Be polite, charm them if you can, but observe and listen. See who sits with who and who avoids each other."

"Who is going to be there?" Mabel said.

"Madame Girron. She will likely have an up-and-coming dragon jockey on her arm. And then there is Mrs. Waverly."

Mabel's heart thudded. "The prime minister's wife?"

"Of course. She feels it is one of her duties to advance the nation's fashion. Unfortunately, her exposure to the fashion world has not improved her poor taste. Try not to insult whatever hideous color she is wearing tonight."

Mabel bit back a giggle. Continuing through the list of names, Elona finished adjusting the dress and painted makeup on Mabel's face. She helped Mabel change into a pair of fine shoes before using a comb and some bobby pins to adjust Mabel's hair. Finished, she stepped back and smiled.

"There. That will make your entrance worth waiting for." Elona crossed to the cabinet and opened a door, revealing a full-length mirror.

Mabel stood straighter as she stared at herself in the mirror. She had thought she dressed well before, but she had never looked so sophisticated and mature. In her quick work, Elona had fitted the dress perfectly, giving Mabel the appearance of curves where she had little. Her hair and makeup were simple yet complemented the dress.

"Thank you." Mabel turned, admiring how the dress hugged her waist before the skirt spread out. "I've never—The dress is beautiful."

"You are beautiful. All I did was enhance it." Elona walked to the door and pulled a satin shawl from a hook. "If there's a photographer there, see if they can provide a picture for you to send to your Antonio."

Mabel's throat clenched and heat flushed through her face.

"I wish he were here," Mabel whispered, picturing him beside her as they entered the room. He was so much more skilled and talented in design than she was. "He deserves this chance more than I do."

"Then charm everyone tonight." Elona gave a soft smile. "And when your lieutenant returns, maybe you can build your careers in fashion together."

Mabel rubbed her thumb against the ring symbolizing their fake marriage. Even if he did forgive her, the chances of seeing him again were slim.

Turning her head, she forced a smile. "It is a good dream."

Placing the shawl on Mabel's shoulders, Elona said, "I'm sure you will do much tonight to build that future."

"I owe him that," Mabel said.

"You owe yourself that." Elona opened the office door and led Mabel into the studio.

She escorted Mabel out of the building and down the street to a grand hotel with a gilded entrance. Along the way, Mabel absorbed every word as Elona walked her through suggestions of topics for the evening.

They reached the ballroom door and Mabel's heart pounded. This was nearly more frightening than her first act of piracy. There, she had been watched over by the crew. Here, she would enter alone and without an ally.

"Trust yourself." Elona squeezed Mabel's arm. "If you're too nervous to talk, just ask them questions about themselves. They'll start chattering and you'll be practically invisible."

Mabel swallowed as she nodded. Glancing at Elona, she said, "Thank you. Life here in Willington would be much harder without your kindness."

Elona smiled. "I had others who were kind to me when I started out. There's a naive part of me that hopes kindness will be the next trend in the fashion world."

"I'm happy to join the effort." Mabel took in a breath before rolling her shoulders and raising her head. "It is time for Madame Sinclair to make her entrance, isn't it?"

"I'm sure it will be grand." Elona rested her hand on the door handle. "Are you ready?"

With Mabel's small nod, Elona opened the door and Mabel entered the ballroom.

CHAPTER 12

In Which Mabel Meets Her Benefactor

The room was magnificent, and Mabel wished she had a moment to admire the high arches, the tiled, domed ceiling, and filigree along the walls. However, fifty members of the fashion industry's elite stared at her with polite smiles paired with a glaze of impatience. There were a few dressed as outlandishly as Mr. Hartavo, but the majority wore extravagantly beaded gowns or fine dinner jackets.

Pushing down the nerves rising within her, Mabel put on her best attempt of a charming smile. If she showed weakness, this room of cheetahs and lions would eat her. Pretending confidence would be her best protection.

Mr. Hartavo glowered as he came to her side. "May I present Madame Mabel Sinclair, the little winner of the contest."

"I'm honored to join you tonight." Mabel ignored the knowing glances Mr. Hartavo was giving others, dismissing her as nothing. "I hope my lateness has only built anticipation."

At least there were some polite chuckles, despite many in the crowd giving her disdainful looks. Mabel's lateness combined with the derisive gossip Mr. Hartavo had already shared likely set Mabel back a hundred steps. But she would not let him drag her down. He might be trying to drown her career before she began, but she would kick her way to the surface.

"We were so worried you couldn't make it." Patricia Evanwind swept up the stairs toward Mabel, her small dog tucked under her arm, wearing a cape matching her dress.

Mabel bit back a giggle. She would have to describe this to Antonio in a letter. A pang rapped against her ribcage. It might be better not to write Antonio until he answered her apology. But how could she not when she was living the dream they both shared?

"I am Patricia Evanwind, president of the Willington Fashion Society. Everyone is quite curious to meet a young designer who has already gained much interest. Come and I will introduce you."

Mabel practiced the nods and greetings she had learned from her mother's tea parties. The people here were wealthier and wore far more elegant clothing, but likely held the same fragile egos. Names and faces blurred together, though she recognized many from *Modan*. Few gave her a real glance, all having a surface politeness, as if waiting for a fly to buzz away.

Within the half-hour of introductions, a string quartet struck up and some of the crowd paired off for dancing. Leading Mabel to one of the tall reception tables made for standing, Mrs. Evanwind said, "I have a few things to attend to, but I hope you enjoy what little remains of your reception."

An emptiness washed through Mabel as Mrs. Evanwind strolled away and joined a circle, her conversation brightening as she spoke to those she considered her equal. Mabel's stomach grumbled as she glanced at the table of appetizers, most of it already picked over. Her throat felt thick.

She was nothing to these people. It would be the same even if she had known of the event and arrived on time. Maybe she should have skipped this and gone with Elona to the café. Then, at least she would have a full stomach.

"Make the most of this," Mabel whispered. Not just for herself, but also for Antonio. The bigger she made her name, the more she could help him when he was finally free from the Navy.

She strode to a circle and tried to slide into the conversation. The group shifted their stances and the opening closed, so Mabel sought another group. Here, the opening remained as the group discussed the latest dragon racing, but there was no glance at her, no acknowledgement she was present.

Moment by moment, she felt more invisible as she sought a chance to say something clever.

Her gaze shifted as a tray of desserts was placed on the serving table. If she was going to be ignored, at least she could have something to eat.

Reaching the table, she took one tart, pudding, and brownie. She considered more but didn't want people to remember her for having a tower of desserts. Carrying the plate to an open cocktail stand, she overheard a woman say in a loud whisper, "I suppose young ladies don't need to watch their figure."

Mabel's cheeks burned, but she kept her head high. As she reached the stand, she took a bite of the tart. It tasted delicious, but the knot in her throat soured the enjoyment. It was awkward to stand alone and eat, but she needed something to get her through. Just a little food and she'd try joining a conversation again.

"May I join you?" a Castallan man in his sixties joined her, his smile warmer than the others and his hair dark brunette, peppered with gray. He held a plate with a mound of desserts. Mabel was impressed with his stacking skills and envious at his boldness to take so much.

"Please." She gestured at the stool across from her, trying to remember his name from Mrs. Evanwind's introductions.

"Arturo Astrellar! There you are!" A nasal-voiced woman drowning in a feather boa came to the man's side and touched his arm. "I have someone I must introduce you to."

A flash of annoyance ran through Arturo's eyes as he gestured toward Mabel. "I was hoping to get to know tonight's guest of honor. Tell them they are welcome to join."

The woman gave Mabel a dismissive glance and condescending

smile before saying in poorly accented Castallan, "The girl is just as dull as Mr. Hartavo claimed. Why waste your time?"

"Because I believe in her talent," Arturo said in the same language, "and I find it rude to hide insults behind foreign languages."

"I agree," Mabel said in Castallan as well. "Fortunately, I have traveled abroad, and understand insults in at least four languages."

A true smile crossed Arturo's face and the nasal-voiced woman went pale.

"I'm so glad you are so clever," the woman said in Barthanian, with a forced laugh. She gulped half of her martini as she glanced to the side. "Oh, I think someone is calling me."

Mabel bit her lip to hold back a giggle as the woman hurried away.

Arturo raised his glass to Mabel. "You are handling this pit of vipers quite well."

Mabel's eyebrows twitched up. His openness was unexpected but refreshing. "They seem more interested in ignoring me than biting."

"I suspect it is their loss, Madame Sinclair." He tapped a finger on his chest. "My loss is that I arranged for my wife and I to be seated next to you at dinner. But you never arrived, and my wife was called away to other business, so I was left sitting between a pair of very dull dinner companions."

"Then I am even more disappointed I missed dinner," Mabel said. Candor appeared the best path, and it was refreshing. "I would have gladly come if I had known about tonight's reception before it started."

Arturo let out a laugh. "No one sent an invitation to our guest of honor?"

"Apparently it was in the welcome packet. I'm sure the packet arrived at my parent's while I was still abroad." A knot twisted in her stomach as realization hit. Her eyes widened as she said, "My mother likely burned it along with Antonio's letters."

"Antonio?" Arturo grinned. "Is he some forbidden love?"

Mabel swallowed, picturing the letters smoldering along with the packet. Her mother had appeared surprised to know Mabel had won, but she had also hidden Antonio's letters. More than anything, this was a reminder she had made the right choice by leaving Cliffshire.

Arturo tapped her arm. "Who is this Antonio?"

"He is—" Mabel wanted to tell this stranger the truth. He probably would be amused. Maybe even sympathetic. However, as long as Antonio was trapped as a lieutenant, it was only fair for Mabel to keep up the lie of their marriage. "He is a lieutenant in the Castallan Navy and my husband."

Arturo grinned. "So young and married to a handsome sailor? I assume he is handsome, of course. How did you meet?"

Mabel ran through the version of the story she had shared dozens of times over the past month. Arturo asked questions and she found herself falling into an easy conversation. As she spoke of ports she had visited, he shared his own travels across the world, from, Castallar to the deserts of Sandar and open fields of Hyun. Mabel found herself smiling as he told stories and enjoyed his bright laughter as he listened to her.

A small crowd formed, seeking to insert themselves into the conversation with Arturo. He deflected their attempts and kept the focus on Mabel.

There was a brief lull as Arturo glanced at the clock. "It is nearing the end of the evening. Would you care to dance with an old man?"

"If you introduce me to him, I'll be glad to." Mabel winked. "But, if you are asking, I'd be honored."

Arturo laughed and offered his arm. They soon joined the small group waltzing. Arturo's steps were smooth with years of practice and Mabel was glad to match him.

Guiding her around the dance floor, he said, "I can see why my wife is so intrigued by you."

"By me?" Mabel frowned. "I am no one."

"You are on the path to become someone. She saw it when she first noticed you. My wife is always seeking new hobbies and projects to fill her time. Some can be quite troublesome, so I try to encourage her safer interests. A few months ago, when she came home from the selection committee meeting and said you had applied, I knew I had to invest."

The muscles in Mabel's neck drew tight. "Sir, there are rumors I only won the contest through bribery. I hate to ask, but are they true?"

He huffed a laugh. "The contest has never been about the candidate's merits. Each year, it becomes a bidding war over whose relative or lover can be given the internship. You're more talented than most winners. I've never played the game before, but it was simple to win. And this evening's conversation has been worth the investment."

Mabel's steps slowed, her smile gone. "I am grateful, sir, but I would rather build my career on my own skills and talents. And I'm not sure what I've done to gain your interest."

From behind her, a familiar woman's voice said, "You gained his wife's interest by shoving her in a pool in Marveth before running off. Then she sought you for hours, trying to fulfill her promise to take you home."

Mabel's spine ran cold as she turned to face Cassandra. The mermaid wore a beaded gown hugging her curves along with a feathered hat pluming over an elaborate white wig. Her blue eyes pierced through the veil hiding her youthful face.

"I do not offer help lightly," Cassandra said. "But I tried to assist you, Madame Sinclair, only to be rejected. Worries of what came of you ran through my mind for months until I happened to see your entry to the contest. It was clear you were alive, but where you were was another question. Rather than scouring the entire ocean for you, I thought it simpler to arrange for you to win and wait for you to arrive in Willington."

"You arranged for me to win so you could find out where I was?" Mabel said slowly, her head throbbing as she tried to follow the mermaid's labyrinth of logic.

"Yes. Though, there were points I was unsure whether you had actually entered the contest, or if you had been captured in Marveth and the entry was a trap.”

“How could my entry into a contest be a trap?”

“You haven’t dealt with the High Witch of Marveth,” Arturo said. “It wouldn’t be the first elaborate trap she has set for Cassandra.”

Mabel stepped back, staring at the couple. “This isn’t—” She shook her head. “I don’t want any part of bribing and scheming, or being anyone’s pawn. I just want to build my life on my own.”

She swallowed the words painful even before she spoke. “I am quitting the internship. I’ll find my own way.”

Before they could speak, Mabel strode way. Tears were threatening to come, but she shoved them back. Winning the contest was only another lie trapping her, just like the wedding ring she wore. Though, the ring was from her own foolishness.

Cassandra reached Mabel’s side and walked beside her. “Madame Sinclair, I am trying to—”

“Let the young lady go,” Arturo said, keeping close to his wife. “A girl that bright will find her way.”

Mabel wished the man was merely a kind benefactor and not Cassandra’s husband. However, she could not trust him nor the mermaid who’d kidnapped her brother and transformed him.

No one else tried to stop her as she strode from the room. Though, Mr. Hartavo bore a triumphant smirk.

Mabel would find her way on her own. She didn’t know how, but if she could learn to become a pirate, she could build her own path in the fashion world.

Her headache grew and her stomach grumbled as she crossed the hotel lobby. The apple and desserts she’d eaten tonight were not enough to make up for the meals she had missed. If only she had gone with Elona. That would have been a far more pleasant evening, and Mabel would be ignorant of those who used money to treat people like puppets.

Reaching the street outside the hotel, she rested her hand on her head. A few tears broke past Mabel’s resolve as she sought where to go.

Returning to her parents was not an option. They would just hold her back. She could stay tonight in the hotel. But, tomorrow, she and her suitcases needed somewhere to go. If she had to, she could sleep a night or two on a park bench while seeking work during the day. She glanced at the ring on her hand. She could pawn it and use the money to get by for a few weeks.

"Or you can go back to being a pirate." She blew out a breath. How she missed Captain Stenton and his crew. They might be pirates, but they treated her as their equal and were honest with her. "But how can you make things right for Antonio if you're traveling with pirates?"

She would just make things worse.

With a moan, she whispered, "I should have never jumped on Cassandra's yacht."

Mabel wiped the tears from her cheeks and raised her head. She would find her way.

"Miss?" a deep voice said from behind her.

She glanced at the stranger, a man in his early thirties with a thin mustache and loose-fitting suit. His smile was polite, but something about him made her uncomfortable. Perhaps it was worrying that Cassandra would be following her.

"You look a little lost, miss. Maybe I can escort you home?"

Mabel brushed her fingertips against the knife hidden beneath her skirt. It would take some creativity to reach it discreetly, but she was glad it was there.

"I'm just getting some fresh air." Mabel turned toward the lobby. Her step paused. Cassandra and Arturo might be waiting in the lobby, ruining it as a hiding place. Pivoting, she began walking, hoping it was the right direction for the hotel she was lodged at.

"You are Miss Mabel Sinclair, the Fashion Society's contest winner?" the mustached man said. "My name is Sam Cadson. I have some connections to the Willington Gazette. Maybe I can get you a profile in the style section?"

Mabel scanned the emptying street, wishing the hour weren't so late. At least several clubs along the street were still open. Perhaps she could duck inside one and avoid this supposed journalist.

"I'm only trying to help you, Miss Sinclair. I know powerful people. I can get you noticed. All you'd owe me are a few favors."

The hair on the back of Mabel's neck rose as she spun on her heel and faced him.

"Just a few favors? What sort? Information? Gossip? Bribery?" She stepped toward him and glared. "Let me be clear, Mr. Cadson: I cannot be bought."

He gave an attempt at a charming smile and shrugged. "I'm not looking to buy. Just bargain."

"For what?" She narrowed her eyes. "For fame? For wealth? For power? If I gain any of those, it will be earned. Thank you for your interest and good night."

She bit out the last words and marched away. As she turned to a less traveled street, the echo of Mr. Cadson's footsteps were joined by others. She glanced at a shop's window and caught sight of at least two heavily muscled men pretending to stroll across the street. Passing another window, it became clear, they were tailing her and Mr. Cadson. Most likely, she was the target.

"The fashion industry's a hard business," Mr. Cadson said. "But it can be easier if you make the right friends."

Mabel pretended to trip and knelt, making a show of fixing her shoe with one hand. She slipped her other hand up the layers of her skirt and removed her knife, the blade the length of her palm. It would do little against a sword or pistol but was better than no protection.

"You all right there, miss?"

Mabel tucked the knife against the inside of her arm and hid the handle in her palm as she waved him off with her other hand. "I only want to be left alone."

Mr. Cadson gave her an empty smile. "Come now. A girl who's come all the way out to Willington on her own has got to have more ambition."

"My only ambition for the moment is to get some sleep." Mabel strode away once more.

Mr. Cadson hurried till he walked beside her. "A mutual acquaintance of ours says you're clever. Now, I work for some powerful people in Willington. If you did them a favor like, say, provide a sketch or two of what Mr. Hartavo's planning for fashion week, I can get you introduced. I'd bet they'd be eager to invest."

Quickening her step, she said, "I am not a thief."

"But you are a former pirate, aren't you?"

Mabel's heart jolted, but she maintained her step. "Who told you that? A mermaid or a fairy godmother?"

Mr. Cadson chuckled. "Let's just say a friend told me how you conned your parents out of your dowry."

Instincts from Mabel's training on the pirate ship snapped into place and she spun on the ball of her foot. She grabbed him by the shoulders and shoved him against a brick wall before holding her knife to his throat. The amusement in his eyes just made her angrier.

"I fulfilled my contract with the Fairy Godmother Society," she growled. "I will do nothing more for anyone associated with them."

"Our organization is much bigger than a few women masquerading as charity workers," Mr. Cadson said. "All you've seen is the surface of a deep pool. I can help you dive deeper. If you're as smart as I've been told, we could make each other quite powerful."

"I paid my debt. I am free." She dug the knife harder against his neck, careful not to draw blood. "Leave me be."

"Everything will be easier the sooner you accept that your future is tied to Madame Blue." He bore a thin smile. "I gave in long ago and have done very well. I can help you."

"My future is mine." She moved to knee him in the groin, but a pair of meaty hands grabbed her shoulders and dragged her back. With a shout, she tried to shift away, but the man held her fast. She twisted her arm and arched her knife toward his leg. He grabbed her wrist and squeezed, forcing the knife to clatter to the ground.

"Let me give you a sample of what will happen if you don't join." Mr. Cadson pulled a vial from his pocket. Mabel let her legs go limp, but the man behind her grabbed her around the middle, holding her up. She tried to bash her head back, but his hand gripped the top of her head and held her still. Mr. Cadson twisted open the vial and removed a dropper before placing a few drops of liquid in Mabel's ear.

A burning sensation followed by itching ran along her ear canal and began spreading down her neck. Her throat quickly felt thick, and she wheezed in breath as her vision became hazy.

"Carry her. We'll talk to her once she recovers in a day or two. Then, I think she'll be more reasonable when discussing her future."

As the large man moved to pull Mabel over his shoulder, a flash of green light smashed into Mr. Cadson. He shouted as he flew back, hitting the wall. Mabel wasn't sure what had happened, but she would take the opportunity. Though her lungs begged for air and the stinging pain was spreading into her chest, she pounded her fists against her captor's back. There were a few thuds as someone else's fists met flesh. Mabel glanced back as Arturo punched the second thug hurrying toward her. Coming around a shadowy corner, her dress billowing around her, Cassandra held one fist up, a sphere of green light swirling over her hand.

"You will set the girl down or you will become ash," she growled.

Mabel's captor tensed before lowering her to the ground. "Just doing what I was paid for, ma'am."

Cassandra glared as the man ran off. Behind her, Arturo dodged the other man's punch. Cassandra glanced back before flicking her fingers. The green orb sprang from her hand and hit the man in the ribs. His whole body jolted as he fell back.

Kneeling, Cassandra helped Mabel sit up. Mabel found herself gripping the mermaid's arm as her lungs burned. She wanted to speak, but she could barely pull air into her lungs.

"How is she?" Arturo panted as he jogged to Cassandra's side.

"You were supposed to wait in the carriage." Cassandra raised her veil, her eyes analyzing Mabel. "You just started your new heart medicine and should be careful."

"How could I abandon Madame Sinclair?" Arturo shook his hand as if it were sore. "How is she?"

"Poisoned." Cassandra focused on Mabel's ear. Mabel's heart thudded. "Enhanced by magic. I don't think it's meant to be deadly but could be if left untreated."

"Deadly?" Mabel wheezed out, her eyes wide. She clenched her teeth as shivers began.

"Shall I send for Dr. Baxter?" Arturo said.

Cassandra nodded before carefully lifting Mabel in her arms, as if Mabel was as light as a small child. "I'll get her to her hotel. Go with Marvin and the carriage and get Dr. Baxter. Pay him double if you must, but he is needed immediately."

Arturo squeezed Mabel's shoulder. "You hold on, dear girl. I'll be back with help very soon."

As he jogged away, a strange shimmering formed in a circle around Cassandra. At least Mabel thought she saw a circle. Her vision was beginning to blur, and her head felt hot as a fever grew.

"Rest, child." Cassandra's fingers brushed the side of Mabel's head. "We will sort out how you got in this predicament later."

As Cassandra cradled her, Mabel's head fell back, and the world became a gray haze.

CHAPTER 13

In Which Mabel
Builds an Unusual Alliance

Mabel rested on a soft bed, her head lying to the side, the effort of turning it feeling too much as the sun warmed her face. A wet rag lay on her forehead and her ear throbbed. The bells of Willington's central clock tower rang, marking it eleven in the morning. Shifting in her blankets, she wished the nightmare of a man grabbing her and pouring poison in her ear would stop haunting her.

"I asked for hot tea. Not this lukewarm mush," came Cassandra's voice.

"I'm sorry, ma'am. I—" a young woman said.

"Go fix it."

The door slammed shut and Arturo said, "You could have just heated it with your magic."

"When I order hot tea, I expect it to be hot. What I can do for myself is irrelevant."

Mabel's head felt as if it were bobbing like a barrel on water as she forced herself to sit up. Her body ached as if recovering from a bad flu. With a moan, she fell back, her head bouncing on her pillow.

"How are you feeling, Madame Sinclair?" Arturo came to her bedside, anxiety on his face.

"Obviously, she still feels terrible." Cassandra arrived beside Arturo, wearing a simpler gown than usual, but finer than how most women dressed for a dinner out. She pressed the back of her hand to Mabel's forehead, her skin nearly ice cold. "She still feels warm."

"You're a mermaid. Everything feels warm to you." Arturo waved away Cassandra's hand before touching Mabel's forehead himself. "The fever's less than it was, but still too much." He looked to Mabel. "You're lucky Cassandra insisted on finding you. If we hadn't been seeking you, I fear what those men would have done."

"I should have turned them into frogs," Cassandra growled. Mabel was glad the venom in the mermaid's eyes was not directed at her.

"There are other solutions besides transforming men and selling them to merfolk," Arturo said. "Madame Sinclair, how are you feeling? Are you hungry?"

Mabel blinked at him, her mind still catching up to the moment and accepting all of this as real.

"I'm starving," she said, pushing a hoarse whisper through her dry throat. "I've barely eaten since breakfast yesterday."

"I'll take care of that." Arturo crossed the room and picked up the telephone near the door.

"Breakfast?" Cassandra scowled as she sat in the armchair beside Mabel's bed. "It's a wonder you didn't faint before the men attacked. It's not advisable to skip meals, even if you're trying to stay trim."

Mabel rubbed her jaw just below her sore ear. "It wasn't by choice. I've no money and the hotel only serves breakfast."

Cassandra looked to Arturo. "Didn't you send funds to the Fashion Society to cover the girl's expenses?"

Arturo glanced over as he finished the phone call. Setting down the receiver, he said, "Of course I did."

"Apparently, no one gave it to her. She's been starving herself because she can't even pay for lunch."

Arturo pulled out his pocketbook and muttered, "Thieves and scoundrels."

"I've told you the Fashion Society is a pack of egotistical fools." Cassandra rested her hands in her lap.

Arturo pulled out a wad of cash as thick as his thumb and set it on the nightstand. "Use this as pocket money. It's only a thousand or two but should get you by for the month if you're careful."

Mabel's eyes widened as she thought of the five macs a week Antonio received as a conscripted sailor or the three thousand macs from her dowry. "I'm sure I don't need so much."

"We have plenty more," Cassandra said.

"I have plenty more." Arturo teasingly prodded her shoulder. "You have your own inheritance to dabble with. I don't mind paying for your clothing or carriages, but not for the whole businesses you buy out when you receive poor service."

Cassandra scoffed. "It is well worth the money when I walk in and announce I'm the new owner before firing someone."

"And then you sell it back to the original owner for a third of what you paid for it." Arturo raised his palms. "But we are not here to fall into old arguments, my love."

He leaned down and kissed Cassandra's forehead. A softness washed through her haughty face as she took his hand. Mabel stared at Cassandra's youthful features and the lines of years on Arturo's face. Listening, it was clear the pair had been married for decades, especially having met their adult children, Isabella and Eduardo. Even knowing this, watching the pair was strange and left Mabel wondering how old Cassandra really was.

However, Mabel had a more urgent question. "Why are you helping me?"

"Because we like you." Arturo smiled warmly. "Also, Cassandra might not admit it, but she feels responsible for you."

"I do not." Cassandra pointed at Mabel. "It was foolish of you to jump on my yacht. I should have turned around and taken you home."

"Shh." Arturo leaned against Cassandra's armchair. "If she hadn't followed you, she'd never have met her husband. Listening to her speak of him last night brought me back to when I found you stranded at sea, and we ended up talking all night." He raised Cassandra's hand

and kissed it. "If we'd been at port and I were a sailor like her young man, I would have eloped with you the next morning."

"You did elope with me." Cassandra leaned forward, analyzing Mabel's hand. "So, it is a wedding ring?"

Mabel flexed her jaw, a thickness growing in her throat. The pair was strange, but they had rescued her. Given the trouble she was apparently in, it would be wise to speak the truth. However, it sent a pang in her heart as she said, "He is not my husband."

Arturo stood straight as he frowned. Cassandra raised an intrigued eyebrow.

"But you are promised to him, aren't you?" Arturo said. "The way you spoke of him last night, you must be."

Tears fell down Mabel's cheeks. She was so tired. "I care for him so much, but—" She raised her hand before letting it flop down. "This is a lie."

A small smile formed on Cassandra's lips, a bright curiosity in her eyes. "Is that so?"

"Yes," Mabel said. "And that lie, along with others, is why I was attacked last night."

The corner of Arturo's mouth curled up. "You get more intriguing by the moment, Madame Sinclair."

A knock came to the door and Arturo hurried over to open it. A bellhop pushed in a dining cart with four platters on it. Arturo paid him a hefty tip before waving him off.

"I wasn't sure what you wanted, so I ordered all of today's soups for lunch." Arturo returned to Mabel's bedside and offered his hand. "Will you tell us your true story, from when you knocked my wife into a pool of other mermaids, to why those foul men attacked you last night?"

Mabel swallowed as she eyed his hand before glancing at Cassandra. The mermaid had turned Malcom into a toad, but she also had saved Mabel's life. And had kept a protective eye on Mabel during their brief visit in Marveth. She wasn't sure she would ever fully trust the mermaid, but perhaps Cassandra could be an ally.

Taking a steadying breath, Mabel accepted Arturo's hand and let him help her from the bed to the table. Sitting in a nightgown and robe as she ate the cheddar and broccoli soup, Mabel laid out the tangled net of her story.

After nearly two hours, Mabel sat with her hands in her lap, her soup and roll long gone and her story finally completed.

Cassandra slowly sipped her second cup of tea as she watched Mabel. "So, you do have a husband, but he doesn't know it?"

"The marriage certificate was forged. All of it is quite fake."

"Except, now the Castallan Navy is making decisions for this young man's future based on your forged certificate." Cassandra glanced at Arturo. "This is far more intriguing than I expected."

"I'm worried for this young officer," Arturo said.

"He's just a tailor." Mabel held up her hands. "The Fairy Godmother Society wasn't supposed to know his real name. He only wants to design clothing once he finishes his required two years as a sailor for the Navy. Then—" Mabel's throat clenched. "Then he'll go home to the girl he's promised to marry."

Cassandra's eyebrow rose. "This has more drama than an opera."

"Everything with the Fairy Godmother Society was supposed to be resolved," Mabel said. "I convinced my father to send them my dowry, and the money has fulfilled the contract. They offered more, but I turned them down."

"There is always more," Cassandra said. "They are like little gnats sneaking into your house. You think you've gotten them all out, and then one nips at your arm."

"I thought I was free." Mabel rubbed her temple. Her fever and soreness were lessening, but she still ached. "But, last night, the man who poisoned me— I know he'll be back. Or someone worse. He mentioned a Madame Blue, as if she's some criminal leader I should know about. All I do know is I want nothing to do with her."

"Avoiding any connection to Madame Blue is wise." Arturo's face was grave. "It is hard to break free when her syndicate gets its talons in you."

Mabel tapped her fist against her knee. "All I want is to make my own future."

"You are quite capable of that." Cassandra rested her hands on the table. "You made that clear when you came at me with an oar after I transformed your brother into a toad."

Arturo snorted a laugh before rubbing his jaw to hide his reaction.

Ignoring him, Cassandra said, "Unfortunately, keeping ownership over your own life will be much harder now that you've gained the attention of Madame Blue's organization. Her operatives do not let go of a potential asset lightly. I've watched them tear down some very influential people."

Mabel's shoulders hung. "How can one woman be so powerful?"

"I'm not sure Madame Blue is simply one woman." Cassandra interlaced her fingers. "The syndicate has been around for well over a century. Madame Blue herself could be some long-lived being like I am or just a persona passed down over time to create an air of mystery. Or she could be some council meeting in shadows with masks and cloaks, and all the regalia of a secret society. Whatever or whomever she is, avoiding any entanglements is essential."

"How do I avoid the syndicate?" Mabel let out a breath. "I've done a poor job so far."

"You've actually done quite well, despite tripping into last night's snare. Most who get stuck in the web aren't wise enough to see the danger in time to escape." Cassandra pointed at her with two fingers. "But more preparation must be done. I can teach you to see through their traps and negotiate a way out. You should also be trained in multiple forms of combat."

"Do you think Isabella would teach her?" Arturo said. "She is skilled and could refine whatever training the pirates gave her."

"To help a woman protect herself and the man she cares for?" Cassandra nodded. "I think she would be glad to help."

"That is very generous of you." Mabel shifted. This was a strange conversation, and she wished she didn't need help. Last night, however, proved she could not protect herself alone. "What would you ask of me in return?"

"Not getting into more trouble, if you can help it." Cassandra tapped her finger on the table. "Think of us as investors. If things go well, we will see a return as you build your future. If it does not, then we accept the loss and move on."

"I am sure we will be well rewarded." Arturo smiled. "For me, I want to see how things turn out with your young sailor."

Mabel shook her head. "He's not mine."

"Of course not," Cassandra said dryly. "Except for in the eyes of your parents and the Castallan Navy."

Trying to ignore the goosebumps along her arms, Mabel said, "Whatever I may feel about the sailor, he has a girl waiting for him."

"Are you sure of that?"

"It was half of what we talked of in our day together." Mabel shrugged. "In between the photograph." She slumped in her chair. "And his kiss."

"So, you don't want him to go marry his betrothed?" Cassandra appeared to be holding back an amused smile.

"Sounds like a woman I know." Arturo pointed at Mabel. "If you do decide to intervene, don't scare the daylight out of him by standing over his bed with a knife in your hand the night before his wedding to the other girl."

"Those were very unique circumstances," Cassandra whispered as she tapped his arm.

Mabel's eyebrows rose. There was much she didn't know of this pair.

"Let me ask more frankly, if there were no girl back home, what would you do?" Cassandra raised a finger. "Those girls are rarely actually waiting for their sailor, by the way."

"He's just a sailor I met." Mabel sat up straight. "Nothing more."

"And Arturo's just a sailor I happened to save from drowning." Cassandra tapped her own cheek. "It's clear your heart is taken, but is this sailor truly worthy of you?"

"I'm not worthy of him." Mabel's heart ached at those words of truth. "I'm a pirate and a liar. He's an honorable man doing his duty so he can take care of his mother and build a good life for his future wife."

Arturo pressed a hand to his chest. "If he's everything she says, I approve of him."

"Few men are everything she's claiming," Cassandra said. "Which is why you are such a rarity, darling."

"This man is." Mabel swallowed, keeping her face stoic even as tears pressed at her. "He sent me a gift when he read I won the contest. But it was only in friendship."

"Sending a gift to the girl you're not betrothed to is sign of far more than friendship." Arturo leaned forward with a grin. "What did he send?"

"Some fabric," she muttered, "that we had discussed when we met."

"Such sweet, young love." Arturo slapped his hand on the table. "We will help you with this too."

Cassandra touched his shoulder. "Let her finish with her internship and fashion week first."

"Of course," Arturo said. "But you know how important true love is."

"I do." She reached over and took his hand while focusing her gaze on Mabel. "We will hire someone to protect you while you complete the internship. Meanwhile, you and I will meet a few times a week to go over some tricks of negotiation and avoiding unwanted attention. Considering longer-term matters, I've some ideas on how to help build the future you want. However, I want to see your final product for fashion week before I decide how much to invest."

"If I agree to this, will my future still be my own?" Mabel said. "I can walk away if I want, nothing owed?"

"Absolutely. In any good agreement, both sides should benefit."

Arturo nodded toward Cassandra. "One benefit is merfolk will always fulfill their contracts. If you have an agreement, Cassandra will keep it." He squinted. "Just be careful about the wording."

Mabel pressed her lips together before saying, "You will train me to protect myself against the syndicate while I finish the internship. And then what?"

"Then I decide to invest," Cassandra said, "and we either continue or not. No matter what, you walk away with more than you started with."

"I'll also make sure to get you a few throwing knives and a small pistol you can hide in your clothing." Arturo pointed toward the nightstand. "And if you need more funds, just ask. I will not have a young woman I am sponsoring starving herself because she can't afford lunch."

"How about we call this an apprenticeship for now?" Cassandra held out her hand. "Do you accept, Madame Sinclair?"

Mabel eyed Cassandra's waiting palm. This was so swift and strange. Yet, Cassandra had kept her word and protected Mabel. She would have to be careful, but the foundations for building trust were there.

She gripped Cassandra's cold hand and looked her in the eye. "As long as I walk away the owner of my future, I accept."

A small smile crossed Cassandra's lips as she gave Mabel's hand a shake. "I am very interested in where this will lead us, Madame Sinclair."

Mabel's own smile formed as she released the mermaid's hand. "I am too."

CHAPTER 14

In Which Antonio Learns He Is Married

Port Suermal, Island in the Wahid Sea, colony of the Castallar Protectorate

Antonio held his stack of mail in his hands, his heart pounding. The last few letters back and forth from his mother, with her wise advice, helped him feel steadier in his decision. Though, it was agonizing waiting three to six weeks for replies to his questions.

He repeated in his mind the words from her last letter.

If your heart has grown beyond your girl from home, let it find a better fit.

His chest felt strange without the locket, but there had been no letters from Sofia in the past four months. Before meeting Mabel, he had thought of Sofia every day. Now, his duty to his promise fought against the air of mystery around the red-headed young woman who was likely in Willington, the clothing she designed about to be shown in fashion week.

He had received more notes from her, but nothing to indicate she had returned home and seen his letters. Or the package he had sent ten weeks before. Maybe she was home, but her letters hadn't reached him yet. Who knew how long it took for mail to travel from a Castallan naval vessel to a town in Barthan.

He tapped the letter addressed to her against his hand.

What did he even hope with the letter? He still had ten months left in the Navy. Then, he would go home to Castallar while she was somewhere in Barthan.

But his words were true. And if they touched her heart, maybe there was a slim opening of a future. Even if it was only a full letter back, something deeper than her quick notes and drawings.

"Are you sending those, seaman?" The port's postal officer glared at Antonio. "Others are waiting."

"Yes." The word was frightening but filled him with hope. He handed over the letter addressed to his mother and sisters before holding out the package containing Sofia's locket.

The postal officer marked it with the stamp and Antonio winced at the high price. It was less than the cost of package he had sent to Mabel. That had been extremely expensive and required digging into the savings he hid in his boots. However, if his heart was no longer Sofia's, she deserved better.

His hand trembled as he passed over the letter addressed to Mabel. The postal officer stamped it and named what Antonio owed. He paid quickly, pushing himself not to lose his nerve. He hurried away from the station, letting the other sailors in line have their turn.

He ran a hand through his hair and breathed out. It was done.

A lightness entered him at releasing the tie to Sofia. His love for her had been great. If he had stayed in his hometown, perhaps he would have been happy with her and their simple conversations. But her letters were so rare, and he didn't connect to the repeated stories anymore. Hopefully, her sorrow would heal in time, and she'd go on to marry a good man.

All of the relief, however, couldn't ease the knots in his stomach as he wondered how Mabel would answer the hopes in his letter.

"Seaman Cortez!" Corporal Hernandez's voice boomed over the dock.

Antonio joined at least ten other sailors in saluting.

"Seaman Antonio Cortez!"

Antonio approached the third mate and saluted. "Reporting, señor."

The third mate glowered. "Come with me. Admiral Guerrero of the Fifth Fleet's called for you."

Antonio tried to hide his bewilderment. "Yes, señor."

Hernandez's jaw was taut. "I thought you were a man of honor, Cortez."

"I seek to be, señor." Antonio's brow furrowed.

Hernandez grunted, eying Antonio. With a huff, he turned and motioned for Antonio to follow.

They traveled along the dock to an officer's hall with brass decorations and polished tables. It was far nicer than the crusty places crowded with bottom-rung sailors like Antonio. They walked upstairs to a small, private dining room and the third mate knocked on the door.

"Come in," came a deep voice on the other side.

The third mate opened the door. "Seaman Antonio Cortez, señors."

Antonio entered and stood at attention. Standing by the small dining table inside was his grim-faced captain and an admiral with at least three layers of fat along his chin.

"Seaman Cortez." The captain motioned for Antonio to step closer.

Antonio's heart raced as the door closed behind him. The purpose of this summons was unclear. Antonio followed all protocol to the letter, but this felt like he was about to be punished.

"I don't like my sailors keeping secrets," the captain said before cracking a smile. "Especially when the young man is to be congratulated."

Antonio frowned as the admiral broke into laughter, the layers of fat along his neck jiggling.

"Pardon me, señor, I'm not sure what you are referring to," Antonio said.

"Still playing innocent, eh?" Admiral Guerrero pulled three tumblers and a bottle of sherry from a shelf next to the table. He then pointed at Antonio's hand. "And hiding the truth."

"I seek to hide nothing, señor."

"After Admiral Guerrero contacted me, I asked the boatswain about you," the captain said as the admiral poured sherry into the tumblers. "My guess is you hid this because your crewmates were already teasing you about mooning over her. I can imagine they would tease you more if they knew she was your wife."

Antonio's forehead wrinkled. "My wife? I have none, señor. The young lady—Her parents rejected me when I asked for her hand."

"Is this why you eloped?" Admiral Guerrero chuckled. "I'm glad your dear father-in-law's come around."

"Again, I have no wife and no father-in-law," Antonio said. "I fear you have the wrong man."

Admiral Guerrero rifled through a packet of papers sitting on the table before pulling out a news article. Glancing at it, he said, "Certainly looks like you."

"I assure you, señor, it is not—" Antonio's mouth shut as the admiral held out the news article. There was the picture of him and Mabel, her pose as if kissing his cheek. His eyes widened. "Señor, I think there's been a grave mistake."

"There was. The marriage certificate had the wrong last name." Admiral Guerrero pulled out a piece of parchment paper and placed it in front of Antonio. "Turns out it was a clerical error at the office in Port Nerama. A letter of correction has been sent."

Antonio's heart quickened as he stared at the marriage certificate. There, Mabel Sinclair was registered as the bride and Antonio Cortez Montero marked as the groom. The location was listed as Port Nerama, where he had met Mabel.

Sweat ran along Antonio's back as he looked to the captain and admiral. "This—" He swallowed. "It is a lie. I'm not—"

She had confessed to stealing his pocketbook, and her crewmates had looked questionable. What the purpose of this lie was, he wasn't sure, but he wanted no part of it.

His fist clenched. The letter to Mabel. He had to get it back.

Admiral Guerrero set a steel ring on the table. "This ring's standard issue to married sailors in the Navy. Wear it with pride, young man."

"It's a lie," Antonio said louder. "I'm not sure why, but—"

"I've spoken with her father." Admiral Guerrero scowled. "Are you trying to dodge the responsibilities of being a husband?" He leaned forward. "Did you mean for this to be one of those fly-by-night marriages, where you trick a girl into believing her time with you is her wedding night?"

Antonio's eyes widened further. "No! I would never."

"That's a dishonorable thing to do, Seaman Cortez," the captain said, his arms folded. "You represent the Castallan Navy, and there is no tolerance for such disreputable behavior. Is this a real marriage or not?"

"The girl's family believes it is, mind you," Admiral Guerrero said. "So, I'd choose your answer carefully if you don't want to risk a heavy mark on your record and risk of a dishonorable discharge."

Antonio rubbed his neck as his gaze flicked between the article and the certificate. He wasn't going to let this lie ruin his name, nor his standing in the Navy. He had ten months left. During that time, he could build the evidence to prove this wasn't true. Or get the fake marriage annulled.

"The marriage is as real as the certificate," he said. At least he could say one truth.

The captain winked at Antonio. "Wise answer, Seaman Cortez."

"Wise indeed," Admiral Guerrero said, "because your new father-in-law's a generous man and has paid for your officer's commission."

"What?" Antonio stared at the two men.

Admiral Guerrero handed over a stack of documents. "This is your new contract. It adds three more years of service, but you'll be immediately promoted to lieutenant once you sign."

"This is where my business is done, Seaman Cortez," the captain said. "Are all your personal items in your trunk?"

"Of course, señor." That was standard protocol. "But I haven't accepted the commission. I—" Antonio gestured at the contract. "I only have ten months left, and would rather—"

"Let me have a word with the boy." Admiral Guerrero winked at the captain. "Go ahead and send the trunk to my ship."

"No, please, I—"

The captain shook Antonio's hand. "Congratulations, Lieutenant Cortez, on the promotion and the marriage."

He patted Antonio's shoulder before exiting.

"There have been several misunderstandings," Antonio said. "I am just a tailor. That is all I want to be. I'm only here because I was conscripted and am doing my required two years of service. The minute I'm done, I plan to go home."

Admiral Guerrero took a shot of sherry before stuffing himself into a chair. He pointed at the seat across from him. "Sit, boy."

Antonio sat immediately at the command.

"I'm going to be honest with you this once, and then you're not to say a word of this to anyone." Admiral Guerrero's thick eyebrows rose. "Do you promise?"

"Yes." There was no other answer to give.

"I'm not sure whether the marriage certificate is real or not, but I've been told by people too powerful to be trifled with to treat it like it is. Someone's got an eye on you, and I've been told you need to sign the contract or my hide's on the line." He took a drink from the second glass of sherry. "I don't know how deep you are in this, but I suggest you cooperate."

"No." Antonio gripped the armrests of his chair. "My mother's waiting for me. She's a widow and I'm saving up for a tailor's shop, and my sisters—"

"Did you look at how much more a lieutenant is paid? And that's on top of the bonus pay the navy sends home for married sailors." Admiral Guerrero pointed at the document. "How much could you save up over three years? Enough to buy a nice little home for your mama." He glanced at the newspaper article. "And enough to start a life with your young bride, if she is your wife."

Antonio moved the documents back toward the admiral. "Please, sir. I asked for none of this."

"Young man, I'm taking you on as my clerk and assistant. I'm very well connected. And not just with the Navy." Admiral Guerrero smiled. "I could help you be very rich before you leave the service. Or, even richer if you stay."

"The answer is still no." Antonio shook his head. "I cannot be bought and will not soil my good name."

The admiral grunted as he scratched one of his chins. "Didn't count on you being so honorable."

"Then, you accept me turning this down?"

Admiral Guerrero barked a laugh. "Absolutely not." He pointed at Antonio. "You think being honest will keep your 'good name'? If you leave without signing, something might happen like finding stolen goods or contraband in your trunk when it arrives on my ship. Then, you'll spend weeks in the ship's brig before being sent back to Castallar to face trial."

"The truth will come out and I will be set free." Antonio felt the lie in his own words. "Please, sir. I've done nothing."

"Other things could happen. Your dear mama could lose her home. Something could happen to your darling—" He frowned as he looked at the marriage certificate. "Mah-belle."

"Mabel," Antonio muttered, correcting the admiral's pronunciation. He held his hands on his cheeks as he stared at the contract. Not signing meant very powerful people would destroy his life.

He was trapped as badly as a fugitive cornered by officers and dogs. But all he had done was have a pleasant afternoon and evening with Mabel Sinclair.

What was unclear was how much she was a conspirator or victim.

With no other choice, Antonio took the waiting fountain pen and signed.

Setting a tumbler full of sherry in front of Antonio, Admiral Guerrero smiled. "Congratulations, Lieutenant Cortez."

CHAPTER 15

In Which Mabel Attends Her First Fashion show

Willington, Barthan

Sweat dotted Mabel's brow as she dodged Isabella Astrellar's rapier. As the mermaid took another swipe, Mabel brought her own rapier up to block it.

Mabel grinned. After a month with these early morning practice sessions a few days a week, maybe she was finally holding her own.

"Better, but still sloppy." Isabella twisted her blade against Mabel's and kicked her in the stomach, sending her flying across the warehouse floor. "You need to work on swiftness and precision."

Mabel grunted as she sat up, the bruise on her backside and her stomach adding to others from the past few mornings of training with Isabella. She glanced over at Arturo as he watched with interest but remained silent. There was a pride in his eyes as he watched his daughter at work.

He was right to be proud. For all of the battles Mabel had been part of at sea, no one had held the finesse and training Isabella showed. And it was clear she was holding back her strength and power.

She was also holding back who she was and remaining enigmatic. Where Arturo was easy to get off topic and chatting, and Cassandra would be closed off but answer Mabel's questions, Isabella would only give her a long, silent look and return to the work at hand.

Approaching, Isabella held out her hand. "Again."

"I should be going to Mr. Hartavo's." Mabel took Isabella's hand and rose. "The fashion show is tomorrow and there's so much to be done."

"Will the fashion show matter if your enemies attack you again?" Isabella's face was hard, far different than the airs she had put on while in a fine gown in Marveth. This morning she wore a plain, military-like uniform.

"I will cut them with my wit." Mabel forced a clever smile.

Arturo chuckled while Isabella's face remained serious.

"You've only seen a sliver of how dangerous Madame Blue's organization is." Isabella rolled her right shoulder before moving into an attacking position. "Your wits will be needed, along with your fighting skills."

She lunged and Mabel barely parried the stab. Isabella pressed another attack, pushing Mabel back across the warehouse. Mabel grit her teeth as she fought to keep up with Isabella's swift blade. Isabella feinted to Mabel's left. As Mabel swiped to protect herself, Isabella used the opening to twist behind her and put her arm around Mabel's neck.

"Stop using those pirate habits." Isabella released Mabel and stepped back before attacking again. As they went through another dance of blades, she said, "Swinging the sword like that might cut off your own arm."

"It worked fine in battle." Mabel grunted as her rapier locked with Isabella's.

Unfortunately, the mermaid was far stronger and easily knocked Mabel back a step. As she swung toward Mabel's middle, Mabel barely blocked it. Isabella's blade twisted with hers and Mabel's rapier went flying, clattering across the floor.

Holding the point of her blunted rapier to Mabel's neck, Isabella said, "It only worked because your opponents were untrained and undisciplined. If you want to protect your future, you must do better."

"Hopefully, the only battles in my future will be wrestling with fixing a seam," Mabel said, "or wounding myself with a needle."

"It is a good hope." A haunted look entered Isabella's gaze as she lowered her blade. "However, your path from my mother's yacht to a pirate ship and then to here, being trained to fight by a mermaid, makes me doubt your life will be so simple."

"I must try." A sick feeling rose in Mabel. "First, though, I must free the man I've accidentally trapped."

Isabella's face was nearly unreadable, but there was a glint of pain in her eyes. "That must be made right."

"Madame Astrellar says you're an expert negotiator." Maybe today, at the end of their training sessions, Isabella would answer at least one question. "Do you have any suggestions on how to break him free of his Naval contract?"

"Human law is more flexible than merfolk law." Isabella sheathed her rapier, marking the end of the training. "Merfolk may be more dangerous, but they will hold to a signed contract as if sacred. Humans do not."

"Some of us do," Arturo said as he picked up Mabel's rapier from the floor.

"Father, you are a man of honor, which is more rare than I like." Isabella walked to where she had set down a canteen and towel. She tossed the towel to Mabel. "As for humans like Admiral Guerrero or the Fairy Godmother Society, you must have leverage to hold them to an agreement."

A tiredness washed through Mabel while she wiped her forehead. "I have nothing and am nobody, and I know so little about them."

"Then learn about your enemy." Isabella took a sip from her canteen. "And use your wits and cleverness to build yourself into a position to gain leverage."

Mabel let out a tired laugh as she pictured Mr. Hartavo's glare yesterday as he said, "I'd rather send a flour sack down the runway than this misshapen travesty."

Elona's calm words and guidance afterward had been a comfort, but Mabel felt sick at the thought of how much work she had to do today.

Glancing at Isabella, Mabel said, "I'm not sure I will ever amount to much, in fashion or out of it."

Isabella's gaze was skeptical. "You charmed my mother enough to gain her interest." She tilted her head and squinted. "I am still not sure if you are a hobby or investment, but you've certainly intrigued her."

"I am not sure there is much power in being 'intriguing,'" Mabel said. "Piquing Admiral Guerrero's curiosity will not persuade him to free Antonio."

"There is more power in being mysterious than you know." A hint of a smile came to Isabella's lips. "Why else would my mother work so hard at it?"

Mabel found herself smiling, though she wasn't sure Isabella had made a joke. Arturo, however, barked a laugh.

Isabella took another sip from her canteen before nodding to Mabel. "We shall see what you become, Madame Sinclair."

Without another word, Isabella walked to the warehouse exit. As she left, Arturo came to Mabel's side.

"I think you are growing on her."

Mabel glanced at him and let out a laugh. "I am grateful for her training, but I doubt she likes me."

"Isabella has endured much in her life, starting from when she was stolen as a child and forced to become a full mermaid." Arturo folded his arms behind his back. "I am proud of my daughter, but I often worry for her heart. Yet, she is strong and, if Cassandra does decide to invest in you tomorrow, I think you can learn much from my daughter."

"Like how to get more bruises on my backside?"

Arturo chuckled. "That, and less manipulative methods of negotiation than what Cassandra uses."

"None of this will matter, though, if I don't finish my dress for tomorrow's runway." Mabel smiled at Arturo. "Thank you, sir, for giving me this chance, and for protecting me."

"Thank you for shoving my wife into a merfolk pool." He winked before laughing and Mabel giggled.

His face grew more serious, and he held out his hand. "Whatever may come, I hope you rescue your sailor and build a good life for yourself."

"I hope I do too." Mabel took his hand. "Though I've no idea how to do either."

There was another goodbye and then she was off across the city. Riding the trolley, sweat ran down her back. There was too much to be done today, but she would finish the dress. It was the key to her hope in the world of fashion, and her best chance to build a future for herself and somehow help Antonio.

The next afternoon, Mabel's stomach clenched as she stood beside Elona while the model swished the skirts. She was exhausted from a late night of fixing hems and adjusting the fit, but this was better than she had envisioned a month ago, the design having developed under Elona's guidance. The dress was as much Elona's as it was Mabel's.

"I love how it moves," the model said as she turned around. "And the smooth elegance."

Mabel grinned proudly while Elona looked toward the curtain hiding them from the runway where an audience of the largest names in Willington gathered.

"Let's hope some potential benefactors like it." Elona turned back to the dress and pulled a string from the sleeve. She glanced at Mabel and smiled. "Remember: even if no one bids on the design, you should still be proud of your work, and that people are hearing your name."

"Your name should be announced too," Mabel said.

Elona gestured at several other dresses being prepared on models. "I get paid to make art that people wear. What greater honor is there?"

"Very little." Mabel rubbed her hands together, taking in the assistants making the final touches on the dresses and models, the preparation space so busy. And here she was, a small part of it.

A pang hit Mabel's chest as she wished Antonio were beside her. He likely would be as wide-eyed as she was, giddy with the energy and excitement filling the space.

He should be here, and not locked into his contract with the Navy.

Mabel pushed down at the sick feeling rising within her. At Arturo's suggestion, she sent weekly letters to Antonio. Each one began with another apology, followed by describing the week's events and all she'd learned from Elona. It was comforting to write to him, and she hoped he could learn some tricks to help him once he was free. Yet, her nerves grew each time she sent the envelope. The letter might not ever reach him. Even if it did, he might never open it. She wouldn't blame him if he never forgave her, but she prayed he would.

"Mabel, my darling, there you are!"

Mabel's back stiffened as she turned to see her parents pushing their way behind the curtains.

"This is a private area," Elona said. "May I help you?"

"They're my parents." They must have gotten Mabel's invitation. That had been another of Arturo's suggestions, and now Mabel was regretting it. "I'll manage this."

Elona gave her a worried look but nodded.

Mabel motioned for her parents to follow her. She led them out to a side area still curtained off from the audience and away from where the models assembled.

"I am very disappointed in you," her father said. "You're a married woman, Mabel. You shouldn't be bothering with these things."

"I had to convince your father not to storm out to Willington and drag you home," Mrs. Sinclair said. "If you were so determined, it was better to let you live out your little fantasy before coming home." She smiled. "Your cottage is ready."

"I told you in my letter that I don't want the cottage." Mabel gestured toward the runway. "I want to be part of this world of fashion. I know it won't be easy, but I will make my way."

"What you want doesn't matter." Her father's face was stern. "You are married. How disappointed Antonio would be."

Mabel stared at him, hating her father's version of her fictional husband. But she would play this game.

"This is where Antonio wants me to be." She looked to her mother. "You saw the fabric he sent to congratulate me. Antonio understands and shares my passion for design. That—" Her chest ached. "That is what first connected us."

"Antonio is a lieutenant in the Castallan Navy," Mr. Sinclair said. "He is a man of the military and of honor. He would not bother with all of these frills and lace."

Mabel's hands shook with anger as she pictured the designs Antonio had shown her. "You do not know my husband."

She didn't really know him either, but she knew him far better than her father did.

"Have you read the recommendation letters?" Her father's face was turning red. "This is a man of action. And he is your husband. You are to obey him and behave properly, as a married woman should."

"I will not." Mabel bit out the words. "Sell the cottage because I will not be living in it. I am not going to idle away my life waiting for my sailor."

"He is a lieutenant. Confirmation came yesterday that Antonio signed. He is building his career for you."

"No. He is being pressed into becoming an officer because you were too eager and didn't listen to me. He doesn't want to be in the Navy. He was conscripted. And now—" Her eyes widened as her heart pounded. "If he's been forced to sign—" She held a hand over her mouth. "Three more years."

Her mother embraced her. "Shh, dear girl. You're still young. Three years is nothing in a lifetime."

Mabel shoved away from her mother. "It is three years he did not want, and it's my fault. He asked for none of this."

"Enjoy your show today," her mother said. "Come home tomorrow, and then all your worries will ease once we can coordinate Antonio's next shore leave. Once you see him, everything will be easier."

She glared at her parents. Cassandra and Arturo had their oddities but treated her better than this. They listened to her and every conversation with them held to the promise of helping her, though it was easy to get distracted as Arturo told a story from decades before.

"I am not going home," Mabel said. "I don't know where I'm going next, but it will not be Cliffshire."

Her mother opened her mouth to protest, but Elona called, "Mabel! Mr. Hartavo is looking for you."

"I must go." Mabel pushed away from her parents. "Please, try to understand how important today is."

She moved back into the preparation area. Mr. Hartavo tapped his foot as he glared at his pocket watch.

"There you are, Miss Wisp," he said. "The show needs to start, and I am contractually obligated to introduce you first."

He held out his arm. Mabel took in a breath for courage as she accepted it and he guided her toward the curtains leading to the runway. Nerves shot through her stomach as violins and horns began playing a dramatic song worthy of a tango. Once the song finished the curtains cascaded open.

Assembled beyond bright lights was a sea of glamorous suits and gowns, many of the women attempting to compete with each other's elaborate hats. Mabel found herself rolling back her shoulders into a formal posture and trying to appear taller, hoping her satin gown and small hat with feathers matched the world she was being presented to for the first time.

The runway was edged with glittering fabric fluffed and arranged to look like clouds along the path with gold, sheer fabric hanging above.

"Welcome!" Mr. Hartavo's voice was projected by a microphone at a podium. The electrified sound was amplified with some static to be heard throughout the room. "Tonight, you will see creatures of the air plucked from clouds and tethered to the earth just long enough for you to glimpse them before they float away."

There were various 'oohs' and light applause.

"But first, I present the winner of *Modan*'s annual contest, Madame Mabel Sinclair."

Through the polite applause, Mabel smiled and waved to the crowd. In the mix, she couldn't see Arturo nor Cassandra and a small pit of disappointment grew. They had promised to come. They had to be here.

"And this is what she cobbled together."

Mr. Hartavo motioned toward the runway entrance. The model entered, her walk accentuating her hips, allowing the soft fabric to cascade around her. Mabel watched the few people she could see in the light. There were some intrigued glances along with a few looks of disgust. Murmurs filled the room, not all of them pleased.

"How middling," one woman whispered within Mabel's earshot.

Mabel kept her smile as the model finished her walk.

"Madame Sinclair, ladies and gentlemen," Mr. Hartavo said.

Mabel waved to the crowd once more before exiting the runway. Reaching the preparation area, Elona hugged her.

"Wonderful job!" she whispered.

"I don't think they liked it."

"At least a few people did. And that's how you get started."

Mabel held onto that thought as she joined the assistants and under designers in a corner where they were hidden from the audience but could see the runway. Watching the completed looks of Mr. Hartavo's full collection, Mabel could see where her dress had too much simplicity and the silhouette did not match what was in style. She had done something which would complement her own figure, not the silhouette of other women.

Once the runway show was complete, the whole crowd was on their feet and applauding rapturously. Mr. Hartavo bowed and blew kisses at the crowd.

Watching the spectacle reminded Mabel this was as much about showmanship as it was about the clothing. Just as Captain Stenton's piracy was more about intimidation than actual fighting.

Maybe Isabella was right. Maybe there was merit to being 'intriguing'.

With the show complete, Mabel walked with Elona to the reception room where the gathered high society crowd looked closer at the gowns as models stood on pedestals.

"How do you feel?" Elona whispered.

"Like I have a lot to learn," Mabel said, pressing her hands together.

Elona grinned proudly. "That is the most important lesson, and worth always remembering."

She guided Mabel to where the model stood wearing Mabel's design. The model was supposed to stand like a statue, changing her pose every time a chime rang through the room. However, she gave Mabel a friendly wink and waved her fingers. Mabel returned the small wave.

As the reception ran on, Mabel stood by her dress at the far corner of the room, a large gap away from Mr. Hartavo's gowns. A few celebrities Mabel recognized paused briefly, giving the dress a casual glance, before walking away. Mrs. Evanwind stopped by, her dog bearing a matching ruffled collar. There was a polite smile, but no words as she returned to the core crowd.

After an hour of being ignored, Mabel was nearly relieved when her parents appeared.

"Your friend Miss Cantor helped us inside." Mrs. Sinclair gaped at the crowd. "Did you see the Prime Minister's wife? What a fine lady!"

"Have you made many connections?" Mr. Sinclair said. "Many important politicians here. They could greatly advance a young lieutenant's career."

Mabel bit back a smile as the model broke from her pose and gave her a sympathetic glance.

"We were just talking to—" Mr. Sinclair glanced over. "Oh, she's on her way." He grinned proudly. "It seems you've interested an investor."

Mabel stood straighter, her nerves rising again. It was most likely Cassandra fulfilling her promise. Maybe she and Arturo had come.

"There you are, Mrs. Autumn," her father said with the grin he gave those who might be able to help line his pocketbook. "Here is my daughter, Mrs. Antonio Cortez."

"You may call me Madame Sinclair." Mabel held out her gloved hand.

The mid-height woman with warm brunette hair gave Mabel a thin smile.

Touching Mabel's fingers in greeting, Mrs. Autumn said, "Such a unique design. Show's much promise."

"We're very proud of our daughter," her father said, putting an arm around Mabel. "As is her husband. Did I mention he is a lieutenant in the Castallan Navy? We're very proud."

"Any father would be." Mrs. Autumn's sharp eyes focused on Mabel. "I represent an investing firm which has taken great interest in you, Mrs. Cortez."

"Again," Mabel said, "when it comes to my designs, please call me Madame Sinclair."

"Oh, be proud of your husband's name." Mr. Sinclair patted her shoulder. "Mrs. Autumn is interested in investing in a set of designs from you. Can you just see it? *Cortez Designs.*"

"What is the name of the firm?" Mabel said.

"Azure Capitol Investors." Mrs. Autumn looked to the gown. "This is unique work, Mrs. Cortez."

Mabel frowned at the investing firm's name, something in it not settling right.

"Elona Cantor helped me plan out the design and craft the dress." Mabel prodded her own memory, seeking where she had heard of the investing firm. "It is the first of what I hope will be many Madame Sinclair designs."

"Our firm admires young women with vision. And you, Mrs. Cortez, come highly recommended."

Mabel's eyes narrowed. "By whom?"

Mrs. Autumn waved her hand. "By associates who find you a quite intriguing prospect."

Mabel's jaw clenched. There were only two entities in Barthan with money who were interested in Mabel's future: Cassandra Astrellar and Madame Blue's syndicate. Mabel doubted Cassandra would send a woman like Mrs. Autumn as her business surrogate, which left one worrying answer.

Deciding on a bit of boldness, Mabel said, "If your organization is at all associated with the Fairy Godmother Society, I must decline the investment."

Mrs. Autumn gave a fluttering laugh. "What a fanciful name! No, I represent a different investment arm."

Goosebumps ran down Mabel's arm at the term 'investment arm,' symbolizing this was just another piece of the larger organization.

"Is Madame Blue one of the investors?" Mabel ventured. It was a gamble, but worth taking. "Because I have already declined other representatives."

Given the slight narrowing of the woman's eyes and moderate tilt of her head, Mabel had struck a nerve.

"Madame Blue has many anonymous investments," Mrs. Autumn said, "and those who are associated with her are wise not to mention her name lightly."

A coldness settled in Mabel. This woman had to be part of the syndicate, which meant Mabel had to be wary. Her hand slipped in her pocket and her fingers reached through a hidden slit to where she kept a throwing knife. She would not be attacked again.

Mrs. Autumn pulled a notepad and small pencil from the handbag dangling from her wrist and scribbled something down.

"This is how much we plan to invest in Mrs. Cortez's first fashion line." Mrs. Autumn showed it to Mabel's parents. Their eyes grew wide before Mrs. Autumn showed the number to Mabel. It was far beyond what Mabel was worth.

"That is quite a lot," a familiar voice said.

Mabel tried not to smile as Cassandra smoothly joined the circle. Her gown was magnificent, with a beading design along the skirt and flowering across the bodice, matching embroidery on her white gloves. She wore a dark brunette wig, and a veil shadowed her face along with her large hat. "But you are late to the game. Madame Sinclair has already begun negotiations with the investor I represent."

Mabel stepped to the side, giving Cassandra's broad skirt more room. What the mermaid had planned was another question, and Mabel was intrigued to find out.

Mr. Sinclair chuckled with delight. "Of course, my daughter has competing investors." He held out his hand. "Mr. Sinclair, manager of the largest bank in Cliffshire."

"Mrs. Granalda." Cassandra delicately touched his fingers. "Agent for the Astrellar estate."

His eyes bulged, the eagerness on his face growing. "Astrellar? As in one of the oldest and wealthiest families in Castallar?"

Cassandra gave a small nod.

"Mabel's husband is a lieutenant in the Castallan Navy," Mr. Sinclair said. "Lieutenant Antonio Cortez. He's likely to be promoted to captain in a few years."

"Is he now?" Cassandra's veiled gaze nearly hid her annoyance.

"Willington is the heart of fashion in Barthan," Mrs. Autumn said. "Wouldn't it be better to support your fellow countrymen and accept our investment?"

"How much is the offer of the Astrellar fortune?" Mr. Sinclair said.

Mabel hated his near-giddy excitement at the prospect of a bidding war.

"Cortez, did you say?" Cassandra said.

"Antonio Cortez of Dorona," Mr. Sinclair said.

"Oh, yes." Cassandra pressed her forefingers together. "The name did sound familiar. I believe he is a distant relative with some ties to the Astrellar family. Rumor is he has quite a large inheritance which he declined so he could build his naval career on his own. I'm so glad he's become a lieutenant."

Mabel shot Cassandra a quick glare. There was no need to expand the lie. Mabel tried not to cringe as her mother pressed a hand to her breast and sighed.

"What a fine young man," Mrs. Sinclair whispered.

"I paid for his commission myself." Mr. Sinclair's chest puffed up enough to pop a few buttons from his shirt. "I'll have to ask my dear son-in-law about his inheritance. See if we can get his wealth restored."

"Madame Sinclair and I'll discuss it." Cassandra turned to Mabel. "That is, if she'll agree to hearing out the Astrellar estate's offer."

Mabel raised an eyebrow at Cassandra, wishing she could see the mermaid's face. Turning to her parents and Mrs. Autumn, she said, "Considering my husband's ties to the Astrellar family, I must accept Mrs. Granalda's interest."

Mr. Sinclair touched her arm. "Wait. How much is the offer?"

"Our true investment will be in a network of potential clients and mentoring Madame Sinclair in the world of design and business." Cassandra looked to Mabel. "Given how vast the Astrellar fortune is, our capital investment is flexible."

"Do you have any guarantees?" Mr. Sinclair said.

"Pardon me, sir, but any negotiations must be only between Madame Sinclair and myself."

"I am her father. It is my duty to advise her, and—"

"She is a capable woman. If her husband were here, we might include him in the discussion, but no one else."

Mabel smiled a little. She only mostly trusted Cassandra, but this was an excellent answer. Especially as her father sputtered, unable to accept such a rejection.

"The reception is ending soon." Mabel gestured toward where the main hall was clearing out. "Mrs. Autumn, thank you for your interest. Father, Mother, thank you for coming and supporting me. Mrs. Granalda, how do we continue this discussion?"

"My employer's carriage is waiting out front. When you are ready, I will escort you myself."

Where the carriage would take Mabel, she wasn't sure. It could be as much of a gamble as jumping on the back of Cassandra's yacht, but it was a better gamble than accepting Mrs. Autumn's offer or returning to her parents' control.

Cassandra turned to leave but paused. "Oh, Mr. and Mrs. Sinclair, I have a niece named Cassandra who made your son's acquaintance. Tell him she thinks of him nearly every day."

Mabel's parents frowned and Mabel could sense Cassandra trying not to giggle as she strode away.

"I would greatly recommend you reconsider, Mrs. Cortez." Mrs. Autumn's eyes were hard. "Our investment firm can be generous but does not take rejection lightly."

"I will never accept an offer from your firm." Mabel returned the glare.

Mrs. Autumn held it before striding away. Mabel's fist clenched as she wondered what the next attack would look like.

"You should have told us of your husband's connections," Mr. Sinclair said. "We could—"

"My life is my own," Mabel bit out. "As Antonio's is his. You are my parents, so I will let you know how I am, but do not dare interfere with my business again."

"Mabel!" Mrs. Sinclair's mouth hung open. "We are only trying to watch over you."

Mabel met her mother's gaze. "I have been better watched over by pirates and someone I thought was my enemy. Thank you for taking the time to come tonight. But, unless you want to ask more about the dress, this conversation must be done."

A deep hurt ran through Mrs. Sinclair's eyes.

"You will not speak to your mother—"

Mrs. Sinclair raised her hand, stopping her husband. Her neck stiff, she looked to the gown. "What sort of fabric did you pick for the dress, Mabel?"

The conversation was stiff, with each question from Mrs. Sinclair feeling forced, but at least her mother was trying. The reception room was clearing as Mabel nodded to her parents and they took their leave along with the other guests.

With most of the guests gone, Mabel offered her hand to the model. "I suppose we are done."

"I'm not sure I could endure parents like that," the young woman said as she stepped down from the stand.

"They are the parents I have, and so I must do my best."

As the reception cleared, Mabel said her goodnight to Elona and others from Mr. Hartavo's studio. It felt strange that the month was at an end, but such strangeness was nothing compared to walking out the front steps of the hall to find a white carriage with gilded filigree waiting with six white horses.

"Madame Sinclair, over here," a footman called as he hopped off the back of the carriage and opened the door. The others lingering on the steps stared, curiosity in their eyes.

"Who sent that?" Elona said as she came to Mabel's side.

Mabel grinned. "The Astrellar estate."

Elona's eyes widened. "Astrellar? Do you have any idea how wealthy the Astrellar estate is?"

Mabel glanced at her friend. "Not really, but isn't that part of the fun?"

Elona let out a laugh. "Mabel, I think you're going to do just fine."

"I hope so." Mabel squeezed Elona's arm before gathering her skirts, walking down the stairs, and letting the footman help her into the carriage.

Inside, Arturo and Cassandra waited, hidden from view of the crowd. Mabel had to duck under Cassandra's hat as she sat across from them. Arturo grinned proudly while Cassandra kept an eye on the door.

Once it was shut, the carriage moved into motion.

"Madame Sinclair," Cassandra said as she raised her veil, "Arturo and I would like to formally offer to be the first investors in the Madame Sinclair Design Company."

Arturo waved his hand. "You are welcome to change the name, if you want. We only need something for the paperwork."

"But before you sign, I need to know one thing." Cassandra held a sly grin. "How do you feel about designing clothing for merfolk?"

Mabel raised an eyebrow. "I am happy to design for anyone, as long as they pay a fair price, and don't try to kill or transform me."

Arturo let out a laugh, his grin broadening. Mabel couldn't help but return his grin.

"As long as we set up favorable contracts, we should achieve both conditions," Cassandra said. "What do you say? Shall we become business partners?"

"There is much to negotiate," Mabel said, using the training Cassandra herself had given her, "but, if the terms are right, I can see myself saying yes."

Cassandra's eyes were bright, clearly enjoying the challenge. "Then, let us discuss the terms."

Mabel leaned back comfortably as she rode in a carriage with a mermaid and her husband, discussing profit shares and ownership percentages. As the negotiation wore on, she tried not to laugh. She felt similar excitement to the first time she had put on a mask and buckled on a sword to join Captain Stenton's crew in some piracy. She wasn't sure where this choice would take her, but she was eager to see where this journey led.

CHAPTER 16

In Which Mabel Makes a Deal with Merfolk

The Northern Merfolk Clan, in the Thalatha Sea

September of the Year 307 B.R.

After two months of endless hours of planning and preparation, Mabel was about to join Cassandra in negotiating their first contract. The concept still felt mad, especially as the yacht passed through a corridor lined with giant stone statues carved from pillars rising from the ocean. The wind had a deep chill as they passed the icebergs surrounding the island.

The wall of ice they approached split open, and Cassandra guided the yacht through. Mabel pulled her fur-lined hood tighter around herself as she shivered.

"Remember, the Northern Mermaid Clan has become reclusive for the past two centuries, but is still reasonable to humans," Cassandra said.

Mabel glanced at her as their breath puffed in the air. "Your sister really is the queen?"

"Yes, though don't expect that to add much friendliness. Even after all these years, she is still sore from me choosing Arturo over my ambassador duties. It made a mess with Marveth which she had to clean up."

Mabel raised an eyebrow. Cassandra had mentioned this before too. She claimed her exile from the Northern Clan wouldn't make a difference in the deals they were attempting to strike. Mabel had more than a few doubts, but it was too late to turn back now.

They reached a cavern with docks carved into the ice and several yachts sat waiting. A group of humans squatted on one platform, speaking to a few merfolk in the water, all laughing like old friends. Cassandra guided the yacht along one dock and a blonde young man wearing a fur-lined leather coat grabbed the docking rope.

"Timson, how are you?" Cassandra said warmly.

"I'm always pleased to see my aunt." He turned his charming grin on Mabel. "And what young goddess have you brought?"

Stepping onto the dock made of ice, Cassandra slapped his hand. "This is Madame Sinclair, the designer I told your mother about." She pointed at him. "She is married."

Timson gave her a mock-disappointed look and pressed a hand to his heart. "You have struck hard enough to bleed."

As Mabel took Timson's offered hand, she felt the wedding ring hidden beneath her gloves. Mabel hated the reminder of a lie she was still trapped in. She had considered removing it, but everyone in Willington believed her marriage was real. And then Arturo had pointed out, "Knowing the Castallan Navy, your lieutenant tailor's stuck wearing his wedding ring too."

The hole within her grew deeper with each passing day where no word came from Antonio himself. She would even take an angry letter, rejecting her and asking to be set free. And she would set him free, once she figured out how.

Cassandra touched Mabel's arm, bringing her attention back to the moment. "Timson, is the waiting room ready?" Cassandra said.

"Isabella came a few hours ago and made sure." Timson moved to guide them, but Cassandra waved her hand.

"I know the way," she said before leading Mabel through the icy cavern and to a tunnel. The floor was clear beneath, merfolk swimming, their whole torsos and arms covered in seal and walrus skins.

The ice ended and Mabel was grateful to step onto warm stone with a carpet running across it. They entered a room with seating made of stone, covered in blankets. At the center was a pool of water with a light steam rising. Isabella sat in the middle, wearing a sharkskin shirt and laying back in a shallow part, relaxing with her fishtail stretched out.

As they entered, she sat up and watched Mabel with her unreadable expression. There had been more practice sessions in the past few months and a few business meetings, but Isabella remained distant.

Cassandra pulled off her fur coat and hung it on a hook carved into the wall. "How was the journey?"

"My yacht is under repairs, so I used the Westom Channel." Isabella kept her gaze on Mabel.

"That is a long journey without a yacht, especially so soon after one of your visits to see him." Cassandra sat on a rock near Isabella. "How is he?"

A stiffness ran through Isabella, and she glared at her mother. Cassandra must have struck a nerve by asking after whoever this "he" was.

"Doing well, despite circumstances." Isabella looked to Mabel. "Which is what I hope you can say of Lieutenant Cortez."

Mabel's stomach clenched. There was something more direct in how Isabella called Antonio by his title. Cassandra and Arturo were more playful, calling him "your sailor" and rarely mentioning him by name.

"I hope he is well, but have had no word from him in months," Mabel said.

"Not even from Mother's informants?" Isabella glanced at

Cassandra with skepticism in her eyes.

"If I had a network of spies, I would have found Madame Sinclair much sooner." Cassandra analyzed her nails. Mabel was finding this was her way of hiding she was annoyed. "Besides, he is being watched by Madame Blue's syndicate. Asking after him might gain their attention, and I would rather remain unnoticed."

"Which is why 'Mrs. Granalda' has made a few appearances?" Isabella folded her arms. "I always wonder how many games you are playing."

Cassandra smoothed her skirt and glanced away. "My business with Madame Sinclair is not a game. It is an investment."

"For how long?" Isabella's gaze bore into her mother.

"For as long as it takes for her to manage the business on her own." Cassandra's sharp eyes focused on Mabel. "With how much she's learned these past few months, I doubt it will be too long. But first, we must have clients if there is to be a business. How warm are the waters here?"

"Frigid, as always." It was unclear if Isabella was saying this ironically or not. "I've spoken with Aunt Miranda, which is why you have an audience." She looked to Mabel. "Are you ready to meet the Queen of the Northern Clan?"

"As ready as I can be, I suppose." Mabel pressed her hands together, trying not to let her nerves rise. "Far more prepared than when I stumbled into Marveth nearly eighteen months ago. At least, this time I know merfolk exist."

"We certainly do." There was a hint of a smile in Isabella's eyes, while her face remained serious. Mabel wished she were easier to read. "How goes the business plan on the human side?"

This was far more comfortable territory. "We've a design studio in Willington and a few warehouses to make and store the clothing. We'll show the designs and get the orders here, make the custom gowns, and then deliver them."

"So simple?" Isabella huffed a laugh. "I do hope you succeed. Just be careful how quickly your business grows. The designs I've seen are good and I think they will catch on, along with the technology we've patented from Perakal. But be careful where you can."

"If there is danger, Madame Sinclair has a gift of improvising her way out of it." Cassandra eyed Mabel. "It is one of her more amusing traits."

"I rather hope there isn't danger," Mabel said. "All I want is to design and sell beautiful clothing."

A chiming sound ran through the room. Cassandra and Isabella sat up and Mabel frowned.

"It is time." Cassandra rose and led Mabel into one of the tunnels, Isabella swimming beneath them but keeping pace.

Here Mabel was, supported by two mermaids, about to meet the Queen of a merfolk clan and promote a business. She chuckled to herself as she imagined explaining this to her parents.

They soon entered another cavern made from ice, this one with sculpted statues. Various merfolk sat on seats carved into the ice. Where the merfolk in Marveth wore their hair large and high, these wore intricate braids, including in some of the mermen's beards.

"Miranda, Your Majesty," Cassandra said to the mermaid seated on a throne made of ice. "Thank you for seeing us."

Miranda appeared a bit older than Cassandra, but still youthful. She sat with her back straight and head high, no humor on her face.

"You have half-an-hour, Cassandra."

Cassandra was a master show woman as she opened the case she carried, revealing a tri-corner hat. "Many of us have lived for centuries and transform regularly into human form."

"For some of us, it is less permanent than others." Miranda gave Cassandra a pointed look.

Mabel held her smile, trying to press down her worry. Though Cassandra had warned her about Miranda's coldness, Mabel had still envisioned her as friendlier than this.

"With an enchanted hat or object, we can walk among humans for a while, inspecting and investigating them. But what if you want to match the style of those around you? Or need to change quickly? My partner, Madame Sinclair, will explain more."

Mabel stepped forward and held up the tri-corner hat. "We have already contracted with merfolk in Perakal to make tri-corner hats, bracelets, and necklaces that will conjure clothing once you transform. They have made a spell connecting an outfit to a pearl pin. Attach the pin to your clothing, tap it, and it will transform your outfit."

She didn't mention the clothing would be stored in warehouses onshore, with a sister pin attached. While the outfit itself would not teleport, the essence of it would be combined with the spell, allowing the clothing to transform. For the transformation to work, the real outfit needed to exist.

"Are any of you interested in trying?" she said.

Isabella nodded to a blonde mermaid across from her. The blonde gave Isabella a wary look but raised her arm before swimming toward them.

As the blonde mermaid sat on the shore, Mabel handed the hat to her. She tried to hide her nervousness she pressed her hands to her side and stepped back. Isabella had tested dozens of hats and bracelets weeks ago, and each had proven to work. Still, Mabel worried.

She breathed out as the mermaid put on the hat and her fishtail transformed into legs. As her body changed, one of the dresses Mabel and Cassandra had designed formed around her. It was a beautiful fuchsia gown with yellow thread creating details along the bodice and hem.

"Press the pins on the side and the outfit will change," Mabel said.

The mermaid frowned as she tapped the pin. She laughed with delight as a shimmer ran over her dress and it transformed to a similar gown in turquoise. Gasps of delight ran through the room.

Mabel couldn't help but smile proudly as she glanced at Cassandra. The mermaid gave her a small nod in return. Too many times, Cassandra had warned her how hard it was to impress merfolk who lived for centuries.

"How much?" the blonde mermaid said, her eyes wide.

"The hat is yours," Mabel said before naming a price in gold. She was still learning how to convert macs and skoons into merfolk currency broken into pearls, gold, and silver. "And we are working on a subscription service where we will send out new pins once per year. You may select the outfit from our catalogue." From one of her crates, Mabel picked up the one-page, full color catalogue. "Our venture is just beginning, but you are invited to be the first to enjoy this new fashion opportunity."

Miranda's blue eyes tracked Cassandra. "Does High Witch Randala know of this yet?"

"We have not contacted Marveth yet," Cassandra said.

"She will want this. And quickly." Miranda narrowed her eyes. "Which is what you want, isn't it?"

Cassandra gave her sister an innocent look. "I am only trying to help a young woman build a profitable business."

Miranda gave her a skeptical look and turned to Isabella. "You will be their liaison with Marveth?"

Isabella nodded. "We've been discussing it from the beginning. None of us would be foolish enough to send a human there."

"We certainly would not." Miranda eyed Mabel and then focused on Cassandra. "This is an impressive scheme. I'll be curious to see where it leads, and what your full plans are."

"The business belongs to Madame Sinclair." Cassandra held her sister's gaze. "I am only an investor."

Miranda's eyes narrowed before she looked to Mabel and raised a pair of fingers. "I do not transform often, but, to support, I want two dresses. Custom made."

Mabel bit back a smile as she nodded. "We will make them the best, Your Majesty, and are honored."

"I expect them to be the best." Miranda eyed her sister. "She would be a fool to invest in you if they were not."

Mabel was not sure if this was a compliment or not. Still, she smiled and gave a nod in acknowledgement. As other merfolk looked over the catalogue page, her grin widened, and a giddy excitement rose in her. After all the preparation, here she was with her first set of clients. They were not what she had ever expected, but they were excited by her designs.

Now, she just needed to deliver on the promises made.

The water frothed around them as the yacht finished its magic-sped journey and they arrived in the underground lake beneath Cassandra's mansion in Pippington. The small city was near Willington, lying across Lake Chalice as if tucked away and sleeping. The underground lake served to provide a portal which took them to the ocean, though Mabel was still unsure how the magic worked.

Staring at the stone ceiling as they moved toward the dock, Mabel let out a laugh. There was so much of the world few knew about, and today had only been a glimpse of all that lay in the Northern Clan.

"I'm glad I jumped on the back of your yacht," Mabel said as she pulled off her fur-lined coat, some ice still on the cuff.

Cassandra stood at the helm, guiding the yacht the last distance back to the dock.

"Part of me wishes you had not," the mermaid said, her face somber. She had been quiet since leaving the Northern Clan. "My sister is right. We need to open business with Marveth, but—" She turned and met Mabel's gaze. "There are only two people I fear: Madame Blue and Randala, the High Witch of Marveth."

A chill ran through Mabel as she sat on the bench along the edge of the yacht. "From the little you and Isabella have spoken of Marveth, I understand. But Madame Blue's organization is only humans committing crimes and blackmail. She can't be that powerful when compared with a mermaid high witch."

"Both Randala and Madame Blue combine power and influence with a ruthless cruelty. Randala is often cruel for cruelty's sake but is limited by the laws of justice of the High Council of Marveth."

"I imagine their version of justice is unpleasant," Mabel said.

"Yes, but Randala enjoys negotiations and a good bargain. If you ever must face her alone, remember to always have something she wants or will amuse her. She's often bored and will be more flexible if she is intrigued." Cassandra glanced at the dock ahead. "Which is part of how I negotiated a kinder exile than she had originally planned for me."

Mabel focused on Cassandra's legs, hidden beneath her gown. Cassandra often hinted at her exile, but rarely spoke of it directly. It would be better not to pry further.

"And what if I'm caught by Madame Blue?" Mabel said.

"Pray you have help to call on, since she and those who work for her are not bound by merfolk law." Cassandra adjusted a lever on the helm. "I honestly don't know much about her syndicate, except she has hidden strings on many powerful people, and it is best to not be touched by those strings."

Mabel's fingers curled into fists. "What if you're already caught in her web?"

"You are not caught, but those strings are seeking to entrap you." Cassandra leaned against the side of the yacht as it moored itself. "However, once your business is established, I think you will remain free. It will give you resources to avoid entanglements."

Mabel pressed her hands to her knees. Guilt rose in her as she stared at the false wedding ring. "I may be free, but Antonio Cortez is not."

"No, he is not," Cassandra said absently as the yacht reached its berth and stopped. "Though, he may be safer by remaining a pawn."

"He deserves better." Mabel rubbed her neck. "He's had three years stolen from his life because of me."

"Then steal them back." Cassandra motioned for Mabel to step onto the dock. "You are a pirate, after all."

Mabel nearly laughed, but her heart wasn't in it. Instead, she hopped onto the dock and looked up at the staircase leading to the mansion above. A whole world of magic and merfolk was unfolding in front of her, but none of it showed her how to rescue Antonio from the mess she made.

Nor, how he felt about that mess. Or about her.

"As promised, here we are in Pippington." Cassandra adjusted a dial on the helm. "The last barge going to Willington will be leaving in—" She pulled a pocket watch out. "Oh dear. A half-hour. You should get going."

Mabel turned toward her mentor. "Thank you and give my best to Arturo."

Cassandra nodded. "It is more than pleasure doing business with you, Madame Sinclair."

Mabel waved as Cassandra began backing the yacht away from the dock before disappearing into a strange fog. Alone with her thoughts, Mabel went up the stairs, into the mansion, and out through the garden gate.

Standing on North Street in Pippington, along a line of mansions, Mabel looked over the city, struck by how ordinary everything felt. As she moved toward the corner with the horse-drawn trolley, she laughed to herself over how far she had traveled and all she had seen, and yet, this was the ordinary world she returned to.

CHAPTER 17

In Which Mabel Receives an Unexpected Letter

Mabel barely reached Pippington's barge on time and spent the hour-long ride across the lake sitting on the upper deck with her sketchbook in hand. She sketched Pippington's skyline, the small city growing with mansions along one end of the shore and wharfs lining the other.

Across the water rose the taller, majestic buildings of Barthan's capital, Willington. It was a gleaming city with bright lights and bustling with life. There was a vibrancy when walking along the large boulevards, as if this were the center of everything happening in the nation and a new opportunity was around every corner.

It was her home, for now. It felt more like a place to begin than to live forever, but she was grateful for her place here.

Near dusk, the barge reached the docks, and she joined the rush of others, many coming for an overnight trip to the larger city.

"Did you hear Dusty Brighton is in tomorrow's dragon race?" a man said as Mabel pushed past.

"The man's a wonder of a jockey. He sits like a feather on a dragon's back. I always put my money on him."

Mabel smiled to herself. She used to love the few times her parents would bring her and Malcom to Willington to see the professional dragon races. Watching those creatures circle the large track was magnificent, and their speed and dexterity was impressive. But, after seeing dragons in the wild on the ocean and spending the day among mermaids, there was a strange ordinariness to the thought of sitting in the stands and watching dragons go in large circles.

Arriving near the small apartment she had found for herself along Sohan Avenue, Mabel stepped into Café Desant on the corner. Many from the design studios came here for a quick dinner before making appearances at the theaters, ballrooms, clubs, and other nightlife near the heart of the city.

"Mabel!" Elona rose from her table with a few others from Mr. Hartavo's studio. "Come join us."

Mabel ordered a sandwich and creamy chicken soup from the counter before joining the others.

"How is our great entrepreneur?" said Denny, one of the design assistants.

"My business partner and I presented to a community of potential clients today," Mabel said, trying not to laugh at how much she had to hide of who that community was. "We've got quite a few pre-orders."

"What sort of clients?" Elona said. "I might have some ideas of what styles they like."

"I'd love to tell you, but my investors consider that proprietary information." Mabel rested her arms on the table. "But I can confirm many of our clients have lived a long time."

"Is it a group of grannies?" Denny said with a laugh.

"In a way, yes, but I cannot say more." She looked to Elona. "How are things for you?"

The conversation turned to current events and gossip from the society magazines and Mabel laughed and joked with the others, feeling fully part of this group. All of them were in various stages of starting their careers in fashion, Elona being the furthest along. They weren't quite as doting toward her as Captain Stenton's crew, but they treated her as a friend and equal.

"We're headed over to the Soria Club after this," Elona said. "Do you want to come?"

"New band's playing and there should be some good dancing." Denny gave her a rakish smile and a wink. "Could be some chances for romance."

Elona glared at him. "Would you stop? She's married."

"Oh, come on. Her man's out at sea." Denny chuckled. "Given the conquests my cousin in the Barthanian Navy writes about, I imagine a healthy young man like your sailor's not sitting on his ship moping over you. So why mope over him?"

"That is not who Antonio is." Mabel held her glare on him. She may not have heard from him in months, but his character was unlikely to have changed.

Elona dropped coins on the table for a tip and rose. "Mabel and I'll be going ahead. You can find someone else to have an evening with."

Mabel gave her a grateful look before following her out, a few other women joining her, and saying, "That was a cad thing to say. You stand up for your lieutenant."

Walking with her friends down the street to the club, Mabel wished he really were hers. The thought weighed on her as they paid the fee to enter the club and stood along the dance floor. Men asked Mabel to dance and would start a conversation until they felt the pressure of her wedding ring. A few would fumble and send her back. Others would start asking of her husband. A few ignored it and she ended those dances quickly as the men got a bit too comfortable with her.

Even with the few good-looking men who seemed polite, Mabel found herself looking at their profile and thinking how Antonio was more handsome and charming.

But he was not hers.

No matter what the forged marriage certificate said.

After an hour of dancing, she found Elona and said, "Thank you for inviting me, but it's been a long day and I need to go home."

Elona hugged her and whispered. "I'm sure you miss him. I'll find something for you tomorrow. We'll have a girl's night to get your mind off things."

Mabel smiled. "Thank you."

With their good night said, Mabel hurried back down the three blocks to her small apartment. She paused at her postal box and pulled out the large stack of mail she hadn't checked in two weeks. It had been too busy to bother with while planning with Cassandra.

She flipped through the envelopes while walking up the four flights of stairs, most of them advertisements for local restaurants and clubs. A frown came as she stared at a thick packet with her mother's handwriting on the address. She turned it over, wondering what business her parents could have with her. They contacted her occasionally, but she had barely spoken to them in the past three months.

Reaching her apartment on the fourth floor, she fought with her key and the door. Once she prevailed, she entered her sparse parlor and dropped the mail on the top of her small table.

Sitting down, she took her letter opener and slid it through the package's side. Six letters spilled out, all weather-worn and with a number of ports stamped on the envelopes. Her heart jolted as she lifted one and stared at Antonio's name in the corner.

He had written to her. Even if he hated her, at least he had written.

Tears began to fall as Mabel lifted the enclosed note in her mother's handwriting.

> *These all came last week from the Lieutenant. Your father and I worry so greatly for you but hope you will be heartened by your husband's words.*

There was more in the note on the status of the cottage and lecturing Mabel on what sort of wife she should be. Mabel tossed the short letter aside and sorted the envelopes from Antonio in order by date. The first two were stamped from the same day, three months before.

Her hands trembled as she tore open the first envelope. Pulling out the folded letter, she wasn't sure she wanted to read this. It could be his rebuke, telling her to leave his life after ruining it.

But he had written. However he felt about her, she would know, for better or for worse.

Taking in a steadying breath, she opened the letter.

Dear Mabel,

I have rewritten this letter a dozen times. Though we only had one afternoon together, I have thought of you every day afterward.

Sobs burst from Mabel, and she rested her face in her hands. She could feel her makeup smearing, but it didn't matter.

There was hope with Antonio.

However, as her tears eased enough to read his earnest, sweet words, it was clear this was written before learning of his promotion.

The letter ended with:

I know you didn't mean to steal my heart along with my pocketbook, but it has been taken all the same. And I find it very rude that you haven't returned it.

So, La Ratera, will you write to me? Something more than your quick notes. When I finish those, I long for more. Write to me like you're speaking to me. Tell me of your life, hopes, and wishes. And, of course, of the latest fashion you see in Willington. Will women ever be rescued from this assault of unflattering ruffles?

Write to me, La Ratera, and ease the loneliness of a tailor who thinks often of you.

She bawled into her handkerchief till it was saturated and had to grab a fresh one.

How she wished she had received this before she had forged the fake letter from him and accidentally set the trap which had snapped on both of them.

She poured a glass of water and drank slowly to calm herself. Pushing air out and in, she picked up the second letter from Antonio. This was postmarked the same day and the handwriting was hasty and loose with many scribbled out words.

Her stomach clenched as she read of Admiral Guerrero personally delivering the news of Antonio's marriage and promotion.

> *I do not know if my anger or worry is greater. Miss Sinclair, are you a charming thief and criminal? Or are you as caught in this trap as I am?*
>
> *My heart prays the second is true. If it is, are you safe?*
>
> *If you are part of the conspiracy, why target a penniless tailor?*
>
> *Please explain. I don't know if you are laughing at me or locked away as a captive somewhere.*
>
> *I hope you are innocent and safe, but I fear only one can be true.*

She set aside the letter and ripped open the envelope postmarked two weeks later. Holding a hand to her chest, she didn't know what to expect. Reading his words, it became clear this had been written in response to the letter she had sent to explain and apologize.

> *On another day, I might laugh at you getting your foot caught in your own net. However, I have little humor when I think of three more years at sea. Especially as I spend time running strange errands for Admiral Guerrero.*
>
> *I see no way out of this trap, and fear that when I near the end of my fifth year in the Navy, some cruel twist will yank my freedom from me again.*
>
> *I am glad you are safe and see how this grew beyond your control. I wish proving the marriage certificate is a forgery would set me free, but, with*

Admiral Guerrero's threats, I doubt it would work.

I have thought for hours on your offer to make things right, but this is out of our control now, isn't it? You have a husband you didn't want, and I am trapped in three more years of naval duty.

How do we make things better?

The greatest challenge in a sailor's life is loneliness. So, I go back to the question I asked weeks ago: Will you write to me?

Do not write to me of troubles we can do nothing about. Write to me of Willington and of the fashion world. Write to me of small stories and send me things that make you laugh. Help me keep my mind off my misery.

In return, I will confirm I am your dutiful husband who eloped with you at Port Nerama and will tell everyone how I miss my darling Mabel.

Strange to say, though, those last words are true. Even with this tangled net you've accidentally caught me in.

If I am only a fool you met at a port, please tell me. But I pray I mean more to you.

~~Apparently, Your Husband,~~
~~Surprised to be Your Husband,~~
Your Unexpected Husband,

Antonio Cortez

P.S. Enclosed are two copies of a photograph of me in my lieutenant's uniform. The first is for when people ask to see your supposed husband. The second is for your father, since he paid so much for the outfit.

Mabel looked in the envelope and pulled out the photographs. Her tears still came, but now instead of guilt and sorrow, they carried joy. She set the photograph against the saltshaker to prop it up and rested her elbow on the table, her chin on her hand.

Smiling wistfully, she said, "I wish it didn't cost three years, but you do look very handsome in your uniform, my dear Antonio."

Taking this letter along with the last three, she moved to her bed and kicked off her shoes. Once stretched out, she read through the other three letters, each responding to letters she had written him of her time in Willington and her life at Hartavo's studio. His sweet words and the clear concern warmed her, and she grinned.

With the photograph in her hand, she looked into Antonio's eyes, taking in the firm lines of his cheekbones and his square shoulders. Her smile faltered. "I don't know how, Antonio, but I will get you home and make things right."

She set the photograph on her nightstand and held her pillow to her chest as she read the letters again.

CHAPTER 18

In Which Mabel Gains a Ship

December of the Year 307 B.R.

The water of the underground lake reflected on the stone ceiling as Mabel ran her hand over the polished helm of the brand-new yacht, feeling the smoothness of the wood and brass.

"Do be careful with it," Cassandra said. "We shall have several hundred very upset merfolk who won't get their orders if anything happens to you. I'd rather not answer to them."

"It's beautiful."

"It transforms too. You can add more ship appearances over time. Similar to the dresses, the actual vessel must exist for this to transform. But it can be any size on the outside and the inside will always remain the same."

Cassandra motioned for Mabel to follow her. Mabel's eyes widened as they went down the stairs and into the hull of a much larger ship. There were bunks for general sailors on one level, a few officers' quarters, cannons, and a lot of room for merchandise.

"It will always be a sail vessel. The magic doesn't work with steamships." Cassandra knocked her knuckles against the wood hull. "But it should serve you well. I'm still wary of the crew you've chosen, but this is your business. It shall rise or sink with your choices."

"This is amazing," Mabel whispered.

"I'm surprised you still can be amazed. You've visited six mermaid clans."

With a smile, Mabel turned to Cassandra. "Thank you. I so misjudged you when we met. You've been far more generous than I deserve."

"First, I turned your brother into a toad, so not trusting me seems a wise choice. Second, if you botch this venture, I will not be kind in seeking repayment. However, Madame Sinclair, I believe in you. Which is why I am handing over an extremely expensive ship to a girl who just turned nineteen." She raised a finger. "Remember. This is an asset of the business, not a pleasure vehicle."

Mabel grinned. "Of course."

"That includes not running off immediately to visit your young sailor. You don't want that horrid Admiral he reports to becoming suspicious of you showing up at every port Lieutenant Cortez has shore leave at."

Mabel's cheeks reddened. The thought had been forming, but Cassandra was right. And it was greatly disappointing. If Antonio had been standing in front of her, speaking the words from his last letter, she wasn't sure if she would stop kissing him.

"Though," Cassandra went on, eyeing Mabel, "a strategic, well-planned visit could be useful in helping your young sailor adjust his circumstances."

She raised her eyebrows for emphasis and then pivoted toward the stairs as if she'd hinted at nothing. Mabel followed her up to the main deck as she tried not to smile. She would be very happy to help Antonio, if she could. However, she needed to be careful in her plan.

Reaching the helm, Cassandra gestured to a map lain out beside it, dots marking ships moving across the paper. "You'll be able to see naval vessels and other ships marked by merfolk." She tapped the paper. "Do remember it is meant for avoiding unwanted attention. Not for piracy."

"I am a reformed pirate, Madame Astrellar."

"We shall see about your crew. Do not let them use this."

Mabel nodded. "It will be in my hands only."

"The conch shells for communicating with me and Isabella are in the captain's quarters. Do you need me to show you how they work again?"

"Tap the side three times in rhythm and then speak your name. You will answer when you hear or are ready."

"Very good." Cassandra held out a naval officer's whistle on a leather string, engravings along the small metal pipe. "This is for emergencies only, in case you get into an unfortunate debacle. I will be able to use it to track you and provide assistance." She placed it in Mabel's hand. "Please do avoid debacles wherever you can. Finesse and charm will get you out of more troubles than a sword and pistol."

Mabel let out a laugh as she put the leather string around her neck. "I don't intend on getting into too many battles."

"No battles is best, even with Isabella's training." Cassandra gestured toward the captain's quarters. "Most of our correspondence will be through your letter satchel. Anything sent to your postal box in Willington will appear in your satchel. You can only send letters out if you know the stamp of other satchels. Any other letters will need to be through ordinary mail."

Mabel sighed. "I wish we could send a satchel to Antonio."

"Getting letters weekly isn't enough?"

"The letters are three to six weeks old." Mabel shrugged. "Sometimes, he sends three a week. It would be nice to get them far more quickly."

Cassandra glanced at her, biting back an amused smile. "While I know who you're focused on, please remember to communicate with your parents. The Astrellar business office in Willington keeps getting phone calls. You and I will continue our regular meetings in person." She handed Mabel a box. "Please protect this. Only Isabella and I have copies."

Mabel frowned as she took the polished wood box and opened it.

Inside were about a dozen divots with names written above them. One was lit-up.

Pointing to the light above a label marked *Pippington*, Cassandra said, "This is where we are." She then pointed at a marble-sized pearl sitting in a hole on the edge of the wood. "Place this pearl in the lighted hole and it will guide the ship to whichever of my mansions I am at. If I need you to come, do come alone. If the crew is still aboard, you can use the captain's skiff. It has a hidden panel with the equipment for traveling spells."

Mabel stared at the box, wondering how the magic worked. "Thank you for trusting me. I don't know if I'll ever repay you, but—"

"Given the profits of our first set of orders, you will repay me soon enough. Otherwise, I would not have commissioned this ship from the Perakan Mermaid Clan." Cassandra pointed at the light. "Where we are is closest to Willington. Use this to travel to your offices there. In a year or two, when the mermaid lines are managing themselves, we'll work on your plan to expand to fashion lines for human clients."

"I've so many ideas." Mabel grinned. "I was thinking of dresses with straight skirts, where—"

Cassandra gave her a tired look. "Your ideas are good, but let's take care of the immediate matters first."

"Getting my crew?"

Cassandra gestured at the helm. "The coordinates are locked in. Just raise the equipment and you'll be on your way. If there is any trouble, there is a conch shell connected to the shipyard. Call them before you bother me."

Cassandra lifted her fine skirts and walked down the ramp to the dock. With a flick of her hand, the ramp rose and slid into a hidden slot in the yacht. "Are you ready, Captain Sinclair?"

Mabel's heart pounded as she rested her hands on the steering wheel. "What if I do the magic wrong?"

"Which is why I've had you practice on our voyages to the

mermaid clans. You know quite well how to manage this yacht. It is the same as mine, though more state-of-the art."

"And with an entire cargo hold," Mabel muttered.

"Go on. I've lunch with Arturo soon and I'd rather not be late."

Mabel chuckled at how commonly Cassandra treated such things. Excitement grew within her as she flipped a lever on the helm and a panel opened revealing a large pearl. She flipped another lever and a set of metal wires rose, spreading out like a weathervane. She pressed a button near the pearl and gripped the steering wheel with both hands.

Though she had done this at least a dozen times with Cassandra, Mabel shouted as the yacht lurched forward at an impossible speed through dense fog. There was a rush of wind, and it was terrifying to stare ahead and watch strange objects pass.

Nearly a half-hour passed before the yacht lurched again. Mabel's breastbone hit the steering wheel and she moaned while rubbing her chest. The fog cleared around her and the sail of the yacht caught the real wind of the sea.

Mabel grinned as she guided the yacht toward a familiar clipper ship on the horizon. Approaching, she raised a red and white striped flag.

Once near, several of the cannons shifted to point at the yacht and familiar faces crouched near the edge of the boat, holding rifles. She lowered her sail to slow the yacht before standing on the edge of her yacht in her tailored trousers, white shirt with puffed sleeves, and maroon vest. Her hair was tucked into a braid, but based on the slow grin on Captain Stenton's face, her red hair was enough to help him recognize her.

"Captain Sinclair of the White Torrent," she shouted, "asking permission to come aboard."

"You're always welcome, Captain Stripes!" Stenton stepped away from the railing and bellowed orders at the crew. Mabel grinned herself as the crew tossed ropes to her and shouted their welcomes.

Mabel straddled the backward chair in Stenton's captain quarters as she rested her arms on the backrest. Leaning her chin on her arm, she said, "So, I need a crew I can trust to travel between mermaid clans and deliver goods."

Stenton sat with a proud smile on his face. "You'd trust a salty band of pirates?"

"I'd trust you and the rest of my friends who rescued a young girl lost in a mermaid's lair."

He squinted. "And you say you've contracts with the mermaid clans? They'll not bother with the crew nor ships belonging to your fleet?"

She nodded. "The crew won't become donkeys in Marveth."

He chuckled before scratching his head. "Stripes, I've been proud of you since the day we've met. I sure hope you're not in over your head, but—" He glanced at the door. "The navies, with their new steamships, are breathing down our necks and let's just say, it's getting harder to turn a profit on this old bucket."

"So, Captain Stenton, you'll join the Madame Sinclair Trading Company?" She grinned.

"I'm not fully sure I trust your business partner, but I trust you." He took her offered hand and gave it a firm shake. "You're my captain now, Stripes. Along with my crew."

"You're still captain. Think of me more like a client. My base of operations will be on the ship much of the time, where I can meet with clients, but I'll often be gone."

"Well, you'll be with good company while aboard."

She smiled warmly. "I can't tell you how much I've missed you and the crew. I love my parents, but I have to remind myself to call them at least once a month. But all of you—" She blinked back a few drops of tears. "You're more family than they are."

Stenton glanced down, scratching his beard to hide a tear. "You're our girl, Stripes. We're all looking out for you." With a sly grin he pointed at the ring on her finger. "Which, now that we're done with business, who's attached to that shiny rock there?"

Mabel grinned. "Remember the young sailor who was my first kiss?"

Stenton sat up, his arms folded and his biceps flexing. "What'd that boy do?"

"Nothing, but I've done a lot to him on accident." She winced. "Have you heard of the Fairy Godmother Society?"

Stenton grimaced. "Oh no, Stripes. What've you gotten yourself into?"

"I've gotten myself out, but now I need to get Antonio out too. I was hoping you might know a way to help."

"If I don't, I might know someone who does. Tell me your troubles, lass."

With a patch of hope in her heart, Mabel told Stenton the whole story of her return home. Henrietta came with dinner and chatted a while, grinning at Mabel, and then had to be shooed away. The sky was dark as Mabel finished, having to answer many of Stenton's questions along the way.

His eyes tired, he rested his chin on his hand. "Despite his girl back home, he seemed a nice boy."

"I hope he's not in more trouble than I think he's already in," Mabel said. "But I've accidentally made him a target for Madame Blue's syndicate. I don't know how large the syndicate is, or how powerful, but I do know he deserves better."

"I'm not much of a conspirator and plotter," Captain Stenton said. "But, with your quick mind and a little help from your new business partner, I'll bet my whole boat we'll find a way for the sailor."

Mabel raised her glass. "To old friends who'll watch out for each other."

Stenton grinned and clinked his glass against hers.

CHAPTER 19

In Which Antonio
Reunites with a Pickpocket

Port Viama, Island in the Wahid Sea, colony of the Castallar Protectorate
April of the Year 308 B.R.

Antonio sat outside the door of the inn's meeting room where Admiral Guerrero met with another questionable looking business liaison. Over the past ten months as a lieutenant, the series of anonymous notes Antonio had dropped at each naval port office had made no difference. Though, as he helped carry the small crates and chests the Admiral often left the meetings with, Antonio made sure he knew as little as possible.

"Keep your head down and stay safe," he whispered as he slipped Mabel's picture from his pocket.

He chuckled at the photograph of her standing in a ballgown with a broad skirt, leading to a lean bodice elongating her form and accentuating the length of her neck. She held a cane and looked out haughtily, though he could see a wink of humor in her eye. Her hat seemed half the circumference of her massive skirt and was an elaborate though elegant display of feathers and ribbons. She looked a high-born lady of wealth about to conquer the world. In the corner was a kiss mark in deep red lipstick.

Leaning back in his chair, he glanced out the grimy windows of another seedy inn in another dirty port.

If things had gone as originally planned, two days ago, he would have finished his two years of service, returned home, and married Sofia. Considering the desperate letter she had sent after his promotion to lieutenant, claiming to have wept an ocean of tears over him, he had chosen the right girl.

Though, that girl was unique. And had accidentally shackled him in three more years of service. And sent ridiculous stories of conducting business with merfolk. He wasn't sure how much of those stories were real. The more she sent, the more he worried they were true.

Even with his questions, he loved every story, every sign of her wit and humor, of her intelligence. Every letter was a delight and every package curated with magazines, colognes, and comfort items.

How he longed to stand with his arms around her as she lightly teased him.

He shifted and pulled out his notepad, flipping through the series of sketches he had made of her. When the time came, he would make every dress he could for her, even if her business failed and he was only a tailor scraping by. Though, he doubted she would fail. With her cleverness, she'd find a way past every obstacle.

His thoughts drifted to imagining how the straight lines of her narrow frame would look in a soft, silk nightgown. He often found himself wandering to them in dress shops when buying her a scarf or handkerchief to send back. He'd twist his steel wedding ring, wondering what it would be like if he and Mabel were really married.

The door opened and Antonio tucked the photograph and his notepad in his pocket as he rose.

"Carry this carefully." Admiral Guerrero handed Antonio a narrow wood box the length of his forearm. "And you'll need to tailor my uniform again. You made it too tight."

"Of course, señor." Antonio decided not to remark on the two pieces of cake the admiral had eaten at dinner last night.

As the admiral left the inn, Antonio stayed at his elbow. They passed merchants beckoning potential customers and crewmen on shore leave, mixing with the bright colors and many sounds of the port town.

As they reached the wharf leading toward the officer's hall where they had rooms for the night, Antonio said, "Señor, I hate to bother you again, but do you have an update on my leave request? I'm two years into service and owed at least a month. I'm here to do my duty, but—"

"Missing your possibly fake wife?" Admiral Guerrero grumbled.

"I am, señor. And my family."

"You're doing important work." Admiral Guerrero patted Antonio's shoulder. "You keep up your loyalty, and I'll start taking you into these meetings. Once you're a captain, I will need you as a courier. As I promised, you're going to be a wealthy man."

"My lieutenant's salary is enough. All I want is to be a tailor."

Admiral Guerrero grunted as he pulled at his military coat as it rode up on his stomach. "You're not much of that. I'd stick to the naval work."

Antonio pressed his lips together, holding back a sharp remark about how it wasn't his fault his client's stomach kept growing.

They went up a set of stairs and a woman called out, "Antonio!"

There were likely many Antonio's around a port with several Castallan ships moored at the docks, so he continued walking.

"Antonio Cortez!"

There were likely other Antonio Cortez's too, but he turned his head. His breath stilled.

Mabel stood on a crate on the other side of the crowded wharf, waving for his attention. She wore a dark green travel dress with a pointed hat and looked just as beautiful as he'd ever hoped. He touched the admiral's arm as he stared at her.

The admiral glanced at where Antonio was staring and squinted.

"Someone you know?"

"My—" Antonio swallowed, unsure what to call her. "She's here."

"Who?" Admiral Guerrero frowned as Mabel pushed through the crowd toward Antonio. He wanted to run and grab her in his arms, but he was standing next to his commanding officer.

"My possibly fake wife." Antonio broke into a grin. He held the box out to the Admiral. "May I—um—"

Admiral Guerrero glowered at him but took the box. "Go greet the girl."

Antonio pushed his way through the crowd until he stood in front of Mabel. This didn't feel wholly real even as he took her hands in his and felt her soft skin.

"How are you here?" His words jumbled through his head as his pulse quickened.

Her fingers brushed his cheek, a softness in her eyes. "I've missed you terribly."

"Me too. I—" He thought through everything he wanted to say, but none of it mattered. Not when Mabel was here, standing in front of him.

Instead, he pulled her into his arms and kissed her for the first time in eighteen months. Deeper longings rose in him as his heart thundered. He tried to push these thoughts away, but they were hard as her hands ran down his arms before reaching up and gripping his shoulders, pulling him closer.

He wasn't sure how long the kiss lasted and didn't care. This was the woman he thought of nearly every moment and dreamed of each night, and she was here. Their kisses the day they had met had started a spark in him, but this was a blaze, and he didn't want to let go. Even as a small crowd formed, and other naval sailors and officers whistled.

"Seems the straight-arrow Cortez's found a girl to meet his needs," laughed one of the other officers from Antonio's ship.

Antonio forced his lips from Mabel's as he kept an arm around her shoulders and shouted back, "She happens to be my wife."

Playful "ooh's" came from the crowd of sailors followed by encouraging grunts and cheers. Antonio kept a protective arm around Mabel, hoping she didn't understand some of the lewder suggestions.

"Why don't you introduce me to your commanding officer?" She kissed his cheek.

Antonio stared at her, sure he looked an idiot with how much he was grinning. "What are you doing here?"

"I was at a nearby port on business and heard your ship would be here," she said. "I thought I'd stop in and kiss you." She fluttered her eyelids innocently. "I think this was a success."

"I think so too," he whispered before pressing his lips to hers again.

Gently pulling away, she said, "We should be careful."

He winked at her. "Why? You are, after all, my wife."

Her face became more serious. "That is exactly why."

Raising her hand, he stared at the diamond ring with a gold band on her finger and the steel ring on his. These symbolized a lie.

He held her hand between his as he looked her in the eye. "What if we— what if you really were—"

Her eyes widened, her light skin growing a touch paler.

"In my heart, we already are," she whispered. "But this is not why I came."

He let himself smile as he put his arm around her waist and held her against him.

"I don't care why you came." He breathed in the soft perfume of her wonderfully red hair. "Only that you're here."

"You'll want to know why I came." She kissed his cheek, angling her head so her hat pointed away from his face. "I suggest introducing me to the admiral."

He frowned, but tightly held her hand as he led her to where Admiral Guerrero glowered.

"Señor," he said, "may I introduce my wife, Mabel Sinclair Cortez."

Admiral Guerrero nodded to her. "The arrival of wives at port is not standard procedure, señora."

"Most wives of officers aren't building a fashion trading company that covers the world," she said with a delightful laugh, her blue eyes bright and her smile wide. "And, I have missed my dear lieutenant."

"The thousand or so letters he's sent you aren't enough?"

"They certainly can't kiss me like he can."

Admiral Guerrero's eyes narrowed before he broke into a genuine laugh. Antonio's shoulders eased.

The admiral offered his arm. "We were heading to the officer's hall. Why don't you join us?"

"I am honored."

She released Antonio's hand and took Admiral Guerrero's arm. The admiral handed Antonio back the wood box and they walked toward the officer's hall. He grinned as Admiral Guerrero and Mabel talked, her manner bubbling with charm and the admiral laughing at her wit through much of the conversation on other ports and towns. It was one thing to read such words from Mabel. Another to watch her smoothly impress his gruff superior officer.

When they walked up the steps to the officer's hall, Admiral Guerrero paused by the door. He took the box from Antonio and said, "You're due some shore leave, aren't you?"

"I had two hours last night when we arrived at port. There are ten hours remaining, unless you have other duties for me, señor."

Admiral Guerrero eyed him. "I expect you and Mrs. Cortez at dinner sharp at six but take a few hours." He grinned while looking to Mabel. "Your husband's a bit stiff. I'm sure some time with you will loosen him right up."

Mabel laughed and gave a confident wink. "I'm sure it will."

Antonio's collar felt a bit tight, but he held his smile.

Admiral Guerrero waved his hand. "Off with you young lovers."

"Thank you, señor," Antonio said. "We'll be back right on time, and—"

Mabel took his hand and led him from the building and further down the wharf. She glanced over her shoulder before pulling Antonio into a narrow alleyway. He grinned, remembering their first kiss, and leaned in to repeat the moment.

"Who else will be at the dinner?" Mabel's eyes were serious.

Antonio stood straight, the pit of his stomach twisting. "The other ship officers." His brows pinched together. "Are you here in port on honest business?"

"It's clear Admiral Guerrero is not." She took his hand, her fingers wrapping with his. "I think I've found a way to make right what I've done to you."

His fingers brushed her wedding ring. "I don't fully mind the trap."

"But you do mind three more years in the Navy." She gave him a quick kiss. "As do I."

He cupped her cheek. "Mabel, whatever you've come to do, I'm grateful, but don't rattle things. If we stay steady, I'll have my way out. And then, I'll come to you—" He coughed uncomfortably. "I mean, if that's what you want."

"Of course, that's what I want." She gestured toward the officer's hall. "But every letter you've written for months mentions another rejection of the leave you're owed. Admiral Guerrero isn't going to let you go."

"I've petitioned naval headquarters. It'll come through." He didn't feel that was true, but he had to believe it.

"You are an honest man." She smiled softly. "Which is one of my favorite things about you. But, when the other players have rigged the dice, you can't play by the rules. You'll only lose."

"Mabel, dabbling in piracy is what got you noticed by those criminals," he said. "And put both of us at risk. Don't step into their world any further."

"I'm not. I'm getting you out."

"How are you going to do that? The people Admiral Guerrero

meets with are dangerous. I hear rumors of people disappearing, of lives being ruined." He rested his hands on her arms. "Staying here and keeping my head down allows me to protect you from them. If I simply keep on, I'll get out."

She hit his chest with the back of her hand. "One of us has lived with pirates. When it comes to backroom deals and smuggling, I think I know more than you do."

"Maybe you do, but he's got decades more experience than you." His eyes pleaded with her. "Don't play their game."

"I'm not. I'm making them play mine."

Given the firmness in her eyes, and how she had come all this way for her plan, he wasn't going to persuade her. Taking her hand, he wished he loved her less, that he didn't read each of her letters a dozen times over, that he didn't lay in his tiny quarters on the ship each night, wondering what it would be like to lay with her in his arms as the moonlight shone down, gleaming on her red hair.

"I don't want you to do this, but it's clear I can't stop you," he said. "So, I want two things in return."

She frowned. "What?"

"First, those stories you write about merfolk and all that. Are they true?"

Her blue eyes searched his face as if considering her answer. Antonio raised his hand and twisted his fingers, sending a line of green flame rolling across his fingertips before puffing into smoke.

"You're an Illuminator," she whispered, her mouth slightly open.

"A what?"

"A human with magic." She smiled while gripping his hand. "And, yes, everything I've told you about merfolk is true. Magic is real. As are merfolk. It's a complicated world, but fascinating."

He breathed in, sorting this truth. It was nearly a relief, but also brought up worries over what danger she faced when entering this world of merfolk. However, that could be discussed later.

Interlocking his fingers with hers, he said, "My second request is for you to come with me."

"Where?"

He gave no answer as he held tight to her hand and led her down the wharf toward the Castallan naval headquarters. As he entered the main doors, one of the officers on duty smiled. "Down the hall and to the left, young man." He nodded to Mabel. "Congratulations, señorita."

Mabel frowned, but Antonio did not give her time to ask a question as he briskly led her to a door marked 'Clerk of Official Records' and led her inside.

He was grateful there was only one couple there and two clerks. He approached the middle-aged man and said, "I need to register a marriage, señor."

Mabel nudged his arm. "What are you doing?"

"Name, sir?" the clerk said.

"Lieutenant Antonio Cortez of the ship Lanzana." He pointed toward the staffing lists for all moored naval ships at the port. "It marks me as married at Port Nerama. However, the registration was under the local law. I just found out that, for my wife to receive my full pension, I need a marriage certified from Castallar."

The clerk thumbed through the staffing lists. He looked to Mabel. "You are Mabel Sinclair of Barthan?"

She eyed Antonio. "You haven't proposed."

"I did, eighteen months ago, before going to the local port's office," he said, barely keeping his face serious. "Don't you remember?"

"It was such a romantic proposal," she said, trying to hide a sly grin. "Down on one knee. Why don't you recreate it for me?"

Antonio kept hold of Mabel's hand as he knelt. "I think it went like this."

"We're getting to our busy part of the day soon, with most sailors half-way through their shore leave," the clerk said. "There'll be many marriages and divorces, so I'd appreciate if you'd move it along."

"Shh." Mabel waved her hand. "My husband is proposing to me."

"Mabel Sinclair." Antonio's heart pounded even as he grinned. "There are many things I'm not sure are true or not about you, but the one truth I know is I love you." He took a breath. "Will you marry me?"

Her grin matched his. "Yes, Antonio. For a long time now, the answer is yes."

"I should hope so," the clerk muttered as he set out the stamps needed. "Your identification, please."

As Antonio stood, Mabel pulled his identification folio from her pocket and set it on the desk along with hers.

"La Ratera," he whispered, "when did you take that from my pocket?"

"When we walked in the building and I was sure of your plan," she said, a proud smile on the corner of her mouth. Antonio leaned over and kissed her cheek.

"Kissing and flirting can happen after we're done," the clerk said tiredly as he filled out a small stack of certificates with their names. "Lieutenant Antonio Cortez, do you agree to wed Señorita Mabel Sinclair?"

"I do." Antonio took both of Mabel's hands in his.

"Señorita Mabel Sinclair—"

"Madame." Antonio winked at Mabel as she grinned. The clerk scowled. "She is Madame Mabel Sinclair, the great fashion designer."

The clerk rolled his eyes. "Madame Mabel Sinclair, do you agree to wed Lieutenant Antonio Cortez?"

Her grin was broad even while her hands trembled. "I do."

"Then, by the authority of the Castallan Navy and Castallar Protectorate, you are officially declared husband and wife, with all legal rights and privileges." He gestured toward some benches. "You are welcome to exchange rings and kiss while waiting for your documents."

Antonio pulled Mabel into another kiss, a heaviness washing away and everything feeling airy. Mabel rested her hand on the back of his head and wrapped her arm around him as she pressed even harder against him.

"Over to the benches please," the clerk said. "Others are waiting."

Antonio kept his lips locked with Mabel's as they shifted over to the waiting area. He felt a greater freedom in kissing her than before and urges he'd long fought against rushed through his mind.

The lie was gone, replaced by a far sweeter truth.

"Lieutenant and 'Madame' Cortez," the clerk shouted.

Antonio kept Mabel's hand in his as he went to the desk and received the marriage certificate. He paid the fee and led Mabel into the hallway.

Handing the certificate to her, Antonio grinned. "I can't think of a better wedding gift."

"I can," Mabel bumped her hip against his and let out a laugh.

Antonio's eyebrows rose, but he couldn't hide his smile.

Mabel's gaze softened and tears came to her eyes as she stared at the certificate. Looking up at him, she whispered, "This is real, isn't it? This office isn't some front and this isn't a forgery?"

"If you had led me here, I'd suspect it was a front," he said with a laugh. He raised her hand holding the ring and kissed it. "But, Mabel, this is real."

He let go of her hand, but she moved her palm to his cheek as she looked into his eyes.

"I would give so much to go back and stop myself from lying about us to my parents." Her hand shifted down his cheek before caressing his neck and then resting on his shoulder. "But I'm so glad to be here."

He put his arm around her as they began walking. He kissed the side of her forehead before whispering, "Happy wedding day, Señora Cortez."

CHAPTER 20

In Which Mabel Duels
for Antonio's Future

The first three hours of their marriage were spent walking the markets to keep their minds off what was to be. Once they joined the other officers of his ship for dinner in a long dining room looking out over the water, Antonio couldn't help feeling both giddy and impatient.

As Mabel dazzled the crowd of naval officers, her hand rested comfortably on Antonio's leg. He sat rubbing her back, longing for dinner to be over and to be alone with her.

Antonio nearly leapt up as Admiral Guerrero excused the dinner table, but his heart fell as the admiral pointed at Antonio and Mabel. "Lieutenant and Señora Cortez, could you wait a minute? I'd like to share a drink."

Antonio silently prayed Mabel's intent had changed as he pressed his sweating palms to his legs. However, he doubted it.

Once the other officers were gone, he remained standing. "Señor, I don't know if you heard, but we registered our marriage with the Castallan Naval Office today, even doing the ceremony again, so the marriage is official in Castallar."

Admiral Guerrero glanced at Mabel and chuckled. "Was the original certificate forged?"

"Were the replacement silver candlesticks you sent to Port Harako actually pewter and covered in silver foil?" She smiled warmly.

Antonio's heart sank further, yet Admiral Guerrero grinned, enjoying the challenge.

"Which arm of our lady's work are you part of?" the admiral said.

"None." Her grin broadened. "As long as we deliver the goods asked for, all is well, isn't it?"

Admiral Guerrero chuckled as he poured port into a glass. He gestured at Antonio. "And was he a good to be delivered or a payment?"

"He was the prize of a bounty."

The admiral huffed a laugh. "I thought the boy was innocent in all this. He's always been too honest." He raised his glass to Mabel. "So, you are the mastermind?"

"Think of me as a negotiator." Mabel leaned against the table and winked at the admiral. "You can see what a fine slice of man my husband is. I'm troubled I only get one night with him. I've heard Castallan Naval policy gives him a whole week off once he's married."

Admiral Guerrero waved his hand. "That's a courtesy rarely given."

Mabel pouted like a disappointed child. "Even for a girl lonely for her young husband?"

Antonio tried not to frown. This was very far from Mabel's true nature. She'd more likely knock over such a girl for being so pathetic.

"I like you, Señora Cortez." Admiral Guerrero gestured with his tumbler. "But I've need of your husband a while yet. There'll be no leave."

"Not even the month he is owed?"

"It's all right, Mabel." Antonio kept his hand on her arm. "He'll provide it."

"Your charm's enough for me to extend my stay here in port by one more night," Admiral Guerrero said. "You are welcome to enjoy that with your husband. But his leave must wait."

"I find that far past disappointing." Mabel reached in her pocket. Antonio frowned as she lifted a vial of glowing liquid. Admiral Guerrero's face paled. "But, while I wait, what if the amber syrup my crew borrowed this morning from your quarters wasn't returned? Wouldn't you find that disappointing? And wouldn't your buyers be disappointed too?"

The admiral held his hand out to her. "Young lady, I am a powerful man. I suggest not threatening me."

"Like you threatened my husband, his mother, and myself?" Mabel raised her eyebrows.

Antonio watched her, both impressed by her and terrified for her. He gripped her arm, part of him wanting to drag her from the room. But he needed to be patient and pray she knew what she was doing. She had said merfolk were real. There had to be something he wasn't seeing.

Admiral Guerrero's smile was cruel. "I've many more threats I can make, Señora Cortez."

"I know." Mabel rolled the vial toward him. He caught it and held it as if precious. "We can play a game of threats, or we can make a profit off each other."

Admiral Guerrero barked a laugh. "What does a young girl like you have to offer?"

"Open sea travel across merfolk waters." She smiled. "Including Marveth."

"Marveth?" Admiral Guerrero said. "Those are dangerous waters ruled by the High Witch Randala."

"She doesn't particularly like me, but I do have a contract for trading goods with her clan."

"Mabel," Antonio breathed, "what are you doing?"

Her eyes were steady as she glanced at him. "I'm negotiating your future."

Facing Admiral Guerrero, she said, "There is an interesting warehouse in Port Harako that I suspect you would deny any knowledge of, but has many goods which were, shall we say, left off ship manifests. I have some goods I need shipped to merfolk clans. This warehouse has connections to smugglers who are familiar with such waters. For the right price, and for free passage of my goods, I could let your ships have shorter paths through dangerous waters."

Antonio sat in a chair on the side of the room and folded his arms. He had to trust Mabel. These were waters she knew better how to navigate. However, he would watch and protect her if he needed.

"Do you have proof?" the admiral said.

Mabel lifted a music box smaller than the palm of her hand from her handbag. "My contract with the Perakan Clan."

She handed it to Admiral Guerrero. He analyzed it before twisting the knob. Instead of music, voices played along with images on the glass top of the small box. Antonio felt the same tingle of magic along his neck as he did when using his own magic to sew.

Passing the music box back to Mabel, the admiral bore a new respect in his eyes. "What's your price?"

From a longer pocket hidden in her dress, Mabel pulled two sets of contracts. "This is for the shipping contract. This is for my husband's commission. I want him to have an honorable discharge in six months. Four of those months, he will be on the leave he is owed."

"He's only owed five weeks, including your sweet honeymoon."

"Your smuggling ships will travel nearly twice as fast. How many more trips can be taken? More trips equals more profits, doesn't it?"

Admiral Guerrero scratched his second layer of chin. "A negotiation then? Since this involves merfolk magic, I request a Tratar con Espada."

"First cut gets an extra request?" Mabel said.

Admiral Guerrero nodded. "I win, any leave he gains will be only taken at the end of his term of service."

"I win, and he gets his first set of leave starting tonight."

"Agreed." He smirked as he unsheathed his officer's sword. "I am an expert swordsman, by the way. Trained by the best masters when I was a young officer."

Mabel glanced at him, unimpressed. "You should meet the woman who trains me."

Antonio rose, his hand on his own sword. "What are you doing?"

Mabel stepped to his side and pressed a small, pearl pin on her hat. Antonio jumped as a haze cascaded over her clothing and her outfit transformed to a white shirt, burgundy vest, tailored trousers and calf-length boots.

"Wondrous!" the admiral said. "How does that work?"

"It's merfolk magic." She touched another pin on her hat. Antonio shouted as her outfit transformed into a black and red evening gown. Though he was bewildered, his eyes tracked the line of her exposed shoulders and the low but modest cut of the bodice.

She tapped his chin, raising his gaze to meet her eyes before she gave him a wink. Antonio swallowed, pushing back thoughts better left for when they were finally alone. With a tap of the pin, she transformed her clothes back to the trousers outfit. Antonio touched the sleeve of her fabric. It was wholly real and complemented her slim figure well.

"So many outfits hidden in a single pearl?" He wanted to ask a thousand questions on how the magic worked and how each outfit was crafted, but now was not the time. Not with Admiral Guerrero standing in a fencer's stance, waiting for Mabel to fight him.

"When striding into danger, one must look their best." Mabel winked, a clever glint in her eye, before kissing him. He stood stiff, not expecting this. However, as she stepped back, she pulled his rapier from its sheath.

"No." He reached for the blade, but she moved away.

"I am negotiating and must be the one who fights."

"Mabel, this has gone far enough. Let this go, and we can leave and just enjoy tonight, and—"

"She has already committed dear boy," Admiral Guerrero said. "By merfolk law, she must see this through."

Holding the flat of the blade parallel to her face, Mabel said, "I fight for you, my love, and our future. I will not lose."

Antonio raised his arms. "And I'm just to stand here and do nothing?"

"You are one of the commodities on the table." Admiral Guerrero chuckled as he slashed his sword before holding it at the ready. "Shall we, Señora Cortez?"

Mabel jumped lightly onto the table before dropping down to the other side in the wide area where servants typically stood during dinner. Standing in a proper fencing pose, her ice-blue eyes determined, Mabel said, "Let us dance, Admiral."

Antonio's fist clenched as the admiral charged toward Mabel like a raging bull, sword raised. Mabel caught his first swipe with her blade and deftly pivoted out of his way. Guerrero huffed as he fought to slow the momentum of his bulk.

Mabel turned on the ball of her foot and met his next few blows. "Six months of leave, no charge for shipping, and one year remaining in his commission, including his leave."

Admiral Guerrero's swipes were slower but carried far more force than Mabel's light, precise movements. "Four weeks leave, eighty percent cost for shipping, and the full three years."

"Five months leave, no charge for shipping, and one year remaining."

The battle of prices and blades sped along, Admiral Guerrero barely lowering his offer while his movement was lumbering yet strong. Mabel raised her offer incrementally while dodging and dancing around the admiral. Antonio pressed his hand to the dagger on his right hip, wanting to dive into the fight and push the admiral back. Especially as Admiral Gurerro's blade made a swipe nearly nicking Mabel's neck.

She leaned back and he swiped at her legs. She launched into a backward somersault before leaping onto the table. Admiral Guerrero grunted as he stabbed at her calf. She kicked away his blade before grabbing the chandelier with one hand and using it to swing her feet into his chest. He oofed as he knocked against the serving counter and fell.

He tried to roll to his feet, but his girth kept him from being able to fully turn. Mabel jumped down, landing with her foot on his rapier. She held the point of her blade to his third chin.

"Ten percent shipping. Four months leave. One year of service remaining, starting at the end of leave." She flicked her rapier, nicking his skin. "The leave starting tonight. Will that do?"

Admiral Guerrero held a hand to the small cut. "And he returns to my ship. I want an eye on my asset."

Mabel flicked her blade, cutting off a button on his uniform. "I don't think you're in a position to ask for anything more."

"I could call the guards." He held up his hand. "Do we have an agreement, Señora Cortez?"

Mabel looked to Antonio. "It's your future, my love. Is that agreeable for you?"

Antonio stared, surprised he was even asked anything. Still, he had to take the opportunity. "What of threats to my family? Including my mother and wife?"

Admiral Guerrero raised his palms. "Gone. As if they had never been."

"Antonio, do you agree?" Mabel said.

He held a hand to his head, watching her.

There, she stood, leaving him with more than a thousand questions, yet she had kept her promise. She had freed him from the trap she had locked him in.

A warmth swelled his breast. He had a lot to learn about his new wife and her dealings with merfolk, but he was proud of her.

He bowed his head. "You have negotiated well, Mabel. I agree."

She took the admiral's hand and shook it. Antonio had to join her to help pull the admiral and his girth to his feet. Admiral Guerrero's face was red from the exertion, and he sweated terribly. Still, the adjustments were made to the contracts, signatures signed, and everything was done.

"Are you sure you don't want to serve our lady?" Admiral Guerrero handed Mabel her copy of the contracts. "You've a sharp mind."

"While I must deal with some questionable associates, I am trying to build an honest and independent business."

"Are you taking investors?"

Mabel leaned toward him. "Not from anyone associated with Madame Blue."

Antonio's eyes narrowed. He had heard the name in whispers through thin walls and doors while standing watch for Admiral Guerrero's business dealings. The name was often said with a small edge of fear.

Admiral Guerrero grunted as he scratched his nose. "My work's made me quite powerful and rich, but, if I could go back, I'd tell a young officer the same advice."

Antonio scowled. "You've been trying to recruit me since I was promoted."

"You've never been more than a patsy, Lieutenant Cortez," Admiral Guerrero said with a laugh. "Someone for me to load a crime on if an investigation gets too close." He nodded to Mabel. "The boy's lucky he has you."

"I'm the one who is fortunate, señor." Mabel's gaze was firm.

She tossed Antonio his rapier. As he sheathed it, she touched one of the pearl pins on her hat and her outfit returned to the dark green one she had been wearing all day.

The admiral nodded to her with respect. "Congratulations on your marriage, Señora Cortez." He glared at Antonio and sneered. "Enjoy your leave, lieutenant."

A slow smile formed on Antonio's face.

He had made it on leave. Standing proudly, he took Mabel's arm, leading- her from the room and into the hallway.

While part of him wanted to hurry to his room to enjoy being alone with his wife, he took his time as he whispered, "What if he goes back on the deal?"

"Merfolk have very strict rules on fulfilling contracts," Mabel whispered back as they walked down the hall. "Since we have sealed it with a merfolk custom, it would be too dangerous for him to break the contract."

He gripped her hand. "I don't understand this world of magic and merfolk, but, for my sake, be careful."

"I always am." Her thumb caressed the back of his hand. "And, if I were ever in danger, I'm sure you would come as soon as you could."

"I'd kick every door down I had to." He scratched his forehead. "Though, you'd probably have convinced your captors that you've actually captured them by the time I arrive."

"I hope I don't have the opportunity." She gave him a long kiss, a deep tenderness in it. Pulling her lips from his, she said, "Shall we go, my dear husband?"

His chest felt warm. "My room's this way."

"Actually, I had your trunk sent to my ship." She kept her face close to his. "There, we can stay in as long as we wish."

"When did you arrange that?" he said.

She played with the collar of his uniform. "While you were buying the silk nightgown at the dress shop."

He grinned. "I'm always going to be at least a step behind you, aren't I?"

"I'll always let you catch up." She tousled a lock of his dark hair. "Shouldn't we be going so you can help me into my new nightgown?"

"Gladly." He gave her a quick kiss before taking her arm.

As they stepped out of the officer's hall and onto the wharf, he put his arm around her waist and held her tight against his side. With the moonlight shining down, he grinned.

There was much he had to learn about his wife, but tonight, he was purely happy. He had the woman he loved and a future outside of the Navy. For the first time in a long while, he truly felt free.

Part 2

CHAPTER 21

In Which Antonio Returns Home

Dorona, Castallar

Antonio polished the buttons of his lieutenant's uniform as he admired Mabel's silhouette. She stood in her corset and undergarments next to the closet far larger than it should be, even for most mansions. It was even stranger with it sitting inside the captain's quarters on a ship. Though, the quarters on this strange ship were also far larger than they should be.

"I was thinking one of these travel dresses." Mabel held up a light blue dress followed by a maroon one.

Antonio leaned into the closet and surveyed the row of ball gowns. He smiled wryly. "What of one of those?"

"Based on what you wrote to me of your mother's shop, I'd look ridiculous," Mabel said. "Besides, those are paid for by my investor and are for conducting business."

"Mother would adore you, no matter what you wear." He kissed her shoulder.

A rare nervousness betrayed itself in her eyes. "I don't think I'm what she's expecting in a daughter-in-law."

Antonio laughed. "You're not what I was expecting in a wife."

"I thought you always wanted to marry a reformed pirate who conducts business with merfolk." She turned to the side to check her profile and held the dresses against herself.

"I prefer pickpockets who prey on innocent, young sailors." He lightly tapped her hip and Mabel jumped before grinning as she turned and hit his arm.

"Are you going to help me or tease me?"

"I'll never stop teasing you." He kissed her. "La Ratera."

The kiss extended, but she pulled away. "We should actually leave the room today."

He grinned. "We left it for some fresh air a few times yesterday. And at least once the day before."

"I thought you wanted to go home."

"I do, but my wife is distractingly beautiful, and I've only four months left before spending a year apart from her. Do you blame me for losing focus?"

She smiled warmly. "No, but your mother has been waiting two years. I'm sure you can spare some time for her."

"I suppose I should," he teased. The past few days of his honeymoon with Mabel had been better than he had ever hoped, but he longed to see his mother and sisters.

Taking the dresses from her, he said, "And neither of these are right. Your red hair and pale complexion are already going to draw stares. For today, I recommend blending in as much as you can." He hung the dresses back in the closet before pulling out a white blouse with a ruffled front, a long black skirt, and a dark green, high-waisted jacket. "You'll still be stunning, but your clothes will match the locals better."

She eyed his selection as he held it out to her. Looking at him, she said, "I suppose if I've asked you to trust me after I've stolen your pocketbook and your rapier, I should trust you in return."

"Only if I've earned it."

Worry returned to her eyes. "Antonio, after everything, have I?"

"I'm taking you to meet my mother, aren't I?" He kissed her cheek. "I would not be your husband or be bringing you home if I did not trust you."

She rested her hand on his chest and smiled as her blue eyes met his. "I love you, Antonio."

"I love you, thief of my heart," he whispered before kissing her. He put an arm around her, pulling her closer as if to anchor her from floating away. They did need to go visit his family, but he could spare a few more minutes alone with this beautiful woman.

At least a half-hour later, Antonio waved off Mabel's crew as they whistled and cheered at the young couple, just as they had every time the pair had emerged from her quarters the past few days. In the conversations and dinners with the crew, he could see why Mabel loved these former pirates who had rescued her from a merfolk lair. Especially as Captain Stenton kept grinning at her like a proud father, trying to hide his tears of joy behind his gruff demeanor.

Standing on the ramp, Antonio breathed in the sea air, the scent of the fish market mixing with the ocean and other smells. He grinned and looked to Mabel. "Welcome to Dorona."

Her gaze scanned the white-washed houses and ramshackle shanties and then the finer mansions deeper in the seaside city. "It's a home to be proud of."

He found himself puffing up his chest as he led Mabel down the ramp to the dock.

"Stripes!" one of the crewmen shouted from the ship. "Quick question before you go."

She touched Antonio's arm before walking back up the ramp and calling, "This had better not be you teasing me again, Gregson."

Antonio chuckled as he placed his polished boots on the dock and strolled ahead as he sought a familiar face among the dockworkers.

Most of his friends worked in the shanty shops, but some might be out here.

"Antonio!"

He stood stiff as a blur in a white dress ran toward him before throwing her arms around him and kissing him.

"My darling lieutenant," Sofia whispered. "I never thought you'd return."

He tried to push her off, but she had the hold of an octopus around his neck. Even with his strength, she grasped on.

"Papa forced me to accept Guillermo's proposal." She kissed his cheek. "We married two weeks ago, but, my love, my heart has always been yours. Always."

Out of the corner of his eye, Antonio saw the glint of a blade just before the point of a rapier pressed against Sofia's neck.

"You will take your hands off my husband," Mabel growled.

Sofia released him and backed away, her eyes wide with fear.

"Sofia," Antonio said. "This is my wife, Mabel Sinclair Cortez of Barthan."

"So, you are the Sofia who stopped writing him when he was at sea?" Mabel held her rapier pointed at Sofia, her glare cold, though Antonio caught the wink of humor in her eyes.

"I got all of your letters," Sofia said, her eyes desperate. "But it was so hard to read them and think how miserable you were, and—"

"Mabel, Sofia married a few weeks ago," Antonio said. "Isn't that wonderful news?"

Mabel raised her eyebrow as she prodded the loose fabric around Sofia's stomach, betraying where Sofia's pregnant belly protruded. It was only a few months along, but the evidence clear. Mabel smiled coldly. "Congratulations to all three of you."

Sofia's face paled, her eyes focusing on the blade, tears falling down her cheeks. "I only was with Guillermo because I missed you, and—things got out of hand, but, Antonio, it is you I've always—"

She stopped as Mabel pressed the point of her sword against

Sofia's chin.

"We have all made our choices." Mabel lowered the blade. "I hope you are happy with yours."

Tears welled in Sofia's eyes before she ran down the dock.

"You didn't need to terrify her," Antonio said quietly.

Mabel handed him a handkerchief. "There are some lipstick marks."

His face felt warm as he wiped at his lips and cheek. "I tried to push her off."

"I know." Mabel pressed the point of her rapier against the dock and held one finger on the hilt. "Any other former girls you've courted?"

"A few short romances, but I thought Sofia was the love of my life when I left." He looked to her. "I was extremely wrong about that."

Mabel gave him an assessing glance before grabbing the rapier's hilt and turning toward her ship. "Paulson!"

The large man leaned over the side of the ship.

"Thank you for the assistance." She tossed the rapier up to him and he caught it by the hilt before saluting her with the sword.

"I hope you don't have use for the pistol, Stripes," he called.

Antonio's eyes widened and he eyed Mabel's skirt while prodding along her thigh and the folds of her ruffled shirt. There was at least one knife.

"Mabel, who are you planning to rob?" he said.

"It's always wise to be prepared." She pulled the pistol from her waistband. "Paulson keeps it loaded with blank shots. It would merely scare off another girl who came too close."

"You are not carrying a pistol into my mother's home."

She eyed him, before turning to the ship and holding up the pistol for Paulson to see before setting it on a crate by the ramp.

"And the knife."

Mabel grunted before turning away from the main dock and lifting her skirt before pulling out a dagger from its sheath along her thigh, followed by at least three knives.

"I'm keeping one," she said. "Just in case."

"And how big is that one?" He leaned as he looked at her skirt. "And do you have a cannon in there too?"

"Habits from piracy," she muttered, "and negotiating with merfolk."

He rubbed his forehead before breaking out in a laugh and taking her hand. "Come. I'm both terrified and excited for you to meet my mother."

As they walked through the narrow path between shanty shops, Mabel grinned at the rich smell of spices and food along with the colorfully painted window shutters and fronts. It was nearly as vibrant as Willington, yet with an everyday simplicity making it feel like home.

"This is La Dulce's." Antonio pointed at the shop with dozens of candies in jars, crowded by children. "When I was a niño, Papa would sometimes take my sisters and me here. He'd buy the cinnamon sticks and then we'd stroll along the wharf as we ate them."

Mabel smiled, her heart warm as she watched the joy in Antonio's eyes as he pointed to another shop.

"And there's the toy shop. I saved up my pennies to buy their wooden figures. I had this little tiger which was my favorite. I'd run around Mama's shop with it and roar at my sisters, and they'd giggle as they ran, pretending to be scared."

Mabel laughed and she ran her thumb over his. His eyes were bright as he took in all of the shops and the crowd going about their daily business.

"When we met," she said, "you claimed you left your heart with Sofia, but I think you were mistaken."

He glanced at her and smiled. "It's clear I was."

"I think Sofia was just a symbol of this place for you." She gestured around them as they walked in a quieter part of the street. "I think this is what your heart was really longing for."

He put his arm around her waist. "It is wonderful, isn't it? The life and warmth. I've missed it every day, but—" He kissed her cheek. "Not as much as I missed you between letters."

A sadness washed through her. "I've never asked you where you want to live, in the long term."

"Not in the trap of a cottage your parents bought," he said. "But I thought your base of business was in Willington? I often thought, if I ever got free of the Navy, that I'd join your life there."

"You would do that for me?"

Antonio gave her a surprised look. "Of course. Why wouldn't I? Besides, it's Willington! It's a city brimming with fashion and life." He raised a finger. "And I've been practicing Barthanian."

He stood straighter and said in a thick accent that muddied the words, "Where esta de train?"

Mabel frowned at him. "Did you say, 'where is the train?'"

He nodded proudly. "I know the accent needs work, but I understand most words when I hear them. By the time I've finished with the Navy, I hope to speak almost fluently."

"We'll work on the pronunciation over the next few months." She kissed his cheek and leaned against him as they continued walking.

Giggling children ran past as a mother called for them down the street. Mabel looked at Antonio's warm eyes and his comfortable smile.

The moment broke as a trumpet played a few notes from a balcony ahead and a man a few years older than Antonio leaned out. "Is that El Emperador Antonio?"

"Esteban!" Antonio shouted and waved in greeting. "Come! Meet La Empresa!"

"'El Emperador'?" she said as Esteban disappeared inside.

"Of anyone, you should understand the importance of dressing well," Antonio said. "I always looked my best, so my friends decided I dressed as an emperador."

More cries of 'El Emperador' filled the street and a crowd gathered. Mabel felt as if Antonio were introducing her to a hundred people at once.

"Step back, step back," Antonio said. "I still haven't seen my mother yet."

Mabel grinned as they pushed through, nearly everyone trying to hug her and Antonio. They reached a small opening in front of a worn building with beautifully made clothing hanging outside.

"Antonito!" a woman a few years older than Antonio burst out of the shop and ran to him, her dress stretched over her round belly carrying a child.

"Juanita!" Antonio embraced his half-sister and kissed her cheek. He moved to try to introduce Mabel, but another woman a few years older with a one-year-old carried in a pack on her back ran to him and held him. Given her similar looks to Juanita, this had to be his oldest half-sister, Luisa.

Wiping tears from her cheeks, Juanita said, "You wrote you weren't able to come home. What happened?"

"Where is Mama?"

The answer came as a woman exited the shop's door, her brown skin tanned by years in the sun and with gray hairs among her near-black hair. She was a woman who worked for a living, but still had signs of her youth's beauty.

She sobbed as she held her arms out and Antonio ran to his mother. He joined her sobs as he held her, and Mabel wiped her own tears from her cheeks. He wrote often of his mother, and it was clear there was great love between them.

Luisa looked at Mabel and broke into a grin before prodding Juanita.

"Have you met Antonio's empresa?" Esteban said as he nudged

Mabel forward.

Unsure how to greet them, Mabel held out her hands. Luisa squealed as she grabbed Mabel's left hand and looked at the ring before pulling her into an embrace.

"You must be Mabel." Luisa stepped back and looked at her. "You're exactly as he described you in every letter the last few months."

Mabel found herself grinning in return. Juanita pulled her into an embrace and kissed her cheek. "Welcome to the family, Señora Cortez. I'm sorry you had to settle for Antonito, but we're glad to have you."

"He's not written as much about you," Mabel said with a laugh, "but, his letters made clear how much he missed you."

"Not like he missed you." Luisa put her arm around Mabel and Juanita joined her. Putting a dramatic hand to her chest, Luisa said, "'Oh, how clever her smile is.'"

"'Her words make me feel like she's next to me,'" Juanita said just as dramatically before laughing. She pinched Mabel's shoulder. "I'm so glad he chose you over that snip, Sofia."

Mabel chuckled. "I'm glad he chose me too."

"Watch out for that one," Luisa said. "He was gone only three months before I went to drop off his latest letter and caught sight of her kissing another young man on the docks."

Mabel stared at her. "What did you do?"

"Gave her the letter, because that is what Antonio wanted, and told her to tell him it was ended. Then, I told Mama."

Juanita giggled. "You should have seen her! I went with her to try to stop her, but Mama was more furious than a hurricane. Sofia was in the yard of her parents' pretty little house, and Mama threw both her shoes at the girl and said—" She made her face stern and wagged her finger. "'You stop writing my son. And when he comes home, you stay away from him, or I'll strike you worse.'"

Mabel's eyebrows rose. "Remind me not to cross your Mama."

"Oh, she's sweet on you." Luisa bumped Mabel's shoulder. "His letters were getting rather gloomy till you started writing him and sending packages." She smiled warmly. "In a way, Mabel, we think you saved him."

Mabel decided not to mention she had put him in danger. Carefully, she said, "Did he tell you how he got the lieutenant's commission?"

"He said it was from some merit he earned for helping an admiral." Juanita grinned proudly. "He's always had a good, honest heart. I'm glad the Navy rewarded him."

Mabel nodded, marking the version Antonio had shared. For how honest he was, he had learned to obscure the truth nearly as well as she had. For him, though, it was clear he was sparing his family any confusion or pain.

She was grateful Antonio had forgiven her and that she had succeeded changing the contract with the admiral.

"I think they're ready." Luisa held an excited grin while nudging Mabel forward.

Mabel's nerves grew as she approached her new mother-in-law. Antonio stood with his arm around his mother and held his hand out to her.

"Mama," he said with a broad grin, his eyes full of tenderness, "this is my wife, Mabel Sinclair Cortez. Mabel, this is my mother, Leticia Cortez."

Leticia closed the gap between them and threw her arms around her. "You sweet girl, he found you."

Mabel stood stiffly as Leticia gave her cheeks about a dozen kisses in greeting and her strong arms squeezed her. Antonio chuckled, his own smile proud.

"You love my niño, don't you?" Leticia whispered. "I could tell from his letters."

"I love him more than my own life," Mabel said. Those words were true.

"I do too." Leticia stepped back and held her hands on Mabel's shoulders. "You're a touch thinner than I'd like, but we'll get some good food in you." She looked to Luisa. "Go to the market. See if Rosita can host us for a good feast tonight. Tell her my boy's brought home his bride."

"Of course, Mama."

Leticia frowned as she squeezed Mabel's shoulder and then bicep. Mabel stood still, holding her smile for Antonio's sake.

"That's firmer muscle than I'd expect in a fine lady like yourself," Leticia said.

"I try to exercise regularly." Mabel didn't mention she went on a daily run and how often she practiced fencing and other combat with Isabella or the crew of her ship.

"I knew I liked you ever since he sent the photograph of you kissing his cheek." Leticia pointed at Mabel. "One look and I said, 'There's a girl with real courage.'"

Mabel's nerves relaxed as Leticia took her hand. "Come, come."

She took Antonio's hand too and they went upstairs. Mabel tried not to gape at how cramped the living space was. It was smaller than the magically enhanced closet and captain's quarters on her ship.

Leticia opened a closet and there lay a cot below a set of suits and shelves of linens and towels.

"I left everything as it was," she said. "Though, now that Juanita's married to Paulo, her room's open. You can stay there while you're here." She glanced at Mabel, and her smile fell. "Though, I'm not sure it's right for so fine a lady."

"Your home is lovely," Mabel said, "and feels so warm. Antonio's told me how happy he was growing up here."

Leticia smiled proudly. "His papa and I tried to raise him right." She reached over and rubbed his arm. "And look at him. A lieutenant. Manuel would be so proud."

"I'm a tailor first, Mama." He glanced at Mabel as he began unbuttoning his officer's coat. Pointing at the clothing in the closet, he said, "Those are second-hand suits I altered myself."

Mabel reached in and pulled a suitcoat out. The hem lines and interior work were precise and clean, with no signs of changes. She frowned. "How did you change it?"

"He took it all apart, cut it to fit his frame, and then stitched it back together." Leticia squinted as she leaned closer and pointed to the hem inside the wrist cuff and tsked. "This one's a bit sloppy."

"No one's looking inside the wrist of a suitcoat." Antonio pulled off his military coat and set it on a chair before stretching his arms. "It's about how it looks on the man."

He began to pull on the suitcoat but stopped as the sleeves got stuck on his upper arms and shoulders. Mabel held her hand over her mouth to hide her laugh, but Leticia giggled and prodded Antonio's stomach.

"You've been a sailor and you've broadened into manhood." She leaned back and assessed him. "I'd guess you've grown at least another inch."

Antonio grunted as he yanked off the coat and hung it back up before pulling out another. This one had stylized flowers embroidered across the back and patterns tracing the shoulders and seam of the sleeve. It was a stunning jacket and had to have taken endless hours of work, even with Antonio's magic.

He grunted as he shimmied it over his upper arms and then over his shoulders. The chest area stretched, and it was clear the jacket was at least three fingers' breadths too tight to ever close. Antonio tried to bring his arms forward, but the sleeves blocked them as it pulled on his shoulders.

"This was my favorite coat," he muttered.

"He wore it out to go dancing almost every day for two years," Leticia said. "As he walked through the market, I always knew where he was as his friends shouted, 'El Emperador!'"

"Then they'd ask me to do embroidery on their clothes." Antonio smiled even as he tried to wriggle out of the coat. "Made good money off the work."

"That he then spent on that fish soup Sofia," Leticia said. "Has she chased after him yet today?"

Antonio gave Mabel a small shake of his head.

Mabel grinned. "She greeted him at the docks while I had stepped away. Once I turned around, there she was, kissing him."

Leticia gasped. "That little rat."

"He looked about as trapped as he is in that jacket," Mabel said. Antonio glared at her as he tried to bend his arm out of the sleeve. "But I held a blade on her to remind her who he's married to, and she scampered off."

Leticia chuckled with satisfaction. "My son chose well."

She gestured toward the small sitting area. "Come, tell me of yourself and your wedding."

"Will one of you help me?" Antonio said through gritted teeth, his arms now stuck behind him.

Leticia eyed him before winking at Mabel and waving her hand at Antonio. "You let a woman other than your wife kiss you. You can get out of your own trap."

"I didn't!" Antonio grunted and finally got one of the sleeves down far enough he could pull it the rest of the way off. "Mabel, tell her."

"I'm not sure what happened," Mabel said with false innocence, returning Leticia's wink. "Except that I found you in the arms of another woman."

Antonio slapped the coat down on the chair. "I was trying to push her off. Why'd I ever want anyone besides Mabel?"

Leticia broke into a giggle first and Mabel's composure fell as she laughed. Antonio rested his hands on his hips.

"I am gone for two years, and I return to have my wife and mother conspire against me." He attempted a glare at Mabel, but his smile broke the illusion.

Antonio crossed to the couch where Mabel sat across from his mother. "Though, I did lie to you, Mama." He leaned down and kissed

Mabel's cheek quickly before saying with a teasing growl, "This is no Empresa. She is La Ratera."

"Innocent girls are far less fun," Leticia said. "I'd much rather have a thief for a daughter-in-law."

Mabel laughed harder, grinning at her mother-in-law. Antonio sat beside her on the couch, his arm around her as they answered his mother's many questions. Juanita and Luisa soon joined the tight space. Antonio tried to look offended and not laugh at the embarrassing stories his sisters shared. Each one made Mabel love him just a bit more.

As she and Antonio retold how they met, the three other women wore sentimental smiles. Together, Mabel and Antonio skipped over the false marriage, focusing instead on their reconnection via letter, and then claiming Mabel had arranged her schedule to meet him at port on the day he started his leave.

Antonio pulled from his satchel their real marriage certificate and Mabel gripped his hand tighter, grateful this was now the truth.

Leticia ran her fingers over the certificate. "You two deserve a proper wedding."

"We're just glad to be married," Mabel said.

"That is far past true." Antonio rubbed her back.

Leticia laughed before looking at them. "Maybe I'm being selfish, but I'd like to give you a proper celebration. If you can stay a week, I think we can manage something small."

"My in-laws still have some of the decorations from my wedding," Juanita said. "And she can borrow my dress."

"I'm a seamstress. She'll have a new dress."

"I can talk to Rosita and my mother-in-law," Luisa said. "We might be able to get the food on time." She looked to Juanita. "And there's the band Paulo's brother is in."

"This is beginning to not sound very small," Antonio said. "I don't want this to be a burden, and—"

Leticia smiled slyly at him before opening a sliding door on the small sitting table and pulled out a rusty tin box. She struggled with the lid a moment before opening it and removing a large bundle of cash. Mabel's eyes widened.

"Mama." Antonio gave a chiding look. "That's the money I sent home, isn't it?"

"It is, and it's going to be used for your wedding."

"It is for you, Mama. To use as you need, and to take care of you when you get older."

"The three of you will take care of me, if needed." She squeezed his arm. "You're the one who's sweat and bled at sea to earn this. Why not celebrate your beautiful wife?"

Mabel's face felt warm under Antonio's gaze, and he whispered, "You do deserve a proper celebration." He looked to his mother and raised a finger. "But not all of it, Mama. Keep some, just in case."

"I'll remember that." She reached in the tin and pulled out a velvet bag. "You don't have to use these, but they served me and your papa well."

She poured out on her palm a man and woman's ring. Holding out the woman's ring to Mabel, Leticia said, "I always felt it was too fine for a seamstress like me, but I think it's just right for a lady like you."

Mabel wiped tears from her cheeks as she stared at the gold band, the top widening into an elegant scallop with delicate diamonds embedded, almost like a starry night.

"I would be honored to wear this." Mabel smiled.

"Do you mind if we start wearing these now?" Antonio held up his hand, showing his steel ring. "My ring is standard issue from the Navy and hers—" He frowned. "Where did you get yours?"

"My mother bought it from a local store when—" Mabel sorted through the lie she needed to give. "When I told my parents you and I planned to marry. It doesn't mean much."

"Go on." Leticia nodded. "They are yours, Antonio."

He took the woman's ring from his mother's hand while Mabel lifted the man's gold ring with small waves engraved in white gold. She pulled off her ring from their false marriage and he removed his. She flexed her fingers before sliding the men's ring onto his.

Her heart pounded as she held out her own hand. Their eyes met as he slid the ring on her finger. It would need to be sized a little smaller, but it felt right and added to the fire within her. It wasn't an out-of-control blaze, but it was like a steady hearth's fire and flared with every pulse as she focused on his brown eyes.

"Do you two need some privacy?" Luisa said with a small laugh.

"Yes." Antonio swallowed.

"We'll be fine," Mabel said, though the way she wanted to kiss him was far from appropriate in front of his sisters and mother. Nor anyone else, really.

"Mm-hmm." Juanita's voice was skeptical. "Except, I doubt you're likely to notice anyone else in the room for a while."

"I never do when she's near." Antonio's smile sent a tingle down Mabel's chest.

Forcing herself to break his gaze, but grateful she was married to this man, she turned toward his sisters. "Luisa, you have two children, don't you?"

As Luisa spoke proudly of her children, Mabel ran her thumb over the gold ring. She felt as if it had always belonged to her, waiting for her to find Antonio.

Keeping her hand clasped with Antonio's, she leaned against him and listened to the sweet stories his family shared. Here, she felt peace, as if finding her true home at last.

CHAPTER 22

In Which Mabel Gains a Monocle

Trumpets rang out alongside the violin and cellos, the singer moving her hips and feet to the salsa beat as her brassy voice sang out over the crowd. Mabel laughed as she tried to move her own hips in rhythm as Antonio spun her, his own hips swinging on a perfect beat. With each shift along her waist, the soft ruffles of her white skirt rippled, moving fluidly. Antonio's white shirt with wide sleeves also swung with his movements.

As the song ended, the crowd clapped and banged their glasses on the tables. They were packed into the garden area transformed into a wedding hall for the night.

Antonio raised his eyebrows in invitation and Mabel giggled as she indulged herself and the crowd by kissing him. Cheers broke out. She wasn't sure her crew or his friends and family were louder, but all competed quite well. Antonio dipped her back and Mabel kicked her leg up, which led to greater cheers.

Rising, Antonio clapped and motioned to the band. "More dancing! This is a celebration!"

Another song played, this one softer, made for a slower dance. Mabel hooked her arms around his shoulders as his hands rested on her hips, the gentle push of his palms helping her follow the rhumba beat.

"Your parents should get back all the money they spent on your dancing lessons," he said.

"In Barthan, women don't have hips," she said. "We are just one straight, elegant line as we waltz."

"What a waste of a beautiful feature." He released her and turned slowly as he rolled his hips, his shoulders moving in sync, creating a smooth motion. When he finished the rotation, he gestured toward her as if challenging her.

She giggled as she attempted to do a similar pivot while rolling her hips, but her movements were far jerkier.

Antonio laughed. "Señora Cortez, you are shaming my family. You are of Castallar now. You must do far better. Here. Let me help."

He came behind her, his hands on her hips as he pressed against her. His body guided hers as they rotated their hips in rhythm together.

"If we want to appall my mother," Mabel said, "we should do this at the reception my parents are planning."

"I'm looking forward to scandalizing your parents." Antonio kissed her neck. His hand drifted to her thigh. "Is that a knife?"

"I only have two on me. Just in case," she whispered.

Antonio chuckled. He took her hand and pulled her into a more formal dance position as the song changed to a faster number. She followed his footsteps as best as she could, wishing she were a better dance partner. He was so smooth and swift but had to slow to help her keep up. At least they had gone dancing the past few nights, giving him a chance to train her.

Another song came to an end, and she said, "Keep dancing if you want. I need to rest a few minutes."

"You are my bride. Why would I be away from you?" He kissed her and the crowd's cheers grew again.

"Because you are having fun."

"I'll at least walk you to our table." He held his hand over his eyes and pretended to scout the crowd. "Don't want anyone trying to steal the most beautiful woman—"

He stood straight. "That woman." He nodded. "Do you recognize her?"

Mabel looked in the direction he indicated. A slight headache formed, and she found herself looking just beyond where he pointed. "Where?"

"The woman alone at the table over there. I don't recognize her." He tilted his head. "How can you not see her? She's dressed to go to an opera gala."

A chill settled over Mabel as she searched the area he was staring at. She felt as if there was something there, but every time she tried to focus on a certain spot, her eyes would drift past. There were several people it could be. One option was good. Others were dangerous.

"Let's go and welcome her," Antonio said.

Walking with him, Mabel slipped her hand in the pocket of her dress and reached through the slit allowing her to remove one of her knives. That was a nice additional feature Leticia had made in the dress at Mabel's request.

Antonio paused at their table and pulled on the bolero jacket he had embroidered the past few days. It was a beautiful work of art and it had been a wonder to watch him work.

They reached an open area shadowed by trees, none of the guests around.

"There's no one here," she whispered. Here, the headache was worse, and her eyes couldn't fully focus.

"Thank you for coming to our wedding," Antonio said with a polite smile to an empty area and held out his hand. "I am, of course, the groom, Lieutenant Antonio Cortez."

"I am here for the bride," came a smooth voice which Mabel would always recognize.

The spell blocking her vision cleared and there appeared Cassandra, sitting at a small wrought iron table. As usual, she was overdressed in an elaborate gown and fine hat. Especially when compared to the shanty town residents and crewmates gathered in their best outfits.

"I am Madame Cassandra Astrellar." She touched the tip of her fingers to Antonio's hand as she gave him an appraising look.

"Antonio, she is my business partner and investor." Mabel smiled.

Antonio's eyebrows pinched together as he stared at Cassandra.

"I'm not as young as I appear." She focused on Antonio. "So, Lieutenant Cortez, which do you prefer? Fake or real marriage?"

Antonio laughed. "Real marriage, Madame, is much better." He kissed Mabel's hand. "Thank you for everything you have done for my dear Mabel. She is a remarkable woman, isn't she?"

"I would not invest in her if she wasn't." Cassandra set her elbow on the armrest. "Do you mind if I borrow your bride?" She waved her fingers, dismissing him. "We can't gossip about you with you standing here."

Antonio laughed before looking to Mabel. "What do you wish?"

"Go dance. I'll join you soon."

He gave her another sweet kiss before nodding to Cassandra and returning to the dance floor. Mabel sat in the chair beside Cassandra's.

"Where is Arturo? I'm surprised he didn't come to see the results of my forged marriage certificate." Mabel grinned.

"He's more than amused and sends his congratulations, as does Isabella." Cassandra's eyes were grave. "But Arturo is not feeling well."

"I'm so sorry. Thank you for taking the time to come."

Cassandra watched the dance floor, assessing the crowd. "You seem surrounded by many kind people who love you and your young husband. Such a treasure is rare."

"I'm very happy tonight."

A soft but sad smile crossed Cassandra's face, a haunted look in her eyes. "Such joy can slip away. Hold onto it tight for as long as you can."

Mabel's own smile fell as she wondered what secrets and tragedies burdened Cassandra from her impossibly long life.

"For example," Cassandra said, her tone lightening, "I imagine this wedding will be far more tolerable than whatever affair your mother is planning."

Mabel laughed. "That will be dull and overdone, but I'll endure it."

"What of your young lieutenant?" Cassandra said. "Does he make you happy?"

"More than happy." Mabel let herself grin, watching as Antonio took Juanita's hand. Though her pregnant belly was round, her steps and hips moved far smoother than Mabel's. "Especially now that our marriage is real."

"He's an intriguing young man. What sort of magic does he have?" Cassandra said.

Mabel glanced at her investor. "He only has a small amount he uses for sewing. How did you know?"

"He saw me before I wanted to be seen." Cassandra focused her gaze on Mabel. "That takes more than a small amount of magic."

Mabel shrugged. "Perhaps there is more, but with all of the magic that I've learned about in the past two years, I'm quite fine if all my husband can do are a few tricks with sewing."

"Simplicity is often something to be admired." Cassandra leaned back and looked at Mabel's dress. "For example, your gown is simple but beautiful."

Mabel beamed. "Isn't it? His mother made it for me." She ran a hand along the stomach area and the small lines of embroidery. "I love it."

"You have every right to. And it is more than clear how much your young man adores you."

Mabel laughed. "That would be impossible to hide."

Cassandra smiled and patted Mabel's hand. She frowned before plucking Mabel's wrist and pulling her ring finger closer. "This is new. Where did you get this ring?"

"It was Antonio's mother's wedding ring." Mabel shifted her finger, letting the diamonds catch the light. "Isn't it beautiful?"

"It would go well with a midnight blue dress of mine." Cassandra leaned closer as she analyzed the band. She pointed with her pinky. "This diamond is actually a crystallized drop of amber syrup, which will amplify the magic of whomever is wearing it."

Mabel's eyebrows rose. "It's a magic ring?"

"Only if you have magic." She tapped her fingers on the table. "Though, if your young lieutenant was holding your hand, his magic might have been amplified. Which could be why he saw me."

Mabel relaxed a little. At least it explained one strange thing.

"Cherish it as a symbol of your bond with the young man." Cassandra pulled a rectangle box from a hidden pocket. "As for my own gift, I was waiting for you to sit down to send it over, and then you would see me. However, you were more enthusiastic about dancing than I counted on."

"Antonio loves dancing," Mabel said with a laugh.

"He is quite good." Cassandra set the box on the table. "Go on. Open it. This is only for you, but it should help you to protect Antonio and your future children."

Mabel frowned as she opened it. Her eyebrows pinched together as she stared at the monocle with a gold rim and matching chain.

"Thank you," she said automatically, wondering why Cassandra was giving her a piece of jewelry usually worn by old men.

"The glass was forged in the Surris Mountains by Illuminators." Cassandra pointed at the monocle. "The spell in the glass allows you to see magic around you. It won't show you the lines of light within magic, like a spectroscope does, but those are more used for looking at details and manipulating spells. This allows you to quickly see an aura around any object or person with magic."

Mabel raised the monocle to her eye and looked at Cassandra. The aura around her was a vibrant turquoise. Looking at her own hand, there was nothing except a bright yellowish light around her ring. She turned toward the crowd. A few people had varying shades of yellow around them while most just had a light dusting of color. Antonio had a similar turquoise color to Cassandra, but it was far less bright.

"I can see where this will be useful in many situations," Mabel said.

"Keep it with you always, just in case," Cassandra said. "Especially with the sorts we have to contract with to deliver the products to the merfolk."

Mabel closed the box and slid it into one of the hidden pockets of her dress. "Thank you, again, for investing so much for me." She smiled warmly. "I hope it will continue being profitable."

"Given your quick wits and determination, I think it will." Cassandra gave her a small, genuine smile before waving her hand, dismissing Mabel. "Go be with your friends and new family. They're likely wondering where the bride is."

Rising, Mabel said, "You are far kinder than you let on, Cassandra Astrellar."

"Never mistake anything I do for kindness, Madame Sinclair." Cassandra gave her a nod. "Congratulations again, Señora Cortez."

The table disappeared as if a fog came through Mabel's vision. She huffed a laugh while Luisa called, "There you are, Mabel!"

Mabel turned to her new sister-in-law and grinned as Leticia smiled warmly at her, waving Mabel over. Walking toward her, part of Mabel hoped this would become her home forever, living a simple life with good people who held such love for each other. First, though, Antonio had to finish his year in the Navy. And she had to introduce him to her parents. She wasn't sure which she dreaded more.

For tonight, she put aside those worries as she accepted Luisa's husband's invitation and returned to the dance floor.

CHAPTER 23

In Which Antonio
Meets Mabel's Parents

Cliffshire, Barthan

"I miss your mother," Mabel whispered in Castallan as she and Antonio followed her parents and brother to where the open carriage waited at the beginning of the parade route.

"I miss food with spices in it," Antonio whispered. "Everything here is flavored with only butter and salt. I've had enough flavorless foods as a sailor."

Mabel giggled and pressed closer to his side. "You've only had dinner last night and breakfast."

"It's enough of a sample."

As they reached the carriage, Mr. Sinclair grinned proudly while patting Antonio's shoulder and gestured while shouting in Barthanian, "Carriage. Go down street. Wave."

Antonio kept a forced smile, though his eyes betrayed his annoyance.

"Father," Mabel said, "I've told you a dozen times since we came yesterday afternoon: Just speak normally and I'll translate what Antonio doesn't understand."

"I'm sure he understands how to get his hand under a girl's skirt, just like every other sailor," Malcom muttered before sneaking another drink from the flask hidden in his coat pocket.

"You're the expert of that," Mabel hissed.

"What is with the pair of you?" Mrs. Sinclair adjusted the furs around her shoulders. "You've been sniping at each other since Mabel came home. Malcom, please be respectful to your brother-in-law."

Malcom's bleary eyes glared at Antonio. "I bet he only married her to get a piece of her but got greedy when he learned her poppy had money."

"Go get in our carriage and try to look sober." Mr. Sinclair glared at his son and pointed. "You will be respectful of the lieutenant."

Malcom jabbed a finger at Antonio. "The bank is mine, you money-grubber."

Antonio leaned toward Mabel and said in Castallan, "What weapons do you have on you? If your brother continues, I might need to borrow one."

"You have one." She tapped his ceremonial sword with her knuckles. "Although, your fists would work too."

Antonio flexed his hand. "I'm a tailor. I don't want to damage my fingers."

Malcom grunted at Antonio as if he'd won some unspoken argument before wobbling toward the carriage.

"I apologize for your brother," Mr. Sinclair said. "Those pirates who kidnapped you seem to have been a poor influence on him. Ever since you returned—" He grunted. "He worries me."

A softness touched Mabel's heart and she brushed her father's arm. "I'm sorry I've worried you so much in the past two years, Father."

He glanced at her, his face trying to be stoic while there was a warmth in his eyes. "You are a married woman now, Mabel, and have the right to live your life with your husband." A grin broke through as he looked up at Antonio, who was at least half-a-head taller than him. "And what a husband this fine, young lieutenant is."

He patted the shoulder of Antonio's uniform and tapped the rank insignia on Antonio's chest before half-shouting, "Good soldier. Good husband."

Antonio bit back a laugh and said in heavily-accented Barthanian, "Thank you, sir."

"See how smart he is." Mrs. Sinclair let out an admiring sigh. "He's already learned some Barthanian."

"I told you last night," Mabel said. "He's been studying the language for the past year. While he does not speak well, he understands most of what you are saying."

"When he comes to work at the bank, we'll get him the best tutor in the county." Mr. Sinclair patted Antonio's shoulder again. "Such an excellent officer. You're going to be a great man around here."

He gestured to the carriage and half-shouted, "Parade start. Should go."

Antonio nodded and guided Mabel to the carriage. Mabel took his hand as he helped her up before hopping in. He put his arm around her waist as he said, "I thought you told him our plans to build a fashion house?"

"At least three times at dinner and twice at breakfast." She leaned her head against his shoulder, not caring if it crinkled the white veil her mother had insisted on Mabel wearing. At least she was able to wear the white dress Leticia had made. The monstrosity of a dress her mother had bought was locked away at her parents, and Mabel hoped it remained there, safe from terrorizing people with good taste.

As the carriage's horses began to march, Antonio said, "I can see why you stayed with the pirates for a year."

Mabel chuckled before taking his hand. "If we can endure what my parents have planned for today, we can endure anything."

Antonio laughed before raising her veil and pulling her into a kiss. Mabel tried not to giggle as they passed through the flowered archway leading onto the main boulevard and the first group of onlookers gasped at such a public display. She broke away and winked at him before turning and at least attempting to look polite as she waved to the gathered people of her hometown, come to gawk at Mabel Sinclair's handsome lieutenant.

Antonio's cheeks felt stiff after hours of forced smiles and nodding as he sat with Mable at the head table. The white reception hall was drowning with flowers, globe lights, and more tulle than anyone should have thought was stylish. He glanced over as Malcom tottered back into the reception hall with a satisfied smile and adjusting buttons on his vest. Within seconds, he was on the dance floor with the third girl of the evening.

Antonio wasn't sure what made him angrier: Malcom or the dress Mrs. Sinclair had commissioned for Mabel without asking. Both seemed satisfying to cut with a sword, though, from the looks of it, the dress might turn out to be made of cake.

"Are you sure you don't want to dance again?" Mabel said as another song started.

"I will, if you want to," he said. "I enjoyed dancing during the first five versions of the same song."

Mabel pushed his shoulder. "They've played dozens of songs."

"All with the same beat." He held his arms in a proper waltz pose. "And the same stiff arms." He leaned toward her. "Dancing is about passion and getting close to the woman you love."

He stole a quick kiss and several of the older female guests around them fluttered their fans as they sighed in adoration. He raised an eyebrow, inviting Mabel for a more passionate kiss. Instead, she gave him a soft, lingering kiss before sitting back properly. This brought a louder chorus of sighs, many young women joining, their eyes longing for such a kiss.

"That was far from satisfying," he whispered.

"I agree, but my parents mean well, and Malcom is embarrassing them enough." She glanced at him. "For their sake, I can wait till we get back to the hotel."

He kissed her hand, leading to more gasps and sighs from the guests. "For my bride, I will be patient."

Mabel smiled warmly at him, but a coldness entered her face as she turned toward the crowd. Antonio sat up, frowning as Mabel glared at an elegant but average middle-aged woman as she reached the table. Though the woman's smile was pleasant, something about her made the hair on the back of Antonio's neck rise.

In Barthanian, Mabel said, "You were not invited. Please leave."

"I helped this marriage happen." The woman's smile was thin as her eyes assessed Antonio. "Why not enjoy the celebration?"

Mabel rose and Antonio joined her, keeping his eyes hard on this stranger with her pale blonde hair.

"Admiral Guerrero told me of your business endeavors," the woman said.

Antonio's chest grew tighter, and he rested his hand on the hilt of his sword. The blade wasn't sharpened, but it still could do damage if needed. Along with whatever arsenal Mabel had hidden under her skirt.

"This is our wedding celebration." Mabel's fingers reached into a hidden slit in her dress. "I do not want to make a scene. Please leave, Mrs. Snow."

Antonio gripped his sword hilt as he recognized the name. This was the woman from the strange organization which had pinned him into becoming a lieutenant.

"I spoke to those I report to and they sent a gift for your wedding." Mrs. Snow set down a midnight blue envelope with gold etching. "Their offer will make the pair of you very rich."

"I have a pistol in my pocket," Mabel said quietly. "You have till I count to ten to take the envelope and leave or I will fire."

"Mrs. Cortez—"

"One."

"There are very powerful people who—"

"Two."

"Who are interested in your future."

"Three."

Mabel lifted the pistol just enough to show the handle. Antonio gave a thin smile while Mrs. Snow's face paled further.

"You wouldn't. Not in front of all of these people."

"Four."

It took Antonio a moment to remember the Barthanian words before saying, "She would."

"Five."

"We have many hidden businesses who need a sharp mind like yours, and—"

"Six." Mabel cocked the pistol. "Seven."

Mrs. Snow held up her hands. "Be reasonable."

"Eight." Mabel began lifting the pistol all the way from her skirt.

Mrs. Snow grabbed the card and hurried from the table. Mabel tucked the pistol into her pocket but watched the woman as she left. Antonio didn't like the danger of the last few moments, but he couldn't help but grin proudly.

Once Mrs. Snow was gone from the reception hall, Mabel pulled her hand from her pocket.

"Mabel," he whispered. She glanced at him, her eyes worried. In Castallan, he said, "I am proud you are my wife."

Her face relaxed and she stepped toward him. She put her hands on his cheeks as she kissed him far more forcefully than any other time tonight. He wrapped her in his arms, holding her tight as he returned the warmth of her kiss. For a few moments, he lost himself in her embrace, his hand rubbing her shoulder as her fingers tangled in his hair.

"Mabel!" came a hiss from her mother.

Antonio panted as he and Mabel drew apart. Their eyes met and Mabel's nose wrinkled before she broke into laughter. Antonio joined her as most of the guests stared with their mouths hanging open. A cluster of young women tittered together while a group of older men gave Antonio approving winks. Murmurs soon swept through the crowd, many of the older women making the appearance of being appalled while also giving Antonio admiring glances.

"What a passionate young lieutenant," a woman nearby said before blowing out a breath as she fanned herself.

He helped Mabel back into her chair

"Do you mind getting me some water?" she said. "I'm starting to have a bit of a headache."

"Was our kiss that exhausting?" He let out a laugh.

"No. But facing Mrs. Snow was."

"I'll be back in a moment, then." He kissed the top of her head, breathing in the smell of her hair before leaving the head table.

He ignored several young women giving him shy smiles and waves as he passed. Even in the ports, he wasn't sure he had had so many women seeking his eye. Perhaps it was his romantic story with Mabel. Or his uniform. Or the crowd of women who had gathered at a café overlooking the water when he went for a morning swim along the beach near the hotel.

Apparently, in Barthan, men were expected to wear a shirt while swimming. Which was a waste of a shirt and would just slow a man in the water.

Whatever the reason, the only woman he wanted eying him was the charming redhead at the main table.

He reached the refreshment table and nodded to several people chatting at him at once. He caught a few words, but so many voices were too much for his brain to translate.

"Water," he said in Barthanian as he pushed through. "For Mabel."

Someone handed him a glass of water and he began pushing his way back toward his bride. He paused as he caught movement out of the corner of his eye. He turned as Malcom and a young woman disappear through a glass door facing the gardens around the hall.

His hand clenched the glass.

He knew too many sailors to not know Malcom's intentions. The man had already been rude enough, and this was not the first girl of the night. It was one thing for Antonio to kiss his own wife passionately in front of everyone. It was completely different for Malcom to sneak off for kissing, or something more, with at least three women at his sister's wedding celebration.

Antonio glanced around him before holding out the glass of water to one of the men talking at him. "Take to Mabel. Please."

He wished he could speak Barthanian better, but his broken phrases seemed to be enough as the man nodded and took the glass. Antonio hurried around the crowd, smiling and waving back to others as congratulations were called to him. He exited out the nearest door and walked down a path. It did not take him long to follow the hush of voices to a secluded area in a semi-enclosed gazebo.

"Come on, Hannah," Malcom said as he panted between kisses, clothing rustling. "Don't you love me?"

"I do, so much."

Antonio's face wrinkled in disgust.

"But, Malcom, I—" There was a break of a cry in her voice. Antonio glanced around the gazebo's corner as the young woman placed a hand on her stomach. "I know you're waiting for an investment before you propose, but we might need to marry sooner."

"Darling," Malcom whispered as he put his arms around her. "Let's not talk of this tonight. Let's just celebrate our love for each other."

"Malcom, I'm worried. I'll be ruined if anyone finds out about our child unless—"

"Don't you worry. Just kiss your dear Malcom. Show him how you love him."

Antonio grunted before marching into the gazebo and unsheathing his sword. Malcom's eyes widened as Antonio held the point of the blade to his neck. Hannah cried out as she stepped away, fumbling to close the top few buttons of her bodice. Antonio's cheek twitched. What a foolish girl caught up by a despicable man.

"No honor," Antonio growled before pointing with his other hand. "Inside."

Mabel deserved better than this scoundrel as her brother. But Antonio would make him hold at least one piece of honor tonight.

Malcom eyed Antonio as he began walking toward the reception hall.

"Take her." Antonio pointed.

Malcom took Hannah's arm and walked slowly while Antonio remained behind him, placing the point of the blade against his back.

"Head table," Antonio said as they reached the doors closest to where Mabel sat.

He sheathed his sword and put his hand against Malcom's back, guiding him to the head table. Mabel took a sip of water before frowning at them.

Reaching her side, he said in Castallan, "Translate for me, please."

She gave him a confused glance but nodded.

Forcing a grin, Antonio stood on a chair and clapped until the crowd quieted and focused on him. Malcom glared and Hannah's face paled.

"My husband has an announcement," Mabel said, watching him.

He hopped down from the chair and stood between the nervous couple, putting his arms around their shoulders. Mable translated as he said, "Mabel and I have had great joy in being married. So, I am grateful to announce my new brother-in-law has chosen to follow our example."

He felt Malcom shaking with rage as the crowd burst into applause and cheers while Mr. and Mrs. Sinclair, along with another couple, who were likely Hannah's parents, frowned in confusion.

Antonio released his arms from around Malcom and Hannah. He gestured toward the crowd and said in Barthanian, "Speech?"

Malcom scowled at him before pulling back his elbow and slamming his fist against Antonio's face. Antonio's head snapped back, but his hand-to-hand combat training from the Navy kicked in and he deflected Malcom's next blow with his forearm followed by an elbow into Malcom's chin. Malcom launched himself at Antonio and grappled him to the ground. Straddling him, Malcom aimed another blow at his face. Antonio brought his knee against Malcom's groin and punched Malcom's gut before twisting himself out from under him.

With a snarl, Malcom swung again. Antonio grabbed his arm and pulled it behind him before shoving him against the ground. Malcom tried to twist his body away, but Antonio knelt on Malcom's back and grabbed his other wrist, holding both arms behind him.

"Pig," Antonio growled.

"Get off me, you fish scum," Malcom spat. "You're a gold-poaching eel."

There was a click and Antonio glanced up as Mabel stood over her brother and held her pistol at her side, out of view of the crowd. Antonio smiled as Malcom glared at him.

"You are going to stand up and apologize to my husband," she said. "And me, our parents, and Hannah. And the crowd. And the other girls you've wandered into the garden with tonight. Then, go home and figure out how to have honor."

"When did you become a common thug?" Malcom said.

"I am a reformed pirate." Mabel raised her eyebrows. "Don't you remember from our year of being captured? What if everyone found out how true your tales of heroics were?" Her eyes narrowed. "You toad."

Antonio looked to Mabel as he said in Castallan, "Should have left him one."

"You wouldn't shoot your own brother," Malcom said.

Mabel pointed the pistol toward Malcom and fired. Antonio

jumped and the crowd screamed, including Hannah, who was breaking into hysterics. Antonio glanced at the black mark on the ground next to them on the wood floor.

"Blank shot?" he said in Castallan.

"Do you think I would bring bullets to our wedding celebration?" she said.

Antonio gave her a pointed look. She sighed and shrugged, acknowledging his point.

"No one was hurt!" Mabel shouted to the crowd and held up the pistol. "My finger slipped, and it hit the ground next to him."

Everyone's eyes were wide as they stared.

"Mabel!" Mrs. Sinclair's mouth hung open, her face pale. "How—why do you have—how can you have—"

"After being kidnapped by pirates, you always stay prepared." Mabel twirled the pistol before sliding it into her pocket.

Antonio released Malcom's hands and rose but did not offer any help to stand. "Leave. Now."

"There will be no apologies." Malcom glared as he stood, straightened his vest, and marched away.

"Mabel," Mrs. Sinclair hissed loudly. "Apologize to your brother."

"Yes," Mr. Sinclair said. "Immediately."

With those words, her parents confirmed Antonio's suspicion on which child they preferred. He held his hand out to Mabel and said in Castallan, "Shall we leave?"

"This is our wedding celebration." Mabel took his hand. "A Castallan tango and then say goodnight?"

Antonio grinned and raised her hand and kissed it. The tango was the most interesting dance she'd been allowed to learn as a youth. That would be enough to cap off tonight's scandals.

He held his back straight and arm behind him as he led Mabel through the room. The crowd parted as they passed, their eyes still wide in shock and everyone silent. They reached the dance floor and the small orchestra.

"Castallan tango, please," Antonio said.

The orchestra leader had a small, amused smile as he bowed in his long-tailed tuxedo before turning to the musicians and counting before they started a slow-paced Castallan tango. Antonio motioned for them to speed the song. The tempo sped and his eyes locked with Mabel's as he took a formal dance pose and they grinned at each other.

With the push of his hand, their feet moved in sync, her lines elegant as they kicked their legs in the steps of the dance. Her hips shifted in precise motion, accentuating as her feet stepped one in front of the other and his own feet led the line of their movement. He kept things crisp and smooth, guiding her across the floor in swift steps, pausing at the end to lean into an extension, their bodies creating a long, straight line, one arm raised, and the opposite leg extended. He then put his hand on the small of her back and pulled her into a series of swift, spinning steps taking them to the opposite corner.

He winked at her before dipping her back. She held her form, her arm around his shoulders as she raised her other arm. He gave her a quick kiss before pulling her into a standing position and spinning her. Shocked gasps ran through the crowd as he shifted his hands to her hips. She placed her hands on his shoulders and moved closer till there was a small gap between them. Then, he guided her through another round across the dance floor, this time rolling their hips more with each step, accentuating the movement.

Hearing the swelling of the end of the song, he spun her one more time. When the spin ended, she pulled herself against him, and wrapped her leg around his waist.

Raising his eyebrows, he said, "La Ratera!"

She raised her own eyebrow before kissing him. Her leg lowered as their kiss ran on even after the song ended. Some of the guests applauded, but the room was still awkwardly quiet.

Pulling back, he twirled her once more and bowed to the crowd. She joined him.

As they rose, she said, "Thank you everyone for coming to

celebrate Antonio and me. If we've offended anyone, we apologize, and you are welcome to take home your gift. As for my husband and myself, we must say goodnight."

Antonio put his arm around her waist, and she stayed close to his side as they walked from the reception hall.

Mabel held her head high as she strolled with Antonio out of the reception hall. Many familiar faces were shocked, while others grinned. Hazel looked worried. Mabel did not care. The tango had been freeing and fun after spending the day pretending to be what her parents wanted her and Antonio to be.

Once outside, both she and Antonio burst into laughter.

"How angry do you think my parents are?" She put a hand on top of her head and blew out air. "I was trying so hard to be polite."

"I'm sorry about bringing in your brother as I did."

"Are you joking?" She hooked her arm around his waist. "It was wonderful to see his face smashed against the floor after how much of an oaf he's been." She brushed aside his fallen hair, revealing the welt on his upper jaw. "Though, the bruise will be colorful tomorrow."

Antonio pressed a finger to it and winced.

They reached their waiting carriage and the driver hurried over from the group of coachmen joking together. As Antonio helped Mabel into the carriage, her father shouted, "Mabel! Come back here!"

"Stop them! You must talk sense into them!" Her mother ran behind her father, holding her skirts delicately to avoid getting mud on them.

Mabel glanced at her parents.

There were moments where she thought she mattered to them. However, their call for her to apologize to Malcom was too far. Still, they had paid for the reception and who knew when she might visit again. A touch of politeness would help ease things later.

"Goodnight, Mother and Father." Mabel stood in the open-topped carriage. "Thank you for how hard you've worked on this. Lunch tomorrow?"

"You will go inside and apologize to your guests for that disgusting display." Her father pointed at the reception hall.

"It was just a dance." She had done it to offend them and had succeeded. But there were far worse things she could have done.

Like fire a pistol at her brother. Which, she had also done.

"You are her husband!" Mr. Sinclair shouted at Antonio, his face growing red. "I made you a lieutenant. You are supposed to be an officer of honor, not a scoundrel."

"Tell him the only scoundrel here tonight is his son," Antonio said quietly in Castallan as he stood beside her in the carriage.

Mabel took his hand and repeated his words. She already loved him, but how each action he took tonight showed trust in her only made her love him even more.

Mr. Sinclair's fists shook, and Mrs. Sinclair's face grew paler as she reached his side.

"After all we have done for you, you insult us?" Mr. Sinclair said.

"I love you," Mabel said, "but my life is my own, Father." She raised her palms. "It has been a long night. Let's talk at lunch tomorrow, after we've both had some rest."

"No. There are important people in that hall. Think of your husband's career."

"I do," Mabel said. "Often. And my husband is a tailor."

"If you do not go and apologize right now, I will not speak to you tomorrow."

"Mr. Sinclair!" her mother said.

Mabel's fists clenched as the deep anger she had long repressed frothed. "There is a young woman whose life has been ruined by Malcom, but I'm the one you won't speak to?"

"I can make your father the second man I've punched tonight," Antonio whispered.

She waved for him to be quiet. This was about more than tonight.

"She'll receive fair compensation," Mr. Sinclair said. "Just like the others."

Antonio's hand moved toward his sword, but Mabel gripped his arm. She squeezed tighter than she planned.

She wished she were surprised there were others, but she was not.

"And what happens to Malcom?" Mabel said.

Mr. Sinclair pressed his hands together. "He's a young man. He just needs patience and a clear name. We can't let a bit of foolishness with a girl ruin his future."

"He is ruining his future, and yours. And the girl's." She gestured at herself and Antonio. "I am married. Yes, we eloped, but those were the circumstances. Everything—" She cringed as she thought of the forged certificate. "Antonio is a man of honor and treats me well."

"A man who brawls with your brother and then dances with you improperly in front of the most important people in town?" Mr. Sinclair held a hand to his chest. "There are investors and important clients in there who are offended by my daughter."

Mabel threw up her hands as angry tears fell down her cheeks. "When Malcom and I walked in the door after a year, you didn't even see me. No one did until I said something, and it was the cook who embraced me first. And my marriage? It was nothing to you until you made an imaginary version of my husband. That lieutenant who'll work at your bank doesn't exist."

She gestured inland, toward Willington. "I am building my own future, Father. The one Antonio and I want. It will never fit into the tiny box you have in your mind. My life is already so much more than you could ever know. But I can tell you none of it because you're so busy trying to imagine Malcom as something he's not."

"We care greatly for your future," Mrs. Sinclair said, tears streaming down her cheeks. It was harder to watch her mother cry, but

Malcom still had a golden aura in their eyes which he didn't deserve. "This is why we fixed up the cottage and planned today so carefully for Antonio to make the proper connections. Please don't be so ungrateful."

Mabel wanted to scream or shout, but it was clear her parents could not see beyond their small world.

"Antonio and I will be leaving for Willington tomorrow morning," she said. "And will be staying at my apartment there for the next month or so. If you want to see us, telephone my office and schedule an appointment."

She turned away and sat as her parents shouted at her, her mother pleading and her father scolding. Antonio sat beside her and put his arms around her. She held her hand on top of his, but remained sitting up, keeping her face stiff.

She would not be returning to this miniscule town if she could help it. She would write to her parents now and then on important events, but there was no need for more.

They soon reached the hotel and she kept hold of Antonio's hand as she hurried inside.

Stopping at the front desk, she said, "What is the earliest train to Willington?"

"Seven in the morning." The gray-haired man gave them a wink. "Though, for newlyweds, I'd recommend the ten or eleven o'clock trains."

"We'd like the seven o'clock train. Can we have our luggage sent over?"

"If that's what you wish." He glanced at the door before whispering, "If you're in trouble, there's a midnight train leaving in two hours. I've got my cart and can get you down there right soon."

"Would that be all right with you?" she said to Antonio in Castallan.

He frowned at her. "I didn't follow the conversation, except that you're looking for a train to Willington."

"We can go tonight."

He brushed a tear from her cheek. "Will you regret not staying and making peace with your parents tomorrow?"

"Would you make peace with them if you were in my place?"

"No." He shook his head. "But they are not my parents."

She gripped his hand. "Then, I am sure."

"Then, we leave at midnight?"

She kissed him softly. "Yes. Thank you."

With the decision made, they went to their room, changed, and packed. Antonio helped the clerk carry their three suitcases to the cart and then push the cart the few blocks to the train station. The clerk huffed a bit by the end and Mabel handed him a larger tip than planned.

They bought their tickets from the half-asleep rail clerk and then sat on a bench and waited.

A cold breeze came, and Antonio pulled off his jacket and put it around her, followed by his arms. She nestled her head into his neck and dozed off until the clack of the train came. He shook her awake and she yawned as he guided her into a private cabin. Before the train moved, she dozed off again, shifting in and out of consciousness for hours, comforted by his steady presence.

With a loud whistle, the train pulled into Willington's Central Station.

She yawned and felt more awake as they walked through the station and then took a late-night horse cab through the dark, empty streets in the dead of night. As they came to her street, there were still flashing signs for the night clubs, dance halls, restaurants, and theaters.

Antonio paid the cab driver and helped Mabel down. She stumbled as she yawned and led him into her building. Her feet tripped halfway up the first set of stairs, so Antonio pulled her over his shoulder before picking up the suitcase she carried along with the two he already held.

"This is not dignified," she said with a yawn. "I can walk."

"You're exhausted and I don't want you to injure yourself. Which floor?"

"Fourth floor. Third apartment on the left."

He huffed a bit by the third flight of stairs, but persevered and they reached her apartment. She handed him the key from her handbag, glad she hadn't left it on the ship. She had done that one night and had been forced to pick her own lock. It became especially uncomfortable when one of her neighbors happened to be walking down the hall.

He carried her inside and set her and the suitcases down.

She sighed in contentment at the small but familiar apartment. "Welcome home, Antonio."

"I pictured something much grander after your quarters on the ship," he said as he shut the door.

"Here in Willington, I'm just a girl starting her career in fashion."

"No merfolk here?"

"Unless Cassandra comes by, no." She yawned again and took his hand as she led him to the bedroom.

"I still can't believe Cassandra's a mermaid." he said.

She waved her hand tiredly. "Just ignore the legs."

Antonio chuckled as he squeezed her hand. "I love how unexpected things are around you."

"I'd like a few days of only calm and normal."

She flopped face-first on the bed and spread her arms out. Within seconds, she began to doze off. She woke a little as Antonio unlaced her travel boots. She rolled over as he helped her out of her jacket and smiled as he hung her skirt and jacket, checking to make sure they were straight and wouldn't wrinkle. Anyone who thought he should do anything outside of fashion did not know this man.

She removed the rest of her layers, including the pistol and four knives strapped to her legs, and pulled on a nightgown. Antonio removed his suit with the same care and changed into his linen pajamas before lying beside her. She tucked her face against his chest as he held her, his hand cradling the back of her head.

"How do you feel about disowning your parents?" he whispered, concern in his voice.

She let out a tired laugh. "That is what I did, isn't it?"

"Mabel, how do you feel?"

Tears came. "I love them, but I'm glad to be free. And with you." Her tears became heavier. "At least, until you have to leave."

He took her hand and moved it to his chest, where she could feel his heartbeat. "La Ratera, you stole this long ago. Even when I go back to sea, it will be with you."

Her gaze rose to meet his, and her chest warmed at the full devotion in his eyes. "You're quite a romantic."

He kissed her before wiping tears from her cheek. "Just sleep tonight so we can enjoy tomorrow."

She rolled closer to him and let her anger and worries wash away as she enjoyed being home with her husband.

<u>CHAPTER 24</u>

In Which Antonio Explores Willington

Willington, Barthan

True joy was the expression on Antonio's face as Mabel stood beside him in the fashion district of Willington. He gaped at all the carts and stores full of fabric, buttons, beading, and other sewing supplies. Mabel grinned, having gaped the same way not long before, and followed him as he dashed between carts, wanting to see everything at once.

"This is real chiffon." He pointed. "And this velvet!"

He ran his hand over another fabric. "Look at the texture on this." He pulled his sketchbook from his pocket and drew the general lines of a dress. "It could lay like this and then, if the lady had a bustle, it would move as she walked, like this."

"She'd need a smoother fabric for a panel on the front of the dress." Mabel ran a finger along the roughly scribbled figure, visualizing what he intended. "It would create a blocking effect."

"Yes, I like that." Antonio grinned as he took her hand and darted to the next booth, gazing at the softer fabrics. He pressed his palm to a yellow print with birds on it. "Mama and I've often talked about how some fabrics feel alive, as if they're calling you, telling you what clothing they were meant to be."

He rubbed his hands together. "I just want to buy a few yards of all of these and go and begin draping and pinning, to let it come to life."

Staring out at all the fabrics and colors, Antonio said, "This is the most beautiful place I've ever seen."

"It is wonderful, isn't it?" Mabel smiled. "We'll spend more time here, but I wanted to show you my studio down the street."

Antonio stared longingly at every booth they passed, like a child bouncing through a toyshop but unable to touch. As they walked, a few people stopped them and complimented the embroidery on his cuffs and lapel matching a stripe down the side of his pants. Where other men would look ridiculous, Antonio looked sharp.

They turned down the side street where her studio lay and went up the set of stairs of an old, worn building.

"We're just starting, and we didn't want to invest too much until the business can pay for itself," she said. "So, try to keep your expectations reasonable."

"I've no idea what to expect, reasonable or not," Antonio said. "Especially with your life. For all I know, you've a batch of pixies in there making the clothing."

"Perhaps I do," she said with a laugh.

A nervous excitement grew in her breast as she reached the worn metal door to the studio and slid it open. She stood to the side as Antonio stepped in. His eyes were wide as he stared at the open floor of the old factory room, tables and dress forms filling the space as the three designers and six assistants worked to create the samples and patterns to be sent to the dress assembly factory.

"Wow." Antonio entered, his eyes taking everything in like it was a sacred space, even with the exposed rafters and dirty windows.

He looked to her. "May I—" He swallowed. "Is it all right if I walk around and examine the work?"

Mabel smiled. "Antonio, it is Madame Sinclair Designs. I think my husband can do whatever he wants."

"Oh, Madame Sinclair, you're here," Mr. Trivay, one of the designers, said while giving a forced smile.

Mabel kept her smile polite in return. If his work wasn't so excellent and his skills so highly recommended by Elona, she would have fired him months ago.

Mabel clapped her hands. "Good afternoon! Can I borrow everyone a moment?"

The small group of employees gathered, Mr. Trivay looking annoyed at the interruption. She grit her teeth. She would be talking to him again later.

She frowned at Mrs. Hennessy, the middle-aged secretary's hair was disheveled and her face pinched. While she always looked worried, this was worse than usual.

Perhaps Mabel should have waited a few more days before returning. Her gut told her she might have lost the rest of her day by coming in.

Forcing a smile, she placed a hand on Antonio's back. "I thought you would all like to meet my husband, Lieutenant Antonio Cortez of the Castallar Navy."

Mr. Trivay gave a bored look while most others gasped and smiled, a ripple of congratulations running through the group.

"I'll make introductions as we walk around so he can see the work we do here."

She nodded to the group, and they headed back to their workstations, Mr. Trivay muttering, "As if she's ever around to actually do the work."

Mabel bit back a sigh. His employment was not going to last much longer, but she didn't feel like dealing with it today. Especially as Mrs. Hennessy approached.

"I'm so glad you're here," the secretary said in her warbling voice as she flipped through a notepad. "We've just had disaster after disaster."

"Not everything is a disaster," Mabel said quietly.

Mrs. Hennessy adjusted her elongated spectacles. "The fabric supplier only delivered half the order this morning to the assembly shop and said the remainder would only be available for delivery in six months."

Mabel's eyebrows rose. This wasn't a disaster yet but would be if those dresses weren't made. She did not want to break contracts with merfolk so early on.

She glanced at Antonio, giving him an apologetic look as she said in Castallan, "I'm sorry, my love. It will take me a few hours to manage things."

"You are captain, and this is your ship." That proud grin of his formed and she found herself standing taller. "I'll be plenty busy watching the designers work."

She gave him a quick kiss that she wished could be longer before walking toward her office. "What else, Mrs. Hennessy?"

"Your parents have called about a dozen times. I've asked for them to wait for you to return their call, but they are being more persistent than usual."

"That is my fault."

They entered her mid-sized office. Mabel winced at the pile of mail and documents waiting for her review. It had been empty when she had left to rescue Antonio two weeks ago.

"The next time my parents call, tell them I am well but made myself clear last night and they are to respect that. Then hang up every time they call afterward. Anything else?"

Mrs. Hennessy gasped. "Pardon me, Madame, I'm not sure I can be so rude."

Mabel rubbed her temple. It was an unfair request of an employee. "You are right. Patch them through and I'll hang up on them while I'm here."

Mrs. Hennessy pursed her lips, but she nodded. Gesturing to the pile of documents, she said, "With your husband being here, perhaps everything else should wait till later?"

"I am here now." Mabel felt tired staring at the pile. "If I want to enjoy time with my husband later, I need to manage it quickly."

Ms. Hennessy nodded before sitting next to the desk and walking Mabel through the documents. As she went on, Mabel rested her forehead against her hand, hating how her to do list was growing.

Antonio was right. She needed to be the captain of her ship. However, it was quickly becoming a very large ship.

Antonio stood by one of the dress forms and watched the pair of assistants and brunette designer in her forties work together to assemble the gown's pieces. His fingers itched to join them in stitching and cutting. Especially as the assistant in her early twenties cut the fabric so it wouldn't lay as smoothly as it should. His mother had emphasized to him and his sisters the importance of cutting the fabric right each time and not wasting a single piece.

As the mis-cut piece of fabric was pinned, the designer, young lady assistant, and balding man assistant tried to adjust it to fit.

"Wait." Antonio wished he could remember more Barthanian words as he stepped forward and raised his palm and motioned for them to step back. Their frowns deepened as he unpinned the piece of fabric and laid it on the table. He carefully trimmed it before carrying it back to the dress form and pinning it into place just as the design showed.

"Are you looking for work as an assistant?" the designer said with a laugh as she held out her hand. "I'm Ms. Devroe. This is Mr. Warren and Miss Sidlow."

Antonio nodded as he shook each of their hands, wishing Barthanian words came more easily. While he understood the language, trying to speak was sometimes like dragging his thoughts through muddy water.

He put a hand on his chest indicating himself and then pointed at the table. "Me help?"

Ms. Devroe smiled. "If you wish, sir. Though, as our employer's husband, you've no need."

"I want." He gestured as he tried to find the right words. "I love—it good work."

He rubbed his forehead and grunted in frustration. There was so much he wanted to say of the design and dress form, but the language was blocking him.

"We would love to have your help." Ms. Devroe pulled out another piece of pattern she had made. "Do you want to pin this?"

Antonio grinned and nodded. Here he was in Willington, helping with a dress to be produced and sold. Though, he was probably the only one in the room who knew the dress would be sold to mermaids.

Over the next hour, he lost himself in the work until Mabel left her office. Her face was pinched, her eyes troubled as she approached.

He stepped away from the table and took her hand. "What's wrong?"

"I need to talk to some of my suppliers," she said. "It won't take more than an hour or two. You can stay here, if you like."

He glanced at the dress form and the clothing being draped. His duty was with Mabel, but he badly wanted to keep working. Still, he said, "If you need me, I will go."

Mabel smiled and rested her hand on his arm. "Enjoy yourself. I'll be back soon enough."

Antonio's cheeks felt warm. "I can go. It's really—"

"Stay and do the work that you love." She kissed his cheek before walking away.

He watched her leave to go be the businesswoman she was at heart. Whatever the trouble was, she would face it with the same determination she had shown when negotiating with Admiral

Guerrero. Whomever she needed to talk to did not know the strength of the woman coming to them.

As the afternoon went on, he set his suitcoat on a hanger and rolled up his sleeves. He grinned as he stood alongside the professionals, joining the debate and problem-solving as best he could when something wasn't laying right or wasn't quite working. It was hard with only understanding their language and struggling to say full sentences. Still, between pantomime and short words and phrases, they were able to communicate.

Mabel had been gone for two hours when Mr. Trivay came to Ms. Devroe's table and circled it as he pretended not to glare at Antonio. "What an interesting look our employer's husband has. With all the fuss on his coat, he looks like a woodpecker dressed up as a peacock."

"Did you spend all afternoon coming up with that?" Ms. Devroe waved him off. "I'm working. Go back to your table."

Antonio glanced at Mr. Warren and Miss Sidlow and joined them in biting back a small smile. Ms. Devroe had strong command of her team and a good eye, especially with how poor of a design drawing she was working with. Mabel's sketches had improved, but it was still hard to build a dress from them. As for the work, Ms. Devroe needed to train Miss Sidlow to be more precise. Though, the sewing and cutting tricks Antonio had shown her were already improving her skills.

"I've done enough for the shoddy design being forced on me," Mr. Trivay said.

"It's a good design, even if the drawings are poor," Ms. Devroe said. "And we're employed. That's more than others in this industry can say."

Mr. Trivay smoothed his collar. "I had my third interview with Mr. Hartavo's studio yesterday. Next spring, you'll see my work in the proper place."

"That's the third position you've interviewed for," Ms. Devroe said. "Not third interview."

"Still, Mr. Hartavo said he's very impressed with how my work has grown. I'll be out of here very soon."

Ms. Devroe pulled on her thread. "We could work for other studios, but Elona Cantor said this one has promise." She gestured at Antonio. "Madame Sinclair's a bit green, but her husband knows his way around a design. With him here, I think he'll help her fill in what she doesn't know."

Antonio grinned and nodded as a thank you for the compliment.

Mr. Trivay scoffed. "You're only here because she's overpaying us with her investor's deep pockets."

"She's paying us a fair wage while others underpay for the work we do." Ms. Devroe finished hand-sewing and began turning the piece inside out. "I don't quite understand who the market is for these elaborate gowns, but the work intrigues me, and she treats us fairly. That's more than I can say for other studios."

"And how did she get the Astrellar estate to invest?" Mr. Trivay gave Antonio a haughty look. "Rumor is the lieutenant here's secretly the heir to the fortune. No wonder she took up with such a greenwind."

Ms. Devroe dropped her work, and the rest of the room went quiet, everyone staring with their jaws hanging. Antonio gave no response as he pinned fabric. Bullies like Mr. Trivay tried to appear bigger through insults and boasts, just like Malcom. Later, Antonio would discuss with Mabel how to deal with him. Though, it shouldn't involve a pistol this time.

Mr. Trivay glared at Antonio and gave a cruel smirk. "You don't understand anything I'm saying, do you?"

Antonio bit back a bitter laugh as he thought of Mr. Sinclair's syllabic shouting. It was remarkable how idiotic others treated him for not being able to speak the language.

Ms. Devroe glanced at Antonio, seeming to check if he was all right. She had clearly picked up he understood more than he could speak. Antonio gave a small wave of his hand, indicating for her to wait.

"Oh, things are so funny," Mr. Trivay said with a false laugh as he approached Antonio, his body language pretending to be friendly. "Isn't it hilarious that little miss Madame Sinclair has barely left her crib and has no skills as a designer? While all of us have been sweating for years to make our way in this industry. But here we are, bought by her wealthy 'investor'." He leaned against the table as he stood beside Antonio, baring his teeth as he sneered. "Proves again: A girl of youth, beauty, and no brains just needs a pretty boy with money."

Antonio's back straightened as a shot of rage went through him. Mr. Trivay's condescending laugh only made it burn more.

"No insult my wife." He glared at the smaller man.

Mr. Trivay smirked. "The wife you bought off some street corner?"

Antonio pivoted on the ball of his foot and swung his right fist into Mr. Trivay's gut. The designer oofed as he bent forward. Stepping back, Antonio shook his fist, trying to quiet his anger. This was enough.

"You all saw that, didn't you?" Mr. Trivay said as he backed away. "He assaulted me."

"Mr. Trivay, you keep losing jobs because you're an ogre at heart." Ms. Devroe nonchalantly worked on pinning the next piece of fabric. "Also, if you were any good at observing, you'd have noticed Lieutenant Cortez understands Barthanian quite well."

"It was a joke." Mr. Trivay attempted a smile. "Just hazing the newcomer."

Antonio gripped Mr. Trivay's shoulder and half-dragged him toward the door.

"I'll call the police," Mr. Trivay cried out. "I was attacked."

The studio door opened, and Mabel entered, her face gray with worry. Her eyes widened as she took in the scene and her hand went into her pocket, where a knife was likely hidden.

In Barthanian, Antonio said, "Mr. Trivay no work here."

"It is only a misunderstanding." Mr. Trivay pulled at Antonio's firm hold on him. "I didn't mean anything by what I said."

"I think he understood you, quite well," Ms. Devroe said. "Would you like me to repeat how you tried to compare our employer to a woman of the street?"

Mr. Trivay's face paled while Mabel's eyes went hard, no mercy in them.

"You have five minutes to collect your things," she said. "My husband will keep an eye on you."

"You don't even know what happened, Madame. Really, I—"

Mabel's eyes narrowed. "Your time here was already growing short, Mr. Trivay, and my husband does not attack without reason."

"I have a deep network," he spat. "I'll tell them how pathetic the designs here are, and—"

"I hired you because Elona asked me to," Mabel said, "so you would have another chance. She told me you are an expert, but an expert who is as rude and disrespectful as you is not worth employing."

"Everyone knows the truth!" Mr. Trivay glared at her. "You have no talent and no skill, except—"

Antonio pulled back on Mr. Trivay's collar and the man choked a bit.

"Leave now," he growled into Mr. Trivay's ear.

He released Mr. Trivay. The man marched to his workstation and threw his belongings into a large bag. He reached the door and glared at Mabel.

"I will ruin you, Mabel Sinclair."

Mabel's eyebrows rose and her face remained cool and calm. "I dare you to try."

Antonio tried not to grin proudly at his wife's strength. Mr. Trivay huffed before marching out. As the metal door slid shut, the rest of the employees broke into applause.

"Pardon me, Madame," Ms. Devroe said, "but I've been wondering why you've been tolerating his rudeness."

"He is a worm," Mabel said quietly, "and I have been dealing with sharks."

She took a step before looking to Antonio. "Will you come in my office?"

There were a few giggles, several of the younger female employees clearly guessing it was for Mabel to kiss him privately. With the worry in Mabel's eyes, Antonio doubted the conversation was on anything so pleasant.

Once he entered Mabel's office and shut the door, however, he was proven wrong as Mabel put her arms around his shoulders and gave him a heavy kiss.

"I don't know what Mr. Trivay said, but I'm sure he deserved the attack."

"It was well-earned." He kissed her cheek. "What's the matter?"

Mabel pulled a midnight blue and gold card from her handbag and handed it to him. It was almost identical to the one Mrs. Snow had tried to give them yesterday. He flipped it open and read the gold-embossed, glowing lettering inside.

Madame Sinclair,

My organizations have reached out to you multiple times with reasonable offers of business arrangements, but these have been refused. Considering how generous the Fairy Godmother Society was in their services, I would think you would have more loyalty.

I do not think you realize what opportunities you are declining, and so I fear I must become more persuasive.

Your fabric shipment is well protected and waiting for you. All you must provide is one thousand macs to my associate who will contact you tomorrow morning. Once the payment is complete, we will happily deliver the fabric. I should hate for your contracts with your very strict clients be broken.

Mrs. Autumn will be contacting you about future business arrangements. It is not just anyone I contact directly, Madame Sinclair. I hope you learn to appreciate my willingness to invest in your future.

Your Obedient Servant,

Madame Blue

"I overheard Admiral Guerrero say he's only received a note from her once." He dropped it on the table, his stomach feeling queasy. "Why is she so interested in you?"

"I suspect Admiral Guerrero reported to higher ups about my contract with him for transporting merfolk goods." Mabel huffed as she sat in the office chair and held a hand to her head. "Every time I think I've pried a tentacle off me, I find myself grabbed by a bigger one."

The telephone rang and a tiredness washed through Mabel's face. She picked it up. A man shouted on the other end, and she pulled it away from her ear.

"Father, this is the tenth time you have called today. As I told you, I am busy conducting business and will talk to you when I have time."

She slammed the receiver on the cradle and moaned as she laid her head on the desk. "Can we go back to your hometown?" She sighed. "Or back to this morning, when I was just lying in your arms?"

"My arms are right here." He held them out.

"Could you bring them over here?" she said.

He smiled, despite the sense of foreboding he felt looking at the midnight blue card. He picked up a chair from his side of the desk and set it beside her before sitting down. She shifted onto his lap, and he cradled her in his arms as she rested her head against his shoulder.

"Maybe I'll not return you to the Navy," she muttered.

"I'd like that too, except I would be flagged a deserter, hunted down, and executed by firing squad." He kissed her cheek. "I can tolerate one more year."

"I'm not sure I can." She rubbed her cheek. "What have I gotten myself into, Antonio?"

"La Ratera," he said softly, "you are the cleverest woman I know. You already have a plan, don't you?"

"Half of one." She pulled out a small map from her handbag. "I got the train's route from the fabric supplier." Her finger traced the railway line. "If I were Madame Blue, this would be in retaliation to how Mrs. Snow was treated last night. The fabric was supposed to be delivered at the train depot early this morning. It would have taken time for the plan to form and be executed. So, the fabric is likely near the destination.

"I think they plan to deliver the goods, so my guess is they are still in crates in a railcar. That will also make it easier to move to another location to sell on the black market if I don't pay. Which means—" She pointed at two spots on the map. "It's most likely at one of these two depots."

Antonio didn't like the situation, but he still smiled, again impressed by her intelligence. "So, we go and rescue fabric?"

"I'll bet the railcar is still among other crates and railcars in the yard, so it's hidden in plain sight, but no one is suspicious." Mabel tilted her head. "And I think the rail depot located before the one my employees were supposed to receive the load is the safer bet. But how do we get there quickly? And how do we find it in a sea of other containers? They likely changed the labeling."

"Cassandra said Madame Blue's organization has magic users, didn't she? If there's magic involved, couldn't you use the monocle?"

She slipped the monocle from her breast pocket and hefted it on her palm. Sitting up, she frowned at the map for a few seconds. She put her arm around his shoulder and said, "It's our honeymoon, my love. Would you like to go on an evening air balloon tour of the countryside outside of Willington?"

Antonio huffed a laugh. "Are you planning a bit of piracy on land?"

She gave him a false-innocent look. "I would never." She grinned. "But I might talk to my friend Mildred Stripes."

CHAPTER 25

In Which Mabel and Antonio Ride in an Air Balloon

A cold wind blew, but the air balloon with its propeller pushed through. Mabel let herself relax against Antonio as he held his arms around her. The air balloon operator had been paid enough to not ask questions, even as they approached the train depot, and she raised the monocle.

"This is nearly romantic." Antonio rested his cheek against hers.

"I've had a pistol under my skirt for most of our honeymoon," she said, trying not to laugh. "How is this different?"

"The rapier has me worried." His arms tightened around her. "And what we have to do once we find the shipment."

"If we're in real trouble, we can use the whistle Cassandra gave me for emergencies. But I'm sure we can manage things on our own."

"Including getting to the ground?"

"It'll be just like swinging between ships or dropping from rigging."

"But, if we fall, there is land below instead of water."

"Then don't fall."

Through the monocle, she scanned the dark area with dots of lights below, some brighter ones illuminating the central office of the train depot. She stiffened as she spied three railcars lined up on one of the side rails, a faint yellow haze around them. All of the other railcars and crates remained dark.

She leaned over and waved to the air balloon operator before pointing. "There. This is where we want to land."

"May I caution you again, Mrs. Corsair?" the operator shouted over the wind.

"Isn't marriage an adventure?" Mabel strapped on the leather harness attached to long ropes spooled on the side of the air balloon basket. "Which is why Mr. Corsair and I want to begin it with a thrill, don't we, my love?"

Antonio looked queasy as he peeked over the edge, but said in a bold voice, "Of course."

"Well, you've paid me enough to accept your stupidity," the operator grumbled.

The operator stopped the propeller, letting the air balloon slow as it drifted. Mabel rolled her shoulders before hopping over the side of the air balloon and standing outside the basket. Antonio was visibly shaking as he joined her, his own harness attached.

Her heart pounded as she stared at the ground far below. However, this was the work needing to be done.

"I love you," she shouted over the wind before letting herself drop. The reel of rope spun, letting her fall at a quick but not deadly speed. Adrenaline shot through her as the ground came closer. The harness jerked her back as she came to the rope's end a few feet above the ground in the field next to the depot. She shifted her weight so her feet were pointed down before hitting the ground. Running, she created some slack in the rope and unhooked the harness. With the tension gone, she fell forward from the shift in momentum and rolled on the ground.

Seconds later, Antonio cried out as he came to the end of his rope.

She ran to him and grabbed him by the harness before unhooking the rope. His arms flailed as he dropped the last few feet to the ground, landing face first.

"Antonio!" She knelt beside him and helped him turn over.

His skin was pale as he panted. His clothing was covered in grass and weeds, but he was whole and alive. She bent down and kissed him, resting her hand on his chest.

"Are you all right?"

"I never want to do that again," he wheezed.

"I thought it was fun."

She gave him a grin before rising and offering her hand. He took it and stood, brushing grass off his plain, dark pants and vest they had bought hours ago. She pressed one of the pearl buttons on her lapel and her dress transformed into her leather knee-length coat, trousers, white shirt, burgundy vest, and calf-length boots. She held her foot out and admired how the boots seemed to lengthen her leg.

Appearances might not matter too much on a dark, moonless night while about to go into unknown danger, but she still preferred looking her best.

From her coat pocket, she pulled the red mask Captain Stenton had given her before her first pirate battle. She smiled fondly, wondering what advice he'd give her now. Hopefully, she wouldn't need too many of the skills he had taught her.

Antonio buttoned up his knee-length coat and pulled on a black leather mask with gold details. They had bought it and a few other items from a theater costume shop at the edge of the fashion district. He stood straight and she admired how the lights from the depot highlighted the smooth line of his shoulders and accentuated his tall frame. He looked very much a hero from some adventure story.

Checking her pair of pistols exposed on her hips, one next to her rapier, she reached his side. "Well, my handsome husband, are we ready?"

He checked his sword and his own pistol tucked in his belt. "I hope we don't have to use these."

"Me too." She wrapped a black scarf around her hair and then helped him put on his own. "But you do make a dashing pirate."

He held his hands out as he looked down at himself. "Mabel, this isn't how I envisioned our life when I proposed."

Her shoulders fell. "It's not what I want, but it is what must be done tonight if we want our own future." She looked him in the eye. "That is what I fight for."

"It is a good cause." He took her hand and kissed it before gesturing toward the train depot. "This is your area of expertise, La Ratera. I follow your command."

She nodded. "Stay low. Stick to shadows. And knock out any potential lookouts. Use the stun darts first. Captain Stenton says the chemical on them will knock a man out for half-a-day. When we run out, use a good double-fist to the head. But, not too hard. Don't want to give them permanent damage."

Antonio glanced at her with an amused smile before giving her a salute. "Aye, Captain."

Mabel led Antonio through the field and over the wood fence before climbing on top of a shed at the edge of the field. She held the monocle to her eye and scanned the depot while Antonio crouched beside her. She squinted as several men strolled around the three glowing railcars. An aura of yellow light surrounded a woman shadowed between the railcars as she gave orders to the men.

"I count four," she said, lowering the monocle. "Including one Illuminator."

"There are six." Antonio pointed toward a man coming around the corner of a container and then one man facing a fence. The second man glanced over his shoulder as he began to unbutton his pants to relieve his bladder. "Let's manage him first."

Mabel nodded and they dropped off the container in sync with each other. Antonio moved with the lightness of a sailor used to climbing rigging. They kept to the shadows of stacked crates and railcars before nearing the target.

"For decency, I'll take this one," Antonio whispered as the target finished his business and began buttoning his pants.

Antonio crept forward and wrapped one arm around his shoulders while jabbing a stun dart into the man's arm. The man struggled a few long seconds before falling limp.

"That shed." Mabel pointed, leading the way as Antonio dragged the man by the shoulders. Once the man was inside, Antonio grabbed some loose chain from the ground nearby and wrapped it around the pair of door handles.

With one opponent gone, they moved together in tandem, Mabel running along the tops of railcars and crates while Antonio ran on the ground. She waved her hand and pointed. Seeming to understand, he flattened against the side of a railcar as one of the men came around the corner. Antonio grabbed the next dart before creeping behind the man and holding him back.

A flicker of movement caught Mabel's gaze and she glanced over as one of the other guards came to the same row, a few paces away from Antonio while he held the struggling man about to collapse. Mabel jumped across a few crates and leapt toward the second guard. She brought her fists together as she dropped down and brought them hard against the side of the man's head. Her fists smacked hard. He fell and hit the other side of his head against the railcar. There was a thud as his skull hit the wood and he landed, sprawling on the ground.

Mabel trembled as she knelt and turned the man over, praying she hadn't killed him. The gash on his forehead from hitting the railcar did not look good.

As Captain Stenton had shown her, she dug her fingers into the man's neck. A small relief came as she felt his pulse.

She glanced back as another thud marked Antonio's target falling. Antonio dragged the man over. Mabel helped him open the railcar door and load the two men aside. She positioned the man with a gash so his back was against the wall and side against a crate so he would stay sitting up.

These might be agents of Madame Blue's crime ring, but that did not give Mabel the right to murder them. Taking their lives over a railcar of fabric was too high a price.

"Three down," Antonio whispered as he shut the railcar door. "This is easier than I thought it would be."

"Never claim victory until you have a full surrender," Mabel whispered. "Though, perhaps this will be simpler than we thought."

She gave him a quick kiss. This sort of work was more fun with her husband at her side. "Shall we, my love?"

He helped boost her on top of the railcar before joining her. She scanned the darkness. Finding their fourth target, she led Antonio across the railcar roofs. Once close enough, Antonio dropped down behind the man and took him out with his last stun dart. With the man secured inside the railcar, Mabel reached down and helped Antonio climb back up. They hopped across another set of crates to the row of railcars where their targets stood.

Anticipation prickled within her as she raised the monocle once more. The fifth man was on the opposite end of the yard. The Illuminator stood beside the three railcars, looking at her pocket watch with a frown. Mabel lowered her monocle as her back straightened.

Though her hair was covered in a dark scarf, it was clearly Mrs. Snow.

Mabel wasn't sure that made things better or worse.

"Is that our wedding guest?" Antonio whispered.

"Shall we say hello and get some answers?" Mabel rested a hand on her pistols.

"You talk to her, and I sneak from behind?" Antonio said.

Mabel nodded. Antonio kissed her hand before dropping down the side of the railcar. She watched for Antonio to move into position behind some crates near Mrs. Snow, crouching with his pistol ready.

With Antonio in place, Mabel leapt across the railcar roofs. Reaching the railcar behind Mrs. Snow, she pulled out both her pistols and aimed. Both were loaded with six blanks, but even those could pack a good welt.

"Mrs. Snow," she called out, "I see you have an interest in fabric."

Mrs. Snow pulled back her scarf, revealing her white-blonde hair. She glanced up at Mabel with a bored look.

"Are you having fun playing pirate, Mrs. Cortez?" she said. "Another associate is scheduled to come to you for the payment, but I'll gladly take it and return your shipment. Both of us can make our evenings much simpler. I'm sure you'd like to be home with your handsome lieutenant. I heard of your passionate dance last night."

"There will be no payment for what I already own," Mabel said. "This is thievery and blackmail. I'll have no part in it."

"You're the one on the roof holding me at gunpoint, Mrs. Cortez."

Mabel held her pistols steady, aiming for Mrs. Snow's chest. Once she fired, Antonio would run out from behind the crates and tackle the woman. Then they would tie her up and leave her for the police to sort out.

Who knew what hold Madame Blue had over the police, but it was the best path.

"I suppose you and I are both just scoundrels after all," Mabel said. "But what is your life worth, Mrs. Snow? I imagine more than disappointing your dear mistress."

Mrs. Snow raised an eyebrow. "You are new to these games, Mrs. Cortez. No one crosses Madame Blue and leaves without scars. Being shot by you is a mercy compared to failing her, but I will not fail."

She stretched out her fingers and blue-white arcs of energy ran along her hand. "Now, come down here and let's have a civil chat."

There would be no more civility with this woman. That was far past clear. Mabel cocked both pistols and fired. As the smoke rose, Mrs. Snow raised both hands and a blue-white orb full of electric energy shot out, slamming into Mabel's chest and sending her flying back.

Her arms and legs flailed as she flew through the air, panic rising in her breast.

She had severely underestimated her opponent, and now it could end in her death.

With a crack and thud, she hit the side of the railcar behind her, both pistols knocking from her hands. She bounced onto gravel and rolled on the ground. The mask protected her face and the leather jacket shielding the skin on her arms. However, her right arm throbbed terribly, the pain becoming agonizing as she tried to move it.

Her heart jolted as another gun fired. Mrs. Snow screamed in pain. A zapping sound snapped through the air, followed by an explosion and smoke.

"Antonio!"

She tried to scramble to her feet, praying her husband was alive. Her bruised muscles along her right leg and hip throbbed, but the adrenaline kept them numb. Gritting her teeth, she rose and hobbled toward the railcar she had fallen from, each step hurting more. She had to protect her husband. Her left hand shook as she pulled her rapier from its sheathe.

A second gunshot rang out.

She prayed this was Antonio's gun and not someone attacking him.

She slid between a pair of railcars as another blast of energy flashed in the air. The railcar to her left lurched, the end jolting toward her. She pushed herself forward, but several large wood crates fell in her path, blocking her exit. As she turned, she glared at the two railcars blocking her in with their corners hard against each other, creating a triangle around her.

Hissing in frustration, she glanced up, looking for a way out. If she had full use of her right arm and leg, she could climb up. She pushed her left shoulder against the crates, but they didn't budge and the pain in her right leg was growing.

She fell onto the ground and laid on her side as a sharp pain ran through her ribcage.

Another zap of energy was matched with another gunshot. Panic shot through her as Antonio cried out in pain.

"No." She panted as she stared beneath the railcars. There was a gap she could pull herself through. But what could she do while alone and injured?

There was one more hope, though she prayed that hope wouldn't be too annoyed.

Mabel's hand trembled as she pulled the Navy officer's whistle hanging from her neck out from under her shirt and blew into it. The tone was sputtering, especially with the sharp ache along her ribcage. She felt a tingle of magic and dropped it.

Hopefully, this would be enough. Until help came, Mabel had to do everything she could.

She sheathed her rapier and rolled onto her stomach. Keeping her right arm and leg straight, she dragged herself underneath a railcar and pulled herself toward the opening on the other end.

CHAPTER 26

In Which a Mermaid Conducts Business

Wearing a brunette wig, lace veil, and gloves, Cassandra leaned against Arturo as he adjusted his poker cards and she rolled the golden bauble in her gloved hand, watching her target like a panther waits for its prey.

"How does an old codger like you get an ingénue of such beauty?" The fifty-year-old Mr. Grisdom's cheeks were red from his fifth glass of alcohol as he laughed. "And how do you get one for me?"

"Money." Arturo raised his glass toward the other man, barely hiding his disdain. His graying hair was slicked back, and his tuxedo framed him quite nicely. No matter his age, he was a handsome man. "Which is what I'll win from you tonight."

"You've plenty of that, Mr. Astrellar," Mr. Grisdom laughed, mispronouncing the name as "As-tray-lar" instead of "As-tre-yar". It was common in Barthan and sent a prickling down Cassandra's neck each time. However, if her information was correct, it was the least of the businessman's crimes.

As Mr. Grisdom chortled, Cassandra faked a delightful laugh, leaning so her excellent profile was accentuated. If she met a girl as idiotic as the one she was playing, she might turn her into a frog too.

"There's always more room in the bank," Arturo said with a wink.

Mr. Grisdom snorted and pounded his hand against the table.

"More room in the bank? Good one, sir."

"I've heard rumor your seeking investors," Arturo said. "The Astrellar fortune is always looking for investments, including ones where we won't ask questions of if the return is satisfactory."

The businessman grinned as he leaned forward, greed betrayed in his eyes.

This man was far past an excellent candidate for Cassandra's purpose. But, for Arturo's sake, she would wait for the proof so they could make amends for others the man had swindled. That was the agreement she had made with Arturo, and she would keep it.

"Isn't that why honest men like us take such business here?" Mr. Grisdom winked. "When I got the invitation from a potential investor, I didn't think it'd be from a man with more wealth than all of Barthan."

"The Astrellar fortune is quite large, but still within reason." Arturo sipped his drink.

Cassandra raised an eyebrow. The family fortune had already been large when Arturo had inherited it. Over the decades, their investments in factories, railroad, shipping, real estate and other ventures had more than doubled it.

Her eyes drifted, focusing on Arturo's face. His skin was a good color tonight but had been so gray for the past few weeks. His health had to be preserved. She could not bear him dying. Merfolk souls lay in water while human souls lay on land. In her current state, if she lost him, their souls would be separated in the afterlife. Preventing that was worth any cost.

"How much, may I ask, are you—"

Mr. Grisdom's eyes widened as Arturo pulled a velvet bag from his pocket and he poured a handful of diamonds on the table.

"There is more, if the arrangement proves worthwhile." Arturo took another sip of his drink before pushing forward a diamond as thick as his pinky. "This could be an advance, if you're willing to share a few names of associates, to provide insurance."

Mr. Grisdom's hand reached for the diamond, but Arturo slapped it.

"You may be embezzling from other investors," Arturo said with a laugh. "But don't expect to embezzle from me."

"Liggerton's Metal Works have books above reproach," Mr. Grisdom said with another wink before taking the diamond. "As does the Horton Shipping Company."

Arturo turned to Cassandra. "My beautiful lady, what do you think of that?"

In a soft, high-pitched voice, she gave a false giggle. "What a clever man."

She hated pretending to be so stupid. However, it gave the right effect as Mr. Grisdom smiled at her, admiring her curves. While her figure was admirable, such looks from men of Mr. Grisdom's poor character were annoying.

"Shall we lay our cards out?" Arturo said, setting his one set of pairs down.

Just as Cassandra had planned when she shuffled the deck, Mr. Grisdom lay down a full house.

"It seems, Mr. Arturo, that I'm your better bet of the night."

Arturo pretended to join the man's laughter before rising, resting his hand on Cassandra's back, and whispering in her ear, "Finish the deal."

He kissed her cheek before saying out loud, "I'll get us some fresh drinks to celebrate."

He picked up the diamonds from the table before tossing one more to Mr. Grisdom. The man chuckled as he caught it and said, "You'll get ten times back."

"We'll all get our fair reward." Arturo gave him a cold smile and strode away.

Cassandra waited till he was a few tables away before gathering the magic to enhance the natural allurement spell merfolk carried and moving to Mr. Grisdom's side. If her beauty hadn't been able to attract his attention alone, he was now lost in that stupor of devotion so many had around her. It was useful but exhausting.

Tracing his nose with her finger, she said quietly, "I've been looking for a man of your handsomeness. Shall we step aside to a private room and get better acquainted?"

His grin broadened and Cassandra took his arm, leading him from the table to one of the night club's quiet side rooms. Once inside the dim space, Mr. Grisdom puckered his thin lips.

Cassandra grimaced, but said sweetly, "Won't you play a little game of toss with me, for my amusement?"

"Anything for you, dear girl."

She gave a pattering giggle before holding up the golden bauble and tossing it toward him. He moved to catch it, but it bounced off his arm and thunked on the ground.

"Hard in the dim light," he said with a laugh while bending down awkwardly to pick it up. Rising, he gave her an attempt at a playful look and tossed the bauble back to her. As it left his hand, his body formed into a toad. Cassandra caught him with one hand while the bauble landed in the other. She grimaced at the small layer of slime on the bauble, formed from the transformation spell.

Carefully, she dropped the bauble into her pocket before placing the now amphibious businessman in the handbag dangling from her wrist.

Wiping her gloves with a handkerchief, she said, "And that's what we do with honest men like you."

Humming to herself, she strode back into the opulent green and gold nightclub, a smoky haze in the air as others conducted less-than-honest business. Arturo was back at their table, a fresh drink waiting for her, but no sign Mr. Grisdom had been there.

"One more drink, a bit of dancing, then home?" he said as she sat beside him.

She raised her veil just enough to kiss him. "Sounds delight—"

She cringed as a high-pitched whistling filled her left ear. Holding a hand to her ear, she handed the bag holding Mr. Grisdom in frog-form to Arturo.

"What is it?" Arturo pressed a hand to her shoulder as he set Mr. Grisdom on the poker table. The bag started to hop away, so he put his other hand on it.

"Madame Sinclair seems to have gotten into trouble." She reached into the hidden pocket of her skirt, grateful as the whistling stopped. She opened a small mirror case and held it in her palm. The top mirror showed Mabel from the side. The young woman was beneath a railcar, climbing through a dark space full of dirt, dragging her right arm and leg. There was a flash of blue-white light outside.

"That does look like trouble." Arturo gripped her arm before kissing her cheek. "Go. Quickly. Protect the girl and her young sailor."

Ignoring a tightening in her stomach which rarely came anymore, she focused on the bottom mirror, watching the map form. It was taking too long. "Looks like she is about fifty miles from Willington."

"You need a faster way there." Arturo glanced out before nodding toward another table. "What if you used your charm on him?"

Cassandra followed Arturo's gaze to a man in his late twenties, boasting to a set of young women fawning over him.

"Have Doctor Braxton ready at the Willington townhouse," she said. "If all goes well, I'll be there within the hour."

She and Arturo rose together. As she began to leave, he put his arm around her waist and kissed her.

"Make sure you come home to me," he said.

"I always do." She squeezed his hand before gliding toward her second mark of the evening.

<u>CHAPTER 27</u>

In Which Antonio Duels for Mabel's Future

Antonio charged as Mabel fired her pistols from on top of the railcar. His heart stopped as Mrs. Snow hit Mabel with an orb of blue-white energy, and she went flying from the roof. Antonio's instinct was to run to make sure she was safe, but she would not remain so for long with Mrs. Snow pressing her attack.

He raised his pistol, aimed, and fired.

He had seen Mabel load hers with blanks, but he had bullets.

If there were true danger, they would need more than a show to save themselves.

The bullet hit Mrs. Snow's left arm. She screamed in pain as she turned toward him and raised her other palm, the white-blue energy glowing along her arm. Antonio dove across the ground and rolled behind a stack of crates. The ground and several crates exploded where he had been seconds ago.

"Antonio!"

He glanced out in the haze as he scrambled toward the next set of crates and hid. That was Mabel's pained cry. Which meant she was alive.

Now, he had only to make sure she stayed that way and they both returned home.

As the haze began to clear, he peeked over a crate and aimed his pistol. Once Mrs. Snow strode through, seeking him, he fired again. He winced as he missed, the bullet hitting the railcar behind her.

He sprinted toward the railcar Mabel had fallen behind. Feeling the crackling of energy, he dove out of the way as Mrs. Snow's blast hit the railcar, making it lurch. He moved toward a set of crates, but Mrs. Snow sent a blast of wind, toppling them over and blocking his path.

Unsure what to do, he kept running, zigzagging to make himself a harder target. He spun behind a railcar on the parallel track and leaned out to fire the next shot. An arc of her blue-white energy hit his arm and his finger pulled on the trigger, the bullet flying wildly as he fell back against the railcar, his body jittering.

"Just give in, Lieutenant," Mrs. Snow said as she approached. "Isn't your dear Mabel's life worth more than a thousand macs? This is all we're asking tonight. Don't make me kill you after all that's been invested in you."

Antonio grunted in disgust. All he and Mabel wanted were their own lives. He pictured Admiral Guerrero sneering at him after another shady business meeting.

That was not who Antonio was, and he and his wife would not be trapped.

He scurried behind another railcar before diving beneath it. Holding his still-numb right arm next to him, the muscles in his forearm tingled like when his leg fell asleep. He'd have use of it soon but switched the gun to his left hand.

"Oh, Lieutenant," Mrs. Snow called in a sing-song voice. "Where are you? All we want is to help your future."

Antonio narrowed his eyes as he looked along the barrel of the pistol, holding the gun steady. One shot might end this night and keep him and Mabel safe. He was a naval officer, and this was a battle. If life was lost, that was the price.

"Imagine the future we can help you build for your dear Mrs.

Cortez."

"One more step," he whispered. The feeling in his right arm returned, so he switched the pistol to his other hand and aimed once more.

"What a sweet life you could have for your little children." Mrs. Snow was nearly in Antonio's line of sight.

"You will touch none of our children!" Mabel yelled as she rose from underneath a railcar and stumbled to her feet. She was covered in dirt and barely standing as she cradled her right arm and held her rapier with her left hand.

Antonio scrambled from underneath the railcar and sprinted as Mabel stumbled toward Mrs. Snow. Whatever she was planning to do, she didn't have the strength for it. He had to protect her.

Mrs. Snow flicked her hand, and a rippling wave of energy ran toward Mabel. Antonio skidded to a halt in front of Mabel, raising both palms by instinct as the energy hit. A surge of power ran along his forearms and a flash of green energy poured out, creating a wall that deflected Mrs. Snow's spell and sent it back into her. As she tumbled backward, his heart pounded and he stared at his arms.

He had never done anything like this before. His magic had only been small spells to make things more convenient. Yet, he felt as if a spring of untapped energy had opened within him, and he could feel a deeper power filling him.

Mabel pushed past him and limped toward Mrs. Snow with the rapier raised. "Yield!"

Mrs. Snow rose to her feet and flicked her right wrist. A blast of wind knocked Mabel down and she rolled across the ground, the rapier falling from her hand. Antonio panted as he let his energy guide his instinct, just as he did while sewing. He held out his palms toward the ground as green energy gathered around his arms. It felt like it was a part of him yet was so unfamiliar. It was frightening and astounding.

And might save them.

Hoping this would work, he waved his arm like throwing a ball. A fist sized orb of green energy sped toward Mrs. Snow. She waved her hand and deflected his spell before returning an arc of lightning. He raised his other palm and breathed out in relief as the green wall of energy deflected her magic.

Sweat covered his brow, and he steadied his feet as he and Mrs. Snow engaged in a barrage of spells back and forth. Each second, he felt he might slip, miss blocking one and be knocked into the railcar behind him. Yet, he held his own as the minutes stretched on. Sweat dotted Mrs. Snow's forehead and her movements betrayed a tiredness matching his own. Especially as more blood stained her left sleeve. He pressed on. He had to stop her and protect Mabel.

"I suppose you won't pay the one thousand macs, will you?" Mrs. Snow said through gritted teeth as she blocked another spell. She twisted her wrist and a ball of red-orange flame formed. "Then, the fabric is no longer an asset."

Antonio's eyes widened. He should have expected this ruthlessness, but it still stung. He sent another ball of energy, but she knocked it aside before sending the ball of flame toward the wooden railcar.

The roar of the sea filled Antonio's ears as he stared at the flame hitting the side of the railcar and quickly spreading. He held his palm in a cupping shape as his instincts whispered to him and he pictured a sphere of water. He jumped as the sphere formed, smelling of the brine of the sea.

Not caring how he'd done it, he gathered another sphere with his other hand and sent the first toward the spreading flame. The fire hissed as the ocean water hit. He pounded his fists forward, hoping this would work, and was relieved as smaller spheres of water shot forward, dowsing the flame.

His arms shook from exhaustion as he turned toward Mrs. Snow. She cocked her head, her eyes curious even as both her hands held an orb of flame.

"Surrender." He panted, his whole body drenched in sweat. "Or just walk away and leave us be. We want none of this."

"Oh, I think you'll be surrendering."

He heard the click of a gun cocking and turned. A coldness shot through him as the one remaining guard stood with one arm around Mabel, the other holding a pistol under her chin. Her blue eyes were full of fury as she glared at Mrs. Snow. Part of Antonio wished Mabel was the one with power, because she would have burned Mrs. Snow to ash already.

However, he raised his palms in surrender.

Nothing was worth risking Mabel's life.

"We'll get you the thousand macs tomorrow," he said.

Mrs. Snow narrowed her eyes before looking to Mabel. "In our original contract, you failed to mention the lieutenant was part merfolk."

Antonio's brow furrowed. "I'm just a tailor."

"It will be quite interesting to see how your merfolk clients react when they find out your husband's heritage. I imagine you'll realize the value of an alliance with Madame Blue then."

Mrs. Snow raised her hand and gathered more flame.

"No!" Antonio cried.

A shout next to him made him turn his head as Mabel used her left hand to stab a knife into the hand of the man holding her and shoving the gun from her chin as it fired. Antonio threw a ball of green energy toward the man. The energy hit and the man cried out as he flew back, his body jolting as if being hit by an electric shock. He moaned as he landed on the ground, curling up on his side.

Mrs. Snow pushed her palms forward, sending two orbs of fire speeding toward the rail car. Antonio raised his fist to send spheres of water but only a small sprinkle came out. He shook his fist and just droplets flew. He stared in horror as the flames rushed up the side of the railcar once more.

He glared at Mrs. Snow and gathered green energy to his hand while Mabel knelt on the ground and raised the pistol.

"What is this mess, Madame Sinclair?" A woman in a blue ball gown strode through the yard toward them, a veil over her face. Mrs. Snow's eyes widened, and she began to run.

"Lieutenant, would you please stop her while I save our assets?"

It took him a moment to recognize the woman as Cassandra Astrellar. She tossed a glass sphere toward the fire. Water rushed out and she pushed her palms forward, guiding the water so it flowed like a stream through the air.

"Go, stop her," she said.

Antonio tried not to gape as the water surged and carved along the edge of the railcar, as if surfing along it. He broke into a sprint. Mrs. Snow shot a wild blast of energy toward him, but he easily deflected it before reaching her and tackling her to the ground.

"Madame Blue will have her revenge," she spat as he grabbed her right arm and held it behind her. An electric shock hit his palms and he cried out as he jerked back. She twisted herself around and brought her knee into his groin. He wheezed as he bent forward, and she scrambled to break free. However, he grabbed her by the legs. She tried to kick, but he held on tight, grateful for his strength as a sailor.

"Mrs. Snow, is it?" Cassandra said as she stood over them. She lifted the veil covering her young face, her expression far from pleased. "I'd ask you to inform your management that the Astrellar Estate has no business with any affiliates of Madame Blue and has worked hard to do so. However, given your persistence, I think that is a waste of both our time."

"I am—"

Cassandra sighed before pulling a golden bauble from her pocket and rolling it across Mrs. Snow's cheek. Antonio's eyes widened as Mrs. Snow shrank down into a frog.

Wiping the golden bauble on a handkerchief, Cassandra said, "Would you be a dear and collect her? I need to go see to your wife."

She strode away with the clear assumption he would follow her command.

Antonio scooped up Mrs. Snow and wrapped her in his handkerchief, tying it to make a pocket. By the time he reached Mabel, Cassandra had another frog in her hand as she stood where the man who had held a gun on Mabel had been. She handed the new amphibian to Antonio before gathering her skirts and kneeling beside Mabel. His wife sat panting, her mask raised and her face betraying her pain as she leaned against the railcar.

Antonio tucked the second frog into his pocket before removing his mask and kneeling beside Mabel. He wiped his palm on his pants before gripping her left hand.

"Madame Sinclair, while your bravery is without question," Cassandra said as she looked over Mabel's right arm, an awkward bend in the forearm where the bone was broken, "your common sense is another matter entirely."

"Thank you for coming." Mabel held her ribs as she hissed. "Did we save the fabric?"

"For tonight, it appears so." Cassandra motioned to Antonio. "Go find a telephone. There should be one over at the signal tower down the yard. Call the police and say there's been some arson and there's stolen merchandise belonging to the Madame Sinclair Company." She looked to Mabel. "Any other 'witnesses' to manage?"

"There are five others, but we knocked them out." Mabel's voice was growing hoarser. Antonio wished his handkerchief didn't have a frog in it so he could use it to wipe her forehead. "Four are in railcars and one in a shed."

"What a bounty," Cassandra whispered, her eyes widening with a hint of greed. She looked to Antonio. "Come back here after you make the call to the police. Tell them there was an attempt at arson, but everyone ran off."

Antonio frowned but stood to follow her command.

"What do you plan to do with the men we knocked out?" Mabel said. "Turn them into frogs and trade them with merfolk?"

"What better way to manage witnesses?" Cassandra ran a hand

over Mabel's leg. Green light swiftly enveloped the leg. A chill ran along Antonio's spine as he watched the light. "That should ease the bruising."

"That is too harsh a punishment," Mabel said. "They should be sent to prison."

"Where Madame Blue's organization will set them free and ask questions?" Cassandra glanced at Antonio. "I suspect you want to keep this Illuminator of yours a tidy secret."

Antonio's mouth went dry as his eyes met Mabel's. Hers were faded by exhaustion, but still worried.

"Mrs. Snow said I'm part merfolk," he said, his voice somewhat hoarse.

Cassandra paused from where she was holding an orb of green light over Mabel's ribs. The light cut off as her fist clenched and she stared at Mabel's wedding ring.

"Madame Sinclair, where is your monocle?" Cassandra's face was cool and serious as Mabel handed over the monocle. Cassandra raised it to her eye and looked up at Antonio. Her frown deepened as she handed Mabel the monocle and rose. She pulled the golden bauble from her pocket.

"Would you hold this, please?" she said.

"Why do you want to turn me into a frog?" Antonio stared at the strange object.

"I don't. I'm testing something." She waved her hand. "Now, be a dear, and hold this."

Antonio shook his head. "I saw what happened to Mrs. Snow."

Cassandra focused on him. "And is it Mrs. Snow or myself who is rescuing you two from this idiotic escapade?"

"Once you transform, all I have to do is kiss you to turn you back," Mabel said tiredly. "But, Madame Astrellar, why—"

Cassandra held her palm out, motioning for Mabel to be silent.

"This is of more importance than I can tell you." There was an intensity in her blue eyes as she stared at Antonio, as if taking a fresh look at his face. "Please, indulge me. It will take just a moment."

Antonio's muscles tensed as he picked up the gold bauble. With the metal against the skin, he could feel the spell within it. He tossed it in his hand and frowned as nothing happened.

Cassandra's stare was strange as she seemed to reassess him. She took the bauble, her voice somewhat distracted as she said, "Thank you."

"I'm glad not to be a frog," Antonio said, "and to have Mrs. Snow be stopped, but—"

"We'll investigate who you are after we return to Willington."

Antonio nodded, but still felt a strange twisting in his stomach as his mind tried to explain everything from tonight. It was complicated and not helping his exhaustion.

Getting out of this place and making sure Mabel was taken to safety were the most important matters.

Within twenty minutes, they had collected the other men as frogs and the police were called, Cassandra used a spell to shift Mabel's broken forearm into place, and Antonio carried her to a clear area at the edge of the rail yard.

Antonio went still as he stared at a red racing dragon standing there, at least twice as long as a horse and one and a half times as tall, its wings flexing as it scratched itself and stretched out its long tongue.

"My darling!" A man in his late twenties wearing a tuxedo ran out from behind the dragon. Antonio's jaw hung open. This was Dusty Brighton, one of the greatest dragon jockeys in the world. "I've waited, just as you asked, but where have you been? I was worried."

Cassandra gave him an almost polite smile. "I found my friends, Mr. Brighton. Thank you again for being such a dear."

"It is easy to wait knowing I'll have you in my arms once more." He grinned and leaned toward her for a kiss.

"Not yet, Mr. Brighton." Cassandra tapped his nose and Antonio felt a tingle of magic along his arm.

"I thought she was happily married," he whispered to Mabel.

"She's treating him as a puppet, just like she did my broth—"

Her voice broke off as she winced in pain and held her ribs. Antonio carefully adjusted his hold of her, though his arms ached.

"Shall we go?" Cassandra gestured toward the dragon.

Mr. Brighton held out his arm to her. "Four people is quite a lot for a racing dragon. I would rather—"

Tapping his arm with her hand, she said, "It's a quick ride, isn't it? Won't you? Just for me?"

Mr. Brighton's chest puffed up with the pride of a man seeking to impress a woman. "For you, darling, I'd carry them to the ends of the world."

Cassandra gave a pattering laugh. "Just to Lamont Avenue in Willington."

She walked past him and led the group to the dragon. Mr. Brighton climbed on first, followed by Cassandra. Antonio helped boost Mabel up while Cassandra used a spell to help support her. Once he was seated on the dragon's spine, ropes tied to the saddle attached to his and Mabel's waists, the dragon rose in the air.

The wind rushed past them, and Mabel whimpered as Antonio's hold tightened.

"Sorry." He kissed her cheek but didn't like the clamminess of her skin. However, there was nothing he could do while the ground was a blur beneath them, and the dragon sped toward the horizon.

He decided to stop looking down as a queasiness rose. He was unsure how much was due to thoughts of falling and how much was from staring at his hand in the dark, seeking signs of webs between his fingers. Contemplating other rumors of merfolk, he felt behind his ear for gills before running his tongue along his teeth. They felt as they always did, but he pictured them growing into needle-like monstrosities.

It had to be a lie.

He had always enjoyed swimming, sometimes feeling as if he belonged in the water. And he could hold his breath longer than most.

However, he certainly had legs and not a fishtail.

"It's not true," he whispered. "I'm just a human tailor with magic."

He shut his eyes, wishing life with Mabel would be as simple as he had dreamed of when he had sent her the first letter asking her to write him. Even with everything, he wouldn't give her up, but he wouldn't mind if mermaids and magic weren't real.

The dragon circled over Willington as fog filled a street full of small mansions packed together, each about a hundred times larger than the small shop and apartment Antonio had grown up in. With the lightness of a sparrow landing on a clothesline, the dragon landed in the middle of the foggy, cobblestone street.

Antonio dropped off the dragon, grateful for steady ground, before helping Mabel down. She moaned in pain as she leaned against him.

"At least we succeeded," she whispered, her voice betraying her exhaustion.

"I'm just grateful we made it out alive." He kissed the corner of her forehead as he watched Cassandra, wondering what strangeness she would lead them to next.

She stood next to Mr. Brighton as he leaned toward her, clearly expecting a kiss as his reward. Cassandra patted his cheek before snapping. Mr. Brighton stood stock still, awaiting her command.

"Return the dragon, go home, and drink this." Cassandra set a vial with a blue potion inside his breast pocket. "You deserve better than the hangover you'll receive tomorrow. But we are all better off if you forget tonight's activities, aren't we?"

He nodded mechanically and marched back to the dragon like a windup tin soldier. Antonio stared as the dragon shot up in the air and flew off into the night.

"Why don't you give me your coat with the frogs in the pockets?" Cassandra held her hand out as she approached. "I'll carry that and you carry Madame Sinclair. I doubt she is walking very far tonight."

"I can manage." Mabel gritted her teeth as she stepped forward but moaned as her right leg faltered and she began to tumble. Antonio grabbed her shoulders to stop her fall.

Keeping one hand on Mabel's back to hold her steady, Antonio removed his jacket and handed it to Cassandra. As she strolled toward a white, marble mansion, he pulled Mabel into his arms, holding her as gently as he could. His own legs and arms shook from exhaustion, but he pushed himself up the stairs and into the small mansion.

"There's our handsome young couple." A Castallan man in his sixties crossed the grand entry hall, a relieved grin growing. He reached Cassandra's side and gave her the casual kiss of greeting between husband and wife.

"Lieutenant Cortez," Cassandra said, "this is my husband, Arturo Astrellar."

"I'm honored to meet you, sir." Antonio carefully lowered Mabel to her feet. That was a better option than risking dropping her on the floor and adding to her bruises.

"What a gentleman this young lieutenant is." Arturo patted his shoulder. "And far more dashing in person." He winked at Mabel. "I can see why you made up a fake marriage with this young man."

Mabel glared at him tiredly. Antonio kept a hand on her back, praying she wouldn't collapse.

"Can you gather some fresh night clothes for the pair to borrow?" Cassandra said.

"Already waiting in the guest restroom." Arturo nodded toward Antonio and Mabel. "I suspected you wanted to be cleaned up."

"Lieutenant, why don't you help your wife?" Cassandra said. "A shower will do both of you good."

Feeling the layer of dried sweat on his skin, Antonio nodded. "Thank you."

He held his hand out to Mabel. "Can you walk, or should I carry you a bit further?"

He waited for some flirty quip, but she held out her left arm and said, "Can you carry me? I'm about to fall."

Antonio rolled his shoulders before carefully lifting her once more. Arturo led them down the hallway and Antonio was grateful the restroom wasn't as far as he feared.

"Guestroom's across the hall." Arturo pointed to an ornately carved door. "Doctor is waiting to check on you. Ring the servant's bell by the door and I'll bring him."

Antonio nodded numbly as he carried Mabel into the enormous restroom which was larger than his mother's apartment. He gaped at the black and white tiled space with a large bathtub and a standing shower.

As gently as possible, he helped her change out of her clothes. It was difficult to assist her in the shower with her injuries, but she soon was clean and wearing the wrap-around nightgown. Freshly clean himself, he pulled on the provided pajama set, a shirt and pants made of Gathrayan linen. It was incredibly light and soft.

He half-carried her into the guest bedroom and helped her lay on the bed. The slit in the wrap-around nightgown slipped and he winced at the deep purple bruising along her right leg. This also matched more bruising on her ribs, hip, and arm.

Grimacing, she lay flat on the bed and said, "I was so foolish tonight. To think I could take on an Illuminator alone."

"At least we were foolish together." He pulled on the servant's bell before sitting beside her and brushing her wet hair from her face. "Though, there was nothing more terrifying than watching you flying off the railcar."

A heaviness gathered in her eyes. "It was terrifying for me too. I'm lucky my injuries aren't worse, or—"

He leaned down and kissed her. "I'm grateful we're here and alive. Let's focus on that tonight."

She attempted a smile, but her eyes remained worried.

He held her left hand even as the white-haired, male doctor came. Arturo stood at the door, watching as the doctor assessed Mabel's injuries. Antonio frowned as a yellowish light flowed from his hands, creating lines of light wrapping around Mabel's body. She drifted unconscious as she floated, the lights flowing around her. Antonio cringed at a cracking sound as her right arm straightened and the bone shifted into place.

Using his palms, the doctor lowered Mabel back to the bed and the yellow light dissipated from around her.

The doctor held out a vial of glittering liquid and said in Barthanian, "Give her a few drops every few hours after she wakes. It will help speed her healing."

Antonio stared at the strange liquid as he held it in his palm. It was another reminder of how much he had yet to learn of magic in this world. And of himself, if he really was part merfolk.

As Antonio set the vial on the nightstand, the doctor nodded to him before walking to the door.

"Thank you again for your good but quiet work." Arturo passed a thick envelope into the doctor's hand.

Saluting with the envelope, the doctor said, "Always willing to help those who show proper appreciation."

As the doctor walked down the hall, Arturo said, "Enjoy some rest, Lieutenant Cortez, and watch over your wife. She is a remarkable young lady."

"She is." Antonio nodded to the older man. "And, we are grateful to you and Madame Astrellar, señor."

Arturo's dark eyes watched him a moment before he gave a stiff but polite smile. "Rest. I will see you at breakfast."

With the door shut and lights dimmed, Antonio lay beside Mabel and rested his head close to hers as he held her left hand.

"Let's try keeping the next few months less exciting than the past few days," he whispered, tears at the edge of his eyes. "Because, whether I'm a human or half-merman, I need you alive if I'm going to spend my life with you."

He kissed her cheek before shutting his eyes, praying sleep without nightmares would come.

CHAPTER 28

In Which Antonio Learns of His Heritage

Antonio held out his hand to Mabel as she sat on the bed. She wore a sky-blue summer dress made of light cotton, her right arm held in a sling, hidden magic serving to hold the healing bones straight. He wore his own dark blue suit with embroidery on the cuffs which had been lain out sometime during the night. How the Astrellars had brought his and Mabel's own clothing, including undergarments, was a minor mystery in the growing catalogue of strange things in Antonio's life.

"Every drop of me aches." Mabel grimaced as she started to move her right arm. "And throbs."

"I can carry you again, if you want," Antonio said, wincing in sympathy. He had discovered a few bruises of his own when waking, but she was in far worse shape. Above everything, he was grateful she had woken this morning alive and whole. "But we're supposed to be at breakfast."

Mabel moaned before accepting his hand. He kept an arm around her, ignoring a twinge in his upper arm, as he helped her to her feet. She shuffled beside him, hissing each time she put weight on her right leg.

"Are you sure you don't want me to carry you?" he said.

"I can walk," she bit out before taking another step and letting out a cry of pain while falling against him. "Perhaps, I could use some assistance."

Antonio pulled her left arm over his shoulder once more before picking her up.

She fluttered her eyes at him. "If I am to be carried as a damsel in distress, shouldn't you kiss me?"

"Considering you stabbed a knife into the man holding you at gunpoint, I don't think you'll ever be a damsel-in-distress," he said. "But I am always happy to kiss you."

She shifted her head toward his but cried out, her neck clearly twinging. Antonio winced before kissing her cheek.

"Rest, Mabel." He carried her to the door and awkwardly opened it.

Trying to remember the directions from the note left with their clothing, he walked down the marble hallway to where he hoped the sunroom lay. Entering the patio area surrounded by glass, the sun was higher than he expected. Arturo sat facing the garden as he sipped on tea and read a book, a blanket across his lap. He glanced at them with an amused smile.

Giving an exaggerated look at his pocket watch, he said, "Breakfast is usually served before eleven."

"Is it so late?" Antonio carried Mabel to one of the cushioned chairs at a metal table with a glass surface. "Pardon me, sir. We lost track of time."

With a laugh, Arturo said, "Cassandra and I expected you would sleep late, with how badly Madame Sinclair was injured last night." He pointed toward a card sitting on the table. "Pick what you want, put it on a note, and then put the note in the portal box. Our chef at one of our other mansions will have it ready for you shortly."

Antonio glanced at Mabel, glad to see her equally surprised for once.

"Portal boxes and doors just shorten distances," Arturo said. "The food will be safe."

Antonio surveyed the menu. "This is real food."

Arturo snorted a laugh and pointed his book at Antonio. "I will never have a Barthanian cook, unless I must have bland food."

"There is good Barthanian food," Mabel said. "Roasted turkey pie or ham casserole or—"

"Compared with grilled meat and peppers served in a tortilla with salsa, with Castallan fried rice and beans?" Arturo said.

Antonio's stomach grumbled. It sounded delicious.

Arturo smiled. "You can order as many items as you want."

Antonio held his thumb to his mouth, the temptation to order all eight breakfast items growing. It was too much food, but everything sounded delicious.

After more agony than he expected, he wrote down his choices on the card.

"Only two?" Mabel winked at him before writing down her choice.

"I'm sure you could eat all eight plates of food on the list and not pack on an inch." Arturo chuckled. "At least, that's what I've seen of other merfolk."

A chill ran through Antonio. His smile fell and Mabel sat up, both of them staring at Arturo.

"Pardon me," Mabel said, "but are you joking or serious?"

Arturo frowned before wincing. "Oh. I'm sorry. I think I was supposed to pretend I didn't know the lieutenant is part merfolk. I am sure that is something you want to keep secret." He raised an eyebrow and smiled. "You can imagine how hard it is to remember what you are supposed to admit to knowing when married to Cassandra."

Antonio's thoughts churned and stomach clenched as he placed the notecard with their food order in the portal box, giving him time to absorb the confirmation. Returning to the table and standing behind his chair, he stared at his hands.

"It is true, then?" he whispered. "I'm not human. How is that possible?"

"You didn't know?" Arturo sat up. "From what Cassandra told

me last night, I thought you knew."

"No. At least, not for sure." Antonio's words were slow. "Everything last night—" He ran a hand through his hair. "This is impossible."

"It is improbable, but very possible." Arturo gestured toward Mabel's hand. "Cassandra only mildly suspected the truth when she saw your wedding ring. It is one she had made decades ago, but had gone missing around when our youngest son, Manuel, had run away. Your use of magic last night may have provided a puzzle piece we have been missing for a long time."

A chill ran through Antonio as his eyes met Mabel's. He focused on the ring as slivers of information gathered, forming into a strange truth. As it became clearer, it felt right, yet he didn't fully believe it.

"My father's name was Manuel." Antonio's voice was hushed. "But there are many Manuel's throughout Castallar."

Anxiety grew in Arturo's eyes. "How many have magic?"

The words were a blow Antonio did not expect.

"Only I knew of my father's magic, and he told me to hide my own magic from everyone, including Mama." Antonio focused on the ring and its fine details. "His friends teased him about how he still looked in his late twenties while nearing his forties. But he aged, so he couldn't be fully merfolk, could he?"

"If we are right, your father would have been half merfolk," Arturo said gently.

Antonio touched Mabel's hand, his finger brushing the ring. "Mama always asked Papa where he got such a pretty ring and he told her he bought it for his future bride while a sailor. But—" He looked to Arturo as his heartbeat quickened. "But my mother's ring was originally taken from Madame Astrellar, who happens to be a mermaid married to a human. And—"

His words stuck in his throat. Speaking them aloud would make them true, but they were too strange to be real. "These are too many coincidences."

"The only coincidence," Arturo said, his face somber as he pointed at Mabel, "is Madame Sinclair happening to meet you and Cassandra, and, ultimately, bringing you here. How these came about, I've no answer. But the rest—" He nodded. "Once Cassandra came home from your wedding in Castallar, she began looking into your father's history, trying to uncover how you had gotten her ring. Your father, Manuel Cortez, signed-up for the Navy in the nearest port from the Astrellar Hacienda a week after our Manuel disappeared."

Antonio's brow furrowed. "Papa said his parents were servants. He didn't say anything about the Astrellar family."

"Our son grew up believing his parents were servants," Arturo said, a sadness in his eyes. "Cassandra and I have three children: Isabella, Eduardo, and Manuel. The first two, Madame Sinclair has met."

Mabel sat still, her eyes wide. "Isabella told me once about how she and Eduardo were transformed into full merfolk as children, but I know little more than that."

"They were stolen by Marveth when Isabella was ten and Eduardo was seven." A bitterness ran through Arturo's face. "Manuel was four. In the attack, he happened to be away with Cassandra for the night. Afterward, we hid him as a child of our servants. I tried not to favor him but did quietly pay for his education." Tears came to Arturo's eyes. "He was a bright boy. A bit mischievous. Sometimes, he would join me on walks in the garden, and we'd chat about whatever discovery he had made for the day. Other days, I'd find him standing on the balcony looking out over the ocean, staring at the waves as if they were calling him."

Antonio's hand pressed to his stomach as a tingling ran through him. "Papa and I'd go swimming often, and then sit on the shore until late in the evening, and he'd tell me to listen to the water." His throat clenched, picturing his father's loose hair blowing in the wind as they sat on the sand as the sunset came. There was a faraway look in his father's eyes as he told Antonio of the ports and islands beyond their town. "Sometimes, I felt I could hear its call, but it didn't draw me like it did him."

A sad smile crossed Arturo's face. "Was he a good Papa?"

Tears fell down Antonio's cheeks and Mabel's hand gripped his. "Yes. And I miss him."

"The report I read said there was an accident at the docks he was working on."

Antonio nodded. "The rigging for a ship being built broke and it started to collapse. He held a beam up for nearly a half-hour as water poured in and other men escaped."

His shoulders shook as he remembered running to the docks as alarms sounded and climbing up a crane. He glimpsed his father just before the beam broke and his father disappeared in a crash of rubble.

That moment still haunted his dreams.

"He saved thirty other men." Antonio's voice was hushed. "What he did was right and allowed others to go home to their families. But I—" A sob broke out. "But I lost my Papa."

The fear he had felt moments before his father died had been close to what he had felt when Mabel had been knocked from the railcar roof.

Maybe, if he had known of his own power, he could have saved his father.

Arturo came to his side and pulled him into a firm embrace. The older man's hold was strong and Antonio clung to him as they wept together, mourning all they had lost. This man was very likely his grandfather. While it did not bring Manuel back from the dead, it gave him a living piece of his father.

"You told him?" Cassandra's grave voice came from the doorway.

Antonio released Arturo and wiped his face as best he could. He glanced at Mabel, and her own face was drenched in tears, the love in her blue eyes even greater. He had written sometimes of his father, but the loss was too great and her letters too much a beacon of hope to be weighed down by this story of tragedy.

Wiping his own face with a handkerchief Arturo grinned proudly. "He figured out the clues on his own."

"But we must be sure." Cassandra slammed down a stack of newspapers on the table and marched toward Antonio. She pulled three sharp pins from her lapel before removing a small piece of paper from her pocket. Standing near Arturo and Antonio, she pricked her own finger and squeezed a drop of blood on the paper before handing the other two pins to the pair of men. Antonio joined the man who might be his grandfather in placing a drop of his own blood on the paper.

Lines of green, electric light ran across Cassandra's palm as she held it over the paper. The drops of blood vibrated before a black line formed from Arturo and Cassandra's drops of blood. The line drew out and a perpendicular line formed before the original line continued to Antonio's drop of blood.

Antonio frowned. "What does that mean?"

"This line means there is a generation missing between the samples," Cassandra said, "but that our drops of blood match the paternal side of your bloodline."

"It confirms I'm your grandfather." Arturo clapped his hand on Antonio's shoulder. "And Cassandra is your grandmother."

Antonio stared at Cassandra's youthful face, though her eyes showed the maturity and weight of her true age. Still, it was hard to believe she was his grandmother. And a mermaid. Which meant he truly was part merfolk.

Taking Cassandra's hand, Arturo said, "After all we've lost, look at what's been restored."

"Too much has still been lost," she said quietly. "And more could be taken."

Arturo's eyes softened. "He'll be less of a target than Isabella and Eduardo because he's a grown man. And only a quarter merfolk."

Antonio breathed in, praying he was wrong about what they implied. But a glance at Mabel confirmed her worry matched his. Being kidnapped by merfolk did not sound pleasant.

Cassandra's jaw was taut, and a cold fury entered her eyes as she flexed her free hand. Green lines of energy crackled across it, but she turned her head and shut her eyes as if trying to calm herself.

Arturo ran his hand along her arm as he said in a soothing voice, "Take this moment of joy. Don't let fears and phantoms steal it."

She relaxed her hand and the energy dissipated. "I'm so tired of fighting."

"Look at him, my darling." Arturo put his arm around her shoulder and guided her to face Antonio. "He has my coloring and look at how the wave of his hair is like mine." He winked at Antonio. "Though thicker."

"Most in Castallan have a similar look." Cassandra's eyebrows pinched together. Antonio found himself standing taller, somehow wanting to gain her approval.

"And most merfolk have a flare for fashion." Arturo smiled. "While I like to dress well, look at the embroidery on his coat. That comes from his grandmother's side."

Antonio almost wanted to hide the cuffs where he had embroidered a pattern of small white and blue birds. He glanced at Cassandra's gown, far grander than was needed for a brunch at home and remembered her elaborate gown she had worn to the wedding celebration in Castallar.

Perhaps this was a family trait.

Pulling in a little courage, Antonio held out his arm, showing the cuff.

Cassandra eyed him as she touched his wrist and leaned closer, analyzing the work. "Those stitches are very precise."

"My mother's a seamstress." Antonio wished meeting his father's parents wasn't so strange. "I learned tailoring and embroidery from her but used some magic to help with the smaller details."

"A far better use of magic than combat." She gave him a pointed look.

"I never used magic in combat before last night, but—" He bowed his head. "All I wanted was to protect my wife and my future."

"And she wanted to protect you and your future." Cassandra released his wrist. "Which led both of you into far more danger than you should have been in. The good intentions are clear, but we'll be discussing later how to prevent such a disaster again."

"Of course. I wish the same." He nodded, accepting the small chastisement. If she had not arrived last night after Mabel had sent the call for help, he wasn't sure how the night would have ended.

"Madame—" Cassandra glanced at Mabel. "I suppose if my grandson is your husband, I should be calling you 'Mabel.'"

Mabel's eyebrows rose high. "I suppose so, but it does feel strange."

"Many things are strange when married to merfolk," Arturo said with a wry smile. "Cassandra and I have lost much, and we have had many strange adventures, but I would not give up a day with her."

Mabel glanced at Antonio and whispered loudly, "I think we know where your romantic side comes from."

Antonio's chest felt lighter, and he grinned. He wished she weren't injured and could be standing beside him.

"Though, it's clear which side his good looks come from," Cassandra said.

Arturo playfully puffed up his chest. "Of course. The Astrellar bloodline is full of many handsome men."

"I would never deny your good looks." Cassandra's eyes grew more serious as she gestured toward Antonio's face. "Look at the strong bone structure, especially his angled cheekbones." She brushed a finger along her own cheekbones. "I may be far paler, but the resemblance is clear."

"Well, I claim the lieutenant's courage." Arturo grinned.

"No." Cassandra's voice softened as her eyes met Antonio's. "Based on what Madame—Mabel has told me of this young man, he's inherited your selfless heart." She glanced at Arturo. "Which is both admirable and worrying."

"You've more compassion than you pretend," Arturo said softly.

She glanced at Mabel. "Only for the few people I actually like."

Mabel's smile was warm while she looked up at Cassandra. "I like you too, Grandmama, if I may call you that?"

Antonio rubbed his jaw, trying not to laugh.

"Never." Cassandra glared, but bit back a smile. "You both may call me Cassandra in private, since that is my name. Use Madame Astrellar, or whatever name I'm borrowing in public."

"And what do I call you?" Antonio said to Arturo. "It would be strange to call you señor in private."

"I am happy to be Grandpapa." Arturo grinned. "Husband of your dear abuelita."

Cassandra glared at him. "I am not a 'little grandmother.'"

"No, but you are a beautiful one."

Cassandra's eyebrow twitched up as she stepped toward Antonio. She eyed him a moment before placing her hands on his cheeks, her skin ice cold.

"You are what remains of my three children, Antonio." He was surprised by the tenderness in how she said his name. "I will protect you, your wife, and whatever children you may have."

"Thank you, señora," he said with reverence.

She hesitated before pulling him into a stiff embrace and holding him for a long moment. Though it felt awkward with a newfound grandmother who appeared close to his own age, he returned the embrace.

"You deserve happiness," she whispered before releasing him.

Arturo clapped his hands. "How should we celebrate the restored heir of the Astrellar estate?"

Antonio stared at his newfound grandfather, his mind moving slowly. "I don't expect anything—Grandpapa. I—" He glanced at Mabel. Her eyes were curious as she watched him. "I just want to live a good life with my wife and make beautiful clothing."

"Of course." Arturo's grin was broad. "But you are my only human, living descendant, Antonio Astrellar. Which eases my heart, because I can pass on our family's estate to you."

Antonio's legs felt weak, and he shifted into his chair as he stared at the room they were in and the manicured grounds outside.

"I would inherit this mansion?"

"It's only a townhouse," Cassandra said. "We've how many? At least seventy of these across the world. They are nice little places to stay when traveling to conduct business. I'd hardly judge the estate's value off this small place."

"It's a mansion," Antonio whispered, air becoming harder to pull in. He was grateful as Mabel gripped his hand.

"No. Our mansions are at least four times bigger than this," Arturo said. "I believe we have fourteen. Is that right, my darling?"

"Plus the three I brought into the marriage." Cassandra nodded to Mabel. "Including the one in Pippington."

"Seventeen mansions?" Antonio rested a hand on his head, his pulse jumping.

"We'd probably best not mention all the business investments, real estate, and capital ventures," Arturo said quietly to Cassandra. "Or the vaults. And family jewels."

Antonio looked to Mabel. "Did I hit my head last night? This can't be real."

Mabel smiled as she squeezed his hand. "I'm shocked too, but—" She laughed. "I think you had an easier time accepting you're part fish."

"We are not part fish." Cassandra's tone was sharp. "And you will not speak of merfolk that way."

Mabel held her fist to her mouth, trying not to giggle. Antonio looked away. If he held eye contact with her, he'd burst into laughter and likely offend his newfound grandparents. He ran his hands over his face before looking toward Arturo and Cassandra.

"It is easier to believe I'm part merfolk because that only means I have more magic than I thought. It changes what I am, but not who I am. Now—" His mouth hung open and tears formed. "Mama. If you'll give me a little of my inheritance, I could buy her house."

"You could buy her a hundred houses," Arturo said. "Or a mansion, if you wanted."

Antonio shook his head. "She'd hate a mansion. But a good house with a few rooms with tile floors, and big windows to take in the sun. And, maybe, if the expense could be spared, even a cook or a maid so she doesn't have to clean up."

"I don't think he understands how valuable the estate is," Cassandra said, leaning toward Arturo.

Arturo rubbed her back as he faced Antonio. "It's clear you need some time to comprehend how wealthy you've just become. I'll set a meeting with my business manager, Mr. Hedley. And my lawyers. We'll talk through how to ensure you will inherit everything."

"Everything," Antonio breathed. How much 'everything' meant was unclear, but it appeared to be a lot more than he ever imagined the word could mean.

He frowned as his stomach grumbled with hunger. "I apologize."

Arturo laughed. "We've been so busy reuniting, we've forgotten your brunch."

He went to the portal box and pulled out the three plates of food and set them on the table.

Antonio's eyes grew large as he breathed in the spicy scents. One plate held a steaming chorizo and egg omelet with pico de gallo along the side. The other plate held chilaquiles, with fried tortilla pieces with salsa, guacamole, and a fried egg on top, all flavored with fresh squeezed lime.

"If being your heir means I can have breakfast like this every day," Antonio said, "that is an excellent inheritance."

He joined the others in laughing as he raised his fork, anticipating eating food with actual flavor. Everything else could wait as he enjoyed a real meal at last.

CHAPTER 29

In Which Mabel Learns
She Has Caused a Scandal

As brunch wore on into comfortable conversation, Mabel felt as if the world outside this sunroom didn't exist. The throbbing pain along her hip, leg, and arm, however, was a reminder of the dangers beyond the room. She pushed aside those thoughts and worries as she sat beside Antonio, enjoying a pleasant meal with his newly restored grandparents.

Having his grandparents be her investors was strange. But Cassandra was more relaxed, her usually aloof exterior softening with genuine smiles as she watched Antonio with a mother's interest. She and Arturo grinned as Antonio told small stories of his childhood and memories with his father.

After two hours of chatting, the plates sat empty and there was a lull in the conversation.

"So, what happens now?" Mabel said. "Is there some grand parade to welcome Antonio?"

"I'd be very happy without a parade." Antonio grimaced. "Your father's going to be terrible when he finds out. He'll toss at me a hundred 'investment' opportunities and then try to convince us to move the whole fortune into an account at his bank."

Mabel grunted. "As long as he plans to hand the bank over to my brother, I'd not let them touch anything."

"We'd never move all cash reserves to a single bank," Arturo said. "That's bad wealth management. I keep accounts in about a dozen banks, sometimes with multiple accounts owned by shell corporations. Makes it harder for someone to know how much I actually have."

"Speaking of your father," Cassandra said with false casualness, a mischievous spark in her eye. "How was your visit to your darling little hometown, Mabel? Did you have a nice wedding celebration?"

"I'm guessing you've read the local paper's report," Mabel said.

"I did." The corner of Cassandra's mouth curled up. "And this report appeared in the papers in Willington this morning."

She reached over and picked up the stack of newspapers which had lain forgotten in confirming Antonio's parentage. Mabel frowned as Cassandra handed one to her.

"Go to page four, where the lifestyle section starts." Cassandra sipped her glass of lemonade, waiting as if springing a trap.

Antonio turned the pages for Mabel. His frown matched hers as they came to a photograph of the pair of them dancing the tango at their wedding celebration. The photograph was a touch grainy, but the passion between Antonio and her was clear.

Above, the article, the headline read, *The Mysterious Madame Sinclair: Prodigy or Imposter?*

Cassandra handed a copy of the same paper to Arturo before pointing at the other papers. "There are versions in three others, but this one is the most complete.

Arturo opened to the page and burst into laughter.

Glancing at the stack of at least three other newspapers, Mabel said, "Do they all have the same photograph?"

"One has a photograph from the parade in your hometown," Cassandra said. "And a wedding photograph I'm guessing your parents sent in. But it appears your tango was quite sensational."

Mabel's cheeks warmed and her forehead wrinkled as she skimmed through the article, Antonio reading over her shoulder. His grunts periodically matched the ones she felt.

"What a nice little biography." Arturo glanced over his paper at Mabel. "The being captured by pirates and taking a year to get home is mostly true, but they wrote the wrong date for your marriage to my grandson. I wonder why they'd be confused."

Mabel glared at him, and Arturo snickered.

"What is this about these battles I fought? And saving my ship?" Antonio pointed at a paragraph next to a photograph of him in his lieutenant's uniform. "I never did that."

"According to the letters Admiral Guerrero and other associates of Mrs. Snow sent my father, you did." She glanced at him. "It was how they conned my father into paying your lieutenant's commission."

"After you conned your parents into believing we were married?" Antonio said.

Mabel cringed. "That lie was never supposed to go past my hometown and was only meant to get me out of my debutante debut. Then, after Mrs. Snow threatened Captain Stenton, I needed it to get my dowry and pay her off. If I had known how far the lie would spread, I never would have forged the letter from you."

"Was it a very good letter?" Antonio said with a smile.

"Not nearly as good as your real letters." Mabel kissed his cheek before continuing reading.

"What I don't understand," Cassandra said as she flipped through one of the other papers, "is where the rumor came from that the Astrellar estate only invested in you because Antonio is secretly the heir. While we now know it is true, no one else knows."

"Mr. Trivay." Antonio pointed at the article. "He must be the anonymous source talking about how amateur and shoddy your designs are, and how you bribe your designers to cover up poor work."

"Of course he is," Mabel said, "but I don't think he has the pull for getting articles in all the papers."

"I think you were already being watched after your design was shown in fashion week last year." Cassandra held up another paper.

"This one has a wonderfully inaccurate exaggeration of the secret bidding war over you as an investment. Two of the papers speculate both investing firms are secretly owned by the Astrellar estate, and set-up the bidding war to make you appear more valuable than you are." She raised an eyebrow. "Which proves they do not know you, my dear Madame Sinclair."

Mabel smiled. "I hope I am still a good investment."

"You are, as long as you don't run off alone into railyards, waving your sword to try and scare off Madame Blue's associates." Cassandra frowned. "But where did this rumor come from? Prior to today, Antonio had no ties to our estate."

Mabel tapped her left hand against the armrest as she bit her lip. A memory came and she held back a laugh. "It was you, Cassandra."

"Certainly not." Cassandra humphed.

"At fashion week, you said it to tease my parents because they were annoying you."

Arturo burst into loud laughter. Cassandra gave him a cold glare, but he ignored her as he held his stomach and wheezed in breath.

"It was just a passing comment," Cassandra muttered. "It was meant as nothing."

"How many more lies are there about me?" Antonio's forehead wrinkled. He pointed at the paragraph about his heroics as a naval officer. "Because it seems every lie about me is becoming true, and I'd rather not live through that one."

Mabel skimmed through the article once more. "At least everything in here is mostly true. I did travel with pirates, I am married to the heir of the Astrellar estate, our wedding celebration in Cliffshire was a disaster, I did shoot at my brother, and my design work is amateur at best."

"I'm sure you're past being an amateur," Antonio said. "But you do need a better figure illustrator. Your drawings have improved, but they are hard to execute."

"I know, but I am trying," she said, a small pain in her stomach.

He was right, but it still hurt.

Cassandra focused on Mabel. "You've caught the attention of the fashion world, for better or worse. The question rippling through the studios is whether you are a true talent or just a girl whose success is paid for by her wealthy husband."

Mabel grunted. "I only want to build up my design business. I don't need rumors, and I don't need threats from criminal organizations. I just want to send fine clothing out into the world."

"Now that you're my granddaughter-in-law, you are part of the family," Arturo said. "The business can be a hobby, since you don't need to live off the income, and the Astrellar estate can pay whatever costs there are."

Mabel stared at him. She had a better idea how wealthy the Astrellars were than Antonio did, but the money still felt separate from her. But, by being married to Antonio, she was an heir alongside him.

"I don't want to be an heiress and spend money because I can." She looked to Cassandra. "Even though we are now family, this is still a business. Just like any other venture, my goal must be to provide a profit, and, eventually, I would like to buy your stake in the business and have sole ownership. I want it to rise or fall based on its own merits, and not have it be propped up because my husband happens to be your heir."

Out of the corner of her eye, she caught Antonio smiling proudly.

"Then, that is the business we will help you build." Arturo gave an approving nod.

"Eyes are on you," Cassandra said. "And these articles create a priceless opportunity to showcase your work." She tilted her head, a clever look in her eyes. "How do you feel about showing at fashion week this year instead of next?"

Mabel's muscles tensed. "There're only two months. I can't design a whole line and produce it in so short a time. Especially with the merfolk products needing to be made and shipped out. There's endless work to do, and—"

"A good captain doesn't run a ship alone." Antonio focused on her. "You need good officers you can trust to command in your name. You need to know your strengths." He gave an apologetic smile. "And your talent isn't in designing. Your talent is in adding to and adapting a good design. I've seen that in the notes you've sent back about my sketches."

Mabel met his eyes. "I enjoy designing."

"You've other talents, Mabel. A million of them."

Mabel glanced at her broken arm. "My skill with a blade isn't very useful in the fashion world."

Antonio laughed before he tilted his head. "There is a talent you've used for piracy which might work here."

Mabel raised an eyebrow. "Pickpocketing?"

"Do you know what makes a good thief?" he said. "Putting on a show to distract your mark while the other hand takes the prize."

"I gave it back," she said with a small smile.

"You are charming, Mabel, and clever, and, when you need to, you put on a good show. You did that with Admiral Guerrero. And, if Mrs. Snow hadn't been an Illuminator, I think you would have succeeded last night when you stood on the railcar holding your pistols on her." Though his eyes held worry, he grinned. "You looked magnificent, with the red mask and swashbuckling clothes."

"So, I stand on a roof dressed as a pirate and hold pistols on everyone to convince them I can be a designer?" she said.

"It would be a good show," Arturo said. "Many would talk about it for weeks to come."

Cassandra gasped and touched his arm. "Why didn't I think of that? With the article, a pirate themed fashion display would be an excellent wink to the rumors." She laughed. "The latest in pirate fashion."

Mabel rubbed her chin with her left hand, picturing Captain Stenton in his coat and elaborate hat as he stood with confidence while intimidating another ship.

She glanced at Antonio. "Others make the designs and outfits, but I put on the show?"

He nodded. "And get a strong manager to run the business side but keep your sharp eye on it. You're a good negotiator too." He prodded her shoulder. "Even when it's not a Tratar con Espada."

Mabel rubbed her forehead before looking to Cassandra. "Two months to put on a fashion show? Most of the venues are sold out."

"The Astrellar estate may own a few or have some connections." Arturo winked.

"No favors." Mabel pointed. "No pulling strings or greasing palms. I want this to be honest work done right. And I want it to succeed because of the quality of the work."

Arturo raised his palms. "If you change your mind, I'll keep my checkbook handy."

"You won't need it," Cassandra said. "Mabel will succeed."

"With help." Mabel nodded to herself. "But only help I can trust." She looked to Arturo. There was one person she needed and then everything would be set. "If you'd like to join your wife as an investor, though, I'm going to need enough money to pay someone very well. But she will be worth every skoon."

Arturo nodded. "Whatever you need."

Mabel looked to Antonio. "How would you like to meet my friend Elona?"

CHAPTER 30

In Which Mabel Puts on a Show

Elona stretched her back as she stood up from pinning ruffles on the bottom of the gown. The two months leading up to fashion week were always the most maddening. Especially as Mr. Hartavo became more irate, snapping at people like a goose whose feathers had been ruffled the wrong way.

"What is this atrocity?" he shouted a few tables down from her. Miss Parker, one of the newest assistants, stood in tears as Mr. Hartavo ripped apart the coat the girl had been working on for two days.

He tossed aside the mutilated garment and sneered. "One more time. And do it to perfection or go home to your little farm town. You'll have no future here in Willington."

The young woman broke into sobs while the studio was silent and Mr. Hartavo marched away, seeking his next target.

Others stared at Miss Parker, unsure whether to say anything, too afraid of how Mr. Hartavo would retaliate. Elona sighed before walking over.

"Miss Parker, I need help with something in my office." Elona motioned to another assistant. "Can you see if anything is salvageable on the coat and leave it on Miss Parker's station?"

She put her arm around the weeping girl and led her into her office. Shutting the door, Elona poured water for her and handed over one of the many handkerchiefs she kept for moments like this.

"Fashion is not for the faint of heart," she said as Miss Parker blew her nose into the handkerchief and sobbed. Elona handed over a second handkerchief. "But, if you love the work, it can be worthwhile. You just have to be willing to work hard. Mr. Hartavo only cares about whether or not you provide quality garments."

"My work's never good enough," Miss Parker said. "I should quit before I'm fired."

"You could quit, and no one would blame you. But that would be cowering to bullies like Mr. Hartavo. You were hired because you have talent, Miss Parker. Now, you need skill to succeed." Elona rested a hand on her shoulder. "Think about what you want tonight. If you still want a career, come in an hour early tomorrow. I'll help you with the coat."

Miss Parker looked up at Elona, her eyes wide. "You would? But you've done so much already, and—"

Elona smiled. "A lot of people forget we all started out on the bottom-rung. Alice Devroe saved me from being fired a few times in my first job, so I'm going to do what I can for you." She held out her hand. "Are you willing to do the work, Miss Parker?"

With her head higher and shoulders straight, Miss Parker nodded before shaking Elona's hand. Elona patted her arm.

"Stay in here until you've composed yourself. I'll say you're doing some swatch work for me."

Mr. Hartavo knew she was usually comforting those he sent crying. She tried not to sigh. Many times, she was sure he berated them on purpose so she would teach them. If only he would just ask her to help instead of terrorizing people.

She moved to leave her office but paused as something shiny caught her eye on the desk. From the pile of new mail, she lifted a red envelope with silver embossing around the edges, *Madame Sinclair Designs* written in silver calligraphy.

With a fond smile, she opened it and pulled out the note on high quality, white paper with embossing to match the envelope. If Mabel was spending her investor's money on such opulent stationary, she was wasting resources. Still, it was intriguing.

Elona,

Would you like to meet the mysterious heir of the Astrellar fortune?

Rue de Fantaras Club, 6:30 PM. A carriage will be waiting outside Mr. Hartavo's studio to take you in proper style.

Your friend,
Mabel Sinclair Cortez

Elona laughed as she tucked the invitation in her apron pocket. Based on what Ms. Devroe had told her of Mabel's studio, she wasn't sure how long it would last, but she still hoped for the young woman. A girl of such spunk and wit was worth believing in.

Throughout the rest of the day, Elona found herself giggling each time she wondered what Mabel had planned for tonight. Most likely, it was a chance to meet Mabel's husband. However, Elona wondered what the 'carriage' would be. Most likely one of those two-person bicycles, or the trolley. Eating at the restaurant would probably be visiting the far cheaper café across the street. Whatever came, Elona would happily play along. An evening with Mabel was always fun.

Though the studio officially closed at five, over half the staff were still there at six when everyone crowded near the windows facing the street. Elona ignored the whistles of admiration as she put away her tools.

"Six horses!" someone said. "No one has carriages like that anymore."

Elona's curiosity pulled her to the window.

Outside was a white carriage with gold details and six pure white horses.

"Who do you think is in it?" another staff member said.

Elona frowned as the carriage footman entered the building. Within minutes, there was a knock at the door and the footman was allowed in.

"Ms. Cantor," he said. "Lieutenant Cortez and Madame Sinclair await you."

Elona's eyebrows rose, her own shock matching everyone else's. "Let me grab my coat and hat."

Wondering how Mabel had pulled this one off, Elona grabbed her personal items from her office. As she crossed the studio, everyone gaped at her. Mr. Hartavo came rushing from his office.

"What is this about you going to dinner with Madame Sinclair?" He walked beside her.

"It's just dinner to meet her husband, the young lieutenant."

"The Astrellar heir?" Mr. Hartavo growled.

Elona laughed. She was one of few people who could get away with laughing at him. "He's just a lieutenant, Mr. Hartavo. Madame Sinclair is quite playful, sir, and is probably only pretending to confirm what was in the gossip column."

"With a six-horse carriage?"

Elona shrugged. "I don't know how she managed to get it. Maybe her investor is lending it to her?" She grinned. "Apparently, I get to ride in it."

"You're not allowed to go to dinner with her. She owns a rival studio."

"I'm going to dinner with a friend. Besides, my latest contract allows me to meet with other studios."

"I have been good to you, Ms. Cantor. Helped build your career.

Remember that. No matter how much of her husband's money she tosses at you."

Elona glanced at him and gave a polite smile. "I doubt any business will happen tonight, but I'll remember how well you treat up and coming talent."

Mr. Hartavo glared at her but said nothing more as she exited. She followed the footman down the stairs and to the carriage. He helped her inside the plush interior and then the carriage was off.

She snickered as they traveled along the main boulevard, many gaping as she passed. Several flashes went off, marking journalists with cameras. Something would be in the social columns tomorrow, with speculation about this carriage. While Elona preferred blending with the background, people confusing her for some fine lady or princess of a far-off country was quite fun. She felt more like the young girl of eighteen who had come to Willington, giddy with excitement, rather than the woman in her early thirties, established in her career and experienced enough to no longer anticipate seeing her dresses walk down the runway.

They weren't really her dresses anyway. These were clothing she had put together for Mr. Hartavo. She had learned a few years ago not to make real suggestions. Only minor ones which wouldn't bruise his delicate ego.

The carriage stopped in front of the Rue de Fantaras Club and the footman opened the door. Elona felt underdressed as she walked into the restaurant and checked in with the maître de. He gave her a dismissive look before she said, "I'm Elona Cantor and—"

He stood up straight. "Ms. Cantor. Of course. We are more than pleased you are here. Let me escort you personally."

He led her through the main room full of high society guests, recognizing dresses and tuxedos she had helped design. As they reached a curtained-off, private dining room, Elona tried not to laugh. Whatever game Mabel was playing, Elona hoped it wasn't as expensive as it looked.

Entering the private dining room, Elona raised an eyebrow.

Mabel sat at the table, holding a gold-tipped cane with her left hand and dressed in an elegant black evening gown with elaborate beadwork. It was excellently made, and likely worth the cost of the whole restaurant. She clearly wore a wig, given the cascading locks of red hair, but it was a good match to her natural color. The wig had a ribbon with jewels woven through and several feathers. While opulent, it was elegant.

The waiter helped Elona into her seat and took her drink order. Once he left, Elona said, "If I'd known of our dinner plans, I would have worn a ballgown to work today."

Mabel broke into giggles. Leaning forward, her light-blue eyes bright, she said, "Did you enjoy the carriage? I thought it would be fun."

"It was, especially with everyone staring and speculating. How did you pull that off?" Elona waved at the room they were in. "And this? And your dress?"

"Some rumors in the paper might be true." Mabel winked.

Elona laughed. "Come on, Mabel. I know your investor is rich, but no investor would pay for something like this."

Mabel's eyebrows rose. "My in-laws would."

Elona waved her hand. "We both know that's not true. Didn't you say your mother-in-law is a seamstress in Castallar?"

"Or, she has a seamstress?" Mabel barely held a straight face, seeming about to sputter into laughter.

Elona shook her head and raised her hands. "Fine. I'll play along. Later, you'll have to tell me how you managed to pull this off."

"I'll tell you as much truth as I can." Mabel leaned to the side, looking past Elona. A broad smile crossed her face. "First, let me introduce you to my husband."

Elona turned her head as a young man from Castallar entered, wearing an excellently tailored tuxedo. She recognized him from the photographs Mabel had shown her as well as the ones in the paper yesterday morning. He had looked dashing in the one of him and Mabel doing the tango. He was stunningly handsome in person.

No wonder Mabel had eloped with the young sailor.

"I've never seen aspirin so expensive," he said in Castallan as he kissed Mabel's cheek in greeting, setting a small glass jar of pills on the table. He glanced at Elona and smiled warmly. Many women would melt seeing a man that handsome with a smile that charming. In heavily accented Barthanian, he said, "You are Elona Cantor?"

Elona smiled back and said in Castallan, "I am, señor. And you are Lieutenant Antonio Cortez, Mabel's young sailor and husband?" She winked. "How do you feel about inheriting the Astrellar fortune?"

Antonio's face paled and his smile disappeared. "Oh. I—"

"She's teasing you." Mabel leaned her cane against the table and motioned with her left hand toward the chair beside her but did not move her right arm. "Elona, I didn't know you spoke Castallan."

"I lived in Castallar for nearly two years working for Diego Valdez."

Antonio's eyes widened. "Diego Valdez!" He sat in his chair beside Mabel. "What was it like? I love his use of colors, and the fringe on some of the lady's capes!" He waved his arm. "How it swoops as the women walk."

Elona's smile broadened at his youthful excitement. This was no naval officer or mysterious heir to an enormous fortune. He was truly a tailor at heart, and his enthusiasm for fashion was as great as Mabel's.

As he opened the bottle of aspirin, he said, "Mabel says you have many dresses which have been in *Modan*. You must be honored."

"It's always an honor to have work admired and shown," Elona said. "I've been fortunate in my career to help make many notable gowns."

She stared at a piece of fabric hanging down from Mabel's shoulder, blending with the dress as it wrapped around Mabel's arm. "Pardon me, but is that a sling on your right arm?"

"I took a tumble down the stairs." She grimaced. "Risk of living in a fourth story apartment, I suppose."

Elona winced. "That does sound painful. I hope you heal quickly." She smiled. "And glad it happened after your wedding celebration in your hometown. It looked like quite a tango."

Antonio broke into a proud grin as he took Mabel's hand.

"If your husband's an excellent dancer, you should take advantage of it," Mabel said.

The conversation eased into discussions of Mabel and Antonio's time together during his leave along with discussions of fashion. Talking with Antonio was as easy as it was with Mabel, though he had an earnestness which balanced Mabel's slyness. The meal came and went, yet Elona let herself linger and enjoy a relaxed conversation.

As a light dessert of chocolate mousse and raspberries came, Mabel said, "You've been at Mr. Hartavo's for eight years now, haven't you?"

"I have." Elona lifted a spoonful of the airy mousse. "You know how ornery he is, but he treats me well."

"You are one of the few people he respects." A rare hint of nervousness entered Mabel's eyes. "With your skills and reputation, you could work for anyone you wanted. Have you ever thought of working for another studio?"

Elona's smile fell, and a heaviness hit her stomach. "So, this is a business dinner, then?"

"I need help from a friend." Mabel's eyes were serious. "But would pay fair compensation."

"Mabel, I heard about you firing Mr. Trivay. I'll help you find another designer, but I cannot leave my position for something three steps back. I manage six other designers at Mr. Hartavo's and am working on half of our studio's outfits going down the runway for fashion week. You can't match what I have." She gestured with her spoon. "Let's forget about business and keep this a friendship."

Mabel pulled a letter from her pocket and slid it to Elona. Skimming through it, Elona's eyes widened. "The Adoraz Hotel's offered you a venue? Mr. Hartavo's tried to use their stage for years, but they keep declining. How did you manage that?"

"By being noticeable in the paper," Mabel said. "Whether my show succeeds or fails, the press will be watching. I am a girl who created a scene at her own wedding celebration, spent a year at sea after being kidnapped, possibly by pirates, and may be married to the heir of a mysterious fortune." She leaned forward. "Wouldn't you go for curiosity's sake?"

"I'd go because it's your show," Elona said. "How are you going to manage putting a whole show together in two months? You've kept telling me you don't have plans for a runway show."

"I didn't, but it seems wise to take advantage when the spotlight's on me."

Elona glanced at Mabel's dress. "And keep the spotlight on you?"

Mabel nodded. "Something I learned at sea: A bit of smoke and mirrors can persuade many." She pressed her left hand to the table. "While I'm good at putting on a show, you've said yourself I have much to learn about designing and actually running a design studio."

"Which is why I'm glad you hired Ms. Devroe. She taught me much of what I know. Her designs aren't innovative, but she knows the business and her way around a studio."

"She is excellent, and more than patient with the shoddy design illustrations I've given her."

Elona couldn't help but wince in sympathy. "But you feel you are in over your head?"

"I'm far deeper than that." Mabel held her gaze. "I'm captaining a ship in a heavy storm. Right now, I'm manning each officer's station alone while the wind's battering the sails and could topple me over at any moment. But, if I can get the right first officer to manage the crew, I can focus on navigating and set the ship right."

Mabel pressed her lips together before saying, "Which is why we are here: I want you as my first mate, Elona."

Elona's forehead wrinkled. "A fashion studio is not a ship, Mabel, but to follow your analogy, if you're sinking, perhaps you should lighten the ship. You're young. You don't need to become the biggest name in fashion immediately. Take time to learn."

"The eyes of the fashion world are on me, waiting for me to fail," Mabel said. "If I succeed, I will have a much larger launch to my career than I could otherwise. The opportunity is right in front of me and worth the risk."

"It may be, but you might also find yourself burning up from going too fast." Elona rested her hands in her lap. "Mabel, I admire your ambition, but I worry for you." She gestured at the room. "How are you paying for this, and the carriage you sent for me? And I've heard of the dresses your studio is designing. They sound elaborate and require expensive fabrics. Such clothing has a very limited market. Who is buying them?"

"I have plenty of buyers," Mabel said. "Who they are must be kept secret and wouldn't be believed."

Elona held her gaze. "I've quietly made gowns for men before. Is that who?"

Mabel shook her head. "No, but that is a market I hadn't considered."

"That market would likely be less treacherous," Antonio said quietly.

Elona frowned before whispering, "Is your business a front? Is that why so much money is being poured into it?"

Mabel's gaze was firm. "My business is legitimate. Everything is honestly paid for. Just—" Her brow furrowed. "We have to be discreet with our current clientele. Which, I know, sounds more suspicious than it is."

"You've found an untapped market?" Elona narrowed her eyes.

"Let's just say it's a foreign market," Antonio said, his face betraying his own nervousness.

Elona thought through a list of other nations. The style of dresses she had heard of didn't fit with anything she recognized.

"Regardless of who my clientele is," Mabel said, "I want to expand to regular markets. I can't do that with my lack of skills and small studio. With the success of my test markets, my investor has offered me more capital."

"And so you're expanding and hope I'll fix it for you?"

"I'm hoping you'll be the head designer, with your name on the building and on each design," Mabel said. "It will be Madame Sinclair's Studio with Designs by Elona Cantor. Other designers who work for you will also have their names attached to their designs. There would be a Cantor gown or a Devroe suit."

Elona's fingers dug into her leg as shattered hopes from her early career began piecing themselves back together. She had to be careful how much smoke was in this offer, yet it was becoming more tempting by the moment. "How many designers would I manage?"

"Eight to start with. All of your choosing. Given your connections, I suspect you will collect the best."

"Who would be deciding on designs?"

"You and I would set the color palette and overall aesthetic for the next set. The other designers would submit designs and you would choose what gets made, with my final approval and consultation. You would also run the day-to-day operations of the studio with a clerk to assist with administrative tasks. And you would stand beside me while your work is shown on the runway."

"Those are some bold promises."

Mabel smiled and gestured at her outfit. "I can't help but be bold."

Elona let out a laugh. "How much would it pay?"

Mabel slid a folded notecard across the table. "A fair salary, I hope."

Elona worked to keep her face calm, but it was hard while staring at a salary triple her current wage. "You can't afford this, Mabel."

"You haven't seen my ledgers."

"I've seen your apartment." Elona glanced at the salary again. "I want five percent more plus ten percent commission on the wholesale price of every piece of clothing sold of my design. And the same commission for all designers."

"Eight percent commission."

Elona flipped the notecard in her fingers. She had worked hard to earn her position. Mr. Hartavo had his temper, ignored her advice, and made at least one staff member cry per day. But he was the best in Willington.

But would he be the best without her steady hand?

And how far could she go if she borrowed some of Mabel's boldness and jumped?

If Mabel's show failed, she could always find other work, couldn't she?

"I want a guarantee of at least half my annual salary if the business fails," Elona said, her nerves rising. "And I want my questions answered honestly when it comes to the business." She looked to Antonio. "Starting with, is the Astrellar estate bankrolling this venture because you are the heir?"

Antonio met her eyes. "The Astrellar estate is investing in Mabel because one of the family members believes in Mabel as a businesswoman. That family member happens to be—"

He glanced at Mabel, and she gave a reassuring nod.

"We are keeping this secret for Mabel and my safety, but—" He breathed in, his eyes betraying how overwhelmed he felt. "The main investor in Mabel's business, Madame Astrellar, happens to be my grandmother."

Elona's mouth hung open. "You are Antonio Astrellar?" She looked at Mabel. "He's handsome, can dance, dresses well, and is rich? I didn't know such men actually existed."

"I'm just a tailor," Antonio said. "At least, I was until we had breakfast with Mabel's investor yesterday and learned my late father happened to be their son who ran away and joined the Navy."

Elona's forehead wrinkled. "Are you conning me, Mabel?"

"If I told you the rest, I think you'd believe I was," Mabel said.

"Like Antonio said, we're not planning on confirming his heritage publicly. We'll hint to play with the papers, but nothing more. The Astrellar estate already invested in me before we knew the peculiar connection. I want to run the business independently and have it be self-sustaining. I don't want to go begging for help from my in-laws, no matter how deep their pockets."

"You have a bewildering life, Mabel." Elona rested a hand on her head. "It's a good offer, but can I think on it?"

"Absolutely. I know how hard you've worked to be in your position at Mr. Hartavo's," Mabel said. "That's why I offer a salary worth the risk."

"It's quite a salary." Elona frowned. "I shouldn't say this in a negotiation, but do you know how much I'm currently paid?"

"Not enough."

"With that answer, I'm nearly willing to accept outright." She pressed her hands together. "How long will the offer stand?"

"Until you say yes." Mabel gestured at Elona. "You're the best."

"There are many designers better than me."

"Perhaps, but you've a good design eye mixed with a strong sense for talent, good leadership, and impressive craft. Also, I trust you, and that is priceless."

Looking at the card, Elona pictured Miss Parker's weeping face. Her hands shook as she met Mabel's gaze.

"Give me three days, and then I'll start with Madame Sinclair Designs."

Both Mabel and Antonio broke into relieved grins.

Digging her spoon into the mousse, Elona said, "With two months before your splash at fashion week, what theme were you considering?"

Mabel's grin broadened further, and her eyes lit up. "How do you feel about pirates?"

Elona let out a laugh and shook her head. "How do we build a fashion line around pirates, Madame Sinclair?"

CHAPTER 31

In Which Mabel and Antonio Dance

Mabel relaxed against Antonio, his arms around her as they stood on the top balcony of the mansion Cassandra called a townhouse. They looked out at the Willington skyline reflecting on Lake Chalice, the lights of Pippington small dots barely visible on the horizon.

"I'm glad the potion is healing you so quickly." Antonio rested his cheek against hers. "Because a week of not being able to take you out dancing has been miserable."

"A few more days of healing and I'll be able to keep up." She rested her hand on top of his. "Though, you seem busy enough between all the training Cassandra is giving you with your magic, and the meetings with Arturo to discuss your inheritance. Plus, helping Elona set-up the new studio space. I love watching you lose yourself in working on a design."

"I do love working with Elona and Ms. Devroe. They are true masters at the craft, and I learn more in an hour than I ever thought possible." He held out his hand and green light gathered around it. "And I am learning useful things from Cassandra."

The green light gathered into a rose made of light, the petals turning a jewel-like red. He held it out to her. She hesitated before holding the stem. It felt nearly solid for a second before bursting apart into small sparks shooting up and flowering like miniature fireworks.

She laughed. "I doubt Cassandra taught you that."

"I figured it out on my own," he said, his voice proud. He kissed her cheek. "But even that is less fun than an hour or two dancing with you."

Waltzing music played from a phonograph at one of the nearby mansions. Mabel smiled as she turned to face him.

"My dear Emperador." She held out her arms in a proper waltz position. "May I have this dance?"

He smiled as he placed his hand on her waist and took her hand. "My dear La Ratera, you may steal a dance from me anytime you wish."

He began to lead her, but paused, his eyes concerned. "What about your hip and leg?"

"It's still sore, but I can manage for at least one song."

He kept his step small as they did the box step of the waltz across the balcony. Each step on her right leg pinched her muscles, but it was bearable as his brown eyes held her gaze and the soft moonlight gleamed down. She pressed closer to him, and the waltz was forgotten. He held her as she rested her head against his shoulder and their steps turned into gentle swaying.

She shut her eyes, taking in the moment while her breast warmed. However, her throat clenched, and tears came. "Are you sure we shouldn't bribe your way out of your last year of service?"

"We have a contract," he said. "And I will fulfill it so no one can use it against us. Not Admiral Guerrero nor the shadows who control him. There are already enough secrets to keep. We don't need more lies or shadowy dealings to trap ourselves in. We must do everything we can in the light of day, openly and honestly."

"I'm having fun being mysterious," Mabel said softly.

Antonio chuckled. "Madame Sinclair is only a version of who you are, not a full lie."

She ran her hand along his shoulder, a pang in her breast. "I know you're right, but it will be a long year with you gone."

"I'll have a letter satchel, so you'll get my letters as soon as I write them," he said. "And, with the merfolk magic on your ship, you can join me whenever I have shore leave at port."

"Would it help if I let you know I am there by stealing your pocketbook?" She smiled.

He laughed. "I'll make sure to keep an extra pocketbook full of pictures of you."

"That will surely make jealous the other girls stealing your pocketbook to get your attention."

"They will be disappointed when I tell them there is only one, true La Ratera who has my heart," he said with a laugh.

Mabel ran her fingers along his embroidered lapel, enjoying the texture. "Less than four months isn't long enough before you leave. Especially with how busy we'll be while getting ready for fashion week. And who knows what Madame Blue's organization will try next."

"But we will be together each of those days." He kissed the corner of her forehead. "And, once the year is done, we will be together every day after that." Leaning back, he winked. "Isn't that what we hoped for when we eloped in Port Nerama?"

She stood fully, taking in his handsome face and smiling softly. "It's what I secretly hoped for the night we met, when we danced, and I stole one last kiss before running off."

"That was both exhilarating and disappointing." Antonio put his arms around her waist. "I had hoped to give you a far better goodbye kiss."

"I know. And it scared me, because I doubted we would meet again." She leaned closer to him. "Still, I wonder what that kiss would have been like."

"I think, my darling Mabel, it would have gone like this."

He held her as he dipped her back. A thrill shot through her as his lips pressed to hers while he slowly returned her to her feet. She kept her arm around his shoulder and ran her fingers through his hair. Holding onto him, she was very glad this was far more than a goodbye kiss.

TO BE CONTINUED IN BOOK 2: THE TAILOR'S ESCAPE

Author's Note

The *Pirate and the Mermaid's Trilogy* began as a Cinderella story.

In 2012, I was finishing the first draft of *The Lady and the Frog*, where we first meet Cassandra and Arturo Astrellar. I knew this mysterious couple had a rich backstory to explore, and one day would have the heir of their fortune restored. Exploring this, I uncovered their long-lost grandson, Antonio Astrellar, a naval officer from Castallar who somehow would be reunited with them.

In seeking the right fairy tale to use, the wealth of the Astrellar fortune made Antonio a strong fit for the prince character in a Cinderella retelling.

All I needed to do was find the damsel he would marry, then build the story.

This version of Antonio was in his mid to late thirties (note: he will be 39 during the events of *The Lady and the Frog*), so it felt more interesting and appropriate to have his love interest be Cinderella's stepmother.

I toyed with the idea for a while, and was introduced to a more mature Mabel Sinclair, close to our prince's age. She was originally a fashion and society writer in Willington whose husband died in a scandal, and so she moved to Pippington to live a quieter life.

This wasn't interesting enough, so I decided she and Antonio needed a past together.

So, how would a fashion and society writer know a naval sailor?

The answer, obviously, is she had been a pirate. I'm sure everyone would reach the same conclusion.

Antonio had met her at sea, they had a romance, and adopted the Cinderella character together. However, he was lost at sea and cursed with amnesia, leaving Mabel to believe he is dead. When he returned to land, he learned he is the heir of the Astrellar fortune. Once in Pippington, he and Mabel reunite. However, he does not remember her and she cannot reveal their past due to piracy. Thus, the Cinderella story would be about love and memory being restored.

It is a great story, full of intrigue, heartbreak, and secrets. However, once I finally sat down to write, the tale of Antonio Cortez and Mabel Sinclair became something more.

I began developing the story in earnest in late 2019 and early 2020. This included reading books on actual pirate (Note: This is why my dog's full name is Edward Thatch AKA Blackbeard the Cuddler). Meanwhile, fashion is a great passion for my sister Natalie. She can give an excellent tutorial on fashion history and how clothing is made. It felt natural to make this a love story of two highly fashionable characters.

In later 2020, while many of us were adapting our lives to COVID, my method for dealing with the underlying stress was to get lost in writing. I wrote about 1 million words during the year, which includes the first draft of *The Pirate and the Mermaid's Tailor Trilogy*.

I started writing, planning only one book. The deeper I went, the more the story grew. So, I found a good point to sew up *The Mermaid's Apprentice* and transition to the second book, *The Tailor's Escape*. I planned for that book to take us to the end. However, a third book rose from the depths of my growing outline, creating *The Pirate's Daughter*.

And, if that is not enough story, over the following year, I uncovered more of Isabella Astrellar's backstory. That project, *The Tale of Isabella Astrellar*, grew from sketching out a few scenes to help me fill in her story. Swiftly, it became an epic story of how she was kidnapped as a child, became a mermaid against her will, and overcame this to become the strong mermaid you meet in her few scenes here in *The Mermaid's Apprentice*. I'm currently working on edits and building plans for its release alongside the trilogy.

So, from the ashes of a Cinderella retelling, there are now four books full of swashbuckling adventure, romance, and excellent fashion.

I dreamt of none of this back in 2010, when I first sketched out *The True Bride and the Shoemaker*, a simple story of Peter Talbot, a nice man who is down on his luck. The world of Pippington has grown enormously since then and I hope you're having as much fun exploring the world of Pippington as I am. And, as always, there are many stories to come.

Acknowledgements

First, to my readers. Thank you to those who have shared their love of the stories and world of Pippington. I hope you enjoyed exploring the Mermaid's Apprentice's tour of further corners of the world. Mainly, I hope you are inspired to dress fantastically.

Second, thank you to my editor Tara Newland for your hard work, excellent revisions, and being an excellent friend. You are a great companion on the journey through Pippington.

Third, thank you to my writers group – nominally, The Writers Squad of Doom. Thank you to the various members who remain and have passed in and out. This includes Alicia Dawn, Benjamin K Hewett, Janeal Falor, Sean Lundgren, Eva Dominga Voorhis, Heike Westendorf, Melinda Erb, and Carolyn Young. You are all fantastic writers who challenge me and push me to be a better writer.

Fourth, thank you to my beta readers – Jacquelyn Vinci, Michelle Algood, Heather Davis, Lauren Grondel, Sara Sell, James Darcy, Sean Acheson, Jacque Stevens. Your constructive feedback and support was essential for polishing this story.

Fifth, thank you to Miblart for a fantastic cover.

Sixth, and finally, thank you to my family and friends. Together, you have been incredibly supportive. Many have helped brainstorm, others have provided quiet support, or shared their love of the world of Pippington with their own friends and family. There are a lot of you and I could probably fill this page with thanking each one of you.

I especially want to thank my sister Natalie, who lives with me and is barraged by my latest idea and patiently provides feedback. She also created the illustrated figure on the cover and inspired Mabel and Antonio's love of fashion and textiles. She is a fantastic companion for exploring a menswear exhibit in London.

To everyone listed here and anyone I may have missed, a final big thank you. I am sure we will journey on to many more tales in the world of Pippington and beyond.

Other Works by L. Palmer

THE TRUE BRIDE AND THE SHOEMAKER

Welcome to Pippington, where motorcars bump down old, city lanes, elegant shoes appear by magic, and an ordinary shoemaker can become a hero.

Peter Talbot could use a little magic. Cheap factory-made shoes are putting his shop out of business, his nagging sisters will never let him rest, and his efforts to find true love are constantly thwarted by worldly fickleness. However, the gift of a wild primrose and a shipment of rare griffin skin are about to change everything. When beautiful, handmade shoes begin appearing in his shop every morning, Peter is determined to find his secret helper. What he finds introduces him to adventure and the hidden world of magic in Pippington.

To read the story, visit <u>tinyurl.com/truebride</u>

When Peter Talbot lifted the mound of dirt carrying a wild primrose, he was not thinking of magic and fairytales. His mind was filled with the fine curvature of Miss Adeline Winkleston's arches, of her small and delicate toes, of her dainty foot dangling from her fine ankle, of her smooth and perfectly proportioned heel. There were few pleasures greater than molding a shoe to cushion and support her feet.

The primrose's delicate petals swayed and danced in the wind as he patted dirt into a pot and added water. Peter steadied his bowler hat as he rose and looked out at the meadow. The field of daffodils was a pleasant sight, but hardly matched the lone primrose's fragile beauty. The flower would now have a better home on Adeline Winkleston's window sill, if the lady accepted it.

Peter meandered along the dirt path leading out of the meadow and onto the cobblestone streets of Pippington. The city had grown much in his twenty-five years. New automobiles puttered along while horses trudged on, pulling old, warped carts. The roar of a crowd echoed from the arena as men far braver than Peter raced dragons around the track. Even if Peter could afford a ticket, he preferred to avoid such spectacle. Though, today, racing a dragon seemed easier than approaching Adeline's door.

Peter kept on his path and walked past factories lining the edge of town, then by the old brick apartments and shops filling the southern region of the city. This was far from the northern bluffs, with mansions and high-rise penthouses rising over Chalice Lake. The cliffs dipped down and became the wharf and docks filled with barges, fishing boats, and the common sort of people Peter understood.

Adeline herself was better than common. Her doorstep lay on Nightingale Lane, in Midtown, among the rows of tightly packed houses mixed in with banks, boarding schools, and professional firms. Each step of his polished shoes brought him closer to knocking on her door and speaking the words his sisters, Mary and Molly, had suggested: How are you Miss Winkleston? The weather sure is pleasant enough for a walk. Would you like to come? Any new hats catch your eye?

The last question had been suggested by Mary, whose husband owned Tevinson's Fine Hats. Peter was surprised Molly, whose husband owned Chancey's Dresses and Suits, didn't mention anything about clothing.

At last, Peter's feet pressed to the walkway outside Adeline Winkleston's house. He wiped sweat from his forehead and held the potted primrose in the crook of his arm. He had attempted to approach the doors of young women before, but had always retreated before reaching the porch. To the flower, he said, "We'll have to do our best, I suppose."

Hoping he had not smudged anything on his finest dark coat and trousers, he approached the door. Molly had given his clothes a full examination before he left, including straightening his collar and polishing his buttons. A fine lady like Adeline would notice anything amiss.

Tensing the muscles of his face into something like a smile, he knocked on the door. He stepped back, holding his hat in his hand just as Mary had demonstrated. His cheeks ached as he kept his face in position as footsteps and giggling approached. . He wished the hot summer day would turn cold so he could excuse his shaking legs.

Adeline Winkleston opened the door, her porcelain face aglow. A genuine smile began to warm Peter's cheeks, when the base tones of a man's voice echoed from the parlor. It was not her father's voice.

"Of course. Thank you, Mr. Talbot. Good afternoon."

The door shut, leaving Peter alone with his bowler hat and potted flower. He considered knocking and offering the plant as an engagement present. A burst of laughter from inside deflated the idea.

light. She lifted her foot, the hem of her skirt slipping, revealing her ankle.

"I'm wearing them right now." She erupted into a batch of giggles that pelted at Peter. "My fiancé, Nathaniel Bronhart, was just complementing the soft point of the toe. They are excellently made, as always, Mr. Talbot. We will surely be coming to you for—" She held a hand to her mouth as her eyes brightened. "The wedding."

"Congratulations." Peter's stomach attempted to join his feet on the ground. "Give my regards to Mr. Bronhart."

"Of course. Thank you, Mr. Talbot. Good afternoon."

The door shut, leaving Peter alone with his bowler hat and potted flower. He considered knocking and offering the plant as an engagement present. A burst of laughter from inside deflated the idea.

Peter's shoulders drooped as he kept hold of the potted flower and he ambled along the lanes until he turned onto Dabbler Street. He came to a friendly, aged building bearing a sign with a fine, sturdy gentleman's shoe with painted letters reading *Talbot's Boots and Other Footwear. We do repairs.*

Once inside with the door locked, having wasted a Sunday afternoon, Peter surveyed the empty shop. About a dozen pairs of his best boots sat on display in the window. Other shoes lay in various stages in the workroom downstairs. He walked past piles of leather and tools on his way to the cramped kitchen. Leaning his elbow on the counter, he set down the flower. It was a delicate thing, too fine for the worn grooves of the wood it sat on. Perhaps one of his nieces might like it.

THE LADY AND THE FROG

Welcome to Pippington, where motorcars bump down old city lanes, frogs transform into men, and mermaids just might be real.

Evelyn Havish is through waiting for Henry Kingston to look up from his ledgers and propose. But, when Henry's brother Jack is transformed into a frog and trapped in a well, Evelyn must join the rescue. Armed with her training as a lady and a solid punch, Evelyn must outwit a scheming heiress, wrestle an octopus, and kiss far more frogs than a girl should be expected to. As she dives deeper into a hidden world of magic, she discovers Jack may not be the one who needs saving.

To read the story, visit <u>tinyurl.com/ladyandthefrog</u>

Jack leaned his bicycle against the fence and used the vines to climb up. Seated on top, he gave her a friendly smile. "Don't mean to intrude, miss, but it sounds as if you've got some trouble. Anything I can do?"

The lady looked to the house. "My father doesn't like strangers coming into the garden."

"That I can do something about." He jabbed his thumb toward his chest and grinned. "The name's Jack. What's yours?"

"I am Cassandra." She dabbed her face with a lace handkerchief. "Please, be careful up there."

"I'll be all right. Tell me how I can help."

Cassandra turned away as a sob shuddered across her shoulders. "No one can help me. It is lost."

Jack leaned forward. "What've you lost? I'm good at finding things."

She clutched her handkerchief as she stared forlornly into the well. "When my dear mother passed away, her last gift to me was a gold bauble. I-I dropped it in the well." She whimpered. "It is lost, just as my mother is lost to me."

Jack's smile faltered as he scratched his head. "Must be precious."

He eyed the well before grabbing a nearby branch and swinging to the ground. "Fortunately, I'm an expert at climbing down wells."

Cassandra stood, her hands shaking. "You should leave before my father sees you. The bauble isn't worth you getting into trouble."

"Not to worry." Jack waved his arm. "I'll have it out faster than you can blink."

He looked into the well shaft. The sun gleamed across the water's surface. Floating on top was a golden ball small enough to fit in the palm of his hand. The well was wider than most of the ones he was hired to clean, with plenty of space for his narrow shoulders. He pulled off his jacket and ran his fingers through his hair. It was already out of place, despite combing it that morning. Well, if he looked heroic enough climbing down the well, she wouldn't notice his hair.

The crank squeaked as he lowered the bucket. It splashed in the water and floated next to the gleaming bauble. Jack locked the crank in place and gripped the rope. He gave a grin and wink to Cassandra before swinging himself into the well. As he descended, he kept his hand against the wall to slow himself. He tried not to cringe as his hands slid on slimy moss and old patches of algae.

Frogs croaked from the bottom of the well, growing louder as Jack approached. There were dozens of bulbous eyes staring up at him. The frogs jumped from stone to stone as if warning each other. Jack rested his feet on a ledge near the water's surface. Once at the top, he should offer to come back and clean the well. It would be a good opportunity to see this girl again.

Holding onto the rope, he crouched down and wrapped his fingers around the bauble. With a grin, he stood and shouted, "I've got it. See, no trouble."

"Would you please put it in the bucket?" she said. "I wouldn't want it to fall."

Allowing himself a happy whistle, he dropped the bauble into the bucket. As it left his hand, he began to fall. The world around him warped as if he were looking through a bulbous lens. His skin grew cold and he splashed into the water. His body felt strange as he kicked to the surface. The well expanded, growing large and vast around him. He reached to grab the ledge, but his hands were slick and mottled green. The bucket rose from the water as Cassandra turned the crank. Jack hopped onto the nearest rock and opened his mouth to call to the girl above, but a long croak erupted instead. Panic rose as he looked down at his webbed feet. He pivoted, seeking a way out, when he found himself nose to slimy nose with another frog.

THE MATCHGIRL AND THE MAGICIAN

Welcome to Pippington, where motor cars bump down old city lanes, carpets can fly, and magic is a secret proper young ladies keep.

One fateful night, a child named Adeline lies alone in the snow. Fading into sleep, her only warmth comes from her matches and the embers of her hidden magic. As she succumbs to the cold of death, she is saved by Rompell, a stranger from a land of deserts and magic with secrets of his own.

Their lives intertwined, Rompell and Adeline become father and daughter. As Adeline becomes an elegant young woman, she fights to control and hide her growing magic in a world full of handsome young men, fine dresses, and her own grand romance.

When an enemy arises from the shadows of Rompell's past, with ancient spells and dangerous magic, Rompell and Adeline risk losing all they have built together. As Rompell fights to protect his daughter, it may be Adeline who must risk revealing her powers and losing true love to save her father.

The Matchgirl and the Magician is the third book in The Pippington Tales and mixes Hans Christian Anderson's Little Matchgirl, Rumplestiltskin, the legend of King Midas, and the magic of the Arabian Nights

To read the story, visit tinyurl.com/matchgirlandmagician

CHAPTER 1 PREVIEW

Only a few months before, Adeline had stood beside her mother as the statue was unveiled. Women in furs and silk handed them a mountain of flowers, pouring out condolences. She posed as her mother told her to, trying to understand the crowd and ribbons. When she asked one of the women what these decorations were for, they pinched her cheek and tapped her nose.

"Your father was a brave, brave fire brigade officer and saved many lives."

Adeline knew why her father was gone. She didn't understand how flowers and ribbons would stop her mother from weeping every night.

During the ceremony, Adeline's grandfather stood apart with her two uncles, taking in speeches about her father's final heroic deeds and thank-you's for funding the statue. Her grandfather and uncles said nothing to her or her mother. Once the ceremony was over, Adeline's mother said, "We are better off without their help."

A shudder of cold ran through Adeline, bringing her attention back to the alleyway. Her hand shook as she lit another match. Images of monsters rose in the illuminated shadows. Adeline sang, focusing only on the flame and its small warmth. It flickered in the wind. She held her hand over it, the flame biting her skin. The fire spread out with her song, as if carried by the soft notes. Her mother had taught her this trick one night when there was little wood for the fire. They had huddled together as their songs carried magic into the flames, helping them grow.

Horse hooves echoed down the street. Adeline blew out the match and huddled in the darkness.

"Never show anyone your magic," her mother had said. "They don't believe in it and won't understand."

Adeline waited till the carriage passed and the echoes were far away. Taking in a few breaths, she took another match from the pile.

She shouldn't use what she was supposed to sell, but the warmth was so inviting.

Striking the match against the wall, she sang and focused on the fire. A feast of goose, potatoes, rolls, pie, and everything delicious arose in the flames. Her mother was at one end, her cheeks pink and full as they had once been. Adeline's father sat at the other end, tall and proud. Her parents smiled at her before disappearing in the smoke of the burnt-out match. She flicked the splinter of wood away. Flakes of ash floated, mingling with the falling snow.

The alleyway seemed darker and emptier. She struck three matches against the wall. Her voice shook as she sang out the melody. She had to recapture her father's smile. The flame flickered, revealing an image of her parents lying in caskets, their faces pale and stiff. She tried to sing the illusion away, but her teeth chattered. The flame started to move, flickering with images of her mother and father dancing. Her mother wore a fine dress with feathers and glittering jewelry. Her father was in a suit, his hair smooth, his face handsome.

Her father had promised always to protect her but had chosen to save others instead. He had gone into the flaming building one last time and it collapsed in a cloud of sparks and ash. Months passed, and winter came and stole her mother away. Adeline shut her eyes, trying to forget waking to her mother's still face only a few weeks before.

The chill settled deeper into Adeline's skin as she curled up on the cobblestone, her cheek to the pavement. Her eyelids drooped. If she fell asleep, she would wake in her parents' arms, wrapped in a thick quilt as they sat by the fire. They would laugh and sing, telling her stories of far off adventures. She would be far away from the frost stiffening her clothes.

The matches burnt out and the warmth of her dream left. She shut her eyes tight, trying to grab onto the dream instead of the pain tingling in her fingers. She sang, her voice little more than a whisper. The song would keep her warm as she faded into rest.

Footsteps crunched in the alleyway and Adeline tried to open her eyes. Hands wrapped her threadbare shawl around her quivering frame. The stranger rubbed her hands between his until her fingers uncurled. In the dim starlight, he pulled one of the matches from her crate and struck it against the wall.

Her eyes opened. The stranger's face was warm-brown, like earthen clay. Snow weighed on his dark hair and goatee. His kind eyes reminded her of how her father had looked at her.

"Little One," he said, his Sandarian accent coloring his words with the warmth of far-off deserts. "What are you doing here alone?"

Her jaw was frozen. The Sandarian removed his overcoat, revealing a layer of jackets and scarves beneath. Taking the crate of matches, he wrapped his coat around her.

He pulled her slender body into his arms, cradling her like a bird with a broken wing, and held the crate by its strap. Though he was a stranger, she nestled her face into the warmth of his shoulder.

The Pippington Tales: Timeline

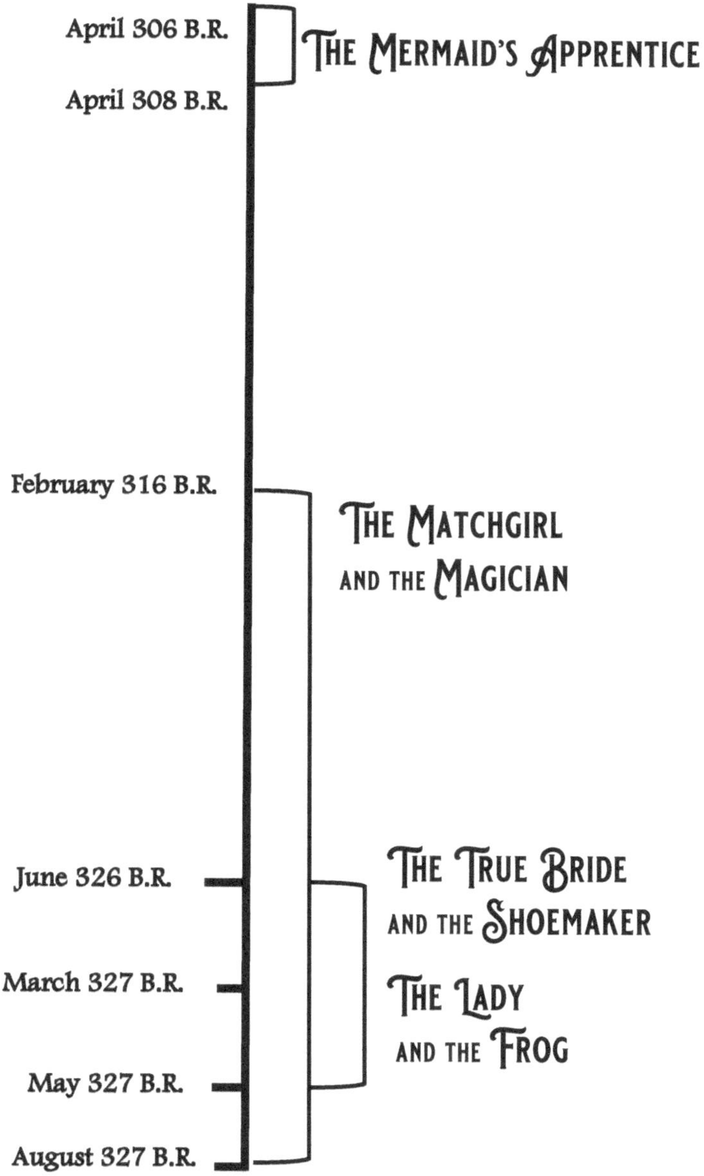

*B.R. = Years since beginning of the Barthanian Republic

About the Author

In between exploring the hidden magic of Pippington, L. Palmer works in public service and lives in San Antonio. She is an award-winning speaker and has presented on various topics at writing conferences, studied English and Film at The University of California Santa Barbara, and has a Masters in Public Administration from Brigham Young University. She developed her imagination and adventure skills through growing up in Girl Scouts, working at resident summer camps, teaching high school English, and reading great books of fantasy and magic. While she doesn't typically host tea parties, she does enjoy hosting some for dragons on Tuesdays. For the latest news, visit: lpalmerchronicles.com

To explore more of Pippington, visit:
lpalmerchronicles.com/pippington_tales

To sign-up for L. Palmer's Newsletter, visit:
lpalmerchronicles.com/about

For updates and free bonus content, visit:
lpalmerchronicles.com/exclusive-preview

If you enjoyed this book, please visit take the time to leave an honest review on the bookseller site of your choice.

Follow L. Palmer on social media:

- Facebook: facebook.com/lpalmerchronicles
- Instagram: instagram.com/lpalmerchronicles
- TikTok: tiktok.com/@lpalmerauthor1